THE VILLA
A NEAPOLITAN LOVE STORY

By
K. BUNKER

"Rome is stately and impressive; Florence is all beauty and enchantment; Genoa is picturesque; Venice is a dream city; but Naples is simply — fascinating."

Quote from Lilian Whiting- American Journalist

CONTENTS

ACKNOWLEDGEMENTS

Writing a novel for the first time is a major undertaking. I have always wanted to write a book but have never had the time to pursue it during my working years. Now that I have retired, I finally have the time. I hope you enjoy the book. I had fun writing it.

I would like to thank my dear friend Amy Dahlin. Amy helped me understand my target audience and avoid land mines. I started, wanting to write a love story which also included my experiences managing Flag Officer Housing. Amy wisely advised against that idea. Instead, she encouraged me to focus on just the love story.

I would like to thank Brianna Bunker, Charlene Larson, George Lea, Melissa Pearson, Henry Turowski and Kurt Benkley who provided me excellent feedback as I wrote the book. I would also like to thank Elena Chiefalo, and Marlena Lea who provided me uniquely Neapolitan points of view.

I would like to offer, a special acknowledgement, to my dear friend and former co-worker Sue Lonigan. Sue wanted to read the book but was not able. She passed away during 2022. Sue is the person who first introduced me to the history of Naples. Afterwards, I began to study Neapolitan history in greater depth to understand its many secrets.

The history of Southern Italy and the Naples Region is extraordinarily rich. Naples is the only place I have ever lived where history and Greek mythology merge. As Sue used to say, "learning Naples' history is like pealing an onion. Each time you remove a layer, you find another layer underneath."

LIST OF CHARACTERS

<u>Main Characters:</u>

- David Moore – A 28 yr. old Navy Officer from Skokie, Illinois

- Elsa Carlsson – A 24 yr. old graduate student from Sweden.

- Harold (Harry) Beeman – a 29 yr. old Navy JAG Officer from Boston, Massachusetts

- Julie Steinman – Harry's 28 yr. old "girl next door," Navy Doctor girlfriend from Evanston, Illinois

- Robert (Robbie) McDonald – a 29 yr. old Navy JAG Officer from Edison, New Jersey. Robbie was Harry's roommate during law school.

- Kimberly (Kimmy) De Gennaro– Robbie's long-time girlfriend from Greenwich, Connecticut

- Antonella Scipione – a 28 yr. old Italian American and Elsa's roommate.

- Marcello DeCarlo: Marcello is a soccer player for the Naples team who lives across the street.

<u>Supporting Characters</u>

- Maria Orsini – Maria is the 80 yr. old owner of the villa who lives on the ground floor.

- Rosa – Rosa is Maria's 80 yr. old housekeeper.

- Fausta – Fausta is the part-time maid hired by Maria to clean up after the three bachelors living upstairs.

- Bari – Maria's Saint Bernard puppy.

- Charles & Silvana Scipione – Antonella's parents

- Max – Max is the Housing Director. David works with Max.

- Enzo –is the Flag Housing Manager. He works for David.

- Commander Cooper – The base Public Works Officer and David's immediate supervisor

- Tony Russo – Antonella's motorcycle racing boyfriend

- Neal Smith– David's sponsor, he introduces David to Elsa

- Kristina Carlsson – Elsa's sister

- John Carlsson & Matilda (Tilly) Carlsson – Elsa's parents

- Sven – Elsa's former boyfriend.

- Frank & Marjorie McDonald – Robbie's parents

- Donatella DeCarlo – Marcello's mother

- Cinzia DeCarlo – Marcello's sister

- Vincenzo (Vinny) DeCarlo – Marcello's brother

- Luciano Carrillo – Marcello's lawyer & former partner of Marcello's deceased father Bruce DeCarlo.

- Donato Malatesta – Elsa's fashion photographer

- Bruto Cativo – Donato's Film Director friend

- Dana – David's ex-girlfriend

- Kimmy's Family (Mother, Father, Grandmother & stepmother Jillian)

PART I: NEW HOME & NEW FRIENDS

CHAPTER 1: THE PROPOSAL

I began my journey to Naples, Italy on a hot August morning in 1989. I was ready to leave the stifling Virginia heat behind. For the past two weeks, I had been living out of a suitcase at the Navy's Breezy Point Bachelor Officer Quarters in Norfolk, Virginia, ever since my household goods had shipped out. My home away from home had been comfortable until the afternoon before my departure, when the AC, as luck would have it, stopped working. I should have changed rooms but decided to gut it out instead, thinking I could manage one night without air conditioning. I forgot how miserable Norfolk could be in August. Falling asleep in the sweltering heat, was difficult, and it wasn't until 2:00 AM that I finally dozed off.

The morning arrived scarcely three hours later when my bedside alarm clock went off, precipitating a quick 5:00 AM shower and rush to the airport. I arrived at Norfolk International just in time to board my flight to Philadelphia. Looking at my watch, it was now 7:00 AM. My next flight, from Philadelphia to Naples, was scheduled for departure at 8:30 AM. It seemed I would have time to make the next flight.

The flight to Philadelphia pulled away from the gate late, however. I arrived in Philadelphia 40 minutes later after circling the airport several times. It seemed for certain I would miss my connecting flight. I raced through the Philadelphia airport, rushing to get to the concourse used for military charter flights. When I finally stopped for a breath, I looked up at the information board. My flight, flight 1508, was "DELAYED." Looking backward now, I realize the simple word "Delayed" was appropriate. Nothing ever happened on time in Naples. Why should the flight to Naples have been any different?

When I finally arrived at the gate with my egg sandwich and coffee in hand, I began fumbling through my backpack, looking for my ticket. Searching each of the pockets, I stumbled upon a small square box, the box containing a ring I no longer wanted. I had tried to return the ring but found I had lost the receipt. I even went to a pawn shop the day before, hoping to sell it, but the shop was closed. Now I was stuck with this thing, this symbol of disappointment. What does a person do with a diamond ring that no one wants, I thought, as I zipped up the pocket and continued to search for my elusive tickets?

After I finished my egg sandwich, I decided to try once again calling the base in Naples. For three days, I had been trying to reach my sponsor, a LTJG. Michael Biggs to confirm my arrival date, but so far, I had not reached him. Instead, I kept getting his answering machine. The message always said that his mailbox was full.

I had last spoken to Michael a month prior and had left several messages since, all of which had gone unanswered. It seemed my sponsor had vanished from the face of the earth. This time the phone rang as usual four rings. I knew the machine would start after the fifth ring. Just as I was about to hang up, however, a voice came on the line. It was a woman's voice with a British accent.

"Pronto, Public Works Engineering, Angela speaking," the voice crackled through the line.

"Angela, this is LT. David Moore," I replied. "I'm the new Flag Officer Housing Officer. I'm scheduled to arrive today on the CAT B flight from Philadelphia. Do you know if Michael Biggs is there?"

"No LT. Moore," Angela replied. "LTJG. Biggs is on emergency leave." For a moment I felt a lump in my throat.

"Do you know if anyone is going to meet me at the airport?" I asked.

"I think so," Angela replied. "I remember hearing about this Monday at the staff meeting. Let me check my notes."

Before I could ask another question, Angela put the phone down and began shuffling papers on her desk. Several minutes later, she picked up the phone again. "The Public Works Officer assigned Neal Smith as your sponsor," she replied.

"Is he there?" I asked.

"No," she replied. "He has gone home for the day."

"Do you have a phone number where I can reach him? I asked."

"No," she replied, "I don't think he has a phone. Most Americans don't have phones. It takes too long to get a phone. My husband and I ordered a phone. It took us five months to get connected and cost us six hundred thousand lire." Angela was giving me way too much information. Clearly, it was hard to get a phone in Naples.

"Do you know if either Michael or Neal made a hotel reservation for me?" I asked.

"I don't know," Angela replied. "Let me look at his desk." Once again, I heard the phone set down as Angela walked away. Ten minutes and three dollars in quarters later, Angela returned to the phone. "I found a piece of paper on his desk with your hotel reservations," she said. "It says he booked a room for you at the Terme Hotel for two weeks."

"How do you spell that?" I asked.

"It's spelled T as in Tango – E as in echo- R as in Romeo- M as in Manhattan- E as in echo," Angela replied. Very clearly, Angela had spent time in the Navy. "It means bath in Italian," she added. "There is an old ruined Roman bath nearby."

"Where is the Hotel?" I asked.

"It's in Agnano, about a kilometer from the base," Angela replied. It seemed we were about to play twenty questions.

"Where is Agnano?" I asked.

"It's on the west side of the city, about 15 to 20 clicks from the airport," Angela replied. "You cannot miss it. Just take the Tange west."

"What is the Tange?" I asked. I was learning a whole new vocabulary.

"It is short for Tangenziale," Angela replied. "It is a freeway, although I would not say it's free."

"Is the toll expensive?" I asked.

"Yes," Angela replied. For a moment, I had a vision of becoming stuck at the airport. I had no Italian money for either a taxi or for toll. My trip to Italy was not getting off to a good start.

"Should I expect Neal to pick me up at the airport?" I asked.

"Yes, he should be there," Angela replied. "His calendar says pick up David at 10:00 PM. Don't worry; Neal is dependable, much better than Michael," Angela remarked. "However, if you do find yourself abandoned, you can catch a taxi at the civilian airport terminal."

"Thanks, Angela, for all your help," I replied. "I look forward to meeting you next week." With that, I hung up the phone. I was glad to have finally reached someone and relieved to learn I had a place to spend the night. I didn't know how to find it, however, nor did I have money to get there. I had better study my Italian phrasebook again, I thought, just in case I need to hire a taxi.

As I fumbled once again in the backpack looking for my Italian phrasebook, I touched the little ring box. Pulling it out, I looked inside at the diamond ring contained therein. Why did I buy such an expensive ring, I thought?

Dana and I had dated for two years before I bought "the ring." From the start, we had a typical, sometimes stormy relationship. At one point, we lived together, broke up and then reunited. During our last six months together, we had often discussed my possible next duty station, and Dana had given me considerable input, dropping hints it was time for us to take the next step. I took this to mean she wanted to get married.

When she expressed a desire to live in London, I pursued that option for several weeks without success. There were no jobs available. When I mentioned the possibility of working in Naples, she seemed interested at first. However, after I accepted the assignment, her interest seemed to cool. "I really had my heart set on London," she said.

I knew I was ready to get married but was not sure whether Dana was. We talked about marriage often but always around the edges, avoiding any difficult discussions. Would she say yes? I didn't know the answer to that question. I finally decided to take the plunge when I learned the Navy would not move Dana's household goods unless we were married. It was now, or never, I thought.

The night I proposed, we went to our favorite restaurant, a place on the water where we had had our first date. It was a lovely romantic evening. Dana was dressed in the beautiful red dress I had bought for her the previous Christmas. It seemed that everything was going according to plan when one of Dana's friends, a woman named Suzy, unexpectedly joined us at our table. The last person I wanted to see at that moment was Suzy.

I hoped that Dana would say "hello," and then Suzy would depart. However, Dana instead invited her to join us. When Suzy arrived, my carefully crafted plan began to go off the rails immediately as both women began talking about nail polish, lip gloss and other things that didn't interest me. I had become invisible. When the two got up to visit the restroom before dessert arrived, I finally saw my chance.

Reaching into my coat pocket, I pulled out the ring box and gently placed the ring in Dana's wine glass. I then refilled the glass with white wine. When the women returned, Dana saw the ring immediately.

"What's this?" she asked, as she picked up the glass to examine it more closely. I could tell that the wheels were turning in her mind. It was then that I asked the big question.

"Dana, will you marry me?"

What followed next came as a surprise. I had expected a look of joy, perhaps a squeal of delight, a hug or even a kiss. Instead, I got a blank stare. What is she thinking, I thought? Out of the corner of my eye, I could see Suzy fidgeting, nervous at the situation.

"Dana, I think I should leave you two alone." she said.

"No, please stay," Dana replied.

After several minutes of the blank stare, I asked Dana what she was thinking. It seemed the gears in her brain had become jammed. It was then that I saw a smile begin to form on her lips. It was not a smile of joy, however. Instead, it was a sneer. This was not a good sign. I wondered if she might say yes. Instead, she began with an apology.

"David, I am sorry I may have led you on with the talk of moving to London," she said. "I really thought you knew." Where was she going with this conversation? She then turned to Suzy and gave her a kiss on the lips. It seemed Suzy was as shocked as I was. Afterwards Dana delivered her line. "David, the truth is I prefer women."

I was stunned. As I stared at my girlfriend, she downed the wine in her glass, catching the ring in her teeth. She tried the ring on, admiring it for a moment and then removed it, firmly placing it in my strawberry cheesecake. I hadn't seen that coming. What should I say now?

As I pondered my next move, I remembered the night before. Dana certainly didn't prefer women that night. What could I say after a line like that! What would father do in this situation, I asked myself? I was deeply embarrassed. It was then that I turned to the waiter standing beside me and said what naturally came to mind. "Check, please!", I said.

I could tell Dana was disappointed by my response. She would not be getting the last word that night. Turning to Suzy, she said, "let's go," and then the two sashayed out of my life. Afterwards, I took a long walk on the beach to collect my thoughts. I felt like my life was over. How could I have misjudged Dana's response so badly?

The next day I tried to return the ring, but of course, I had lost the receipt. I considered throwing the ring into the ocean but then thought better of the idea. Who needs women anyway, I thought? I was going to Naples with or without Dana. It was time to move on with my life.

After my night of disappointment, I never saw Dana again. She did, however, get the last word. I later learned from a mutual friend that she had lied to me and was seeing another man. Shortly thereafter they got married. As I sat there in the airport lounge, remembering the past few months, I noticed people were getting up to stand in line. Our flight was now boarding.

FLIGHT TO NAPLES

The flight to Naples was seven hours in length. I tried to focus on the movie; however, I had seen "When Harry met Sally" before. I couldn't stay interested. All it did was remind me of the last time I saw the movie with Dana. These movies aren't realistic, I thought. In the real world, Sally tells Harry she is a lesbian.

To keep my mind off my ex-girlfriend, I started to read a book. This worked for a few hours until I got sleepy and decided to take a nap. When I awoke, the cabin was dark, and it was clear we were beginning to make our descent into Naples. Lifting the window shade, I looked out the window. Below everything was black except for a glow of light in the distance. We were still over the water. As I shifted my weight to keep my leg from falling asleep, the pilot came onto the intercom announcing that we were beginning our descent into Naples.

For the next several minutes, I peered out the window as the lights onshore came closer and closer to our plane. It was clear we were approaching a large city. Below I could now see the outlines of several Islands, including one with a large mountain. We then banked towards the left, revealing a long ridge covered in lights. At the bottom was a ribbon of light that swung in a wide arc along the water until it passed under our plane. We then made another sharp turn to the left.

Below I could now see the outline of a mountain. It was a large mountain ringed with lights. At its center sat a deep black crater. I was looking into the mouth of a volcano. I was looking into the mountain that destroyed the city of Pompei. I was looking into the mouth of Vesuvius. We had arrived.

We continued to fly north for several minutes, following the line of some tall mountains now visible on the right side of the plane. We then made another banking turn to the left and began our final approach into the airport. The ground was coming up fast now, as our wheels gently touched down. The passengers applauded our safe arrival. After touching down, we taxied for several minutes, passing a large passenger terminal until we came to a stop at a small building with an American flag. We had arrived at our destination.

ARRIVAL IN NAPLES

After several minutes waiting, a rolling stairway pulled up to our plane, and everyone began to get off. Seated as I was, in the back of the plane, I had to wait as everyone slowly got up and began to pull their luggage from the overhead bins. It seemed everyone was moving in slow motion, like people in a zombie movie.

After what seemed an eternity, I was finally able to stand and begin moving down the aisle myself. As I approached the door, I felt a rush of hot, muggy air as I stepped off into the night. The climate in Naples, was just like Norfolk.

The walk to the terminal was at least two hundred yards, but it felt good to stretch my legs. When I finally stepped inside, I saw the bags, all of which were black, beginning to spin around the baggage carousel as hordes of yawning people pushed forward to claim them. My luggage was tan, which would make it easy to spot. As luck would have it, however, my bags were the last to be loaded onto the carousel.

When I finally emerged from the terminal and stepped out into the night, I found myself alone as the last group of people departed. It was clear Neal was nowhere to be found. He had forgotten me. Welcome to Naples, I thought. I suddenly felt very alone and far from home.

Turning to a man cleaning up for the night, I asked him for directions to the civilian terminal, hoping it was not far away. "I need to find a taxi," I said.

"It is about a mile away," the man replied. He then gave directions. "Walk out to the main road," he said, "and then follow it to the main gate. After you walk out the gate, walk for another several hundred meters and then turn right at the first street. You cannot miss it," he said. I felt like a mouse about to begin a search for cheese.

Great, what a wonderful way to begin my life in Naples, I thought, as I started down the road towards the main gate carrying my two suitcases. I made a mental note that I needed to buy new suitcases with wheels. Already my arms were tired. When I passed the main gate, I stopped once again to ask for directions, this time in Italian, from the guard seated in the booth. When the guard replied in Italian, I had no idea what he said. So much for the usefulness of the Italian phrasebook, I thought.

Then, as I walked down the long dark road towards the civilian terminal, I saw a truck coming toward me. When the truck reached me, it stopped, and the man inside rolled down his window. "Are you LT. David Moore?" he asked. It was Neal. Boy was I happy to see him! Throwing my bags into the bed of his truck, he welcomed me to Naples. "Sorry, I am late," he said. "I was at a soccer game party tonight and lost track of time. I thought I gave myself enough time to get to the airport, but the traffic is terrible tonight," he said.

Climbing into the front seat, we turned around and set off into the night. It turned out the civilian airport was remarkably close, barely three hundred yards from where Neal finally picked me up. "I almost missed you," I said. "I was walking to the terminal to hail a taxi."

"Glad I reached you in time," Neal replied. He then turned right and accelerated down a ramp into fast-moving traffic. Ahead of us was a sea of brake lights. Somehow Neal squeezed us into the flow of traffic narrowly avoiding sideswiping a concrete wall. Up ahead, I could see five lanes of traffic, shifting into two lanes. "There must be an accident up ahead;" Neal remarked, as he shifted over to the left. Behind us, I could hear someone honking. They were displeased with Neal's sudden merge. It had begun to rain, turning Neal's windshield into a sea of mud.

"Do you ever wash this thing?" I asked.

"No," Neal replied. "I did when I first got here, however I quickly learned it was a pointless gesture. I have decided to leave the dirt as-is. My feeling is that the dirt protects the paint." As he said this, I heard a loud crack as a car passed within inches of Neal's truck removing his driver-side mirror. "Fuck!" Neal exclaimed, "that's the second mirror I've lost this month!"

Welcome to Naples, I thought. I wondered what might happen to my new car. The thought sent shivers up my spine as I pictured my BMW creased with a million dents. Why did I buy a new car? I should have bought a beater instead. "Is Naples traffic always this crazy?" I asked.

"No," Neal replied. "Sometimes it's worse. Normally the city is empty during Ferragosto." Neal continued; "however, today, the Naples team won their match, and everyone is out driving around celebrating."

"What is Ferragosto?" I asked.

"During the last two weeks in August, the entire country goes on vacation," Neal replied. "It's impossible to get anything done at work. Normally Naples is empty as everyone goes to the beach. However, this week it seems everyone has returned to watch the soccer match. The Naples team is good this year. There is a real chance they may win the Italian Cup."

After several minutes of stop-and-go traffic winding through a long tunnel, the cars began to move again. Up ahead, I could see three smashed cars behind a large orange bus. The smell of auto exhaust was heavy in the air.

"Does anyone ever pass out in these tunnels?" I asked. Neal did not answer. "Should we roll up the windows?" I asked.

"The AC doesn't work," Neal replied. He was puffing away on a cigarette. "Just think of this as smoking a pack of cigarettes," he said. "Every day you get to smoke a pack of cigarettes for free." As he said this, I noticed everyone around us smoking. Apparently, the exhaust from a thousand idling cars, stuck in a tunnel, was not enough smoke for the other drivers. Like Neal, they had a death wish.

"Does everyone smoke here?" I asked.

"Of course," Neal replied. "This is not America. When it comes to smoking, Naples is still in the 1960's. Wait till you meet Donatella at work. She must smoke at least five packs of cigarettes a day."

As we sat in the traffic, trying not to breath, I noticed the cars begin to move again. We were about to exit the tunnel. "What is that pile of spaghetti up ahead?" I asked, pointing to something resembling an interchange.

"That's the exit for the Vomero," Neal replied. "That one interchange empties into an entire quarter of the city. If you drive up that ramp, you will be presented with a plethora of choices after the toll booth. Never go there," he said. "I got off there once by accident and ended up spending three hours trying to get back on the freeway. The Vomero is a complete zoo with one-way streets that change directions every other block. There are several good restaurants up there, however. Just remember, always take the funicular."

"What's a funicular?" I asked.

"It's a type of train that goes up mountains," Neal replied. "As you can see, Naples sits in a mountain range." Looking around, I noticed Neal was right.

We finally reached the Agnano exit after passing through the fourth or fifth tunnel, just as Angela predicted. "I reserved a room for you at the Terme Hotel," remarked Neal. "The reservation is for two weeks; however, you can extend it for longer if you want. I stayed at the Terme when I arrived two years ago," he added. "It is a pleasant hotel in a quiet location and only a short walk from the base." As he said this, we turned into the long tree-lined driveway of the Terme Hotel, leaving the Naples, chaos behind.

"Do you have any plans for tomorrow?" Neal asked.

"No," I replied.

"How would you like to join a friend of mine and me on a trip to the Amalfi Coast?" he asked.

"Sure, but I don't have any Lira," I replied.

"Don't worry; I will cover you until you can get to the bank on Monday," Neal replied. I will pick you up at 9:00 AM."
"Ok, see you then," I replied, as we unloaded my bags from the bed of his truck. That night I slept well, enjoying the nice air conditioning in my room.

CHAPTER 2:

DAVID'S FIRST DAY IN NAPLES

I awoke to the sounds of women's laughter in the hallway. Glancing over at the clock on the nightstand, I noted it was 8:00 AM and time to get up. After showering and shaving, I proceeded to the lobby downstairs.

As the elevator neared the lobby, I could hear the din of hundreds of young women talking. The sleepy hotel from the previous night had come to life. As the doors opened, I was greeted by Neal sitting on a marble window ledge in front of me.

"Welcome to Naples," he said. "You sure picked a good week to stay here!"

"What's going on?" I asked.

"The hotel is hosting a beauty pageant today," Neal replied, motioning to a sign nearby. Glancing to my right, I saw a sign in bright colors. The sign read, "Benvenuti Ragazzi, Miss Campania 1989."

"Let's get a café," Neal suggested, as he motioned for us to move towards the bar. At the end of the hall stood a crowd of beautiful young women in front of a bar. They were waiving their hands at four men behind the bar, who were rushing to fill their orders. It was chaos.

"Do you think we will ever get to the bar?" I asked.

"Follow me," Neal replied. "The first rule to remember in Naples is there is no such thing as a line."

With a few "mi scusi's" and some gentle touching of bare backs, we quickly pushed to the front of the pack. It turned out most of the women had already ordered. In typical Italian fashion, none of the women had thought to move away from the bar so other people could order.

"What would you like?" Neal asked. "I am buying."

"A Cappuccino and Cornetto," I replied. I had studied my Italian phrasebook that morning.

"I think they are out of Cornetto's," Neal replied, pointing towards a glass case behind the bar. In the case, I saw two types of pastries. One that looked delicious in the shape of a butterfly and the other that looked like a rock. Neal saw the choices also.

"I suggest ordering the pastry that resembles a rock," Neal continued. "Lesson two of living in Naples," he said, "is if the pastry looks good, it is probably not. The best-tasting pastries are always the ones that look like rocks." Not knowing the name, when it came to my turn to order, I pointed to the dessert within the case.

After a few minutes, the bartender set two meticulously crafted cups of coffee in front of us with our pastries. "What is this called?" I asked, pointing at the pastry.

"Sfogliatella Frola," the bartender replied with a deep voice, rolling his R's.

Looking into my cappuccino, I noticed it had a perfect heart shape of coffee in the center, sitting on top of a mound of perfectly whipped milk. It was a work of art, almost too beautiful to drink. I wanted to add sugar but knew it would spoil the effect.

The pastry was excellent. It was warm inside with a filling of ricotta cheese and candied fruit. "You were right about the pastry Neal," I remarked. "How do they get the cups so hot?"

"Look behind the bar," Neal replied as he tipped back his head to finish his coffee. Peering over the back edge of the bar, I saw a row of cups sitting in steaming hot water. Welcome to Naples, I thought.

After our small but filling breakfast, we set out for the center of the city to pick up our partner for the day, a Swedish exchange student named Elsa.

"Do you live near here?" I asked Neal, as we departed from the Terme hotel.

"I live about a mile away," he replied, motioning to a street we had just passed on the right. "I live on the old Roman road, the Via Domiziana, about halfway between the NATO base in Bagnoli and the city of Pozzuoli," Neal replied. "I should invite you over some time. You can't miss it. Just turn left at the billboard with the picture of the naked woman."

"Billboard with a naked woman?" I was intrigued.

"Yes," said Neal. "The old billboard was replaced last week with this new billboard for a car stereo company. It has a picture of this incredible pair of wet tits. No face, nothing below the waist, just this incredible pair of tits!"

"Have you bought a stereo yet?" I asked.

"No, but I'm definitively thinking about it," Neal replied, laughing.

As we passed through the busy intersection, not bothering to stop for the traffic light or even slow down, I noticed a string of traffic lights up ahead, each without a cross-street. "What's with all the traffic lights?" I asked.

"I think the contractor got paid by the light," Neal replied.

We traveled down the road for several miles, passing rows and rows of tall, rather ugly apartment blocks towards a wall of solid rock ahead. At one point, we passed a large stadium on the left.

"That's where the Naples soccer team plays," remarked Neal.

When we reached the immovable rock wall, we entered a dark tunnel and then came to a stop midway into the tunnel. In front of us was a large orange bus belching exhaust into my open window.

"Is there another accident?" I asked.

"No, I think it's just a traffic light," Neal replied. "Most traffic lights are optional, however, this one is not."

When we finally emerged from the tunnel, we entered a large piazza with a statue in the center. We had entered the Piazza Sannazaro. Directly in front of us stood a policeman standing on a small stone pedestal. He was waving his arms like an orchestra conductor, being completely ignored by the motorists whizzing by.

Easing into the traffic, Neal moved to the right, exiting the square at the first street we encountered. The street ahead was blocked in many places by cars double and triple parked. On the right, I saw a fish market. Behind a group of mustached women, I could see a man cutting off pieces of a large fish while onlookers watched.

"Is that a swordfish?" I asked.

Neal quickly glanced to the right, narrowly missing a moped that suddenly cut in front of us. "Yes, I think so," he replied. He then swerved again to avoid a man crossing the street. The fish must have been at least 10 feet long and perhaps a foot in diameter. I had never seen a fish that big before.

When we emerged from the street filled with parked cars, Neal turned onto another wide street running along the water. "This is the Via Caracciolo," remarked Neal, as another moped raced by carrying two young girls. They were incredibly cute and scantily clad in miniskirts. On their backs, they wore tiny wallet-sized backpacks held on by long leather straps.

"Did you see that?" I asked.

"I try not to look," Neal replied. Then he hit the brakes as two women resembling Sophia Loren suddenly stepped out in front of us to cross the street.

Neal continued talking. He was used to stopping for beautiful women, whereas I was not. "We're meeting Elsa at the end of this long park on the opposite side," he said. "I hope she is there, so we don't have to keep circling the park." I was barely listening at this point, taking in the intoxicating sights and sounds of the world we had entered. All around us was a sea of beautiful women.

As we neared our rendezvous location, I spied two tall blond women standing on the corner of a narrow alley entering the main road. Above the alley hung dozens of clotheslines, decorated with colorful laundry drying in the morning sun. One woman was dressed in a yellow sundress and fashionable white straw hat. The other woman had perfectly tanned skin with short blond hair and sunglasses perched on her forehead. She wore tight pink shorts which accentuated her narrow waist and wore a white loose-fitting blouse tied just below her chest, leaving her tanned stomach totally bare.

As we pulled to a stop, the woman with the sunglasses leaned into my open window and asked Neal a question. "Neal, do you mind if my sister Kristina comes with us?" she asked. Rather than answering, Neal turned to me.

"What do you think?" he asked. "Can we fit all four of us in the front seat?"

Our day trip suddenly took on a whole new dimension. I did not sign up for a two-hour ride with someone sitting on my lap. I could have said, no, but instead was intrigued by the woman peering into my open window. She was one of the most beautiful women I had ever seen. I decided to go with the flow and replied in the affirmative. "Sure," I replied, "the more the merrier!"

Within a few short minutes, we managed to fit in the truck. The woman with the sunhat, Kristina, sat in the middle next to Neal, in front of the stick shift, while Elsa, the woman with the pink shorts sat on my lap.

The road on the backside of the park was quite bumpy. Several times Elsa had to catch herself on the front dashboard to avoid hitting her head.

"Can you please hold me more tightly around the waist?" she asked.

"Certainly," I replied, "if you will shift slightly to the left."

"Sorry about my bony ass," Elsa replied. If I had known I was going to sit on your lap today, I might have worn some jeans with a little more padding."

"It's not your bony ass that's bothering me," I replied. "What but what do you have in your back pocket?"

In response to my observation, Elsa reached into her back pocket and pulled out a key. It was a giant skeleton key with large nobs on the end.

"Is that the key to the Bastille?" I asked, hoping to provoke a smile.

"It could be," remarked Elsa, smiling. "It certainly does look medieval. It is just my apartment key," Elsa replied. She was now smiling the most beautiful smile. "Sorry about that," she continued. "I forgot to put it in my purse after we left the apartment."

"Where do you live?" I asked.

"Somewhere back in that rabbit warren of streets," Elsa replied. "The building is positively decrepit, but the apartment is quite nice, although a bit tiny."

Kristina had been listening to our conversation. "Tiny is an understatement;" Kristina chimed in. "It's so small I need to step outside to change my mind."

"Kristina doesn't appreciate where I live," Elsa giggled. "She would prefer to stay at my roommate Antonella's parents' house."

"Now that's a house," Kristina exclaimed! "You should see this place. It's a huge mansion by the sea in the Marechiaro quarter. It has its own beach and swimming pool, plus it has a cave underneath the house where Antonella's father parks his boats."

I tried to picture such a magnificent house in my mind. It was not easy.

"It's OK," confirmed Elsa in a rather nonchalant manner. "Antonella and I prefer living in our own place closer to the University." Clearly Elsa was not impressed by large houses.

"You speak very good English," I remarked. "Where are you from?"

"My sister and I are from Stockholm," Elsa replied. "Would you believe Kristina and I are twins? We certainly don't look alike. I speak seven languages; Kristina speaks six."

"Good for you," I replied. "I barely speak one."

Elsa laughed. "I like your accent," she replied. "Where are you from?"

"I am from Skokie, Illinois," I replied. I could see from Elsa's face she didn't recognize the town. "It's a suburb of Chicago, on the north side," I replied. At this reply, Elsa's face changed.

"I've been to Chicago," she replied. "My father attended graduate school at Northwestern University back when we were young. I like Chicago, especially the tall buildings," she continued.

"When did you live there?" I asked.

"We lived on the north side of Chicago in Rodgers Park just below the Evanston city line from 1966 to 1968," Elsa replied.

"Do you realize we were only a couple miles apart?" I asked. "Skokie is just north of Rodgers Park, next to Evanston."

"No, I didn't know that" Elsa replied. "I was only four years old at the time. Perhaps we met? You seem familiar."

As I listened to this conversation, I felt the same way. There was something about Elsa, something quite familiar. Listening to Elsa's voice was like music to my ears. There was something soothing and melodic about it. Perhaps, it was her Swedish accent. It reminded me a lot of my father's cousin, Aunt Vivian.

She shifted her weight several times to keep my leg from falling asleep, and each time I reembraced her waist afterward. "You have warm arms," Elsa noted.

"Am I too warm for you?" I replied. "If so, I can change positions."

"No, it feels good," she replied. "It's been a long time since a man has held me in his arms -"

"We live in the land of endless winter," Kristina interjected, interrupting our conversation. "Summer is a two-week winter holiday in Sweden. My skin hasn't seen the sun since last summer during our vacation to the south of France –."

"I've been getting plenty of suns this summer, Elsa interrupted. Do you like my tan David?"

As I gazed down at her body from behind, I couldn't help noticing that her skin was tan as far as my eyes could see. For a moment, I wondered if she sunbathed topless. It was hard not to look. For the first time, I saw a hint of her nipples behind her blouse.

"You look good," I replied.

Elsa looked up at me and smiled. "You're not so bad yourself," Elsa replied.

Our trip to the Amalfi Coast took about two hours, but it seemed to pass in a matter of minutes as we engaged in animated conversation. Elsa and Kristina were naturally sociable and able to carry on a conversation with complete strangers with relative ease.

My initial fears of a drive filled with awkward silence were never realized. It was clear both women were highly educated. As the topic shifted to inquiries about whether we were seeing other people, Elsa startled me by asking a rather provocative question.

"Could a boy like you fall in love with a girl like me?" she asked, as she looked up at me with inquiring eyes.

"Of course," I replied.

I dismissed the question as a casual flirtation between people getting acquainted. I was certain it didn't mean anything. Elsa just smiled, seeming to drop her inquiry for the moment. Later that day, however, she would ask the question again two more times.

After climbing to the crest of a mountain range on a looping switch-backed road, we crossed over the top and began our descent towards the water below. It was then, as we rounded a bend in the road that I first gazed upon the Amalfi Coast. For a moment, we all stopped talking as we took in the magnificent view.

When we reached the first wide spot on the road, we pulled over to take pictures beside a wooden cart selling hot peppers and garlic. A few miles further up the road, we encountered a large flock of sheep crossing the road. We had entered a parallel universe, only thirty miles from Naples.

After several more miles we arrived in the village of Positano around 11:30 AM. We parked the car in front of a coffee bar and went inside to order. After we got our coffee, we stood on the edge of a terrace looking out over the coast, sipping our drinks.

Elsa pulled at my hand and wrapped it around her waist. "Isn't it beautiful?" she said. She had a dream-like quality to her voice. I was mesmerized by the view in front of me, as well as by Elsa. "I wish I could stand here forever," remarked Elsa, as she squeezed my hand and began commenting on the sites below.

In front of us sat the dome of a church, covered in colorful majolica tiles, and beyond that, stood a beach completely covered with colorful beach umbrellas. It was like a scene from a painting.

"Have you ever been to that beach?" I asked, pointing towards the beach far below.

"Just once," Elsa replied, "two years ago while on vacation. It's expensive to lay on the beach, but there are some great restaurants down there. My favorite is Chez Black," Elsa remarked.

I smiled and nodded. "We should go there sometime," I responded, making a mental note of the restaurant's name.

After our coffee stop in Positano, we continued onwards towards our lunch destination, the tiny village of Ravello, perched high on the side of the mountain. When we reached the outskirts of the village, Neal parked our truck in the village parking lot just below the main square, which was closed to vehicle traffic. Walking up a staircase, we emerged into the main square.

Taking stock of our surroundings, we took in the sights of the square. There was the quintessential village church perched atop a tall staircase, the central feature of so many Amalfi Coast towns, and scattered around the edges of the square were a coffee bar, a gelateria, a store selling brightly painted dishes, a road tunnel passing through an outcropping of rock and a stone tower which looked quite ancient. Turning to Elsa, who seemed to be a font of knowledge, I asked her about the old stone tower.

"It's part of the Villa Rufolo," she replied, "and it's very ancient. Most scholars think it dates to the 13th century. However, I think it is older. According to one story, a Pope abdicated there in the Middle Ages. Do you know that Richard Wagner lived there for a time in the 19th century?"

"No," I replied. "I did not know that."

Elsa continued her story. "The Villa Rufolo gardens, inspired Wagner to write his opera "Parsifal," about a knight's quest for the Holy Grail." I was mesmerized by Elsa's speech. It wasn't so much what she was saying that amazed me, however. I couldn't take my eyes off her face. She was incredibly beautiful to watch.

"Let's visit the villa <u>after</u> lunch," Kristina interrupted, perturbed by her sister's ongoing litany of historical trivia. "Right now, I'm hungry!" Clearly, Kristina was not as enchanted with her sister as was I.

Not wanting to offend Kristina's grumbling stomach, we walked through the tunnel to reach the restaurant on the other side. When we emerged at the other end, we saw a hotel as well as an iron gate seeming to lead to someone's house.

"Where is the restaurant?" Kristina inquired.

"It's below the road," Neal replied. "Open the iron gate and walk down the stairs."

At the bottom of the stairs, we entered another world, a large dining room filled with people and beyond an even larger terrace overlooking the sea.

"Let's sit outside near the railing," Elsa suggested.

After a few words exchanged in Italian with the hostess, we were seated at an immaculately furnished table near the railing.

"Vino Bianco or Rosso," the waiter asked.

"I would like white wine, Elsa replied. "What does everyone else want?"

"White is OK with the rest of us;" we chimed in.

As the waiter stood nearby patiently waiting for our order, the four of us pondered the large menu.

"What do you recommend?" Neal asked the waiter.

"The risotto fruiti de mare is exceptional today," the waiter replied. "The fish is also very good."

"I will have the fish," Kristina replied!

"I will have the risotto," Neal replied.

"I will have the risotto, also," I chimed in.

Looking toward Elsa, I noticed she was still reading the menu. "What are you getting, Elsa?" I asked.

"I'm tired of Italian food," she said. "I want something different. How is the chicken?" she asked the waiter.

"It's very fresh," he replied. His response seemed a peculiar answer.

"OK, I'll have the chicken," Elsa replied.

After the business of ordering was completed, we leaned back in our chairs, sipped our wine, and began to take in the view. I had seen pictures of the Amalfi Coast before, but no picture could compare to the stunning and majestic vista in front of us. The sun was shining brightly, and yet there was a misty quality to the air which seemed to enable the merging of the sea with the sky, without a perceptible line between the two.

"It seems almost like an impressionist painting," remarked Elsa, noticing the same effect as I.

"I wonder how high we are?" mused Kristina. "We must be at least a thousand feet above the sea."

"I think perhaps two thousand," said, Neal.

"I have never seen such beautiful blue water," remarked Elsa. Then she looked at her travel book. "The book says that Ravello is 1,200 feet above sea level," she replied. Only I was listening.

"I could sit here forever," Kristina remarked. "Let's stay here and never go home!"

As we pondered the beauty of the vista in front of us, Neal pointed out another sight equally interesting below. "Look down there," he said, pointing towards a woman carrying an ax. "Can you guess what's going to happen next?"

Listening to Neal, I glanced towards Elsa, who was noticing the same thing. Elsa had a look of horror on her face. When the woman entered the shed, we heard a cackling sound, followed by a thump, and then silence. The chicken was dead.

I could tell from Elsa's face that she understood what had just happened. Neal smiled at Elsa.

"The waiter warned you the chicken was fresh," he said.

"I feel so bad," remarked Elsa. "Honestly, I had no idea. I thought they would just take a package of chicken out of the refrigerator."

Kristina laughed at her sister. "Where do you think chicken comes from?" Kristina teased.

"I know," Elsa replied, "but it's always been dead beforehand, not murdered at my request." It seemed Elsa had just lost her appetite.

After forty-five minutes and a refill of our wine pitcher, our food finally arrived. The first plate to be served was Kristina's fish. The fish was served with the head still on and was about 12 inches long. It was artfully presented, swimming in a sauce of white wine and butter, surrounded by a ring of cherry tomatoes.

"Do you know what Pesce means in Neapolitan?" Kristina remarked with a twinkle in her eye. She then began poking at the fish's eyeball with her fork.

"Don't spoil my appetite," Elsa interjected, not wishing this line of questioning to continue further. I looked at Elsa and asked her what the word "pesce" meant in Neapolitan. Leaning over, she whispered in my ear, "It's a penis," she replied.

The next course to arrive was the risotto fruiti de mare. As I examined my plate, I saw all sorts of seafood mixed with rice. There were scallops, clams, mussels, calamari, and tiny little octopi, all topped with a large prawn.

"Let me take a picture first," Elsa said, as she hastily pulled the camera out of her purse. The last dish to arrive was Elsa's scrawny murdered chicken surrounded by a ring of French fries.

"Is that a pigeon or a chicken?" I teased. Elsa looked at me, smiled, and then stuck out her tongue.

"Don't make fun of my food," she teased, reaching for her knife and fork.

"You're supposed to eat chicken with your fingers;" Kristina chimed in.

"You eat your fish the way you want, and I will eat my chicken the way I want," Elsa replied.

Watching Elsa eat a whole chicken was entertainment in and of itself. Somehow, she managed to eat every bit of meat without ever touching the bird with her fingers. When she finished, she placed her fork in the meatless carcass and then draped her napkin around the fork, topping off her tiny grave marker with a flower from the nearby vase. "We have gathered here today to say goodbye to our dearly departed chicken," she mused.

After witnessing Elsa's ceremony, I reached for the flower, cut the stem with my knife, and placed the flower in Elsa's hair. "Thank you," she said. I was thinking about doing that.

After lunch, we stopped for gelato in the village square and then proceeded on a long walk through the village streets towards the Villa Cimbrone gardens on the edge of town.

"You must see this David," Elsa whispered in my ear. "It will be the highlight of our trip."

When we reached the garden entrance, a castle tower with a large wooden door, it seemed the gardens were closed for the day. Behind the wall, we could hear construction sounds.
"Push on the door," Elsa urged. "Maybe it will open."

A closed door was clearly not a barrier to Elsa. At her insistence, I pushed on the door, which opened easily once we decided to turn the large bronze knob. As the door swung open, we were greeted by a lovely sight. On the left was a large stone building with small arched windows in an unfamiliar yet ancient style. Ahead of us was a long pergola lined with sculpture beckoning us towards a terrace overlooking the sea. Just as we closed the door behind us, a cute young woman approached us from behind.

"Sorry about the closed door," she replied. "I had to use the restroom. That will be five thousand lire each."

After we had bought our tickets, we began our walk towards the terrace, admiring the sculpture and occasionally stopping to smell the flowers.

"I love this place," Elsa exclaimed! "This is the place where I someday want to get married. There is simply no more beautiful place in all the world."

At the end of the pergola, we emerged from under the purple bougainvillea stepping out onto the sculpture-lined terrace overlooking the sea.

"This is the Balcony of Infinity," remarked Elsa.

Looking downwards towards the sea, I could see, for the first time, hundreds of terraced fields climbing the mountainside. Far below, I could make out the outline of the winding road we had taken to reach Ravello. I had no idea all of this was here when we were driving up that road.

"Isn't it breathtaking?" Elsa whispered in my ear.

I nodded my head in the affirmative as I wrapped my arm around her waist. Then Elsa did something I didn't expect. She leaned over and kissed me on the cheek. When I turned toward her, she blushed and apologized.

"I'm sorry I did that," she said. "I couldn't help myself."

"Don't apologize," I replied. "It was nice."

Elsa then asked me a question. "Do you think a boy like you could ever fall in love with a girl like me?" she asked.

"I don't know Elsa," I replied. "You need to know that I have some baggage."

"We all have baggage, David, even me," she replied. It seemed at that moment like the entire world around us had disappeared, and the only thing remaining was just Elsa and me.

Then Kristina intervened and broke the spell. "What are you two lovebirds up to," she asked. Elsa did not reply. "Neal wants to drive down to Amalfi to see the Cathedral before we drive back to Naples," Kristina continued. "Are you game?"

"Sure," Elsa replied. "Can we stop in the ceramic shop on the way back through the village? I want to see if they have some of those vinegar and oil decanters I really like."

I felt disappointed. I would rather have stayed on the terrace with Elsa for a little while longer.

During the trip to Amalfi, Elsa and I barely spoke while Kristina and Neal continued to chatter away. It seemed nice to sit together without talking. After our visit to the Cathedral, to see the tomb of St. Andrew, we decided to sit in the back of the truck for the ride home rather than continue to sit in the front seat with Kristina and Neal.

The bed of the truck was a mess with crates, trash and other debris randomly scattered about. Clearly, Neal had never cleaned out the back of his truck. Somehow, despite the bumpy roads, Elsa and I managed to bring a small bit of order to the chaos, creating a space near the cab where we could comfortably sit. Elsa even managed to find some cushions which were hidden inside a wooden box. Once we were settled, we began to relax and get to know each other better.

"What has brought you to Naples?" I asked.

Elsa smiled. "I am pursuing a graduate degree in history at the University of Naples," Elsa replied. "I have always been fascinated by history, particularly the history of ancient Italy. One of my goals is to participate in an archeological dig while I am here. I find the history of this region fascinating. Do you know that Naples is over 2700 years old and that there are places in the Naples area mentioned in Homer's Odyssey?"

"No, I didn't know that." I replied. "Perhaps you would show me sometime?"

"What are you doing tomorrow?" Elsa asked.

"I have no plans other than perhaps to hang around the hotel," I replied.

"I need to drop my sister off at the airport in the morning but could be at your hotel by 11:30 AM," Elsa replied.

"That would be great," I replied.

"So, what brings you to Naples, David?", Elsa asked.

"I'm starting a new job on Monday as the Flag Officer housing manager at the U.S. Navy Base," I replied.

"What is a Flag Officer?" Elsa replied. She looked puzzled.

"In the U.S. Military, all Generals and Admirals have the right to fly a flag at their headquarters," I replied. "A Flag officer is an Admiral. Given that Naples is the headquarters for NATO Southern Europe, the American Military has an assortment of Admirals and Generals stationed here. Some are assigned to NATO, and the remainder are stationed here as part of the U.S. Sixth Fleet. I will be managing their houses."

"Sounds like an interesting job," Elsa replied. "Have you ever worked with so many high-ranking people before?"

"Not yet, wish me luck," I replied. "My main goal for the next two years is to somehow survive and not get fired."

Moving on to more serious topics, I asked Elsa if she was seeing anyone.

"I was seeing someone before I moved to Naples," she replied. "It's over now, however."

"Do you care to tell me more?" I asked.

"Do you want to hear the short story or the long version?" Elsa replied.

"Either story is fine with me," I replied.

Elsa nodded her head and then began her story. "Sven and I have dated off and on during college. We even lived together for one year after college."

"How did that work out?" I asked.

"Not well," Elsa replied. "Living with Sven was vastly different from dating him. I found him super jealous of my time. I had no privacy and felt suffocated. Eventually, I moved out. I think that even when two people live together, they need to give each other some privacy."

"Did you ever live together again after that?" I asked.

"No, but we continued to date," Elsa replied. I moved out just before I moved here."

"So, what eventually caused you to break up?" I asked.

"I guess we just wanted different things," Elsa replied. "Sven wanted to settle down and get married, and I didn't. Don't misunderstand me," Elsa continued. "It's not that I'm against marriage or having children. It's that I didn't want to get married yet. I also have dreams, and I wasn't willing to give them up. I still want to travel, to see more of Europe and continue my education."

"Is it over?" I asked.

"For now," Elsa replied with a tentative note in her voice, indicating perhaps it wasn't. I could tell there was more she was not telling me.

As I listened to her story, I realized that perhaps, I might have made the same mistake with Dana. Had I asked too much of her, more than she could give? What dream had I asked her to give up? I wasn't sure.

"So, tell me your story, David. Why are you still single?" Elsa asked.

"To tell the truth, Elsa, I think I fell into the same trap as Sven," I replied. "Before I moved to Italy, I had a girlfriend named Dana for the past two years. Just before I moved here, I asked her to marry me, and she said no. At the time, she told me she was a lesbian. Afterwards, I learned that she lied to me. She was in love with someone else." As I said this, I noticed Elsa's face change. She was listening to me intensely. "I realize now, in hindsight, we failed to communicate," I continued. "We talked a lot, but often not about the things that were most important. I think perhaps after two years we didn't really know each other as well as we thought we did."

"Did you want to get married?" Elsa asked.

"I'm not sure I did," I replied. "I think maybe I asked Dana because I thought that was what she wanted. Don't misunderstand me. We were close, and I realized I would be losing my best friend if I moved to Italy and didn't ask."

"So, you had already committed to moving to Italy at that point?" Elsa asked.

"Yes, I was committed," I replied. "You see, I didn't make that decision on my own. I thought Dana and I made it together. The problem was I misinterpreted the signals she was sending."

"So, you were certain if you asked, that she would say yes?" Elsa asked.

"Yes, that's what I thought," I replied.

"It must have been horrible to learn she lied to you and said yes to someone else," Elsa replied.

"It was," I replied.

"Have you spoken to her since?" Elsa asked.

"No," I replied. "There is no putting that genie back in the bottle."

"I am sorry, David," Elsa replied. "I really am." Then she wrapped her arms around me.

"Thanks for listening to me," I replied. "You are the first person I have told this to."

As our conversation wrapped up, we entered the city. Neal decided to drive directly into the center rather than around the city on the Tangenziale, as we had done on the way to Positano. We exited the freeway at the port of Naples and then quickly turned into Piazza Garibaldi, in front of the main train station. From there, we drove the length of the Corso Umberto, through the historic heart of the city.

The streets were deserted for Ferragosto. As we drove by the University, Elsa began to speak again. "Did you know that the University of Naples is over 700 years old?"

"No," I didn't know that I replied.

"It was founded in 1224 by the German Emperor Frederick II," Elsa replied. "I am attending one of the oldest universities in the world."

After we passed the University, we continued down the Corso Umberto until we veered left into another street and entered a large square, the Piazza Municipio. On the far end of the square next to the harbor, sat a huge feudal castle with giant round towers.

"What is that?" I asked Elsa, pointing towards the castle.

"That is the Castle Nuovo," Elsa replied. "It was built by the Angevin Kings of Naples in the 13th century. Did you know that Naples was an independent country for seven hundred years?"

Elsa was full of historical facts. "No, I didn't know that" I replied. Elsa, you seem to be a limitless font of knowledge.

Elsa smiled. "As I said before, I love history," she replied.

Just as she said this, our truck drove past the San Carlo Opera House and entered another small piazza with a fountain in the center. We had entered the Piazza Trieste et Trento. Next to the fountain stood a bride posing for a picture.

"This is where we get out," Elsa exclaimed, picking up her backpack from the floor of the truck! "I live just up that street behind the funicular station on the edge of the Spanish Quarter. I will see you tomorrow around 11:30 AM," she said.

"That sounds good," I replied, climbing down from the truck to sit in the front seat. "Did I tell you the name of the hotel?"

"Neal did," she replied. "He said you are staying at the Terme Hotel in Agnano."

"Yes, that's correct," I replied.

Before we could exchange another goodbye, Neal put the truck in gear, and we sped off. My first day with Elsa was at an end.

"You two seemed to hit it off;" Neal commented as we drove away. It was then that I realized that Neal might have wanted to spend the day with Elsa himself.

"I didn't steal your girl, did I?"

"No," Neal replied. "I met Elsa last week at my roommate Peter's going away party. Apparently, Peter met Elsa earlier this summer at someone else's party." Neal then changed the subject. "What do you think of Kristina?" Neal asked.

"She's very pretty," I replied.

"I would like to spend some more time with her," Neal continued.

"I hate to be the bearer of bad news," I replied. "Elsa told me that Kristina is flying back to Sweden tomorrow morning."

"Fuck!" Neal exclaimed! "Just my luck that the girls I'm interested in always move away. I should have asked for her phone number in Sweden. Can you do me a favor? When you see Elsa tomorrow, can you ask her for Kristina's phone number?"

"OK," I responded, not paying attention.

CHAPTER 3:

EVENING CONVERSATION BETWEEN KRISTINA & ELSA

KRISTINA'S NARRATIVE

As the boys sped off towards the Royal Palace, Elsa and I lingered in the piazza to take in the sights. Beside the fountain, there stood a woman clothed in the most beautiful wedding dress I had ever seen. "Is that one of Antonella's creations?" I asked.

"I do not know," Elsa replied, "but it's certainly magnificent."

As we watched, the woman did a graceful pirouette, turning towards one of her bridesmaids to straighten her veil. It was then that I noticed there was no groom. "Do you think she is really getting married," I asked, "or are we watching a modeling photoshoot?"

"My guess is she is a model," Elsa replied. "Wedding dresses are a big business here in Naples. I bet that dress sells for at least 25,000,000 lire."

"Seems like too much money for a dress that someone only wears once," I replied.

"I agree." Elsa responded. "That is the ironic thing about the Neapolitan people, many are so poor, struggling to make ends meet, and yet they spend huge sums on weddings and dresses."

"Is it true that Naples has a 30% unemployment rate?" I asked.

"I do not know," Elsa replied, "I think the 30% figure is an urban myth. I have heard there is a lot of petty crime here. It is mostly invisible, however. No one has ever tried to rob me."

"So, why do they spend so much money on weddings?" I asked.

"Living in the shadow of Vesuvius does that to people," Elsa replied. "The Neapolitans say that the nearness of death, exalts life. I suppose that is what I like about Naples," Elsa continued. "It's not just a place. It is a feeling that seeps deep into your soul."

I could sense it also, even though I had only been in Naples for two weeks.

"Would you like to see the San Carlo before we return to the apartment?" Elsa asked.

"Sure," I replied.

On the other side of the square stood the San Carlo Opera, one of the oldest opera houses in Europe. It was not a stand-alone building like the other later opera houses built in Paris and Vienna but was instead an extension of the Royal Palace itself.

"Did you know that comic opera was born in Naples?" Elsa asked.

"No, I did not know that." I replied.

"The San Carlo is the Royal Court Theater. It is a part of the palace," Elsa replied.

"Do you think someone will let us look inside?" I asked.

"We shall see," Elsa replied, as she stepped up to the ticket counter. Beside the counter, I stopped to admire a poster announcing La Traviata would be playing that evening as Elsa spoke to the clerk inside the window.

After several minutes, Elsa turned toward me with a smile on her face. "She has offered to show us inside," Elsa said. Moments later, the large grey door opened, inviting us to enter. Behind the door was a long room beautifully appointed with a long red carpet. Motioning us to follow her, the woman led us up two flights of stairs into another long gallery. "Now comes the good part," Elsa whispered.

The woman fumbled in her purse, producing a long skeleton key which she inserted into the door in front of us. Once she opened the door, we stepped inside the magnificent theater. What a sight! In the center was an enormous stage surmounted by a white and gold arch. As I peered around the theater, I could see hundreds of extravagant box seats arranged in five rows overlooking the stage. It was one of the grandest theaters I had ever seen.

"Look behind you," Elsa said as she motioned towards the Royal box behind us. The Royal Box was several stories tall and surmounted by an enormous crown. "That is where the king once sat," Elsa remarked. I had no idea the San Carlo was so beautiful inside.

"Did you know that Naples was an independent Kingdom for seven hundred years?" Elsa continued.

"No, I didn't know that" I replied.

"You are looking at the remains of an ancient kingdom that no longer exists," remarked Elsa. I noticed she had a tear in her eye.

"Have you ever been to an opera here?" I asked.

"Not yet," Elsa replied, "but I should like to attend at least one before I finish my degree."

"How about tonight?" I asked. The sign at the entrance said La Traviata is playing tonight.

"I can't afford it," Elsa replied. "I am tapped out. My credit card has hit its limit. I don't want to use father's card anymore. We can go to the opera next time you visit. Perhaps then, I will have more money. Do you know when you plan to come again?" Elsa asked.

"No," I replied. "Mother wants to come next summer; I will come with her if I can get off work."

"Where would you like to go for dinner during your last night in Naples?" Elsa asked.

"I am still full," I replied. "Let's get a pizza later this evening and take it to the apartment. I read that "Il Colpo Grosso" is on TV tonight and would like to see that. Also, my feet are tired from all the walking we did today."

"Ok," Elsa replied. "That is fine with me; my feet are tired too." After touring the San Carlo, we stepped back into the street.

"Which street do we take to your house?" I asked. "All these streets look the same to me."

"That one," Elsa indicated, pointing to a narrow alleyway behind the fountain.

"What is the name again?" I asked.

"Via Nardone's," Elsa replied.

Crossing the square once again, we began our long walk up the dark alley towards Elsa's apartment deep within the labyrinth of the Spanish Quarter. The streets were deserted. Everywhere the shops were closed, their large graffiti-covered metal shutters hiding the stores within.

"Do you think we will be able to find a pizzeria open?" I asked.

"For sure," Elsa replied. "The pizzeria next to my building is always open, even during August."

We walked up the long narrow street for what seemed a kilometer and then turned left, right, and left again as we wandered through the labyrinth of ancient narrow streets. All the streets looked the same to me as I became hopelessly lost in the maze. Looking upwards towards the sky, I could see hundreds of clotheslines crossing the street, each festooned with colorful laundry. The facades of the buildings looked ancient, positively decrepit, with large chunks of plaster missing revealing the dirty volcanic stones underneath.

"Aren't you afraid something will fall on your head?" I asked. "All these crumbling buildings give me the creeps."

"I was afraid at first," Elsa replied, "but after a while, I no longer notice."

"How old are these buildings?" I asked, admiring their advanced state of decay.

"Three to four hundred years old," Elsa replied. "Despite their appearance, these are not the oldest buildings in the city. The oldest buildings are on the other side of Via Toledo. Some of those buildings are a thousand years old."

"They look like they could collapse any minute," I remarked. Elsa laughed, and then smiled.

"That's the secret," Elsa replied. "They all want to collapse but cannot because they are too close together. Somehow, they prop each other up like a house of cards." As she said this, we turned the corner, passing through a large archway into a courtyard within. Stepping back into the archway, I took one last look at the street, hoping to frame a picture in my mind.

"What is that museum across the street?" I asked.

"It's the entrance to an underground catacomb," Elsa replied.

"Early Christian?" I asked.

"Parts of it are," Elsa replied. "I visited there once with Antonella. Behind that door is a long staircase that leads underground to a deep vertical spiral stair, which goes down 8 or 9 levels. At each level there are tunnels that branch off in various directions."

"Did you see any rats?" I asked. "I hate rats!"

"Me too," Elsa replied! "No, we didn't see any rats in the catacombs, however I have seen some in the streets. Inside the catacomb were many tunnels and rooms. Some rooms were used as air-raid shelters during World War II, and one of the rooms was a first-century church."

"Did you see any bones?" I asked.

"Yes, I saw some bones," Elsa replied, "where some tombs had been vandalized."

"Sounds creepy," I replied.

"One thing the visit taught me," Elsa noted, "was that Naples has an entire world under the streets. There are kilometers of tunnels under the city."

"Who built them?" I asked.

"I suppose the Neapolitans did," Elsa replied.

"Why?" I asked.

Elsa laughed. "They were not looking for buried treasure," she replied. "They are stone quarries." Then she motioned to the many buildings around us. "All this stone had to come from somewhere," she said! For a moment, I began to grasp the extent of the tunnels under the city. The labyrinth under the city might be larger than the city itself? The thought sent a chill up my spine as I pictured the subterranean world.

"How old is Naples?" I asked.

"Officially it is 2,700 years old," Elsa replied. "I think Naples is much older, however. Remember the word, Naples, means "The new city." There was a much older city next to Naples known as Parthenope. The Greeks named the city Parthenope after a legendary Siren from Greek mythology. No one knows what the ancient inhabitants called their city."

"Do they know where Parthenope stood?" I asked.

"The scholars think it is under the Pizzofalcone Hill in the Santa Lucia quarter," Elsa replied. "We are currently standing next to that hill."

"How old is Parthenope?" I whispered.

"Nobody knows," Elsa replied, "because no one can dig there. It is one of the densest parts of the city, and there is a fear that more digging might cause buildings to collapse. The archeologists at the university where I study have found buried agricultural settlements outside the city, however, dating back to 3000 BC. My guess is Naples may be older than that, perhaps dating back to the first agricultural settlements in Italy."

"How old is that?" I asked.

"Perhaps, six to seven thousand years old," Elsa replied.

For a moment she stopped talking, letting her last words sink in. Then she continued. "Naples is thought to have been first settled in the later part of the stone age, during the Neolithic period, when people first began practicing agriculture. Naples may be one of the oldest continuously inhabited cities in Europe." I was now beginning to get an appreciation for why Elsa wanted to study archaeology in Naples.

As we finished the conversation, we stepped into the apartment building elevator, a small wooden antique box no bigger than a phone booth, and I pushed the button marked "5". "Why isn't it moving?" I asked.

"You need to close both the gate and the door," Elsa replied.

Reopening the door and closing the gate, I pushed the button once again, and the elevator began to move. When we reached the top floor, Elsa pulled out the "Key to the Bastille," as David called it, and pushed it into the heavy steel door. After three turns of the key, the door unlocked, and we stepped inside her apartment.

"Do you mind if I take a shower and wash my hair?" I asked.

"Go ahead," Elsa replied. "Do not use up all the hot water however, as I want to take a shower after you."

"How long until you move?" I asked from within the shower, hoping she could hear me.

"Two more weeks," Elsa replied. "After that, Antonella and I are moving back in with her parents. Don't tell mom and dad about the needles and condoms on the street, please."

"Don't worry," I replied. "Your secret is safe with me." From behind the door, I could hear Elsa continuing to talk. "Moving here was Antonella's idea, not mine," she said. "It sounded fun at the time. I had no idea it would be so expensive or potentially dangerous."

"What do you pay for this place?" I asked.

"Would you believe $1,000,000 lira per month?" Elsa replied. The amount sounded astronomical.

"What are you doing for money these days?" I asked, "besides using your credit cards."

"I have started modeling again," Elsa replied. "Mostly I do work for Antonella's mother's fashion magazine. You remember Silvana. I introduced her to you last Monday. I also do shoots that she recommends. The work is good, and it pays very well. Would you like to see my Portfolio?" she asked.

"Certainly," I replied.

After several minutes I turned off the shower and emerged from the bathroom wrapped in a bath towel. "It's your turn," I remarked. "Where is your Portfolio?" I asked.

"It's next to the nightstand," Elsa replied as she stepped into the shower and closed the door.

"Do you mind if I open the window?" I asked. "It's very stuffy in here." When I opened the window, a flood of street noises entered the apartment. It seemed as if the streets were coming back to life after the afternoon siesta. Everyone had not left town for a holiday after all.

From below came the busy humming of the city with the sounds of people talking, children playing, vendors selling their wares and motorbikes whizzing by. As I waited for Elsa to finish her shower, I decided to remove the clothes from the line stretching across the street. It was then that my towel slipped, accidentally revealing one of my breasts.

Below I heard an old man say, "Ciao Bella!" He tipped his hat to me and smiled.

I smiled back and said, "excuse me." I had just made his day.

A few minutes later, Elsa emerged from the bathroom in her bathrobe, with a towel wrapped around her head. "Did you find the Portfolio?" she asked.

"Not yet," I replied, "I've been entertaining your neighbors trying to retrieve my bra from the clothesline."

"Do you need help?" Elsa asked.

"No, I figured it out," I replied, blushing as I dropped the towel slightly to show Elsa my nipple. Elsa smiled.

"Did you give someone a show?" Elsa asked.

"Yes," I replied. "It was an accident."

Sitting down on the bed, still wrapped in my towel, I opened Elsa's Portfolio and looked inside. There were pictures of Elsa in wedding dresses, pictures in sundresses, a picture in a swimsuit at the beach and a very elegant closeup picture taken for a perfume ad. The last picture, however, was quite provocative. It was a picture of a naked woman's breasts emerging from the water, with a caption below advertising a car stereo company.

"Tell me about the car stereo picture," I asked.

"I learned about that shoot from Antonella's mother," Elsa replied. "It paid eight million lire. Silvana didn't know the shoot was a nude shoot. I used the money to buy my motor-scooter."

"Don't ever show that picture to mom and dad," I replied.

"What is the big deal?" Elsa asked. "Women take their tops off at the beach every day in Italy. Even mother removes her top when we visit the French Riviera!"

"I know," I replied, "but this is different. It's like taking your top off on TV."

"Don't worry. I'm not going to be a contestant on "Il Colpo Grosso,"" Elsa laughed.

"Their loss," I replied, admiring the picture.

"What do you think would happen if Sven found out?" Elsa asked.

"He would lose his mind," I replied!

Elsa laughed. "Should I tell David?" Elsa asked.

"I'm not sure," I replied. "You better get to know him better before you show him the picture. American men can be strange animals. They seem to enjoy looking at naked women until they find out it is someone they know."

"What do you think of David?" Elsa asked.

"He seems nice enough," I replied. "He is quiet, however."

"Do you think he looks like Robert Redford?" Elsa asked. It took me a moment to picture Robert Redford in my mind. Eventually, the image of the famous actor wearing a White Navy uniform came into mind.

"Yes, I think so," I replied, "however I also think he looks a little like father."

For a moment Elsa stopped talking and stared at me. "Do you really think he looks like father?" she asked.

"Just a little," I replied. "Of course, he also looks like the boy you had a crush on in the seventh grade."

Elsa laughed. "He doesn't look anything like Christian," she replied. "You're just playing with me. Are you trying to say I am attracted to men who all look the same?"

"No," I replied. "Sven doesn't look like either David or father," I replied. Once again Elsa laughed.

I then changed the subject. "Do you remember that movie Robert Redford was in with Barbara Streisand?" I asked. "What was the name of that movie?" It was made in the 1970s.

Elsa smiled. She knew the movie instantly. It was her favorite movie. "The movie was "The Way We Were,"" Elsa replied.

"I wonder if David looks that good in his white uniform," Elsa remarked. She had a distant quality in her voice.

"I noticed you two spent considerable time today together," I replied. "Are you falling in love with the man or the image of Robert Redford in his white uniform?"

"I'm not in love, at least not yet" Elsa protested. "I just think David looks like Robert Redford!" It seemed to me that Elsa was falling for David, (or perhaps for a man who looked like father).

"What about your old boyfriend, Sven?" I asked.

"Sven and I have broken up again, this time for the last time," Elsa replied. Sven & Elsa were always breaking up.

"What happened this time?" I asked.

"Sven accused me of seeing another man. He saw me at the library sitting beside one of my classmates from school. When I told him I wasn't cheating, he didn't believe me and took a swing at me," Elsa replied.

"Did he hit you?" I asked.

"No, he missed, but he did knock a hole in the wall of his apartment," Elsa replied.

"What did you do?" I asked.

"I threw a potted plant at his head and walked out the door," Elsa replied.

"Is that why you came to Italy early?" I asked.

"Yes," Elsa replied. "I had to get away from Sven and find time to think." It was clear from the tone of her voice that the relationship was not over.

"Do mother and father know?" I asked.

"No, and please don't tell them," Elsa replied.

"Do you still have feelings for Sven?" I asked.

"I don't know," Elsa replied. "I feel very confused. One part of me still loves him, and yet part of me is also terrified of him. Sven has major jealousy and anger issues that he needs to resolve."

"Has he tried to contact you since you moved to Italy?" I asked.

"Yes," Elsa replied. "He sends a letter to Antonella's parents' address every week. Fortunately, he doesn't have their phone number."

"Have you responded or called him back?" I asked.

"Not yet," Elsa replied. "I have been ignoring him."

"Do you want to know what I would do?" I asked.

"Sure, what would you do?" Elsa replied.

"I would dump him," I replied. Once a man gets violent, he's finished, as far as I'm concerned. Better to find this out before you get married rather than after. I say dump him!"

"Thanks for the advice," Elsa replied. "I am tending towards your point of view but am trying a more subtle approach of ignoring him first, hoping he will just go away."

That night we split an exceptionally good pizza from the shop nearby, while we watched "Il Colpo Grosso" (The Big Score) on Elsa's tiny TV. "Listen closely," Elsa whispered. Outside the window, we could hear the noise of hundreds of TV sets all turned to the same show. The entire neighborhood was watching "Il Colpo Grosso." Elsa and I tried not to giggle. "I read in the newspaper this week that "Il Colpo Grosso" is currently the most popular TV show in Italy," Elsa whispered. "Can you imagine a TV show where women remove their tops on Swedish TV?"

"Never," I replied. Little did I realize that Swedish TV would eventually create its own version of the show.

"You and I could win this show if we wanted to," Elsa suggested.

I gazed down at our breasts and had to admit she was right. "Yes, we could win," I admitted, "but father would have a heart attack afterwards. Don't even think about it!" I remembered the car stereo ad. What would father think if he saw that picture? I shuddered to contemplate the ramifications.

After the show ended, we turned out the light and went to bed. Elsa fell asleep the minute her head hit the pillow; however, I couldn't sleep. All night I kept replaying in my head our day on the Amalfi Coast. It had been a wonderful, beautiful day. The last thing I wanted to do was get on a plane and return to Sweden. I am going to miss this apartment, I thought, even if it is a dump.

CHAPTER 4:

DAVID & ELSA TOUR NAPLES

I didn't sleep well during my second night in Naples. Just before dark, the hotel air conditioning, which had been so pleasant the night before, stopped working. It seemed the A.C. gremlins from Norfolk had followed me to Naples. When I enquired at the front desk how long it would be until the A.C. was repaired, the man behind the desk shrugged his shoulders and said, "Domani or Dopo Domani." I would learn this meant tomorrow, the day after tomorrow or maybe never.

When I returned to the room, I opened the windows, which seemed to help cool the room, but then another problem presented itself. From behind the hotel, I began to hear a chorus of frogs. There was a swamp behind the hotel. At first, it was just one frog, not too terrible a distraction, but then other frogs joined in until there was a symphony of frogs all trying to out-croak each other. Imagine if you can if frogs could scream. That is the sound that kept me from falling asleep.

By 12:00 pm, I had had enough and got up to close the windows. That, of course, raised the temperature in the room to a level just below sauna. Glancing over at the alarm clock, it was now 12:30 pm. I wondered how long the symphony might last. Around 1:00 am, after sweating profusely, I opened the windows again, letting the amphibious chorus back in, and so it went all night. It wasn't until 4:00 am that the chorus finally stopped.

No sooner had I drifted off to sleep than my alarm went off. It was 7:00 am, time to get up. I thought of hitting the snooze button but decided against it. I wanted to find the American Base nearby before Elsa came to pick me up. When I stepped outside of the hotel, I was engulfed by a blast of hot, muggy air. Today is going to be hot, I thought to myself.

Following the directions provided by the coffee barista, I proceeded down the hill until the street merged with a wide street, the Via Beccadelli. From there, it was a short walk to the intersection with Via Scarfoglio. As I stood at the corner waiting to cross, I noticed that no one was stopping for the red light. It seemed I might have to wait forever. Finally, I saw a break in traffic and started across. Remarkedly motorist started to slow down and weave around me, but they didn't stop. Many of the cars had NATO plates. They were Americans. When I made it to the other side, I began walking towards the Base, somewhere between my location and the rim of the Agnano crater beyond.

Even though it was Sunday morning, there was already a stream of cars with AFI NATO plates going towards the Base. After passing several car dealerships, and auto repair shops, at last, I arrived at what looked like an American strip mall surrounded by a tall steel fence. I had found the American Base. It looked small. Inside the fence, I saw a familiar sign for an American hamburger chain. I walked up to the first gate into the Base, thinking I might be able to enter there, and was turned away. "This gate is for vehicles only;" the Italian guard proclaimed! "You must enter at the pedestrian gate!"

Afterward, I walked another hundred yards down the fence to a second gate, a gate resembling the entrance to a prison. After several minutes of answering questions, and showing ID, the guard hit a buzzer, letting me in through the heavy metal turn-style.

That morning I ate my breakfast on base, experiencing my first small taste of America outside of America. It was good to be back home, if only for an hour. After breakfast, I returned to the hotel, now soaked with perspiration. The front desk clerk had good news. "The A.C. will be repaired today," he said.

"Where are the beauty contestants today?" I enquired.

"They just left on buses for the Island of Ischia," he responded. "Today is the swimsuit competition."

"I am sorry I missed it," I replied, picturing hundreds of scantily clad women in my mind.

"Are you with the contestants?" he asked. "If so, I can arrange a cab to take you to the ferry at Pozzuoli. The ferry does not depart until 10:00 am."

"No," I replied. "I am not with the pageant. I was simply curious."

When I returned to my room, I took a shower and prepared to wait for Elsa's arrival. It was stifling hot, so I decided to wait outside under the shade trees. No sooner did I sit down than Elsa arrived on her motor scooter, an adorable, new, red motor bike. This time she dressed in white capri pants with a blue and white horizontal striped blouse, her sunglasses perched as usual on the top of her forehead.

"I like your motor scooter!" I exclaimed.

"Thank you," she replied! "I just bought it back in July."

"Did you have any trouble finding the hotel?" I asked.

"No, but I was a little late leaving the airport," Elsa replied.

"Have you had anything to eat?" Elsa asked.

"I had a coffee and roll for breakfast, but that is all," I replied.

"Good," she remarked! "I have brought a picnic. It's here in my backpack." She removed the bright red leather backpack from her back and set it on the ground. For a moment, I was mesmerized as she stood in front of me, tossing her blond hair and readjusting her sunglasses. I thought of telling her how beautiful she looked but decided not to. I didn't want her to think I was too needy. But still, I couldn't help admiring her beauty.

"Do I have something on my nose?" she asked.

"No," I replied. "I was just thinking of something."

"Have you been waiting long?" Elsa asked.

"No, I just came down from the room," I replied.

"I know a beautiful spot above a lake where we can have our lunch," Elsa offered.

"Where are we going today?" I asked.

"You said you were interested in seeing the ancient sites in the area, so I thought I would take you to Cumae," she replied. "After that, we can work our way back through Pozzuoli and Naples. I thought we could have dinner near the Egg Castle. Does that sound good?"

"Perfect," I replied. "That sounds like a plan!"

"Can you please carry my backpack?" she asked, "so that you can wrap your arms around me while we ride. I would hate to have you fall off the bike!"

"Ok, with me," I replied. It seemed that wearing the backpack was a small price to pay to embrace Elsa for the entire day. As I climbed onto the bike behind Elsa, I noticed the smell of her hair. It was intoxicating.

Within a few minutes, we were on our way. After several turns, we crossed a busy intersection and began to climb a long steep hill. Before long, our moped was barely moving.

"Do I need to get off and push?" I asked.

Elsa laughed, "I hope not," she replied. "I have never tried to go up this hill before with two people." Up ahead, I could see the billboard with the naked woman that Neal had told me about the day before.

"Did you know that Neal lives near that billboard?" I asked.

"Yes," Elsa replied. "I attended a party at his apartment last Friday night." Elsa then changed the subject. "What do you think about the billboard?" Elsa asked.

"It seems a bit brazen just to sell car stereos," I replied. "Don't get me wrong, the woman looks great, but really, it's a little over the top."

"That's what I think, too," Elsa replied. "They must think that only men buy car stereos. What about us women?"

"What do you suggest?" I asked.

"A picture of a naked man, not, of course, his face, but like the other picture, his, you know what?" Elsa giggled.

"Wouldn't that cause an accident?" I replied. I was enjoying this line of flirtation.

"I' don't think so," Elsa replied. By now, we had reached the top of the hill. "On the right is the entrance to the Solfatara," Elsa remarked, waving her right hand in the air. "This is just one of the many volcanic craters in this area."

As we drove by the entrance, I suddenly smelled the smell of rotten eggs. "This area is known as the Campi Flegrei," Elsa proclaimed. "The name means the flaming fields." After the Solfatara we passed a small church on the left surrounded by cars double and triple parked.

"What is this church on the left?" I asked.

"That is the church of San Gennaro, the patron saint of Naples," Elsa replied. "According to the story, he was martyred at that spot back in the fourth century. There is a vial of his blood kept in the Cathedral, which changes to liquid three times each year."

"Have you ever seen that?" I asked.

"No," Elsa replied, "but that is on my list of things to do."

"What happens if the blood does not turn to liquid?" I asked.

"Dreadful things," Elsa replied! "Vesuvius might erupt!"

"Has it ever happened?" I asked.

"Yes," Elsa replied. "The last time the blood failed to liquify, Naples lost in the Italian Cup final."

"So apparently, San Gennaro cares about soccer?" I asked.

"Apparently so," Elsa replied. "Did you know that the blood failed to liquify in 1944?"

"No, I did not know that" I replied!

"The Italians lost the war, the Germans occupied the country, and Vesuvius erupted, all in one year," Elsa exclaimed!

"Let's hope the blood turns to liquid, at least for the next two years," I replied.

"I agree," replied Elsa!

By now, we had entered the town of Pozzuoli and were driving around a long bend in the road, passing a large, ruined structure on the right. "What is that" I asked!

"The Roman Amphitheater," Elsa replied. "That is the third-largest Roman Amphitheater in the world. At one time, Pozzuoli was a major Roman city and the principal port for Rome. According to historians, St. Paul first visited Pozzuoli on his way to Rome, and he preached here in the marketplace."

"Where is the market?" I asked.

"Down the hill towards the water," Elsa replied. "We will go by that in a minute." After a few minutes, we arrived at the top of a cliff overlooking a deep excavation below. At the bottom of the excavation was an ancient, paved plaza with a cluster of Roman-era columns.

"Is that the market?" I asked?

"Yes," Elsa replied. "Do you see that area on the columns which have many holes?" she asked.

"Yes, I see it," I replied.

"Those holes were created by marine boring insects," Elsa replied. "The land in this area sits on top of a large underground magma chamber. Sometimes the magma cools, causing the city to sink, which in turn causes the market to flood. Sometimes the lava heats up, causing the city to rise."

"Is it hot right now?" I asked. I noticed that the plaza was dry.

"Yes," Elsa replied, "this area began to rise rapidly in the early 1980s. We will see that down by the harbor. The expansion of the caldera almost shook the city of Pozzuoli to pieces. At one point it got so bad, the Italian Government thought an eruption was imminent and decided to relocate the entire population of 30,000 people, to an area north of here known as Monterusciello."

"It appears they moved back." I replied, motioning to the crowds of people, buses and cars below busily streaming into and out of the port.

"Yes," Elsa replied. "Thankfully, the eruption never happened. The people are now moving back. Let's go down to the port, and I will show you the fish market."

When we arrived at the port, Elsa chained her bike to a sign. Afterward, we walked across the street to the fish market. In front of us spread a long wooden trestle covered with pans of fresh seafood, recently caught that morning. Some of the fish were still moving. At the end lay a large fish, a swordfish, being sliced by a fisherman.

At the other end of the trestle were several pans of shellfish. One pan was filled with little squid, still squirming in the pan. One pan was filled with mussels, and one pan was filled with clams. On top of the shellfish was a purple octopus, still alive, attempting to escape.

"Do you think he will get away?" Elsa asked, with an impish smile.

"Let's watch and see," I replied.

Three times the octopus crawled across the pans to the edge of the table. It seemed he might be able to make it to the water, but at the last moment, the man behind the counter grabbed him and put him back in the first pan.

"Poor Mr. Octopus," Elsa exclaimed! "I think he's stewed! Let's see if the clams are fresh," Elsa remarked, beckoning me to place my face closer to the pan. Taking her cue, I put my face near the pan, not realizing what was about to happen. As I turned to face Elsa one of the clams' spit water in my eye, causing Elsa to laugh.

"You knew that would happen," I remarked.

Elsa just grinned. "I'll never tell," Elsa replied with an impish smile. "Let's go," she continued. "I'm hungry, and it's time for lunch."

Hopping back on the motorbike, we rode along a long bumpy road near the port. The road was so bumpy I felt like I might lose my dental fillings. We followed the road for several miles past factories until we arrived at another busy intersection.

"This is Arco Felice," Elsa proclaimed. "Welcome to the "Happy Arch!"

"Are we there yet?" I asked.

"Almost," Elsa replied as she turned left onto a road leading under a freeway overpass. Soon thereafter, the road ended at a sandy trail. "We will need to walk from here," she replied.

We had arrived in a vineyard overlooking a deep lake. "This is Lago Averno," said Elsa, as she started to set up our picnic, pulling a white and red checked cloth out from under the seat.

"What's for lunch?" I asked. I reached into the backpack and began pulling items out.

"There are two sandwiches, a small bottle of wine, various plastic containers filled with leftover antipasti, two glasses and two forks," Elsa remarked, as she began taking things from my hands and spreading them out on the blanket. "We will have to eat direct from the containers as I could not fit two plates into the backpack."

"Looks delicious," I remarked. I began opening the lids on the antipasti.

"There is eggplant in this one, zucchini in that one, and Tuscan white beans in that other one," Elsa replied, pointing to the dishes arrayed on the blanket.

"Would you like some wine?" I asked. I opened the wine bottle. On the front was a label which said "Lacryma Christi."

"Yes, please," Elsa replied.

"What does Lacryma Christi mean?" I asked.

"Tears of Christ," Elsa replied. "It's made from grapes grown on the slopes of Vesuvius."

"What is on the sandwiches?" I asked, biting into one of the crusty round rolls.

"Prosciutto and Mozzarella di Buffalo," Elsa replied. "They are my favorite sandwich."

"The cheese is like a sponge filled with milk," I replied. "It's not at all like the Mozzarella in America."

"This is the real Mozzarella," remarked Elsa, "not that stuff you buy in the States."

The sandwich tasted excellent, even though I now had milk running down my arm. For a moment, we stopped talking and began to admire the view as we ate our lunch. Below us, I could see a ruin sticking out of the hillside. On the other side of the lake, I could see a restaurant beside the water.

"What is the name of this lake again?" I asked.

"Lago Averno," Elsa replied. "This is the legendary Lake Avernus. Do you know that the Greeks and Romans considered this lake to be the entrance to Hades?" For a minute, I stopped chewing my sandwich to take in Elsa's words. It now seemed fitting that we should drink Tears of Christ wine while dining at the entrance to Hell.

"Nice touch," I replied, complimenting Elsa on her choice of wine! "I never pictured the entrance to Hell would be so pretty."

"Yes, it's nice today, but it hasn't always been pretty," Elsa replied. "Do you see that mountain on the left side of the lake? That is Monte Nuovo. It wasn't there at the beginning of the 16th century before the eruption of 1538. The mountain was created in just three days. Under our feet is lava. There is a fire here, that runs deep into the earth."

"How deep?" I asked.

"Hundreds of miles," whispered Elsa.

"Perhaps the ancients knew something?" I mused. "Perhaps this is the entrance to Hell?"

"Yes," Elsa whispered. "Perhaps it is. Would you like some more eggplant?"

"What is the ruin beside the lake?" I asked.

"That is the remains of the Temple of Apollo," Elsa replied. "In ancient times it was the location of the Oracle of the Dead." Once again, I paused to slowly chew my sandwich.

"Sounds spooky," I replied.

Elsa nodded her head and then continued her story. "Do you want to hear something else interesting?" she asked.

"What," I replied.

"This lake was once used as a base for the Roman fleet," Elsa replied. "During the age of Caesar Augustus, the Roman General Marcus Agrippa built a canal linking Lago Averno to the Bay of Pozzuoli. It may have been where Monte Nuovo stands today. The harbor he created was named Portus Julius after Julius Caesar. At one time, this lake was filled with Roman war galleys."

For a moment, I stopped eating to imagine the scene. Elsa's story brought a whole new dimension to the lake below. In my mind's eye, I pictured the naval battle scene from the movie "Cleopatra."

After lunch, we put away the food and wiped off our blanket. It was a beautiful place for a picnic. Elsa lay beside me on the grass, gazing up at the sky as we watched the clouds roll by. Once again, I was mesmerized by her beauty. Where have you been all my life, I thought? As I gazed at her perfect body lying on the blanket, Elsa turned to face me. It was then that I noticed her eyes. Elsa had the most beautiful blue eyes. They sparkled in the warm afternoon sun. The moment only lasted for a second, unfortunately, as Elsa broke the spell, starting to pack everything up. "Let's get going," she remarked! "There is more I want to show you today!"

Within a few short minutes, we were back on the motorbike and headed towards Cumae with my arms wrapped tightly around her waist. Just before we reached our destination, we passed under a large ruined Roman Arch. "That is the aqueduct that once brought water to the Roman port," Elsa pointed out. We then hit a patch of Roman cobblestones, which nearly threw me off the bike. "Sorry about that," she remarked. "I should have slowed down."
When we finally reached the ruins of Cumae, the parking lot was empty. The gate appeared closed for the day. "Cumae looks closed," I observed.

"Fences are like traffic lights," Elsa responded. "Let's push on the gate and see what happens." Within a few short moments, we were inside. The guard had forgotten to lock the gate. I wondered if we would have to climb the fence later to get out.

Ahead of us ran a long path through the woods. After several hundred yards, the path passed between two cliffs and entered a strange courtyard carved out of living rock. Below me, on the right, a large tunnel appeared extending deep into the earth. "Is that the cave of the Sibyl?" I asked. I had read about the Sibyl's cave the night before.

"No," Elsa replied. "That's a tunnel built by the Romans to connect Lago Averno to Cumae. The entrance to the Sibyl's cave is over here towards the left."

We walked another fifty yards until we came to the cave's entrance. The cave was not like any cave I had ever seen. It had a strange trapezoidal shape, following an ancient design, and penetrated deep into the hillside with shafts of light at regular intervals along its length. As we walked quietly along its length, I realized that the cave was running parallel to the sea and that the shafts of light I had seen at the beginning were openings, looking out towards the water. At the end of the cave, we entered a larger chamber whose walls were covered with green-colored moss. Looking upwards, I noticed the roof was covered with a heavy layer of soot from thousands of years of burning candles.

"This is the Sibyl's chamber," remarked Elsa. "Do you know anything about the Cumaean Sibyl?" she asked.

"No," I replied, "but I am sure you are about to tell me."

Elsa smiled. "Sit down beside me," she said. She then began her story. "The Cumaean Sibyl is one of many Sibyls from the ancient world. Sibyl is a title, rather than a name. It is used to designate a priestess of the god Apollo. According to the myth, the god Apollo seduced a woman. In exchange for her virginity, she asked to live for as long as the grains of sand in her hand. The god granted her wish however, she did not think to ask for the one gift that mattered more, the gift of perpetual youth.

"The priestess is said to have lived for a thousand years, gradually shrinking, and withering with age, until she was so small that she was kept in a jar hanging on the wall. Eventually, before she disappeared, only her voice remained. It was said she wrote her prophecies on oak leaves which she laid on the floor of this chamber. She let the wind shuffle the leaves to hide their meanings from mortal men.

"It is also said that she was the keeper of nine ancient books of prophecy, which were brought to Cumae following the destruction of Troy. According to an important story, she traveled to Rome and attempted to sell the books to the last Roman King, Tarquin, for an exorbitant price. When he refused to buy the books, she burned three of the books and offered to sell the remaining six books at the same exorbitant price. Once again, the king refused, and once again, she burned three more books. When only three books remained, the priests of Apollo begged the king to buy the books before the knowledge contained therein was lost forever.

"Eventually, he agreed to purchase the three remaining books for the same price originally proposed for all nine books. After the purchase, the books were kept in the Temple of Jupiter on Rome's Capitoline Hill, where they were stored for hundreds of years. Then in 83 B.C., the books accidentally caught fire and were destroyed.

"After the fire, the Roman Senate began an exhaustive search of the then known world to find copies of the books lost in the fire. Eventually, copies were found, which were returned to the Temple of Jupiter in 76 B.C. The oracle of Apollo and the Sibyl were especially important to the Roman State. For us today, it would be like losing the only copy of the Holy Bible in existence."

"Whatever happened to the books?" I asked.

"They were destroyed in 408 A.D. by the Roman General Stilicho, just before the destruction of Rome by the Visigoths in 410 AD." Elsa replied. "Some suggest that the destruction of the books was an omen for the destruction of Rome which followed. There is one more thing you ought to know about the Sibyl."

"What is that?" I asked.

"It is believed she predicted the birth of Christ," Elsa replied.

As we sat in the dimly lit chamber, a gentle breeze blew into the room, shuffling the leaves scattered on the floor. For a moment I thought of Elsa's story. "Did you see that? I asked.

"Yes," Elsa whispered. "Perhaps the Sybil is still here?" I was beginning to understand why Elsa loved Naples.

As we walked out of the cave back towards the entrance to the park, Elsa provided me with another story of another cave nearby in Baia. "There is another cave," she explained, "also associated with Sibyl. It is nearby in Baia. That cave runs from the surface to a point deep underground, where it ends at a steaming underground river. It is said that the river might be the inspiration for the river Styx."

Elsa had promised a glimpse into Naples' ancient mythic past. It wasn't just Naples's past, however. It was everyone's past. Her tour that summer afternoon did not disappoint. I was hooked, just as she had been years before.

After our journey back in time, Elsa and I retraced our steps, riding back through Pozzuoli, driving along the sea until we arrived at a giant rusting steel mill. Turning left after the steel mill, we drove up a road, hugging a cliff until we turned into another road, driving under a large arch. We had entered the Posillipo Quarter. I did not know it at the time, but the Posillipo hill would be my home for the next two years.

After the stone arch, we reached a small park and broad intersection with roads branching off in many directions, where we stopped for a moment to get reoriented. Pointing to the right, Elsa indicated that her roommate Antonella's parents lived on that road. "At the bottom of the hill is a small fishing village named Marechiaro, with several excellent restaurants," she said. "Straight ahead is the Via Posillipo, the oldest street which runs along the water. I am going to turn to the left so that we can see a better view of the city from the top of the hill." In my mind's eye, I remembered this hill. It was the long low hill with lights that I flew along during my arrival two nights before.

We turned left onto Via Boccaccio, which became Via Manzoni after a traffic circle. As we rode up the hill, I noticed a strange sight. On the right side of the road, parked under the pine trees, were several cars parked on the sidewalk. Each of the cars had newspapers covering the windows.

"What is with that?" I asked, motioning to the parked cars as we whizzed by.

"You should see this stretch of road on a Saturday night," Elsa remarked. "On Saturday night, this sidewalk is occupied by hundreds of cars, all with newspapers covering the windows."

"What are they doing?" I asked.

"What do you think?" Elsa replied.

"Having sex?" I asked.

For a moment, Elsa said nothing; then, she finally gave me a cute reply. "Welcome to Naples, David. You're not in Kansas anymore."

We reached the crest of the hill shortly thereafter and proceeded down the other side on another wide road. The road was named Via Petrarca. When we reached a bend in the road, we stopped to admire the view. I now could finally see the hill in both directions. To the right, there were hundreds of beautiful mansions and gardens riding on a gentle slope to the sea. Beyond sat the beautiful outline of an island far in the distance. To the left, I saw the city with the Egg Castle sitting out in the water like a child's sandcastle beckoning us to dinner. Beyond the city, across the water, loomed the outline of Vesuvius.

Starting on the right, I asked about the island. "That is Capri," Elsa replied. "Do you see that high point at the far-left end of the island?" she asked.

"Yes, I see it," I replied.

"That is where the Villa Jovis is located," Elsa replied. The Villa Jovis was once the palace of the Roman Emperor Tiberius."

"Can you tell me about these mansions below?" I asked.

"You are looking at the richest area of Naples," Elsa replied. "Rich people have been living on this hill since Roman times. The Posillipo may, in fact, be the oldest continuously inhabited wealthy neighborhood in the world."

"What is that house surrounded by gardens?" I asked. I pointed towards a large mansion in the distance.

"That is the Villa Roseberry," Elsa replied. "It is the official residence of the Italian President, in Naples. I have one more place to show you before we go to dinner," Elsa continued, as we set off down the hill once again. It seemed to me like we had just eaten; however, when I looked at my watch, I realized it was nearing 7:00 pm. Where had the time gone? Elsa was right; I was ready to eat again.

It seemed we were driving towards the water, but then Elsa turned to the left and began traveling up another winding street until she suddenly veered off to the right onto a narrow lane. After a few short yards, we came to a stop in front of a large square hanging off the hillside. We were now directly above the Mergelina tunnel. "This is my favorite place in the city," Elsa exclaimed as she jumped off the bike and took my hand to lead me to the railing.

In front of us was the grandest urban panorama I had ever seen. I had seen downtown Chicago at night from high above Lake Shore Drive. I had even seen Los Angeles from above the Hollywood Bowl, but I had never seen a sight like this before. This view was on a different level, like viewing Rio from the top of Corcovado.

In front of us lay the ancient City of Naples in all its glory. Below us, I could see Piazza Sannazaro, the large square I had driven around the day before with Neal. In front of us ran three-wide streets, the Via Caracciolo on the right, which ran along the water, the Viale Gramsci in the center and the Riviera di Chiaia on the left. Between these wide streets sat large Renaissance palaces, each occupying a full city block with large interior courtyards. At the end of these buildings sat a large white building with an American flag. It was the American Consulate.

Beyond the Consulate lay the long green arc of the Villa Comunale Park, once a garden of the king. The Villa Comunale now provides a green space in the center of one of the densest parts of the city, the Chiaia Quarter.

At the far end of the park sat the oldest part of the city, the Pizzofalcone Hill, the site of the original city of Parthenope. At the base of the hill sat a ring of luxury hotels lining the waterfront, across from Naples's oldest castle, the Egg Castle. This area is known as the Santa Lucia Quarter.

On the left side of the park rose hundreds of apartment buildings climbing up the hill like multi-colored stairsteps to the top of the Vomero Hill. At the far end of the Vomero stood the mighty fortress of San Elmo, a giant star-shaped fort which once protected the city from foreign invaders.

As we gazed out admiring the view, Elsa made a comment that I found most interesting. "Naples has three castles," she said. "They are the Egg Castle, which is the oldest, the New Castle, which is not new, and the Castle San Elmo. Only one castle, the Castle San Elmo, was designed to protect the city. The other two castles were designed to protect the king from his subjects. So, what do you think?" Elsa asked after a prolonged period of silence.

"It is magnificent," I replied!

"My thoughts also," Elsa replied.

Elsa then did something unexpected. Elsa was always doing unexpected things. She leaned against me, wrapped her arms around me and gave me a long kiss on the lips.

"I just had to do that," she said! "It seemed such a shame to waste such a beautiful view."

"Would you like to do that again?" I asked. I noticed there were several other people kissing beside the railing. Elsa did not reply, but instead closed her eyes and leaned over to kiss me a second time. Her kiss was like magic. For a moment time stood still.

Afterward, we gazed out at the city for what seemed like hours as the sun began to set. As we stood there a large van pulled up to the square and began selling ice cream. Soon a crowd was gathered. "Lets' get something to eat," Elsa suggested. I nodded my head in agreement, realizing I was hungry again. It was twilight time and almost dark.

CHAPTER 5:

ELSA & DAVID'S FIRST NIGHT TOGETHER

ELSA'S NARRATIVE

Our first night together, David & I had pizza by the sea, in the shadow of the Egg Castle. I had a pizza resembling an Italian flag, with tomato sauce and garlic on one side, mozzarella cheese on the other side and a stripe of green broccoli rabe with sausage in the center. David had a pizza with prosciutto, mushrooms, artichokes, and peppers, which was also particularly good.

We started out eating our own pizza but soon decided to share. After the first course, we proceeded to the meat course. I ordered scallopini (a tender, thinly sliced cut of veal) with lemon, and David ordered scallopini with white wine. Both were excellent. After the second course, we ordered dessert, Rum Babas (delicate cakes formed in the shape of mushrooms and soaked in rum). I should have realized I had had enough alcohol for the night, but I didn't. After two bottles of wine and a shot of rum in the form of a cake, I ordered shots of Limoncello thereafter. It was the best meal I had eaten in weeks. Unfortunately, we both had too much to drink.

After the meal, our check arrived, I was aghast at the bill. The bill was 150,000 lire. I didn't have that much money, nor did David. Between us we only had 140,000 lire. What would we do? As we contemplated our next move, David reached into his wallet to take stock of our options. His wallet was empty. For a few moments he opened all the compartments until he found a credit card. Thankfully, David had a credit card. We both felt relieved.

As we waited for the waiter to return with the card, David offered an observation of our condition. "We are in no shape to ride the moped," he said. He was right, of course. "Is your apartment nearby? I can walk you back and then perhaps take a cab back to the hotel," David offered.

David's suggestion sounded sensible; however, there was one problem. The cabs had stopped running for the night. "I suppose you can spend the night at my apartment," I suggested. As I said this, I instantly regretted my offer.

David paused for a moment to think and then asked a question. "What day is it?" he asked. "Is it Sunday?" He had lost track of which day it was.

"Yes," I replied, "it is Sunday."

"Tomorrow is my first day at work," he replied. "I need to be there by 7:30 am. Do you think you can get me to the hotel by 7:00 am?"

"Certainly," I replied, not certain if I could wake up that early. On a good day, I often did not get out of bed until 8:00 am. Tonight, I said yes, however. As David said previously, I was in no shape to drive.

As we got up to leave, my legs felt wobbly, but also happy. In fact, I was incredibly happy. I wondered what I was getting into. "You must understand," I blurted out. "I do not want you to think poorly of me, but I'm not the kind of girl who invites men to her apartment on the first date."

"I understand," David replied.

I wondered, however, if he really understood or was one of those men who thought he was about to get lucky. As I pondered David, I asked myself a question. Would he stop if I said no? I wasn't sure.

The walk back to the apartment was long, much longer than it usually seemed. As we passed through the Piazza Plebiscito, we stopped for a moment to take in the view of the long façade of the Royal Palace. "Have you seen this yet?" I asked. I could not remember if we visited the palace the day before. The wine was affecting my brain. Why did I keep drinking, I asked myself? Did I really need that last shot of Limoncello?

"No, not yet," David replied. "Perhaps you can take me to the palace next time?"

Next time, I thought. I wondered if there would be a next time. Should I tell David I would soon be moving? Perhaps not tonight, I thought. I wondered how the evening would turn out.

After what seemed like hours but was only minutes, we finally arrived at my apartment. David was thoroughly confused about where I lived. Good, I thought, just in case I did not want to see him again. I had gone a little out of the way to confuse him. When we entered the apartment, I stepped into the bathroom, inviting him to take a seat on the bed.

I was so nervous, positively beside myself with worry. I stayed in the bathroom for 30 minutes, maybe longer, brushing my teeth, adjusting my hair, and changing into my sleeping clothes, a pair of gym shorts and a tee-shirt. I took my bra off out of habit and then decided to put it back on again. When I finally got up the nerve, I opened the bathroom door and returned to the bedroom. It was now past midnight.

There on the bed nearest the window, lay David, fast asleep. He had taken his shirt off but had not removed his shoes, socks, or trousers. As I stared at him, a smile came to my face. This was not so bad, I thought. Perhaps David was the nice guy he appeared to be. Sitting on the side of my bed, I began to heat water to make a cup of tea. I needed something to help relieve the hangover I was sure I would have in the morning. I also set the alarm for 6:00 am, just for David.

As I sat there drinking my tea, David slept like a baby in front of me. He really did look like Robert Redford, I thought, as I admired his slender arms, not much larger than mine. Thank goodness you are not muscle-bound, I thought. I wasn't interested in muscles anymore, not since Sven had put his fist through the wall.

After I finished my tea, I gently removed David's shoes and socks and then took the brave step of removing his blue jeans. Somehow, I got them off without waking him up. I thought about peaking under his underwear but decided not. Better not tempt fate, I thought. If we ever live together, there will be plenty of time for that. Just before I turned out the light, I decided to remove my bra. I really hated sleeping with my bra on. No sooner than my head hit the pillow than I fell asleep.

At 6:00 am, the alarm rang, waking me from my peaceful slumber. It also awoke David. "What time is it?" he asked.

"It's 6:00 am," I replied.

Looking around at his surroundings and lack of clothing, David asked another question. "Did we, do it?" he asked.

"Yes," I replied, teasing him. "It was wonderful!" David stared at me and then smiled.

"Was I good?" he asked.

"Of course," I replied. I blew him a kiss.

He could tell I was lying. "You're full of it," he replied! "Did anything happen?"

"Nothing happened David," I replied. "Honestly, nothing happened! When I came out of the bathroom, you were fast asleep."

"Did you take my pants off?" he asked.

"Yes," I replied. "Your secret is safe with me."

That brought a broad smile to his face. He tossed a pillow at me and laughed. After a few minutes of friendly banter, we each took a quick shower and changed back into our clothes. Afterward, I drove David back to his hotel. When we arrived at the hotel, he invited me to come up to his room, so he could change into his uniform before proceeding to the base.

As he changed in the bathroom, I saw his white uniforms hanging in the closet. Sure, enough, he had with him one of those beautiful white uniforms with the stiff white collar and brass buttons. It was the same type of uniform that Robert Redford wore in the opening scene of the movie "The Way We Were." When David emerged from the bathroom, I asked him to put the uniform on for me.

"Sure," he replied. He looked at his watch to confirm he had time. When he emerged from the restroom a second time, I was mesmerized! David was gorgeous. He was the spitting image of Robert Redford.

"Do you mind if I give you a kiss?" I asked. David didn't bother to reply. Instead, he leaned over and gave me a kiss. David was starting to grow on me.

After a second brief change of clothes back into his work uniform, we hopped on my motor scooter and rode to the base. I gave David one last kiss after he climbed off the bike and then watched him walk through the pedestrian gate. It was not until I returned to the apartment later that morning that I realized I had forgotten to get his phone number. That evening I returned to his hotel, hoping to find David, but he wasn't there. I left a message for him at the front desk, which he apparently never received. I was very depressed that evening. It seemed for a moment that my personal Robert Redford was suddenly gone forever.

CHAPTER 6:

DAVID'S FIRST WEEK AT THE OFFICE

DAVID'S NARRATIVE

My first day at the office went quickly. From the start, I was pulled into meetings with my many new bosses. I didn't have one boss or even two. I had five bosses.

First, I met with the Public Works Officer, my immediate supervisor, then with the Base Commanding Officer, his boss, and finally with the Commander Fleet Air Mediterranean (COMFAIRMED), the man responsible for all the Navy's bases in the Mediterranean. I would not meet with my ultimate boss, the Commander in Chief, U.S. Naval Forces Europe, (the CINC), until the following week.

At each meeting, my new bosses explained their expectations, reciting their interpretations of the year's past events. It was the events which led to the creation of my position. It was like drinking from a firehose.

As I listened to their problems, several points became clear to me. First their litany of problems seemed minor to me. Second, Admirals, Generals, and their wives can get into trouble when they become bored. Third, poor communication can lead to misunderstandings and hurt feelings, and finally fourth, none of the leaders seemed to understand how to deal with our property owners. It seemed everyone wanted to get out of the housing management business. Hence the reason my job was created.

At the end of the final meeting, the Admiral summed up my new job best. "A house is a very personal thing," he said. "If you have a nice place to live, your home life will be happy. I know our wives can sometimes be difficult. They mean well, however. Please try to keep them happy. Also, please keep us out of the newspapers." The Admiral's instructions could not have been clearer.

MEETING THE REAL BOSS

After the first round of meetings, I walked to the other side of the base, the side outside the fence line, to meet the people I would be working with. It was now 3:00 PM and time to meet my fourth boss, the Housing Director. I realized I had not had lunch. No time for lunch today, I thought. I need to meet the Housing Director before he goes home for the day.

As I opened the door to enter the housing office, I was enveloped in a cloud of cigarette smoke, even though the Navy had banned smoking in Federal Buildings the previous year. The waiting room was full of people. As I walked toward the director's office, I counted the ashtrays on each of the worker's desks. Each desk had an ashtray filled with cigarette butts. Each desk was also empty. I noticed that the butts had a heavy coating of lipstick on them and wondered where everyone was. I would later learn they were all next door at the Personal Property Office having late afternoon coffee.

When I opened the door to the director's office, I met Max, the Housing Director, for the first time. He was alone, sitting in the dark. I would learn that Max never turned on his light, preferring to sit in the dark, as it made it easier for him to see the computer screen on his desk.

"Hello Max," I said, extending my hand to shake his. "I'm LT. David Moore, the new Flag Housing Officer."

He seemed very tense, not particularly happy at my arrival. After a brief pause, he smiled and then shook my hand, welcoming me to Naples. Motioning for me to sit on his long couch, he called for Enzo, the man responsible for the day-to-day management of the Flag housing, to join him.

Max appeared to be in his mid-sixties, past retirement age, and in poor health. I wondered why he was still working but thought better than to ask. I read beforehand that Max had been working as the Housing Director in Naples for 20 years. Before that, he had served as an enlisted person in the Navy for 25 years. He was, what we call in the Navy, a "double-dipper." He was a person working to obtain two pensions from the Federal Government (an active-duty military pension and a civil service pension). Years earlier, the pension system had been reformed, however, there were still a few people in the system who had been grandfathered. Max was one of those people.

For the next four hours, we discussed each of the houses and their occupants in detail, as I listened to Max and Enzo put their spin on recent events. Both seemed worried about losing their jobs.

During the meeting, Max made a point of reminding me several times that I did not work for him, nor did he work for me. He also firmly stated that Enzo worked for him and not for me. Max was defining his turf, making sure to leave little remaining for me. When I asked him if he had a workspace available for me in the office, he politely said "no." It was clear he did not want me around.

As our meeting closed, I began to ask Max about the many signed pictures hanging on the walls of his office. I recognized a few of the names and faces, but not all. Max knew some especially important people. There were signed pictures of two Presidents, as well as signed pictures of many former Navy Admirals. I only recognized a few of the faces.

"How did you get to know all these people?" I asked. Max just smiled.

"I suppose I've been around," Max replied. Then he pointed to a picture on the wall which I did not recognize. "I used to be his flag secretary during the Cuban Missile Crisis," he said. "Several of these people have lived here in Naples, and I worked for others in Vietnam."

"How long were you in Vietnam?" I asked.

"From 1967 until 1972," he replied. "I suppose I was too good at my job. The Admirals would not let me go home."

I had heard about people like Max during my four years in the Navy. I had even met a few men who had been held prisoner at the "Hanoi Hilton." I had never, however, met a direct witness to the Cuban Missile Crisis. My respect for Max grew considerably that day. "How did you get the picture of Kennedy?" I asked.

Max smiled. "I worked at Camp David," he replied, "before the Cuban Missile Crisis."

I knew that a man like Max could be a dangerous man. I understood how he kept his job. He was a "sand crab." Max knew all the secrets. He probably had a file on everyone. He also controlled the money.

After studying Max, I then turned towards Enzo, still sitting in the chair beside me and wondered, how he managed to survive for forty years in his job. Clearly, Enzo had more cards than Max. He was not displaying them, however, on the walls of his office.

It would take me several months to uncover Enzo's secrets. When I did, I would learn where Max got a few of his pictures. They came from Enzo. Enzo collected signed pictures like baseball cards. He had been doing so ever since the Second World War.

As the meeting wrapped up, I asked Max one more question. "I thought we were not supposed to smoke in the office," I said.

He tipped back his head and laughed. "I tried that for the first week," he said. "I told the staff they had to smoke outside. Shortly thereafter everyone went outside. After a week, trying to implement the new policy, I gave up. It simply doesn't work here in Italy."

"Is CDR Cooper ok with this?" I asked.

Max laughed again. "He has the same problem I do," Max replied. "Would you like a cigarette?" Max pulled a pack out of his coat pocket.

"No, thank you," I replied.

Max continued speaking. "I started smoking these in Vietnam," he said. "I have tried dozens of times to quit but cannot, even though it's damaging my heart." He offered to show me the scar from his recent triple-bypass surgery, but I declined. Then he lit up his cigarette and leaned over towards Enzo to light Enzo's cigarette. For a moment in time, I watched the two men perform an act I would learn to call the cigarette kiss. The two men stood close, cigarette tip to cigarette tip, sharing a light. I would see this ritual performed many times in Naples.

FIRST WEEK ON THE JOB

During my first week on the job, I worked wherever I could find space. I didn't really need a desk anyway. That first week I met each of my customers, working my way down the list, until I met with my last customer, the CINC. For a few days, I used the phone on LTJG. Biggs desk until he returned to work that Thursday.

Working in the Public Works Building was very distracting. Every two minutes or so, the secretary would ring a bell, get on the intercom, and tell someone they had a call on lines 2 or 3. I grew to detest Angela's British accent. It felt like I was working in an old-time department store. Someone named Antonio was getting most of the calls. Unfortunately, he was slow to pick up the phone. Pick up the dammed phone, I thought!

When the noise got too annoying, I carried my office, a new leather briefcase I had purchased at the Navy Exchange, over to our burger joint, where I used one of the booths as my desk. It was during one of these escapes that I had my first personal one-on-one conversation with the Public Works Officer, Commander Cooper.

"So, I see Max hasn't given you a desk yet;" he kidded me as he sat down across from me in the booth. "Do you mind if I join you?"

"Make yourself at home," I replied, motioning for him to sit.

"If you would like, I can send LTJG. Biggs down to the motor pool and give you his desk," he offered.

"No thanks," I replied. "I really need to sit in the housing office."

"I agree," he replied. "Do you want me to tell Max he needs to find you a desk?"

"Thanks, but no," I replied. "I need to do this on my own."

"Can I give you a suggestion?" He offered again.

"Sure," I said.

"Try sitting on his couch for a few days," the Commander replied. "I did that when I first arrived. Don't be fooled by Max," he said. "He comes across as a grump at first, but inside he is a nice man."

"How long did it take to get him to talk to you?" I replied.

"About three days," the Commander replied. "I took up residence on his couch. Trust me; he will get tired of you sitting on his couch and will eventually give you a place to sit."

"Do you have any other tidbits of useful info that will help me deal with Max?" I asked.

"Yes," he replied. "How long have you been in the Navy?"

"Four years," I replied.

The Commander studied me and then began to talk. "I know that the Navy teaches its officers to follow their chains of command," he said, "but that is not necessarily how the Navy works. There are people who have power on paper but not necessarily in real life. Take, for example, our Commanding Officer. He has never run a base before. All he knows how to do is fly planes.

"On paper he runs the base, however in reality we do. We tell him what he needs to know, to make him look good. Then we send him out to shake hands, cut ribbons and hobnob with the other brass. He likes that, and we do too. The real powers in the Navy are the people who control the resources, the workforce and especially the money. Max is one of those people.

The Commander continued. "On paper, Max works for me, but the reality is that Max's budget is three times the size of mine. He controls half of the base's real estate, whereas I only control less than twenty percent. Between Max and the Navy Exchange Officer, they control most of the base's assets.

"When I first arrived, I attempted to take control of Max's budget, thinking it was mine. I was soundly rebuffed. The people in Norfolk who control the housing money wouldn't let me touch it.

When I appealed to their Admiral, he told me to "pound sand." It turns out Max manages his money well. He knows how to pinch a penny until it screams. For the past ten years, Max has saved their bacon numerous times. Max is a hero to the folks in Norfolk. Have you seen the pictures on Max's wall?"

"Yes, I have," I replied.

"Max has many friends and important people far above my paygrade," the Commander continued. "Unfortunately, sometimes he cashes in his chits. That's how your job ended up being created."

"What happened?" I asked.

The Commander leaned back in his seat. "Max squashed a three-star with a four-star," the Commander replied.

"Did Max prevail?" I asked.

"Yes," the Commander replied, "however the people who were squashed were none too happy. One of your jobs is to prevent Max from doing things that get the rest of us into trouble. Do you understand?"

"Yes," I replied. At last, I understood the reason for the Commander's visit.

He then continued his speech. "If Max wants something, he gets it, whereas when I ask, I get a Seabee salute!"

"What's a Seabee salute?" I asked.

"The Admiral pats me on the shoulder, tells me he appreciates my hard work and then ignores me."

"So, I guess you have learned to live with Max," I asked.

"Yes," the Commander replied. "Max knows how to get things done, and that type of person can be a valuable friend to have. I suggest you work hard to become Max's friend."

"What about Enzo?" I asked.

CDR Cooper smiled. "People like Enzo make us all look good," he replied.

"I see where he has worked for the Navy for 40 years," I commented.

"Yes," the PWO is confirmed. "There are many people on this base who have worked here that long. They know how to get things done here in Naples. Without them, nothing would be accomplished."

THE LUIGI STORY

As the conversation went on, the Public Works Officer became more relaxed. Sitting back in the booth, he began to relate a story to illustrate the point he was making. "Let me share a funny story," he began. "There is an engineer upstairs named Luigi. Most of the time, he sits at his desk and reads the newspaper. He also falls asleep. One day I asked the Engineering Director why Luigi still works here. He was clearly past the age when he could retire."

"Luigi knows people," the Engineering Director replied. "Luigi was once the Chief Engineer for the City of Naples."

"That is a good reason for hiring him initially, but why is he still on the payroll?" I asked. "It doesn't look good to employ a person who spends their day sleeping at their desk."

"Do you remember that road we needed to be paved to Carney Park?" the Engineering Director replied.

"The road to Carney Park was awful. It was nothing but potholes large enough to break an axle. For months, the C.O. had been pressuring me to repave the road even though I could not. It was not on our property. Guess who got the city to pave the road?"

"Luigi?" I asked.

"Yes," CDR Cooper replied. "Luigi called the Mayor of Pozzuoli, who was an old friend and asked him to pave the road. He told him that President Bush wanted to go jogging at Carney Park during the G-7 summit in Naples."

"Did the President ever go jogging in Carney Park?" I asked.

"No," replied the PWO laughing. "He never went anywhere near the park."

"So, I suppose Luigi still works in engineering," I smiled.

"You bet!" the PWO replied. "He can work there for as long as he wants." It was nice to get to know my new boss and learn he had a sense of humor. I had heard rumors he was quite intense, but now I understood he was a regular guy.

FRIDAY NIGHT HAPPY HOURS

My first week at the office ended on Friday afternoon when at last, I finally ran into Neal. "Do you know Elsa's address or phone number?" I asked.

"No," he replied. "I just met her last Friday before I picked you up at the airport. I did learn, however, from Kristina that Elsa and her roommate are moving soon."

"Do you know where they are moving to?" I asked.

"No," Neal replied. "Kristina said that Elsa and Antonella were moving in with Antonella's parents."

This was not much help. I remembered Elsa pointing towards a street where Antonella lived but could not remember the street location. "The Posillipo hill is a big hill," I replied. "Do you know where on the Posillipo?" I asked.

"I haven't the foggiest," Neal replied. "Sorry that I'm not much help."

Hearing Neals's assessment of the situation was depressing. All week I had been kicking myself for not getting Elsa's address. I was in such a hurry to get to the office that morning, that I neglected something more important.

"I can see this is really bothering you," Neal replied. "Would you like to drown your sorrows? I know a good place to go for happy hour."

I accepted Neal's invitation and soon we were off, driving towards the NATO Officer Club at AFSOUTH. In those days, the Allied Officer Club was the place to go on Friday nights. Enjoying a drink at the bar, soon became my favorite way to end the week. The evening would begin at the bar for happy hour and then move from there to the dining room for an excellent Italian dinner. The food was exceptionally good.

Sometimes we varied the ritual. We would eat at one of the local restaurants in nearby Bagnoli instead. My favorite restaurant in Bagnoli was O' Calamaro. They had wonderful antipasti dishes. Thinking of the food still makes my mouth water. They also had a charming head waiter who reminded me of my favorite waiter from the local pizzeria back home.

Another favorite place we liked to visit, was a pizzeria named De Gennaro, also known as Bagnoli Joe's. They had excellent wood-fired pizza. I often stopped there on the way home from work to pick up a pizza to go.

While the men drank at the bar of the "O-club" on the second floor, the women would go to the first floor to play the slot machines. It was not the restaurant or the bar which made the Officer Club solvent; however, it was the slot machines.

Unfortunately, the slot machines turned out to be the club's downfall. When the workers went on strike, the Italian police discovered the slot machines. Once that happened, the slot machines were hauled away. Within a month the club went bankrupt, ending our Friday night happy hours forever. That night, however, the club was still open and doing a brisk business.

"So how did your day with Elsa go?" Neal asked.

"It was great, although very warm," I remarked. "Elsa took me on a tour of the creepier places in Naples. Did you know that the entrance to Hell is in Arco Felice?" I asked.

"I heard a rumor of that, Neal replied, liking where this was going. "Personally, I think the backdoor to Hell is in Washington D.C.," he added.

"So, you've been to D.C. in the summer also?" I asked.

"Yes," Neal replied. "I am awfully familiar with D.C. summers," he added. "I swear the sun is a little closer to the earth in Virginia," he remarked.

After this sidebar about D.C.'s steaming summers, I continued with my story. "After Elsa and I toured Cumae and Pozzuoli, we had dinner near the Egg Castle."

"How did that go?" Neal asked.

"It went well until we discovered we didn't have enough money to pay the check. We forgot to consider the cover charges, I replied."

Neal was now laughing at my misfortune. "Did you end up doing the dishes?" Neal asked.

"Fortunately, no," I replied. "As it turns out, they accepted my credit card."

"So how did the evening end?" Neal asked.

"She invited me up to her apartment," I replied.

"This is getting good;" Neal responded, rubbing his hands together.

"Don't get your hopes up," I replied. "I was so jet-lagged I fell asleep while she was in the bathroom."

Neal laughed. "So, nothing happened?" Neal asked.

"Nothing," I replied!

"What a bummer," Neal replied. "Your date sounds like one of my dates! Would you like another beer?"

After hours at the bar, followed by more hours in the restaurant, Neal finally dropped me off at the hotel around 10:00 PM. As I attempted to get to sleep, I decided to try and find Elsa's apartment the next day. Perhaps if I retraced my steps, I thought, I might be able to find her apartment before she moved. It seemed like my best shot, although it was a long shot at best.

That night I slept well. The air conditioning was finally working again after four days on the fritz. For some reason, I never stopped to check the front desk to see if she had left a message. As usual, I ignored the simple solution and instead chose the harder one.

SEARCHING FOR ELSA'S APARTMENT

The next day I hired a cab to take me to the Egg Castle, and from there, I attempted to retrace my steps. While on my expedition, I visited the Royal Palace that we passed the previous Sunday night, as well as the Castle Nuovo that I had admired the previous Saturday. Afterward, I wandered the Spanish Quarter for hours, trying to find Elsa's apartment building and getting hopelessly lost in the process. Everywhere I went, the buildings all looked the same. It seemed there were hundreds of blocks of crumbling ancient buildings. I was trying to find a diamond on a beach. When it began to get dark, I finally gave up. It was clear I had lost Elsa, my diamond, for good.

CHAPTER 7:

DAVID MEETS HARRY

DAVID CONTINUES HIS NARRATIVE

I thought about returning to the old city the following day but decided against it. What is the point, I thought? I have already spent an entire day wandering there. The only chance I had to find Elsa again was by accidentally passing her on the street! That day, I decided instead to do my laundry at the base. It seemed a much better use of my time. Easy come, easy go, I thought. Perhaps it was not meant to be.

The next Monday, I resolved to focus my attention on getting an office to work from, finding a place to live and looking for a car to buy. Living in the hotel without wheels was already getting old. It would be at least another six weeks before my car, and household goods would arrive from the States, but I was anxious to get on with life.

On my second Monday in the office, I tried CDR Cooper's idea, taking up residence on Max's couch. The idea worked as suggested. By Tuesday afternoon, Max capitulated and gave me a desk.

On Wednesday, I began the process of getting to know Enzo. He invited me to lunch at the Carabinieri Mess. It was pasta fagioli day, his favorite day!

As an aside, the Italian Carabinieri is Italy's version of a national gendarmerie, part police and part military. They wear dark blue uniforms, with policeman-style hats emblazoned with the image of an exploding bomb. They also carry lollipops, small white and red paddles about the size of a ping-pong paddle, with which to stop traffic.

I learned the hard way that you must stop for lollipops, regardless of what you are doing. If you do not, the next thing you will see is the barrel of an Uzi sub-machine gun pointed at your face.

My favorite Carabinieri, however, were the women. They dressed in miniskirts, with tall black boots sporting Uzi's as if they were the latest fashionable purse. It was hard not to stare.

When we arrived at the mess, we were greeted by a long queue of people waiting to get in, most of which were not Carabinieri. Apparently, pasta fagioli day was popular at the NATO base! As we waited in line, I saw people walking away with large bowls of steaming hot, good-smelling food. When we finally reached the large pot, I was ready to eat.

Pasta fagioli is a particularly good, thick type of Navy Bean soup filled with broken pieces of pasta, whatever happened to fall off the pasta assembly line that day. It goes down easy, making you want a second bowl; however, you pay the price later, as it sets up in your stomach like a soccer ball. Once you eat a bowl, you are full for the day.

After our filling meal, Enzo invited me to go with him to the supermarket nearby. "My wife and children are coming home from vacation today," he replied, "and the refrigerator is completely empty." As we loaded up the cart, I wondered where Enzo would put all this food, perhaps in the office refrigerator? Thinking Enzo's family had gone to a far-off location, I asked him where they went for the summer.

"Each year, we rent a house at the beach in Bacoli," he replied. Bacoli, I remembered that name from my visit to Cumae with Elsa.

"Isn't that on the other side of town?" I asked.

"Yes," he replied. "The house costs me four million lire per month, but it's worth it to have one month alone as a bachelor. They are happy, and I am happy!"

"Do you visit them on the weekends?" I asked.

"Heavens no," Enzo replied. "When you have a family with six kids, some of whom have children of their own, you sometimes just need to get away from them! Last summer, my wife joked that we should send the kids to the beach and that the two of us should remain at the apartment in Casoria! Even my wife wants to get away sometimes!"

"Do you all live together?" I asked.

"Yes," he replied, "all ten of us live together in a three-bedroom apartment in Casoria. Would you like to see a picture of my wife? he asked."

"Sure," I replied.

Enzo reached into the glove box of his car and pulled out a picture of his wife, Carlotta. It was their wedding picture, taken in 1952. Enzo's wife was dressed in a beautiful white dress, like the wedding dress I had seen the previous Saturday with Elsa. Enzo was dressed in a black tuxedo.

"You look good in that picture," I remarked. "You look like that famous 1960's Italian actor from the movie "La Dolce Vita." Who was that actor again?" I asked. "I cannot recall his name."

"Marcello Mastroianni," Enzo replied. "His name is Marcello Mastroianni. Even my wife thinks I look like Marcello! I wish I had his money!"

As we drove back to the base with a trunk full of groceries, I used the opportunity to get better acquainted. "I read that you have worked for the Navy for forty years."

"Yes," he replied, "although technically, I have worked for the American military longer."

"When did you start?" I asked.

"In 1943," he replied, "just after the Americans liberated Naples."

"Liberated?" I asked. It seemed like an odd way to refer to a conquering army.

"Yes, liberated," Enzo replied. "You see, the Italian Government surrendered after the fall of Sicily. When that happened, we thought the war, at last, was over. Then the Germans came and occupied our country! The Germans were awful! We hated them! I still hate them!

Before the Americans arrived, we endured bombing raids, naval bombardment, famine, and the Gestapo. We even ate the fish in the city aquarium. Even Vesuvius erupted, trying to eject the Germans." Enzo laughed.

"The day, the Americans arrived was the happiest day of my life! It was the day I met my wife, Carlotta."

"After the Americans arrived, I started shining shoes for GIs in exchange for chocolate bars and cigarettes," he went on. "Would you like a chocolate bar?" he asked. "I have a half-dozen in the glove box."

"No thanks," I replied. "I am still trying to digest the soccer ball I ate for lunch."

Going on, he continued his story. "After that, I worked as a valet to a three-star general and then as a driver in the motor pool. I started working in housing in 1970 when the prior flag housing manager became the on-site housing manager at Pinetamare, the Navy's main housing area. I have been working for the Flags now for 29 years, twenty of which I have spent working for Max."

Enzo and I were becoming friends. It turns out he was not afraid of our powerful customers or of me. Enzo's biggest fear was of offending Max. This would be the start of an incredibly good friendship.

THE HOUSE

Later that week, on Friday, a second unexpected blessing occurred. Max called me into his office and closed the door. "I have a house here; I think you will like it," he said, as he pulled one of the housing office data cards from the top drawer of his desk. "I pulled this out of the showing book earlier this week," he said. "A newly arrived Navy JAG officer is looking for a roommate to share the rent on a house in the Posillipo. This house has been rented to Navy JAG officers since the 1960s and rents for two million lire per month. There are two issues, however, you should be aware of it. First, the house has no heat."

"Do I need heat? I asked.

"That depends on how cold, you like to be," replied Max, smiling. "My wife and I run the heat for three months each year in the winter, usually from the beginning of December until the end of February. Naples does not get snow, but it can get down into the forties, plus these old stone houses can get cold. The house has a heating system, but it has not worked in years. We have asked the property owner to repair it, but she refuses. That said, the JAG officers have still wanted to keep the house, despite the lack of heat."

As I listened to Max, I weighed this information in my mind. I had lived in Southern California, where some houses also had no heat. The climate seemed the same as here, I thought. Perhaps this is no big deal. The Romans lived here for thousands of years without heat. Little did I realize that the Romans did have heating systems. I would learn that later, on a trip to Pompeii.

"What is the second problem?" I asked. "You mentioned there are two problems."

"The house is next door to Villa Nike," Max replied!

For a moment both of us were silent. It took several minutes for that fact to sink in properly. Did I really want to live next door to my most powerful customer, the four-star Admiral? The Admiral seemed genuinely nice however I wasn't sure yet about the staff. The thought of endless streams of aides coming to my door asking to borrow things came to my mind. I was not sure.

Finally, I asked Max the question weighing heavily on me like an anvil. "I met the Admiral earlier last week," I began. "What is he really like?"

"The current occupant is a good man," Max replied. "He prefers that the Italians maintain his house. He doesn't want the U.S. Government to get stuck with the bills. You should understand that Villa Nike is a money pit. The current occupant will not give you a problem," Max continued. "I cannot guarantee, however, what his successor might be like. We get all kinds here," he said. It was Max's way of saying the next Admiral might be difficult.

"Do you have a phone number for the JAG officer?" I asked.

"No" replied Max. "He sits upstairs on the next floor. You may be able to catch him before he goes home for the day. His name is Harry Beeman."

No sooner than we finished the conversation, I went upstairs to find Harry. When I arrived in his office, I found Harry seated behind his desk, collecting his things in preparation to depart.

"Are you Harry?" I asked. "I understand you are looking for a roommate. My name is David Moore. I work downstairs in the housing office."

"Nice to meet you, David," he replied, reaching across the desk to shake my hand. "Would you like to see the house?"

"Sure," I replied.

"Has Max told you about it?" he asked.

"Yes," I replied.

"I just assumed the lease this week from the current resident," Harry replied, "and I am feeling quite tapped out. There is no way I can afford two million lire per month on my own. A friend of mine, an old roommate from law school, is arriving in two months. I promised him a room; however, we need an additional roommate to share the expense. Are you interested?"

"Yes," I replied. I quickly did the math in my head. "So, we would each pay about $400 per month after the other man arrives, I asked?"

"Yes, that's about right," Harry replied.

"Does the house have appliances and kitchen cabinets?" I asked.

"Yes," Harry replied.

This was exceptionally good news! Earlier in the week, I had looked at several vacant apartments, which all lacked the essential fixtures of modern life. When I spoke with Max after the tour, he confirmed that to be a widespread problem with all the rentals on the market.

"The Italians view kitchen cabinets, appliances, and wardrobes as furniture," replied Max! "It creates a tremendous problem for military families when they come here. I have been trying to solve this problem for years."

As I listened to Max, I began to understand why the Navy had designated duty in Naples as a "hardship tour." Setting up a place to live was extremely expensive.

The day before I had tallied up the cost to move into an apartment without these essentials and had determined it would cost me six to eight thousand dollars (for first and last month's rent plus appliances.) I had not anticipated the high cost when I agreed to move to Naples. Living with Harry would enable me to avoid those expenses.

I next asked Harry about the heat. He confirmed the furnace did not work. "I thought long and hard about taking the house," he replied, "given the lack of heat, but decided it was worth the price. When you see the house, you will understand why. I have brought an electric blanket," he added. "You may want to buy one as well."

Leaving Harry's office, we proceeded to walk towards Harry's old beat-up car in the parking lot.

"Where did you find this gem?" I asked.

"I bought it two months ago for $500," he replied proudly!

It was one of the ugliest cars I had ever seen. Harry owned a 1960's era German automobile, with highly oxidized snot-green colored paint. Looking into the back seat, I saw that the upholstery was torn, as if a family of raccoons had moved in.

"I know it looks like crap," Harry smiled, "but it runs."

"Does it burn oil?" I asked.

"Yes," Harry replied, "lots of oil."

Harry then started up the car, discharging a thick cloud of blue smoke behind us. Soon we were on our way. Riding with Harry was an exhilarating experience. While most people would slow down when approaching a traffic jam, Harry would instead look for a way around it.

Harry had only been driving in Naples for two months, and yet he had fully assimilated the driving style. I would learn this was typical in the American community. There was something about Naples which turned ordinary law-abiding Americans into red-light running Neapolitans during their first month in the country. I suppose it was the cowboy in our genes.

Harry drove as crazy as the natives. His favorite response to every situation was to honk his horn. As we approached the end of Via Scarfoglio, we stopped for the traffic light. "Some lights are optional," Harry remarked, "but this one is not."

Towards the left, I saw a terrible traffic jam. "I hope we are not driving in that direction," I remarked.

"That's "The Squeeze,"" Harry replied.

I had heard about "The Squeeze" before I left Norfolk. The Squeeze was legendary within the Navy. It was a terrible two-lane road with a reputation for destroying cars. The problem wasn't the road, but rather that people parked on the side where they shouldn't. This caused the road to become one lane in many places. Everyone trying to access the freeway had to run this gauntlet. It was a real clusterfuck!

During my first week in the office everyone complained about "the Squeeze." I heard horror stories about how it sometimes took two to three hours to get home every night. Looking in the direction of the traffic, I resolved in my mind that there was no way I would ever drive my new car into the squeeze. That day, I decided to buy a "beater" car like Harry's car.

As my mind returned to reality, Harry reassured me that we would not be entering the Squeeze, although he seemed disappointed. Instead, we would be turning right onto Via Beccadeli, a nice wide street running in the opposite direction.

As we drove towards the NATO base, we passed another Naples institution. Sitting on a wall beside the road was an aged, egg-shaped woman and legendary prostitute. It was a woman known affectionately by the American community as "Humpty Dumpty."

The road was beginning to look familiar, as this was the same route, I had traveled with Neal two weeks before. We drove past the stadium, through the tunnel, around Piazza Sannazaro, up the street blocked by parked cars at the fish market and towards the Mergelina.

When we reached the intersection to turn onto Via Caracciolo, however, we turned right instead of left. "This is Via Orazio;" Harry remarked, as we began to drive up the steep switch-backed road.

At one point, we stopped for traffic on a steep slope. As we sat there waiting for the traffic to move, I noticed a truck was rolling backward towards us in slow motion, threatening to crush Harry's radiator beneath its rear bumper. I could see what was about to happen but could do nothing about it.

Harry however would not allow the finest feature on his car to be damaged. He honked his horn and then swerved into the oncoming traffic lane. He managed to pass the truck as well as several other cars, just before we encountered a tourist bus coming down the street. For a moment, my life flashed before my eyes. Afterwards Harry smiled at me. "Sometimes, you have to do, what you have to do," he said.

A mile after this harrowing incident, we turned left into a one-lane road running parallel with the hill. "This is our street, Via Scipione Capace," Harry remarked.

Beside the street were elegant apartment buildings on the right and large grand villas on the left. Harry continued speeding down the street. Then he slammed on the brakes.

On our left stood a large green gate with a sign reading "Villa Maria." Beside the gate stood another gate painted white with cameras and one-way glass, with a sign that read "Villa Nike." "This is the house;" Harry exclaimed, pointing towards a large mustard-colored house behind the green gate. After he opened the gate, we drove the car inside and then closed the gate behind us.

The house in front of me stood two stories tall and had large windows. The top floor of the house was a bright mustard yellow color which was now slightly blackened by decades of air pollution. The base of the house was a deep red color, which I would later learn, was called Pompeian Red. The windows were painted green, the same green used in the Italian Flag.

As we exited the car, I proceeded towards the large wooden front door to go in. "That door is a fake," Harry indicated. "Behind the door is a brick wall. The real front door is in the back."

As we walked down the sloping driveway towards the back, it quickly became apparent that the house was not two stories tall but was, in fact, three stories tall. Like the front door, the house had its illusions.

FACE TO FACE WITH THE PUPPY

As we walked down the driveway, I was greeted by a large St Bernard Dog drooling profusely as he shook his shaggy head. Within seconds my white Navy uniform was slimed with thick globs of dog slobber mixed with dirt.

"This is Bari," Harry remarked, laughing at my misfortune. "He means well but is still just a puppy." The dog was large enough to ride. All he needed was a saddle.

As Harry stood by, completely amused, Bari decided to greet me properly face to face, placing his large dirty paws on each of my shoulders.

It was then that I met Rosa, a feisty but tiny 80-year-old woman who struck Bari with her broomstick. "Basta!" she exclaimed, sending Bari scurrying for safety deep within the garden!

"This is Rosa," Harry remarked, introducing me to the maid.

Behind Rosa emerged another woman stepping out from behind the nearby kitchen door. "This is Maria;" Harry announced, "our proprietor and gracious host!"

Maria was an elegantly dressed woman, similar in age to Rosa but significantly more an aristocrat. She had a thick mane of snow-white hair immaculately coifed about her head. "Maria's husband was a General in Mussolini's Air Force," Harry added, to further my interest.

"Como Si Chiama," she asked. She wanted to know my name.

Maria had an irritating voice. It seemed like the same high pitched nasal voice used by General Burkholder in the TV sitcom "Hogan's Heroes."

"My name is David," I replied, "David Moore."

Maria repeated my name several times. Then she smiled and welcomed me to Naples. Afterwards she whispered something in Harry's ear. "What did she say?" I asked.

"She said that she needs to find you an Italian wife," Harry replied.

After we exchanged pleasantries with Maria, we joined her at a table in the garden for a shot of her homemade strawberry liquor. I would learn that twenty minutes of pleasantry's was always required before conducting business in Naples.

After we finished, Harry offered to give me a tour of the house. "The ground floor of the house is where Maria lives with her maid Rosa and their dog Bari," he explained. "The upper two floors belong to the rental."

As I looked at the house from the garden, I could now see three tall floors with large windows at each level leading out onto balconies. In front of us stood a long, wide marble staircase, at the top of which was a large terrace leading into the dining room.

At the top of the stairs on the left were two large wooden doors leading into the upper two floors of the house. "Be careful on the stairs;" Harry remarked as we proceeded up the stairs. "They can be very slippery when it rains."

At the top of the stairs, we entered a large terrace complete with a blue and white metal table and chairs and an old worn-out rusting barbecue grill. Facing us were two large wooden doors eighteen feet tall.

After Harry unlocked the door, we entered the wide entrance hall, which extended the length of the house. I could now see the brick wall blocking the front door. In front of us was a wide marble staircase leading to the third floor, where the bedrooms were located. In front of the stairs sat an old harpsichord piano. "Do not try to play the piano," Harry remarked. "It has not been tuned in years and sounds awful." Behind us, I could see Maria following us, her cane in hand.

At the bottom of the stairs were two large archways. One led into the living room, a long room running the length of the house. It was twenty-five feet wide and fifty feet long with 20-foot ceilings. At the end of the living room led a doorway into the front porch. "We don't use the porch," Harry remarked. "The windows are painted-shut and will not open. I use that room to store boxes."

In the center of the living room, on the exterior wall, was a small fireplace. It was our only source of heating within the house. As I passed out of the living room back into the entrance hall, I noticed that the house's interior walls were three feet thick. I wondered to myself how cold the house might get during the winter once those thick walls got cold.

Across the hall was the dining room, another large room 25 feet by 25 feet in size. In the center of the room was a large inlaid wood table and chairs, which were in turn surrounded by three large matching cabinets. One of the taller cabinets had glass doors and contained a large assortment of Liquor bottles.

"You have quite a collection here;" I remarked as I opened the glass doors to look inside.

"Yes," replied Harry. "Navy JAG officers have been living here since the 1960s. The movers will not let us ship bottles filled with liquid back to the States, so each resident has left their alcohol behind."

There must have been at least 50 bottles within the cabinet. It seemed there were liquors from every country on the planet.

Behind the dining room was the kitchen, a small room with a white marble table in the center, and behind the kitchen, a small bathroom. It was nice to see the kitchen had a stove, refrigerator, cabinets, washer, and dryer. I was ready to move in. Who cares whether the house has heat, I thought?

After touring the downstairs, we proceeded upstairs to see the bedrooms. The top floor contained four bedrooms, each with its own large wooden wardrobe, another major expense I could avoid. The floors on this level were covered with wood in a fancy herringbone type design. I would learn later that wood floors were rare in Naples.

Harry's room was the largest, 25 feet by 25 feet in size, with its own attached bathroom. My room was the second largest, with a third bedroom behind leading out onto the back terrace. This room had a spare bed, not in use. The bed was in rather poor shape and apparently the bed came with the house.

"You can use that bed," Harry indicated, "until your household goods arrive."

On the terrace stood a spiral green staircase leading up to the roof. "You must see the view;" Harry remarked as he led me up the spiral staircase.

As we stepped out onto the large flat roof, the entire bay of Naples from Capri to Vesuvius spread out in front of us. The water of the bay was now brilliant deep blue in the late afternoon sun.

Immediately below to the left, I could now see Villa Nike, the largest house in my inventory. It was gigantic. In front of the entrance canopy, stood one of the large grey limousines I had seen yesterday in the motor-pool garage.

As I stood there watching, the Admiral emerged from the house in his dinner dress uniform and climbed into the limousine with his wife. I was struck by the fact that the Villa Nike, while a larger house than the Villa Maria, had a much smaller garden.

I remembered as I saw the Admiral depart that Max had mentioned that my new property owner, Maria Orsini, had once lived in Villa Nike before World War II. It seemed there might be an intriguing story behind that comment. Clearly, my landlady had been an important person before the war.

Returning to the view from the roof, I gazed across the waters of the bay. On the far side, I could see a long mountain range running the length of the Sorrentine Peninsula. I knew that the villages of Positano, Ravello and Amalfi were on the opposite side of those mountains. At the base of the mountains, I could see several towns perched on the water's edge, including the town of Sorrento at the far west end of the peninsula. Sitting opposite the end of the peninsula sat the Isle of Capri, like a mighty ship anchored at the mouth of the bay.

At the opposite end of the mountain range, towards the east, I could see the still higher Apennine Mountains, which form the backbone of the Italian Peninsula.

In front of the Sorrentine Mountains sat the mighty Vesuvius looming over the city of Naples like a Damocles Sword.

I remembered what Elsa had told me at Lago Averno. Deep beneath the tranquil blue waters of this bay lay a sleeping colossus. It was a titan of mythic proportions, a giant pool of molten lava extending deep into the Earth's Mantle.

I had read a translation of Pliny the Younger's account of the famous eruption in 79 AD. His description sounded like the end of the world. God, I hope it doesn't erupt while I live here, I thought.

Switching to less ominous thoughts, I gazed east towards the ancient city of Naples lying in the shadow of Vesuvius. Somewhere beneath the dense jumble of buildings lay the ancient grid of narrow streets first constructed by the Greeks 2700 years ago. I had wandered that grid of streets several days before, looking for Elsa's apartment. What a sight! It was the grandest view I had ever seen! It was even better than standing on the South Rim of the Grand Canyon!

"You should see it at night," Harry remarked, indicating that the view was even better in the dark.

I knew I would be spending time on this roof.

The remainder of the house was anticlimactic after the roof. There was one more small bedroom and a large bathroom. That was it.

"When can I move in?" I asked. I was ready to sign whatever papers were required.

"Tonight, if you like," Harry responded.

That night I moved into my new home away from home, The Villa Maria on Naples's famed Posillipo Hill.

CHAPTER 8:
HARRY MEETS JULIE

HARRY'S NARRATIVE

I first met Julie towards the end of May 1989, during my first week living in the American Hotel. Each morning we passed in the lobby around 7:00 am. I would be headed to the office; she was returning from her night shift at the hospital. At first, we just nodded heads acknowledging each other's existence. This went on until the end of June. Then one day, I finally mustered up the courage to say hello. It was the start of something, or so I thought. Wanting to keep the conversation going, I asked her an obvious and, in retrospect, stupid question.

"Are you a nurse at the hospital?" What was I thinking? Of course, you fool, she's wearing scrubs, I thought.

"No," she replied, "I'm a doctor!" Seems I had opened my mouth and inserted my foot.

Julie wasn't the type of woman who would stop traffic. She was more like the girl next door. She could look plain, or she could look pretty, depending on her mood and how she dressed that day. The woman I met at first was the serious Julie, the professional doctor always deep in thought who didn't have time for a smile. This was Julie, who hid behind dark-rimmed glasses and a pair of scrubs.

After our first attempt at conversation, we didn't see each other again for many weeks. It seemed she might have moved out of the hotel. The next time I saw her was at the end of July, coming out of the Navy Exchange. For once, she was not in scrubs but was instead wearing a pair of yellow shorts with a sweatshirt with the word "Wisconsin" emblazoned across the front. It was a chilly day for the month of July. I almost didn't recognize her at first. She was not wearing her glasses, and her hair was down.

Like many women officers, Julie had long hair, which she wore tightly compacted on the top of her head to comply with Navy Regulations. Seeing her with her hair now down revealed an entirely new Julie.

Julie was a rebel who deliberately kept her hair long despite the Navy's pressures to keep it short. Julie had a beautiful long mane of chestnut brown hair, which caressed her shoulders in a jumble of waves and curls. She was really stunning with her hair down. I wondered how she managed to keep all that hair under her hat.

She didn't see me, however, passing by on the sidewalk, serious as usual, walking towards the burger joint. Following behind at a safe distance, I saw Julie from behind for the first time. She had an extremely cute butt, something I had missed under the scrubs before. From behind, she was an entirely different woman. I had no idea she had such a trim, narrow waist.

When we stepped inside, we encountered a lengthy line. It was Saturday, the day when every American in Naples went to the base for the day to get their hamburger "fix." As we stood there gazing at the menu board, Julie finally noticed me.

"Hi," she said. "I remember you. I'm Julie Steinman. What's your name?"

"My name is Harry Beeman," I replied with a smile.

"What do you plan to get?" She asked.

"I'm not sure," I replied. "What are you getting?"

"I think I'm going to get the cheeseburger," Julie replied. "I've been craving a hamburger all week. Would you like to split a French fry?" she asked.

"Sure," I replied. It seemed a good opportunity to continue our conversation over lunch.

"Have you decided yet?" Julie asked.

"Yes," I replied. I am going to order the fried chicken sandwich.

After we got our food, we decided to sit at a table near the window. "So, what do you do, Harry?" She asked, assuming I already knew she worked at the hospital.

"I work at the Legal Service Office over in Edilizia 2," I replied.

"What type of cases are you working on?" She asked, showing interest in my work.

"I'm working on several adoptions at present," I replied.

"That's an interesting coincidence," she responded. "I work in the maternity department; of course, the entire hospital is a maternity department. That's what we do here in Naples; we deliver babies."

"I didn't realize having sex is the primary business here," I replied.

Julie missed my attempt at humor. "It's not," Julie replied in a deadpan fashion. "Navy wives come from all over the Med to deliver babies here. We get women from Gaeta, Rota, Sigonella, La Maddalena, Greece you name it. Our nickname is "The Storks Nest." Do you know that there are twenty women right now staying in the barracks waiting to deliver?"

"No, I didn't realize that" I replied. "So where are you from?" I asked.

"I'm from Evanston, Illinois" she replied.

"Did you go to Wisconsin?" I asked.

"No," she replied. "I attended the University of Michigan for Undergrad and finished Med School at Northwestern University. My brother attends Wisconsin. He bought me this sweatshirt last year for Christmas."

Changing the subject, Julie asked me an unrelated question. "Have you seen the movie "Ferris Bueller's Day Off?"" she asked.

"Yes," I replied. I had seen the movie and thought it quite funny.

"My parents live in the neighborhood where "Ferris Bueller" was filmed," Julie remarked. "I remember when they filmed the movie. The traffic was diverted for hours."

"That's interesting;" I replied now wanting to hear more. "Has anyone ever told you that you look like Ferris Bueller's girlfriend?" I asked.

"No," Julie replied "but thank you for the compliment. I loved her in "Dirty Dancing.""

Julie clearly did not understand who I was talking about, but that didn't seem to matter anymore. For the first time, I saw her smile. She had a beautiful ear-to-ear smile, which made her eyes light up. Julie was not a "plain Jane" after all. In fact, she was very pretty. I was now on a roll. Seeing my opportunity, I took the plunge.

"Would you like to go out some time?" I asked. "I found this nice little trattoria nearby in Bagnoli."

Without hesitation, Julie replied yes. "I would like that," Julie replied! "I don't get out much. It seems every time I try, my pager goes off, summoning me back to the delivery room. We need more doctors! The hospital here is so short-staffed. Would you like to go out tomorrow?" Julie asked. "I need to work the night shift tonight but could go out for dinner tomorrow, after my shift ends, provided no one goes into labor."

"Sounds like a date," I replied. It was nice to be asked out by a woman for a change. "Where should we meet?" I asked.

"You can pick me up at the hospital at 11:00 am after my shift," she replied.

As we parted company after lunch, I watched Julie walk into the commissary to grocery shop, admiring once again her cute little bottom.

FIRST DATE

The next day I arrived at the hospital promptly at 11:00 am, expecting Julie to be waiting at the entrance. She was not, of course, but still working upstairs. At 11:10, an orderly came down to find me now seated in a row of chairs near the entrance.

"Julie's running late," he said. "She is finishing delivering a baby. She should be down by noon."

When noon arrived, there was no Julie. What should I do, I thought? I decided to wait until 1:00 pm and make my decision then. Then I did something particularly stupid. I decided to get in the elevator and go upstairs to the maternity floor while fidgeting with my car keys.

As I stepped into the elevator, I encountered an orderly pushing a stretcher who knocked the keys from my hand. As I watched, the keys fell in slow motion towards the gap between the elevator and the floor landing. The keys fell cleanly through the crack, not hitting either the elevator or the landing. "Fuck" was the first word that came into my mind. Clearly, the gods did not want Julie and me to date!

At that moment, the other elevator door opened, and Julie stepped out. "Sorry, I'm late," she replied. "Where are we going for lunch?" Instead of answering, I stood there looking at the crack between the elevator and the floor. "What's wrong, Harry?" She asked.

"I just dropped my car keys down the elevator shaft," I replied.

For a moment, we stood there silent, each thinking of what to say next. "Do you have a car we can take?" I asked.

"I wish," she said. "My car has been in the shop ever since I bought it. I think I've ruined the engine this time! The last time I drove it, I heard a loud banging sound, followed by smoke."

"It sounds like you cracked the engine block," I said. "How much did you pay for the car?"

"Two thousand dollars," she replied.

"Sounds like we're both screwed," I replied. "How do we get my keys out of the elevator shaft?"

"We can ask the duty officer," suggested Julie. "They will need to call in Domenico, the elevator technician."

"Do you think he will come? It's a Sunday," I asked.

"Who knows," Julie replied. "This elevator breaks down all the time."

As we stood by the elevator talking, the duty officer walked by, overhearing our conversation. "This elevator is a piece of junk," he exclaimed! "I will call Domenico. I will tell him that a patient headed to surgery is stuck in the elevator. That will get him to come in on a Sunday!"

For the next three hours, Julie and I spent time together in the lobby, getting to know each other better. At 3:00 pm, Domenico finally arrived, annoyed that we dragged him away from his Sunday dinner. If there had been a patient stuck in the elevator, it would now be dead. He was even more annoyed when he learned the real reason for the call. That afternoon we learned several new Neapolitan curse words.

We waited another 45 minutes for him to shut down the elevator cars, enter the pit and retrieve my car keys. Then just as we were about to leave for dinner, five hours later than planned, another nurse came down to the lobby.

"Julie, we need you to work another shift," she said. "Kim has called in sick, and Mrs. Barker is going into labor."

It seemed that day I could not catch a break. That night I ate some sort of mystery meat submerged in a tasteless grey gravy in the hospital cafeteria. Our first date was a bust.

SECOND DATE

I was not willing to give up, however. I asked Julie out two more times, but each time she had to work. Finally, on the third attempt, now in September, she said yes. This time I ran into Julie at the base library.

"Would you like to see my new home?" I asked. "We can grill steaks and afterward go for gelato."

"That sounds wonderful," she replied. "I have off for the next two days. If you want, we can go now, before my pager goes off!"

This was a little sooner than I had planned, but I decided to go with the flow. With Julie, I had learned I needed to strike when the moment was right.

After quickly checking out our books, we departed the library and headed toward my house. The traffic was chaos as usual. I thought about taking the back way, cutting through Bagnoli but decided instead to take the shorter route, driving directly through Fuorigrotta. That decision turned out to be a big mistake.

As we drove through the densely populated Fuorigrotta quarter, we began to see large crowds of people exiting a train station, crossing the street in front of us. It was soccer day, and we were stuck in the middle of people entering the Stadium.

Ahead of us were several police officers directing traffic, flailing their arms, completely ignored by the river of people crossing the street. It seemed we were stuck for the duration. After 20 minutes or more of waiting for the crowd to clear, we began to inch forward again, passing the train station. It seemed the worst was over.

Up ahead, five cars in front of us, stood a bright orange city bus inching forward in the congested traffic. Behind the bus stood a three-wheeled farm truck bringing produce into the city from the farms to the north. Piled high in the bed of the truck was a stack of crates, perhaps fifteen feet tall, held in place with a spider's web of bungee cords. It was a vegetable version of the Leaning Tower of Pisa.

As we sat there waiting, slowly inching forward, I noticed that the farm cart started swaying back and forth. With each oscillation, the load tipped further to the right and then to the left. Turning towards Julie, I asked the obvious question. "Do you think it will fall over?" I asked.

"Maybe," she grinned, obviously enjoying the scene in front of us. We were now driving on a stretch of road approaching a tunnel straddling a streetcar track. As we sat there waiting for the traffic to move, I noticed a bright orange city bus coming towards us on the opposite side of the road.

Then it happened. The pile of crates leaned far to the left and struck the on-coming bus. Splat! there were tomatoes everywhere, instant Pizza sauce, completely covering the front windshield of the bus, which now swerved into a parked car on the opposite side of the road!

As the traffic came to a full and complete stop, bedlam ensued. I could see grapefruit and oranges rolling everywhere. Smashed melons lay beside the road. It was a scene of complete pandemonium. Only in Naples, I thought, laughing hysterically.

At this point, Julie was in stitches. "Did you see the look on the bus driver's face just before the tower collapsed?" She laughed. For several minutes we laughed so hard we cried. Then Julie added some urgency to our situation. "I need to pee," she exclaimed!

Looking for a quick exit, I noticed that the sidewalk was clear. Perhaps I could navigate around this cluster, I thought. As luck would have it, the idea worked, and soon we were on our way again, enjoying a stretch of roadway not encumbered by cars, busses, or melons.

When we arrived at the house, we found my new roommate David playing with Maria's St Bernard puppy in the driveway. Bari was clearly having an enjoyable time playing fetch with a ball, his tail wagging so hard it could break.

"Better wait before we get out of the car," I explained, pointing towards the dog, who now had a long string of drool hanging from his muzzle. Bari was clearly excited to greet us. Finally, he shook his big shaggy head, wrapping the hanging drool around his nose. "There" I said, "it's now safe to get out."

After we exited the car, I introduced Julie to my new roommate, David. "We are going to grill steaks" I exclaimed, inviting him to join us!

That afternoon we each enjoyed a large T-bone steak accompanied by a baked potato and a tall can of British beer. David had visited the British store at AFSOUTH that morning, making use of his new wheels, an old beat-up gray car. While there, he purchased a bottle of British steak sauce in addition to the beer to complement our steak.

After dinner, we turned on the TV, hoping to watch baseball on the only TV channel available. Today there was no baseball, just reruns of the Love Boat. Turning towards Julie, I asked her if she could get Italian TV on her TV set.

"No," Julie replied. "The only thing I can get is AFN. I have the same problem as you."

No one had told us that our American TVs did not work in Italy. For two years, we only had three TV choices. We could watch AFN, watch a movie on the VCR or turn the TV off. The most profitable business on base was the video store.

After dinner, we piled into the "Green Machine" and headed towards the gelaterias at the bottom of the hill. The soccer game was now over, and all of Naples was in the streets. As we sat in traffic, inching our way towards our destination, dozens of young girls on mopeds passed us.

"Guess we won," I remarked to Julie, wondering if I would be able to return to the house after ice cream.

We lived across the street from Savio Mendoza, the hero of the Naples Team and one of the best soccer players in the world. I knew tonight that the street in front of the house would be overflowing with hundreds of children chanting his name. This happened every time Naples won a home game.

When we reached the bottom of the hill, I turned onto the wide street, running along the water, merging into the dense flow of traffic.

"Where are we going to park?" Julie asked.

"Here," I replied, spotting an open space ahead on the right.

The parking gods had smiled upon us. With the help of a white cap, who helped to stop traffic, I parked the car. "Quanto Costa?" I asked the man who was now standing next to me as I exited the car.

"Due mille, cinque cento" he replied.

I reached into my wallet and handed him a five thousand lire note, to which he replied "grazie molto," doffing his cap.

"Why did you pay him?" Julie asked as we walked away. "This is a public street, and he is clearly not a parking attendant."

"Let me tell you a story;" I said as I wrapped my arm around her shoulder. "Every week I read the police blotter that comes across my desk. This week three American cars were stolen, and four American homes were burglarized. It was a normal week. The same thing has happened every week I have been here.

I realize the man is not a parking attendant. He could be someone's father just trying to earn money to buy a pizza for his family, or he may be a car thief. One thing I know for certain is this. The minute he takes my money, he will be honor-bound to protect my car. That is why I gave him five thousand lire.

"You are very trusting, Harry," Julie replied! "I am not so certain I believe in honor among thieves."

I then related a second story that happened to me my first weekend in Naples. "A small boy approached me in the old city. At first, he seemed to want to be my friend, and then he picked my pocket. I tried to chase him in the crowd but quickly lost him when he ducked into a doorway. I thought I had lost my wallet for sure but then encountered the boy again three blocks later."

"What happened?" Julie asked.

"He sold me back my wallet for a portion of the contents," I replied. Julie laughed.

When we arrived at the gelateria, we encountered a large crowd of people all milling about the counter making their orders. It seemed like Neapolitan chaos as usual. Following David's lead, we pushed through the crowd towards the counter to order our ice cream.

"Shouldn't we wait in line?" Julie asked.

"Only if you want your ice cream tomorrow," I replied.

Following David's example, we soon had our ice cream. I ordered a cone with strawberry and lemon. David ordered a cone with vanilla and pistachio, and Julie ordered a cup of chocolate with hazelnut.

Moving away from the crowd to sit on a nearby wall, we took in the sights. Behind us stood the busy Mergelina port, a small harbor providing shelter to many large yachts and fishing boats, as well as the numerous hydrofoils traveling to and from Capri. I enjoyed watching the hydrofoils from the roof of the house, their sleek forms flying across the water at high speed until they slowed to enter the harbor.

In front of us strolled hundreds of people on the wide sidewalk enjoying the cool evening air. Everywhere there were people enjoying the evening walk by the sea.

As we sat there eating our ice cream, Julie and I counted at least a dozen couples kissing, some sitting on park benches, some on walls, and even a few, seated on mopeds. The author Mark Twain had described this scene in a book written a century before. The only thing different was that the horse-drawn buggies had been replaced by automobiles.

"I need to get out more often," Julie remarked, absorbing the view. It was the first time she had visited the historic center of the city.

After finishing our ice cream, we returned to the car, still diligently guarded by the white cap. Climbing into the car, we inched our way into traffic and joined the passeggiata. Within minutes we managed to cut across four lanes of traffic into the Piazza Sannazaro as we tried to go back through the tunnel towards Fuorigrotta to return Julie to the base to retrieve her car.

The traffic was heavy, very congested and moving very closely with cars on either side of me barely inches apart. I was becoming used to this game of slow-motion chicken. The secret to the game was to keep your front bumper slightly in front of the car next to you. If you did that, you would have the right of way. The second rule was to never make eye contact. If you did, you would lose the right of way.

I was doing well for a few minutes until a large city bus began encroaching upon my position from the right. City buses didn't play fair. They just claimed the right of way, whether they had it or not. I couldn't go to the right, so I veered towards the left, beginning a deadly game of chicken with a tiny car driven by a middle-aged woman.

I thought I knew where she was; she thought she knew where I was. Turns out we both misjudged. As I moved forward, she moved forward at the same time resulting in a crunch of metal which left my front bumper dangling and her right front fender dented. I was screwed. I needed to get out of the car to view the damage, but it was too dangerous. I decided to wait for the police to arrive.

Fortunately, the police were nearby. Within 5 minutes, they arrived, and soon thereafter, the Navy Shore Patrol arrived as well. I expected the police to ask us questions, but they did not, unable to reach us because of the many people now getting out of their cars. As we watched the melee unfolding in front of us, a Navy Chief Petty Officer walked up beside my car window.

"What's happening?" I asked.

"Everyone is telling their version of what happened," he said. "The group on the right is arguing that the woman in the tiny car is at fault. The smaller group on the left is arguing you are at fault."

"Who's winning?" I asked.

"You are," he replied.

After 15 minutes of this scene, the police officer walked over to the tiny car and handed the driver a ticket. Apparently, I had won. The Petty Officer smiled at me. "You won the argument," he said.

"How?" I asked. "I didn't say anything."

"The distinguished man in the suit argued that you are obviously a man of importance, as you drive a large German car, whereas the other party is clearly less important as she is driving a tiny car," the sailor replied. "Clearly, you could not possibly be at fault."

It took everything I could muster not to burst out laughing. For the second time that day, Julie was laughing hysterically. I had finally broken through her serious doctor veneer. After the accident, we drove back to the base, where we parted company.

"That was fun," Julie remarked, shaking my hand to say goodbye!

Before I could appreciate how our date ended, she sped away in her new, slightly used car. "Do you think she wants to go out again?" I asked David.

"I have no idea," he replied. "Let's go home and sample the liquor cabinet."

Chapter 9:
Conversation Between David & Harry

DAVID'S NARRATIVE

I could tell that Harry was disappointed after we dropped off Julie at the base. "What's wrong?" I asked.

"Nothing," he replied. "I was expecting too much. Dating Julie is work. Do you know I have been trying to date this woman for five months?"

"No," I replied. "I didn't realize that."

"What do you think about Julie?" Harry asked.

"She seems nice," I replied. "Quiet but nice. She is very cute, at least on the face. I cannot tell what her body looks like under the sweatshirt. She has a nice smile. She is clearly very smart." I was trying to say nice things, not knowing where the conversation was going.

"I'm still trying to figure her out," Harry replied. "Sometimes, she's serious, like a heart attack and other times, she's cute, like the girl next door. I thought I was making progress, but then tonight, I got the handshake. It seems with each date I move two steps forward and then one step back."

"Maybe she's shy," I offered. "Not every woman feels comfortable kissing on a first date."

"It's not our first date," Harry replied!

It seemed he was quite bothered by the handshake. He then began to unload all his frustrations. "I stepped on my crank the first time we spoke when I thought she was a nurse," he said. "Ever since then, it has been an uphill battle. Dating a doctor is much harder than I thought. She works crazy hours and is always on call. We can't plan anything! On top of that, I feel like I'm doing all the work. She shows no initiative."

"Is she moody?" I asked.

"I don't know," Harry replied. "I haven't spent enough time with her to figure that out. She seems to have a good disposition."

"That's good," I replied. "At least she is not manic-depressive." Harry agreed. There was at least one bright spot in his otherwise frustrating relationship.

"Do you think I should keep trying?" Harry asked.

"Do you have any other prospects?" I replied.

"Nope," Harry replied, "this base is like the Sahara Desert! All the women here are either engaged or married."

"Maybe where you work, but not where I work," I replied. This piqued Harry's interest. "So, you've met single women?" He asked.

"Not at work," I replied, "but there are some cute girls at the housing office. Come by some time, and I will introduce you." Harry, however, did not seem interested. Instead, he changed the subject.

"Have you had any luck yet?" Harry asked.

"Not yet," I replied. "I met a Swedish exchange student named Elsa during my first day in Naples."

"So how did that work out?" he asked.

"Good at first," I replied "until I forgot to get her phone number. I haven't seen her since."

"Do you have any idea where she lives," Harry asked?

"Yes," I replied. "I visited her apartment once. She lives somewhere in the city center. I couldn't find it again, however. Every building looks the same down there." Changing the subject, I asked Harry a question. "Are you going to ask Julie out again?" I asked.

"I might as well," Harry replied. "I've got nothing else happening right now. Naples isn't like my last duty station, Washington D.C."

"So, you had better luck there?" I asked.

"A little better," Harry replied. "I dated a young Congressional staffer for nine months. Her name was Gwen. She worked for a Congressman from Alabama. I forget his name."

"What happened?" I asked.

"I'm not sure," Harry replied. "It seemed everything was going well, and then she unexpectedly stopped returning my calls. I have no idea what happened."

"Did she move away?" I asked.

"I thought so, at first," Harry replied, "but then later, I saw her walking in the mall with the Congressman. A few weeks later, I read he was getting a divorce. Maybe she ditched me for him."

At this point in the conversation, we had arrived home. The street was filled with children, just as Harry had predicted earlier that evening. There were hundreds of children all standing outside of Mendoza's apartment building, calling his name.

"Do you think he is there?" I asked.

"No," replied Harry. "Would you come home?"

"No," I replied.

We then entered the driveway and opened the green gate. "You may want to pull your car into the driveway," Harry suggested. "It's not good to leave on the street after soccer games. Last month, the crowd painted a nearby car light blue (the color of the Naples team). They did not just paint the metal. They painted the windows, the tires, everything."

After this suggestion, I started up my car and pulled into the driveway behind Harry. Thank goodness we have a large gate, I thought.

We proceeded upstairs to the dining room to continue our discussion over drinks. "What's your poison?" Harry asked.

"Let's try the Russian Vodka," I replied. I had been eyeing the tall bottle since my arrival. "So, who went to the Soviet Union?" I asked.

"I have no idea," Harry replied.

I then changed the subject. "Why did you join the Navy?" I asked.

"To pay for law school," Harry replied. "That and I also wanted to get experience as a trial attorney. Most of the graduates in my class went off to corporate law firms in New York, but I decided to take a different path."

"How long do you have to serve?" I asked.

"Six years," Harry replied. "I have already done two years and have four years remaining. What about you?" Harry asked. "Why did you join Uncle Sam's boat company?"

"I joined for the same reason you did," I replied. "I was out of money with a year to go until graduation. When Uncle offered to pay me $1000 per month to sign early, I signed up. I recently completed my four-year commitment and am now in extra innings."

"Are you going to make a career of it?" Harry asked.

"Maybe," I replied. "I still have not decided. For now, my plan is to enjoy Naples for the next two years. After that, who knows." I then changed the subject. "So, tell me about our new roommate," I suggested. "When is he supposed to arrive?"

"Robbie's supposed to arrive at the end of the month," Harry replied. "I have known Robbie for a long time. We first met as undergraduates at Yale, then we lived together in law school. During our last year, we both joined the Navy. After JAG School, our paths diverged. I moved to D.C., and he moved to San Diego."

"Sounds like you two are close," I replied.

"Yes and no," Harry replied. "We used to be close; however, in recent years, I hadn't heard much from Robbie, except when he heard I was moving to Naples. It will be nice to see him again. We've always had fun together. Robbie is a chick magnet. For some reason, all the women like him. They think he looks like Harrison Ford. During our undergraduate, his nickname was "sugar britches." He could get laid any night of the week and often did. That's how he met his current girlfriend, Kimmy."

"I take it you weren't so lucky," I asked.

"Not hardly," Harry replied. "I don't resemble anyone famous. I'm just an average-looking joe. Women like the pretty boys, not the average joes."

"Nonsense," I replied. "I think there is someone for everyone. I had a roommate in college who was rather ugly. He had his pick of beautiful women."

"How did he do it? Harry asked.

"I don't know; perhaps he was, you know, well endowed," I replied. "It just never caused him a problem."

Harry laughed. "Perhaps, your right," Harry replied. "Perhaps I'm just too picky." He then changed the subject. "Speaking of pretty, wait until you see Robbie's girlfriend, Kimmy. She's like sex on a stick! We went out a couple of times until I introduced her to Robbie. After that, she didn't give me the time of day."

"Is she coming here also?" I asked.

"Yes," replied Harry, "although I think she's not invited. Robbie told me she invited herself and is supposed to arrive in mid-October for a two-week visit. My guess is she will never leave."

"So, what's their story?" I asked, now intrigued by the conversation.

"Kimmy and Robbie have been on-again, off-again dating for a long time," Harry replied. "They met during undergraduate. Kimmy is two years younger than Robbie.

Two years ago, Robbie asked Kimmy to marry him, and she said no. She wanted to finish graduate school first. Afterward, she attended graduate school at the University of Pennsylvania, while Robbie lived in San Diego. After they moved apart, Kimmy thought the relationship was still ongoing, whereas Robbie thought it was over. He started dating again."

"Do you think they will get married?" I asked.

"No," replied Harry, "but Kimmy doesn't know that yet! Would you like another drink?" Harry asked, offering me a glass of brandy.

"Yes," I replied. It was now midnight.

We sipped our brandy for another hour, sharing our "war stories" about life in the Navy. I even told him about Dana and showed him the ring. Afterwards, I retired to bed. Outside, the children were still calling Mendoza's name, and he had still not appeared on the balcony. Go home, I thought. Get a clue; he's not home! Just as I finished that thought, a red Ferrari turned into the driveway across the street. It was Mendoza, and the crowd went nuts.

CHAPTER 10: THE ROBBERY

HARRY'S NARRATIVE

The day began like every day. I arrived at the NLSO office by 7:30, met with David for coffee at 9:00 and prepared to go to lunch at noon. Today, however, would be different as I planned to meet Julie for lunch at a pizzeria in Bagnoli. Ever since the cookout, Julie and I had started to see more of each other as Julie began to take a more active role in our relationship. We still had not kissed, but at least we were becoming friends.

As we spent more time together, I realized that Julie's quiet, reserved character was not who she really was. She was just shy, a characteristic which I mistook for coldness. Once she became comfortable with me, she began to be more talkative. It was an amazing transformation that made me want to spend more time with her.

At 11:55, just as I was about to leave the office to meet Julie, the phone rang. I debated whether to pick it up, thinking it might cause me to be late for our date, but I decided to pick it up anyway. It was Julie, and she was distraught about something.

"What is wrong?" I asked. "Slow down. I can't understand you."

"I've been robbed," she replied with tear-soaked sobs.

"What did they take?" I asked, thinking they stole money or jewelry.

"They took everything Harry!" Julie replied.

"Everything?" I replied.

"Yes, everything," Julie replied! "Please come to my house. I need you," she pleaded! "I don't know what to do!"

"Have you called the shore patrol," I asked? "They will need to make a report."

"I haven't but will," Julie replied. "Please come to see this. I cannot describe it over the phone."

"I am on my way," I said, not sure what to expect when I got there.

I had read about other burglaries. The problem was, unfortunately, all too common in the American Community. This time was different, however, as someone I knew was now part of the statistic. Before I stepped out of the office, I reviewed the police blotter for the area where Julie lived. Ten burglaries had been reported in that area during the past six months. So far, there have been no arrests.

Petty crime was a frequent problem in those days. There was the case of the Navy weapons contractor who had three rental cars stolen from him in a single day. It turns out he kept telling the clerk at the rental car counter the name of the hotel where he was staying. The thieves, who likely worked for the rental company, stole the car, selling it to a chop shop, while the car company made a claim against the insurance. It was what Neapolitans referred to as a victimless crime. Crooks in Naples could be both ingenious and brazen, becoming admired local heroes in the process.

I read about one such case where someone stole all the cars parked in front of the San Carlo Opera House during an evening opera. They showed up with several car hauling trailers, simply loaded all the cars onto the trailers and then drove away. The crime happened during the evening hours while thousands of people walked nearby enjoying the evening. There were no witnesses, even though it happened in broad daylight in a busy public square.

I arrived at Julie's house after forty minutes of driving. Like so many Americans, Julie had chosen to live twenty miles to the north, out in the water buffalo fields, northwest of Naples. They lived in places with lots of single-family homes. Towns with names like Monterusciello, Licola, Lago Patria and Varcaturo.

When I arrived at Julie's house, I could immediately tell why she liked it. She lived in a spacious villa with a green front lawn with fruit trees, surrounded by a stone wall. It seemed she had chosen well. The house had the security features that houses should have, a robust front door made of steel hidden behind a wooden veneer, as well as green painted steel shutters on every window. Everything seemed to be in its place.

It was not until I pulled into the driveway that I began to get an inkling of what had happened. I saw a pile of rubble in front of the garage door. Walking towards the back of the house, hidden from the road, I found the source of the problem. The reason Julie had been crying on the phone. The entire back wall of her kitchen had been removed.

Why go through the front door, I thought, if it was easier to knock a hole in the back wall? The hole was large, as large as the back end of a moving truck. As I climbed up into the opening, I found Julie sitting on the kitchen floor sobbing.

"They took everything," she exclaimed, "literally everything."

Peering around the kitchen, it seemed she was right. Only the sink remained. Gone were the stove, the refrigerator, the washer, the dryer, and the kitchen cabinets. The thieves had left the gas bottles and the food. That was all.

"Let me show you the rest of the house," Julie sobbed as she staggered to her feet, trying to regain her composure.

The living room was barren, with only nails remaining on the walls where her pictures had once been. The dining room was the same, as was a small den where she kept her books. I had visited Julie's house only three days before and could not get over the transformation. The once crowded den was completely bare. They had even taken her family photo albums which were still in a box.

After touring the ground floor, we proceeded upstairs. The upper floor was a disaster area, not as clean as the ground floor. The furniture was gone as well as the wardrobes. However, the thieves had left Julie's clothes, which were now scattered across the floor. By this point, Julie was sobbing again.

"Did they take any of your papers?" I asked.

"No," she replied. "Thankfully, my papers are at the office. What should I do?" Julie asked. "I cannot stay here tonight. I don't want to spend another night in this house! I want to go home," she said. "I want to return to the States! I've had enough!"

At that moment, I made a major decision, a big decision, a life-changing decision. I invited Julie to move in with me. For a moment, she stopped crying.

"Are you sure, Harry?" She asked.

"Yes," I replied. "My house is safe. Perhaps the safest house in the city. We have a proprietor who never leaves the house. We have two Carabinieri who guard a four-star admiral next door, as well as a man who protects the Naples Soccer team across the street. No one's going to bother you at my house."

"Do you have a spare room?" She asked.

"Yes, we have plenty of room," I replied. "We have a spare bedroom in the back complete with a bed, wardrobe, and dresser."

"Isn't David using that room?" She asked, remembering the layout of the house.

"He is for one more week," I replied, "until his household goods arrive. After that, he will move into his own room. Can you sleep on the couch for a week?" I asked.

"I suppose," she replied.

I could see the gears beginning to move in her mind now that the waterworks had stopped. That night, Julie moved in with me. In a brief period, she would be joined by two additional people. Our house was beginning to fill up.

PART II. FORMING RELATIONSHIPS

CHAPTER 11:

DAVID VISITS THE VILLA SCIPIONE

DAVID'S NARRATIVE

During the fall of 1989, Enzo and I went to inspect repair work recently completed at one of our newest leases, the Villa Scipione. This house was owned by a wealthy businessman named Don Carlo Scipione, who would be joining us at the house for the inspection.

"I hope the repair people did a decent job this time," Enzo remarked, as he pulled up to the compound front gate. The last attempt was not to the owner's satisfaction. Enzo seemed clearly worried the latest attempt would not be much better. "I do not want to replace the entire floor," he said.

"How did the floor get damaged?" I asked.

"It was damaged by the movers a month ago when Captain Bailey moved in," Enzo replied. "They did not adequately protect the floor before they tried to bring in Mrs. Bailey's piano."

As we pulled up to the gate, Enzo got out of the car to speak into the entrance intercom. Within seconds the gate began to open. Once inside, we turned towards the left into a short driveway. We had arrived.

"This is the Villa Scipione," Enzo proclaimed as he walked around the car to open my door! His days as a chauffer had not left him.

The house looked small compared to our other rented villas, perhaps two thousand square feet or less. It sat in a ravine surrounded by slopes on three sides which were all covered thickly with flowering vegetation. In front of the house stood two magnificent palm trees, standing thirty feet tall.

"Are those Canary Island Palms?" I asked Enzo.

"Yes," he replied, "I think so. The house is much bigger inside than it looks," remarked Enzo. "Would you guess it is almost 3000 square feet?"

"No," I replied.

When we stepped inside, we were greeted by Mrs. Bailey, the Captain's wife. Standing beside her was the property owner, Don Carlo, admiring the floor. Our landlord was a giant man with broad shoulders and robust muscular arms. He had a large wide face with a bald head encircled by a wreath of light brown hair. His large nose seemed like it had been broken more than once.

He reached out his hand towards mine. "Call me Charles," he said. "I hate when people refer to me as Don Carlo. It makes me feel like a character in "The Godfather.""

"They did a respectable job," remarked Charles, as he congratulated Enzo. It seemed to me they had as well, as I could not tell where the repair had been made.

"Sorry for the inconvenience this has caused you, Mrs. Bailey," Enzo said, turning towards the Navy Captain's wife.

"No problem," she replied. "I feel a shared sense of responsibility for the damage. I am glad this all worked out well."

After we engaged in small talk with Mrs. Bailey for a few minutes, we left the house to return to the car.

"Would you care to join me in the house for lunch?" the proprietor asked.

"Ok," Enzo replied. "LT. Moore and I have another appointment at 2:00, but we should have time."

"That should be more than enough time," Charles replied.

For the next several minutes, we walked down the driveway, following Charles as he pointed out the exotic plants in his garden. One of the trees was quite striking.

"What is that tree?" I asked.

"It is a Cedar of Lebanon," Charles replied. "My wife's father planted it back in the 1920s."

When we reached the end of the driveway, we walked past a four-car garage and through a wooden gateway that appeared almost Japanese. There was no indication of what lay beyond the gate.

As we stepped through the gate, we entered an expansive terrace decorated with small potted palms. In the center sat a large swimming pool. On the left stood a large two-story villa, painted in pastel colors, with a red-tiled roof.

The house looked immense, perhaps 10,000 square feet in size. It had several floor-to-ceiling windows overlooking the terrace. Beyond the pool, at the far end of the terrace, sat a large rock outcropping with a white statue of a naked woman pouring water from a jar into a pool below. To the right of the fountain ran a long stone railing with several marble busts of Roman Emperors overlooking the sea. Across from the pool on the far right was a small flat-roofed building perched on the side of the cliff, which seemed a changing house for the pool.

After gazing about the terrace, I saw an even more interesting sight, a beautiful, tanned woman lying on her back, sunbathing topless beside the pool in a beach chair. Beside her on a table sat a cocktail with a little pink umbrella in a glass.

Picking up a towel, Charles pitched it at the woman, the towel landing on her chest. "Put some clothes on Antonella; we have company," he said!

As I stood there trying not to stare, the woman, draped the towel around her shoulders and sat up to look at us, shading the sun with her eyes.

"Is this David Moore?" She asked with a smile. The towel was now covering everything of importance.

"Yes," her father replied. "Now get dressed."

"I have heard interesting things about you," Antonella said as she stood up slowly and walked towards the changing house.

As soon as she closed the door behind her, Charles reached out his hand toward me, inviting me to enter the house. "I apologize for my daughter," he replied. "I told her you were coming and asked her to look more presentable, but she did what she wanted. She takes after her mother."

After this, he invited us to retire to his office to discuss business. Following Charles, we proceeded through the house, up a wide staircase and into the living room overlooking the pool. At the far end of the room, I noticed a black grand piano sitting atop a raised glass floor. Walking over towards it, I noticed that the room sat atop a hot tub below. On the floor of the hot tub was a coat of arms. An oval shield with red and white horizontal stripes.

"What does this signify?" I asked.

"That is the coat of arms of the Carafa family, my wife's family," Charles replied. "She comes from an old and distinguished Neapolitan family who once produced sixteen Cardinals. You see, this house once belonged to her father. We inherited it after his death in 1973."

"Where did you live before that?" I asked.

"Silvana and I lived in New York," he replied. "I worked for an engineering firm, and my wife worked as an editor at a major fashion magazine. My wife and I met in Naples in the early sixty's while I served as an officer in the U.S. Navy. After we married, we returned to the States, where we lived until Silvana's father passed away. We decided to return to Italy after his death to care for Silvana's mother, who was in ill health at the time. Mother has since passed away."

"So, you are American?" I asked.

"Yes," Charles replied, "I am originally from Birmingham, Michigan. I am a graduate of Michigan State University."

"I graduated from Northwestern University myself," I replied. "How many children do you have?" I asked.

"Just two," he replied, "Antonella and her twin brother Tony."

"Are they American?" I asked.

"Yes, they were born in New York," Charles replied. "Our citizenship is a complicated thing. At this point, we are all dual citizens, American and Italian. I am also a citizen of Monaco through my mother."

Charles sounded fascinating. I wondered if any of our other property owners had such interesting stories. I was beginning to understand from Enzo that our proprietors were significantly more interesting than our tenants.

Changing the subject, Charles maneuvered towards a topic of special interest to him. "I understand you are looking for more houses to lease;" he smiled, turning towards Enzo.

"Yes," I replied. "We are always looking for more houses to lease."

"I have a small two-bedroom bungalow by the sea," Charles said, "which was leased by the U.S. State Department for the past five years. They recently gave it back after their employee returned to the States. I am now trying to find another tenant. Would you like to see it?" Charles asked.

"Yes," I replied.

"It is the small house to the side of the pool as you came in," Charles replied. "We can look at it after lunch." By this point, we were seated in the living room.

"Let me show you my office," Charles continued, walking over towards a large door. Enzo and I followed him into the office, where we sat down on another set of couches in front of his desk. The desk was quite large, built in a neo-classical style with inlaid wood panels on the sides.

Looking behind the desk, I saw a credenza covered with pictures. One photo particularly caught my eye. It appeared to be a photo of Charles and a woman standing next to the Pope. Seeing that the picture had caught my attention, Charles picked it up and brought it closer.

"This is one of my prize possessions," he said.

"When was that taken?" I asked.

"This picture was taken at Antonella's christening," he said. "It is a picture of my wife, Silvana and I standing next to Pope Paul VI."

As we were admiring the picture, a tall, much tanned, beautiful, middle-aged woman with long dark hair walked into the room. She was dressed impeccably in high-heel shoes, wearing gold jewelry, with sunglasses perched on her forehead.

"This is my wife, Silvana," Charles replied, patting her on the bottom.

"Is this LT. Moore?" she asked. "I have heard so much about you!"

How did these people know so much about me? It seemed a strange conversation, given that I had never met this woman before in my life.

"Silvana is the most important person in our family," Charles teased, kissing his wife on the cheek. "She is my fashion goddess." Brushing her husband aside, Silvana changed the subject.

"Would you like to join us on the terrace for lunch?" she asked. "I have set out an assortment of antipasti."

As we walked out onto the terrace, I saw a beautiful blond woman wearing a bright yellow bikini coming out of the pool. I could not see her face, only the perfect form of her body from behind. For a moment, it seemed as if time stood still. Somehow the woman looked familiar.

"Is that you, Elsa?" I asked. Slowly the woman turned around to face me. It was Elsa.

"Where have you been all my life?" she asked as she walked towards me.

She gave me a big hug, forgetting about her wet bathing suit. In an instant, she thoroughly soaked my khaki uniform. I didn't mind, however. The feeling of her wet body against mine was like magic. Then she pulled back.

"Sorry, I got you so wet," Elsa remarked as she pulled away from me. "Let me get you a towel. I am sorry I forgot to give you my new phone number," she apologized. "Did you get the message I left for you at the hotel?"

"No," I replied. "I was not aware you left a message."

"I came by twice," she replied, "each time leaving messages."

For a moment, I paused. How stupid, I thought. I had never bothered to check for messages. "I spent an entire afternoon wandering your old neighborhood looking for your apartment," I replied. It seemed we had both been looking for each other.

After our initial exchange, Elsa invited me into the cliff house to change my clothes. As we entered the house, I saw Antonella coming up the stair, now impeccably dressed like her mother. She gave me a big smile and winked at me just before we passed on the stair.

At the bottom of the stair, Elsa pointed me towards a bathroom to change. "There is a robe hanging on the back of the door," she remarked. "Hand me your clothes after you change into the robe, and I will put them in the dryer." After a few minutes, we re-emerged from the cliff house to join everyone for lunch. It was then that I realized how silly I looked in the robe.

"The flowered collar really completes the ensemble," Silvana remarked, as everyone had a good laugh at my expense.

After our lunch, I toured Elsa's apartment with Charles and Enzo, still wearing Elsa's bathrobe. I wondered if Elsa realized that Antonella's father was attempting to lease her apartment out from under her. After quickly touring the house, which was small, I realized it was not suitable.

"You have a nice house, Charles," I replied at the end of the tour, not wishing to displease him. "I need something larger that can accommodate a family. If you have something with 3-4 bedrooms, I would be interested."

After changing back into my uniform, we departed the house. During the drive back to the base I asked Enzo how much money Charles wanted for his tiny house.

"Six million lire per month," Enzo replied.

The amount was truly staggering. It was much more than we paid for the largest villa in our inventory. Then, as we drove toward our next appointment, I realized once again that I had left Elsa without getting her phone number. Well, at least this time, I knew where she lived.

"Did you know that was going to happen?" I asked Enzo. His smile indicated that he did.

CHAPTER 12:

CHANGES -OCTOBER 1989

David's Narrative

The month of October brought many changes. During the first week, my household goods arrived after their six-week Atlantic crossing. It took them three weeks to cross the ocean and another three weeks to clear customs in the port of Naples. It was wonderful to finally sleep in my own bed again.

During that same eventful first week, Harry's new love interest, Julie, moved into the villa. Initially, she was very depressed following the loss of her possessions. However, she quickly warmed to her new surroundings. She enjoyed living with people again after living alone. We seldom saw her, only the traces of her, a wet towel in the bathroom or perhaps some dishes left in the sink. She continued to work crazy ever-changing hours while Harry and I worked days. Occasionally our paths crossed, but often they did not.

During the second week, Robbie arrived and moved into the house. Harry's description of Robbie was exactly as he described. Robbie resembled a young version of Harrison Ford. Not the Harrison Ford of the "Indiana Jones," films but rather the Harrison Ford of the first "Star Wars" Movie.

The thing that struck me most about Robbie, however, was his penchant for grilling. Robbie cooked everything he ate on the barbecue. For breakfast, he had sausages, half of which went to Bari, and for dinner, he had steak. He loved giant Texas-sized steaks that Fred Flintstone would be proud of. If it did not have black stripes on it, he didn't eat it.

During the third week, Robbie's girlfriend Kimmy arrived. From the start, it was clear she would be the star of the show. Kimmy was a delightful ball of energy, no more than five feet in height, with a weight of around one hundred pounds. She had a beautiful Italian face, with a contagious ear-to-ear smile and dancing brown eyes which could light up a room. Everything about Kimmy was miniature, and yet everything was perfectly proportioned. Once her perfume entered a room, it stayed long after she left. She was like an overflowing champagne bottle, decorating our home with an effervescent cheer from dawn till dusk. But most of all, she never stopped talking.

"Now you understand," Harry remarked, one night while we were enjoying a beer.

Yes, I did. There was a reason Robbie hadn't broken up with Kimmy yet. He could not bring himself to do it. She was irresistible. I now understood why Harry said she would never leave.

As the days passed into weeks, I learned the secret of Kimmy's control over Robbie. It was sex. They did it constantly. They were like bunnies, never seeming to get enough. During their first Saturday together, Harry and I counted them going upstairs at least five times.

"How can he do it?" I asked. "She is insatiable!" Harry smiled as he tried to suppress his laughter. Even Julie, who had joined us on the couch, cracked a smile.

As we settled into our communal life, I attempted to begin building relationships with my roommates. Julie was easy to get to know, given our mutual connections to the Chicago area. We became friends quickly within a few days. Harry was also easy to relate to; He was an open book; what you saw was who he was. Robbie and Kimmy, however, were a challenge. Robbie seemed to relate to his old friend Harry but not to Julie or me. We were not worth his time. As for Kimmy, her relationship with Harry was tentative at best. It was clear they had some unresolved issues.

I was not surprised to learn after several weeks that Kimmy had once dated Harry briefly before she met Robbie. While this did not seem to bother Harry or Robbie in the least, it did seem to affect Kimmy.

Kimmy and Julie bonded well, sharing observations about their men. Kimmy, however, had little use for me. I was invisible to her, someone not worth knowing. I suppose it was because she didn't want anything from me.

The month of October also brought good things for me. Elsa was back in my life again. From the moment we met at the swimming pool, we became inseparable. That first weekend, I brought her to the house and introduced her to Harry & Julie. Afterward, all four of us visited the Archaeology Museum in the center of Naples.

VISIT TO THE MUSEUM

The Naples Archaeology Museum is housed in a large Pompeian Red building, which had once been the King's barracks, deep within the old city. Within its galleries are the treasures of the ancient Roman world. It includes the finest art recovered from the excavations at Pompeii and Herculaneum, as well as the sculpture collections of a Renaissance Pope. Many of these works of art had once decorated the palaces of the King, only becoming the property of the common people following the reunification of Italy.

I was most impressed by the giant sculptures, which included the colossal torso and head of the Greek God Zeus, recovered from the acropolis at Cumae, as well as the largest sculpture from the ancient world, the Farnese Bull, which once served as a centerpiece in Rome's Baths of Caracalla.

The museum has many other fine works of art. My favorite works of art were the fine mosaics and bronze sculptures from Pompeii and Herculaneum.

The average Roman of the first century AD lived much better than we do now. One work of art best captured this sense in my mind. It was a large mosaic, which once covered a dining room floor in Pompeii. Depicted on the mosaic in tiny little stone squares, delicately assembled, was the image of a famous battle between Alexander the Great and the Persian King Darius. The image captures for eternity the moment when Alexander breaks through the line and the Persian King is about to flee. It was Elsa's favorite and mine too.

VISIT TO POMPEII

After our visit to the museum, we visited Pompeii the following day. I had three impressions of Pompeii. First that it was a decent size city accommodating 30,000 inhabitants; secondly, the inhabitants lived comfortable luxurious lives and thirdly that Pompeii was a typical city for its time.

The visit dispelled a basic assumption I had made when I first moved into the Villa Maria. Roman houses did, in fact, have heating systems. The houses were heated using hot water, which circulated under the floors.

Most of the houses in Pompeii were quite spacious, with entrance atriums that opened to the sky. The atriums were used to collect rainwater which was stored under the floors. In addition, many houses had gardens in the rear of the house, which were surrounded by columned arcades. The gardens often contained fountains, which were fed by the aqueducts supplying water to the city. Each of the houses also had many rooms. Some of the houses had second floors, and a few of the houses had bathrooms with running water.

The thing that struck me most, however, about the houses was that every house had walls covered with paintings. Pompeii had acres of original art frescos. They were everywhere. Visiting Pompeii taught me something remarkable about the ancient world. They lived better than us. I now understood something essential about the Italian Renaissance.

The houses tended to fill the center of the blocks, and each house had several shops and stores, built into its walls, facing outwardly towards the streets. Houses were not just for living. They were also places for business.

I remembered the thousands of one-room shops I had seen while wandering Naples' city center, looking for Elsa's apartment. While the buildings were much taller than Pompeii, the fundamental retail aspects of the city of Naples had not changed in over two thousand years.

In the center of Pompeii stood a large square surrounded by government buildings, temples, and markets. Within the square stood the pediments of statues, which had long since been removed to fill Naples's museums. The square also had two triumphal arches.

The square sat at the intersection of two main streets. One street ran north-south, and the other ran east-west. From these streets extended a grid of streets. Some of the streets were wide, once housing the rich, and others were narrow, forming the back alleys where common people lived. Many of the streets had deep wheel ruts in the paving stones, revealing the city was once very congested with horse-drawn carts.

I remembered reading that ancient Rome had once had city ordinances forbidding horse-drawn carts to enter the city during the day. The nights must have been very noisy, making it difficult to sleep. I wondered if Pompeii might have had similar laws. They clearly had designated one-way streets.

At the opposite end of the city stood a large arena surrounded by arcades, which were said to include more markets as well as a training school for gladiators. One of the buildings was once a multi-story hotel.

After touring the city, we visited the covered arcades surrounding the main square. Behind iron gates, we could see hundreds of clay pots, statues and stone furniture recovered from the excavations. Some of the furniture looked as if it might easily fit into a modern Italian home today.

Within several glass cases, we saw plaster casts of the bodies, which had been buried in volcanic ash during the eruption of 79 AD. After the eruption, the city of Pompeii was abandoned.

TIME SPENT WITH ELSA

Spending time again with Elsa was simply wonderful. I never tired of her company. One of our favorite pastimes was walking from her house to the small fishing village nearby.

The fishing village was called Marechiaro. It was not really a fishing village per se, but rather a dead-end street with many excellent restaurants. At the end of the street beyond the restaurants was a set of stairs leading down to a small harbor where fishermen parked their boats. It was an evocative place with many ruins.

There were ruins offshore rising out of the water, as well as broken columns standing beside the narrow alleyway walls. Behind the walls lay the luxurious gardens of giant houses hidden within.

The neighborhood rose like stairsteps up the side of the hill. From the streets above, we could see the remains of a large villa partially submerged offshore, as well as many other splendid mansions hidden behind garden walls. This was the part of the city where the elite lived.

The submerged villa was said to be the remains of a palace built by the first Roman Emperor, Caesar Augustus. The Posillipo was an enchanting place, not part of the real world. For two brief years, however, it became my home.

CHAPTER 13:

JULIE AND THE GIRLS VISIT SORRENTO

JULIE'S NARRATIVE

It was late October 1989 when Kimmy, Antonella, Elsa, and I spent a beautiful Sunday in Sorrento. I had been working odd hours at the hospital for seven days straight and finally had two days off. I wanted to get out and enjoy the beautiful summer-like weather, which was expected to be in the eighties. It seemed perhaps the last warm day until spring.

Harry, however, had other plans. "Today is football day," he exclaimed! "AFN is broadcasting three games. David, Robbie & I plan to spend the entire day in front of the TV set!"

"Have fun with that," I replied! The last thing I wanted to do was spend the entire day watching football.

"Kimmy, would you like to go to Sorrento?" I asked. "I plan to do some shopping, eat out at a nice trattoria, and spend the afternoon at the beach."

I had noticed that Kimmy seldom went anywhere during the day while Robbie was at work. Instead, she sat around the house reading and watching TV. The "cutesy act" that she did around the boys ended when they left for work. The real Kimmy was quiet, nervous, and bored. Something was bothering her.

"Yes, I would like that," she replied. She turned towards me and smiled.

"Let's invite Elsa," I suggested "and see if she wants to come!"

Kimmy had not met Elsa. However, I wanted to spend more time with Elsa after our day at Pompeii. Elsa would provide good company, just in case Kimmy turned out to be less than sociable.

When I reached Elsa, she asked if she could bring her roommate. "Certainly," I replied, "the more, the merrier!" Within 30 minutes after hanging up, Elsa arrived with her roommate Antonella, riding her motor scooter. It was still early in the morning, barely 9:00 am.

Elsa had already told me some things about Antonella. I knew that her mother was an Italian and that her father was American. I also knew that Antonella had spent her early childhood in New York before moving to Italy at age seven. None of that, of course, was visible from looking at her. Antonella was a classic Italian beauty. She was tall with dark hair. She had a killer body and deep blue eyes. Clearly, she was a woman capable of leaving a trail of broken hearts. That day, I would also learn she had a great sense of humor.

Our lively and animated drive to Sorrento took about an hour and a half, enabling us to reach the central square by 10:30 am, just in time for a quick café. After enjoying our coffee, we wandered the narrow streets of the ancient town, stopping to visit the many jewelry stores and inlaid wood shops.

Sorrento is known for two specialties, beautiful inlaid wood furniture and jewelry. The jewelry shops specialize in selling cameos and other jewelry made from the local red coral. I particularly liked the coral neckless' which resembled strings of pink pearls. All the girls loved the shopping. We were in our element.

Kimmy and Antonella bought some jewelry. Kimmy bought a lovely pink coral neckless. Antonella bought some pink coral earrings. Elsa and I decided to buy inlaid wood. I bought a small, beautifully crafted music box with a violin on the cover. Elsa bought an inlaid wood tray with a floral design. Afterward, we bought a bottle of Limoncello for the boys.

When we finished our morning shopping, we returned to the main square for lunch. The square was not really a square in the traditional sense but rather a wide spot on the road in the center of town. The town had many excellent restaurants hidden within its narrow streets, however, I wanted to find a place to sit outdoors in the sun.

We found a lovely restaurant in the main square opposite the coffee bar we had visited previously. Once seated, we each ordered pasta for lunch. That afternoon we supplemented our lunch with a bottle of local white wine. By the end of the meal, we were feeling quite relaxed.

"Does anyone know a good beach nearby?" I asked. "Someplace that does not charge a lot of money and has some nice sand." I had been to the Amalfi Coast before and had learned that it was hard to find a free beach with sand.

For a moment, Elsa and Antonella spoke to each other in Italian. It seemed they were discussing various options. I heard Elsa mention going to Positano, an idea which Antonella firmly rejected. She didn't want to spend 10,000 lire for a beach umbrella.

Finally, they settled on a selection. "Elsa and I know of a small beach just outside of town," Antonella suggested. "It is called the Baths of Queen Giovanna, and it's free." We all agreed that free was good.

After lunch, we retrieved our car from the lot and proceeded to the beach, driving up the long sloping hill on the west side of town. When we reached the top of the hill, we stopped to enjoy the view and take some group pictures, using the town of Sorrento as a background. It was an incredibly beautiful day!

No sooner did we get back on the road than we drove around a bend and turned right into a long shade-covered street, where we parked the car. The beach was closer than I thought. We could have walked.

"The beach is at the end of this street," Elsa remarked as we got out of the car.

Following Elsa and Antonella, we walked to the end of the street and from there entered a narrow trail through some tall grass, leading to the bottom of a cliff. As we approached the bottom, it became clear that the Baths of Queen Giovanna were, in fact, the ruins of a large villa beside the sea.

"This place is named for the last Angevin Queen, Queen Joan II, who lived in the 15th century," Elsa explained. "The ruins are much older, however," she added. As I looked down at the ruin, I could not see a beach.

"Where is the beach?" I asked.

"It is inside," Elsa replied. "It is hidden within."

When we reached the bottom of the cliff, we walked around the remains of several walls until we came to a deep hole. Below us sat a small crescent-shaped beach and a beautiful round pool of blue water, sitting inside of a round ruined structure. It was then that I noticed that the hole was not, in fact, a hole at all but rather the collapsed remains of what may have once been a large domed building.

"That's it," Antonella replied, pointing towards the beach. "Follow me; the stair to the beach is on the left."

When we reached the stair, we found it was not really a stair at all, but rather the crumbling ruins of a stair. Fortunately, someone had installed a heavy chain along the wall, enabling us to reach the beach below.

When we reached the bottom, we encountered a beautiful sight. In front of the beach and its blue lagoon were the remains of a crumbling Roman arch. Beyond the arch, we could see the perfectly framed view of Mount Vesuvius. Gazing around us, I admired the secret place we had found.

"Was this once a room?" I asked.

"It may have been," Elsa replied. "However, there are no traces remaining of the roof. It's also possible it was constructed to look this way."

Elsa's observation was intriguing. Had the Romans built a structure intentionally designed to look like a ruin? Perhaps they had. "How did this place get its name?" I asked.

"There is a legend that Queen Joan, the last Angevin ruler of Naples, brought her lovers here," Elsa replied.

That afternoon we had the beach all to ourselves, enjoying the clean sand and warm sun. It was our own private little paradise. After we had settled in, laying out our towels and removing our clothes to reveal our swimsuits underneath, we decided to go for a swim.

Antonella and Elsa quickly jumped in and swam through the arch out into the open water beyond. Kimmy and I proceeded cautiously into the water, fearing it might be cold. While the air was warm in the mid-eighties, the water was, in fact, cold. It was too cold to swim in the open bay. Instead, Kimmy and I decided to sit in the shallows and soak up the sun. It was also my chance to speak with Kimmy alone.

"How are you doing?" I asked. "You seem distant today and not your normal cheerful self."

"I am sorry," Kimmy replied. "I have a lot on my mind."

"What's wrong?" I asked, hoping to appear helpful without being too nosy.

"I need to make a big decision," Kimmy replied. "You see, Robbie and I have been a couple for a long time, almost six years now. Two years ago, following his graduation from law school, Robbie asked me to marry him. At the time, I wasn't ready. I still wanted to go to graduate school. I asked him to wait two years until I finished school."

"Where did you go to school?" I asked.

"I went to Yale as an undergraduate," Kimmy replied. "That's where I met Robbie. I went to the University of Pennsylvania's Wharton School for my master's." She then continued with her story. "Robbie seemed to agree to this arrangement at the time, even though it meant we would be apart for two years."

"Did he ever give you an engagement ring?" I asked.

"No," Kimmy replied. "He didn't offer an engagement ring either when he asked me to marry him or afterward. The more I think about that, the more it bothers me! Why didn't he give me a ring?"

"What happened next?" I asked.

"For the past two years, while I have been in graduate school, we've been maintaining our relationship long-distance, spending our holidays together and talking on the phone," Kimmy continued. "At first, we spoke every day, sometimes more than once. Gradually over time, however, our phone calls became less frequent. We were drifting apart."

"So, what kept you together?" I asked.

"We began having sex whenever we were together," Kimmy replied. "It seemed necessary to keep the flame going during our long absences. The best tryst occurred back in March when Robbie invited me to visit him in San Diego, just after graduation. We stayed in bed for two days. During the trip, I thought he might propose, but he never did. There was no proposal, nothing! It was a giant disappointment! Instead, he invited me to visit him in Italy. He did not ask me to move here. He just asked me to come to visit! What's with that!"

"Have you asked him to marry you?" I asked. "There is nothing in the book which requires the man to be the one who proposes."

"Not yet," Kimmy replied. "I would prefer to have him do the asking. I have dropped many hints. Robbie isn't, however, taking the bait. I guess I am old-fashioned. I want the man to propose."

"Do you still want to get married?" I asked.

"Yes," Kimmy replied! "I am crazy about Robbie! I have been in love with him for six years. I can't tell, however, if he is still in love with me. Do you know if Robbie has spoken to Harry about us?"

So, this was her angle. She was trying to use me to understand what Robbie might be thinking. I could see the wheels turning in her mind. She thought I might know the answer to her question. The fact was, I did not know. Harry and I were still getting acquainted. He hadn't yet confided in me about Robbie.

"Harry and I are just friends," I replied. "We only went on two dates before he invited me to move in with him. You see, I was robbed just before you came. The robbers took everything I owned. In my time of distress, Harry came to my rescue."

"So, you're not a couple?" Kimmy replied.

"No, not yet," I replied.

Kimmy seemed disappointed. Then she said something interesting. "I've known Harry a long time," she said. "I think he likes you." I hadn't realized that fact yet.

"Do you plan to stay?" Kimmy asked.

"I would like to," I replied. "I enjoy living in the house. It is nice to live with other people again. However, whether I stay or not depends on Harry."

"What do you mean?" Kimmy asked.

"I mean that I am not ready to sleep with him," I replied. If he expects me to sleep with him, I will move out."

"What's wrong with Harry?" Kimmy asked. "He's a nice guy. I've known Harry for seven years."

Changing the subject, I asked Kimmy what she needed to decide. "I need to decide whether to return to New York next week as planned or stay for several more weeks," she replied. "I have until December 1st before I need to start a new job in New York. If I stay beyond that date, I will need to give up the new job." I could tell by the tone of her voice that she wanted to keep her options open just in case Robbie wouldn't commit.

"Where do you plan to work?" I asked.

"I have been offered a job at the World Trade Center in Lower Manhattan," Kimmy replied. Clearly, Kimmy was a smart woman about to enter a fast-track career. Why was she hanging on to Robbie?

"Do you think he will propose by December 1st?" I asked.

"I don't know," she replied. "When I bring the subject up, he keeps asking me why I'm in a hurry. He thinks I should give up my career and live with him in some sort of marriage limbo."

Hearing this, I decided to ask the obvious question that needed asking. "If he is not willing to give you a commitment, why are you still having sex with him?" There it was, I said it!

The response Kimmy provided seemed incredibly naïve or deceitful. "Because I love him," she replied!

It seemed she was not willing to tell me the real reason. Dump him, I thought! He's using you! I did not, however, share my opinion with Kimmy. She needed to learn this on her own.

As our conversation reached an end, Elsa and Antonella returned from their swim. Both seemed to be enjoying themselves and laughing. Then as Kimmy and I lay on our towels, both Elsa and Antonella removed their tops to sunbathe. It was the first time either Kimmy or I had been with women topless sunbathing. I wrote it off as just another experience. We were in Europe, after all. I could tell, however, that Kimmy was uncomfortable. Eventually, she removed her top as well, leaving me the only woman still wearing a top.

"Are you going to join us?" Kimmy asked.

"No," I replied, laughing. Peer pressure would not force me to remove my top. "I see boobs all day long at work," I replied. "It is no big deal. Remember, I deliver babies." My excuse seemed to work. Kimmy lay back on the towel and covered her face with her arm. As we lay there, soaking up the sun, Antonella began to speak. "Do you want to know a secret?"

"Sure," I replied. "What is your secret?"

"It is not my secret," Antonella replied. "It is Elsa's secret. Have you seen the car stereo billboards all over town?"

"Yes," I replied. I remembered seeing the billboard on the road to Pozzuoli. The billboard was quite brazen. It used a picture of a woman's naked breasts to sell car stereos.

"The woman on the billboard is Elsa," Antonella replied with a whisper.

For a moment, I turned on my side to confirm what Antonella was saying. Elsa lay on her back, smiling. Her boobs did look familiar. Clearly, she had no hang-ups regarding her figure. Why should she, I thought? I wondered, however, if David knew. It was not my place to tell him. He would need to hear that news directly from Elsa herself.

It was now about 4:30 in the afternoon. The most beautiful part of a beautiful day. Turning over onto my stomach, I closed my eyes and took a nice long nap. I had not slept since my shift began the day before. When I awoke, it was 6:00 pm and starting to cool down. Kimmy was still lying face up, sound asleep, while Elsa and Antonella were now standing, fully dressed, and beginning to shake the sand from their towels.

"It's time to go," they said. "We need to get going if you want to catch the football game which starts at 8:00 pm. Driving home from Sorrento on a Sunday night can sometimes be difficult." They were right about the difficulty. That evening, it seemed the entire city was headed back towards Naples.

We arrived back at the villa at half-past 8:00, missing the first part of the game. That night we all watched football with the boys. Afterward, Elsa and Antonella crashed on air mattresses scattered across the living room floor. It was a great end to a perfect day.

CHAPTER 14:

FOOTBALL AND BARBECUE

After the girls left for Sorrento, it was a normal Sunday. I went to the base to run errands, return videos, browse the music store, and buy tailgate supplies for the afternoon football games. Robbie went to the office to catch up on paperwork, and David went to one of his Flag villas to deal with a problem. Apparently, a light bulb needed changing or something. I was glad I didn't have his job! The last thing I wanted to do was play servant to some Admiral's wife on a Sunday.

When I returned to the house around noon, I found Robbie cleaning the grill on the terrace. "Is David back yet?" I asked.

"No, but he's on the way," Robbie replied. "He called a few minutes ago. I asked him to pick up beer at the NATO base. We're almost out."

I knew I had forgotten to buy something. "How many beers do we have left?" I asked.

"There's a six-pack in the frig," Robbie replied, "as well as a six-pack in the bathroom."

That seemed like more than enough beer for me, I thought. There are only three of us. "Would you like a beer?" I asked.

"Yes," Robbie replied.

Within a few moments, we were both sipping cold ones while Robbie continued cleaning the grill.

"So, what's going on with Kimmy?" I asked. I had been dying to ask that question for several days. "Is she headed back to New York next week?" Robbie didn't reply but instead kept rubbing the grill.

"This wire brush is worn out," Robbie exclaimed. "We need to buy a new brush and, while we're at it, a new grill. This grill is on its last legs."

"I agree," I replied. "We need to start a collection. I priced grills at the Navy Exchange this morning. A grill this size costs $450." Robbie did not reply. It seemed he was deep in thought. "So, what's happening with Kimmy?" I asked once again.

"I don't know," Robbie replied. It seemed he didn't want to discuss the topic. "I don't know what she's going to do," he replied again! "Ever since she got here, she's been obsessed with getting married. She wants me to quit the Navy and return with her to New York! I've told her I can't just up and leave, but she keeps thinking it's possible. She thinks her daddy, who happens to work at the Justice Department, can pull some strings to get me out of the Navy. She thinks the Navy will just let me go. She doesn't seem to realize that I like the Navy!"

"Do you want to get married?" I asked.

"I don't know," Robbie replied. "I thought I did two years ago when I first asked Kimmy, but now I'm not certain. Living a single life in San Diego was fun. I got to meet many beautiful girls, and of course, I "knew" a few, if you know what I mean. It was like living in a candy store. How can I go back to one type of candy every day?"

As I listened to Robbie, I remembered our college days before I introduced him to Kimmy. Robbie had sampled every candy in the store before he met Kimmy. That was how he met Kimmy. In fact, he had stolen my girlfriend. Robbie seemed to forget that important fact, even though Kimmy nor I did.

"Don't misunderstand me," Robbie continued. "I like Kimmy, she's beautiful, and she's the best lay I've ever had, but she's also so controlling. Do you know that she has our entire life planned out? I'm supposed to work for her father while she works as an investment banker on Wall Street. Then a few years from now, we are supposed to move to Scarsdale, buy a big house and have four kids. She has even named the kids. Then after we work for thirty-something years, we will retire to the Hamptons.

"Do you know her father offered me a job? He offered to pay me twice my current pay to return to New York and babysit his corporate law practice while he works at the Justice Department. I hate corporate law," Robbie exclaimed!

"Did you turn down his offer?" I asked.

"No," Robbie replied. "Kimmy's father is an important man, and I don't wish to offend him. I want to keep the option open for now."

"You know if you work for Kimmy's father, she will own you," I pointed out!

"I know," Robbie replied. "It's like being sold into slavery. Kimmy gets a ring for her finger, and I get a ring for my nose!"

"So, what are you going to do?" I asked.

"I have invited her to stay here for the next two years and give us time together as a couple," he replied. "I told her not to rush into anything. Many couples live together for years without getting married. Some even have children. I don't understand her obsession with a piece of paper. If she wants to live together, we can do that now, without a piece of paper." It seemed Robbie had a rational answer for everything and couldn't bring himself to understand Kimmy's point of view.

"What about her career?" I asked. "Didn't she just finish a master's degree in finance?"

"I am not asking her to give up her career," Robbie replied. "I am not asking her to give up any of her dreams. I am just asking her to put them on hold for two years as she asked me to do. Is that too much to ask?" Once again, Robbie was not willing to listen to reason.

"No," I replied, "it sounds like a good plan." As I listened to Robbie, it seemed he was more interested in getting even than in marrying Kimmy. Theirs was a struggle for dominance, and Robbie was losing. First, he needed to win, to somehow regain his manhood. Then, after that, he might be willing to settle down ----maybe.

"So, what's happening with you and the Navy Doctor?" Robbie asked.

"Not much," I replied. "We are taking it slow, day by day. I am still trying to figure Julie out. She is clearly very smart, perhaps much smarter than me." I could tell Robbie wasn't listening. He was just making small talk while he thought of the next thing to say.

"She seems plain to me," Robbie replied. "Your last girlfriend, Gwen, was much better looking."

"Yes, but looks are not everything," I replied. Gwen was like Kimmy. She wanted to organize my life. "I don't want an organizer. I want a real genuine person, someone who is not trying to make me into something I am not. So far, Julie seems real, which is enough for me just now." I wasn't ready to tell Robbie what I really thought about Julie.

"So, what about Elsa's friend?" Robbie asked, changing the subject. "You know the Italian one, the real looker with the deep blue eyes. Do you remember her name?"

"Her name is Antonella," I replied.

Robbie repeated her name several times. "Antonella, he pondered; I like that name!"

"I saw you looking at her," I replied. "You need to be careful. Kimmy saw you also!"

"Can't I look?" Robbie exclaimed! "It's hard not to look. Do you think her eyes are really that blue?" Robbie asked.

"No," I replied. "I think she is wearing tinted contact lenses."

"I could get lost in those eyes." Robbie replied. Once again, he was not listening to me. He was daydreaming about Antonella. "She's really stunning." he continued. It seemed clear to me that Robbie was not serious about Kimmy. He was instead thinking about his next potential conquest.

At that moment, David arrived on the terrace carrying a case of beer. "It's time to fire up the grill and turn on the TV," he exclaimed. "The first game starts in twenty minutes. What do we have to eat?" David asked.

"I bought hamburgers, hot dogs, bratwurst, and buns," I replied. "We also have a full selection of condiments, cheese for the burgers, sauerkraut for the dogs, and munchies." David smiled and began opening a bag of corn chips.

That afternoon we ate well, enjoying a burger, a dog, and a bratwurst each. We also made short work of the two six-packs and even started into the new case of beer. By the time the girls returned, we were having an enjoyable time and "three sheets to the wind."

That evening, as we watched football, I learned that Julie could be one of the guys. She liked football as much as I did. It was a pleasant surprise. Even Elsa and Antonella had an enjoyable time. They didn't understand the game but seemed to like it just the same. Kimmy, however, did not join us. She hated football. Instead, she went up to the bedroom she shared with Robbie.

When the game finished after midnight, we set up air mattresses for our guests in the living room. As I left to go upstairs to bed, I saw Elsa lying on the couch, fast asleep. I also saw Robbie lying on an air mattress next to Antonella, whispering in her ear. I hoped Kimmy did not come down to find him like that. I liked Robbie. I had known him for a long time, but I didn't like the way he was treating Kimmy. He was stringing her along, giving her just enough to keep her from leaving while trying to get a better deal with someone else. Robbie had moved on, but Kimmy didn't know it yet.

CHAPTER 15:

KIMMY'S DISCOVERY

KIMMY'S NARRATIVE

I was very tired when I returned from Sorrento and decided to go to bed early. I had no interest in watching football, nor did I want to be around Robbie, who had been drinking. For the most part, Robbie did not drink; however, when he did, he could be obnoxious. I was simply not in the mood. It wasn't until nearly 1:00 am before Robbie finally came upstairs to bed.

"Who won the game?" I asked. Robbie did not answer my question.

"It was a good game; you should have stayed," he replied.

"Good night," I replied, kissing him on the lips. He still smelled of beer. However, it was clear his buzz had worn off.

That night, I slept soundly until 5:00 am when I was awakened by a sound downstairs. Robbie had left the bed, perhaps going downstairs to make coffee. It was still dark, and I was cold, but I decided to join him, donning my slippers and bathrobe. At the bottom of the dark stairway, I could see a flicker of light coming from the living room. Someone had lit a fire in the fireplace. I could hear a woman's voice and Robbie's voice as well. I recognized the woman's voice. It was Antonella. Why was Antonella still here? Didn't she go home after the football game?

When I arrived at the bottom of the stairs, I peered into the living room. There, sat Antonella and Robbie, seated on the coach in front of the fire with their backs towards me. Robbie had his arm around her shoulders and was whispering in her ear. I recognized what he was doing, as sometimes he did the same thing to me.

Clearing my throat, I interrupted their secret conversation. "Would anyone like some coffee?" I asked.

For a moment, they stopped what they were doing and turned toward me. I could see a surprised look on Robbie's face, realizing he had been caught. Antonella looked relaxed and confident.

"Let me make some coffee for you;" she said, "while you and Robbie sit by the fire." As she passed me walking towards the kitchen, she beckoned me once again to join Robbie on the sofa. "The fire is nice," she said. "You look like you need warmth."

After Antonella left the room, I turned towards Robbie. "What was that?" I asked.

"It was nothing," Robbie replied, pretending I had seen nothing. "I could not sleep," he said. "It was too cold upstairs, so I came downstairs to start a fire. Antonella joined me. It was simple as that," he said!

Somehow, I didn't believe him. He knew Antonella was there. "Where is Elsa?" I asked, thinking perhaps Elsa had spent the night as well.

"She's upstairs with David," I think, Robbie replied. He wanted to provide no further explanation.

After a few minutes, Antonella returned with a tray containing three cups of Cappuccino and three croissants. The coffee did taste good. As we relaxed by the fire, I tried to forget what I had seen. Antonella seemed nice. It was not her fault that Robbie was acting like a Don Juan. My issue was with Robbie, not Antonella.

"What time is it?" Antonella asked.

Looking at my watch, the hands now said 6:30 am. "It's 6:30", I replied

"I need to get going," Antonella replied, remembering it was Monday. Within minutes the house began to come to life as Antonella ran upstairs to wake Elsa while I went to make another cup of coffee. By 7:30, everyone had departed for work except Julie.

"What are you going to do today?" I asked.

"I need to go to the office and catch up on paperwork," Julie replied.

I was disappointed to hear her say that, as I was hoping she might spend the day with me. I had already spent too many days alone in this big house. Julie could tell I was disappointed and offered a suggestion.

"Why don't you take a walk into the city?" she suggested.

It sounded like a promising idea. "I think I will do that," I replied. It certainly sounded better than sitting around a cold house, reading a book.

Later, when I finally stepped outdoors, the sun had come up and was shining bright. The air was still crisp and cold, but it seemed it would be a beautiful day. As I walked to the end of the street, towards the funicular station, I could hear the birds chirping, just as I stepped into a pile of dog poop.

Why can't the Neapolitans pick up after their dogs, I thought to myself. Clearly, I needed to watch more closely where I was walking, as there were piles of dog poop everywhere.

After cleaning my shoe with a tissue from my purse, I continued my walk, making sure to put the tissue in a trash can. The Neapolitans would simply throw the trash over the railing onto the street below, but I was determined to be better than that.

As I walked down the hill towards the water, I decided to explore a narrow street running towards the left under the road. In front of me was the roof of a house, completely covered with a beautiful garden. There were so many of these in Naples.

Beside the house stood a tall Umbrella Pine overhanging the roof. I had seen this view before in paintings and decided to stop and take a picture.

It was then that I saw a beautiful square nearby overlooking the city. The view was simply breathtaking, but even more beautiful still was a tall Italian-looking man standing next to the railing.

He had long curly black hair, matted with sweat and a finely sculpted face with a square jaw covered with razor stubble. It was obvious he had been jogging. He was wearing gym shorts, running shoes and a sweatshirt emblazoned with the words "New York" on it.

I wondered if perhaps he was American but quickly dismissed the notion. Certainly, he was Italian, I thought. Perhaps he had visited New York on vacation. Walking up to him, I asked him a question in English, expecting him not to understand me. He looked at me and smiled, shading his eyes.

"What is your name?" he asked.

"Kimmy," I replied. "What is your name?"

"My name is MARSHMELLOW," he replied.

"That's a funny name," I replied, misinterpreting what he had said.

Realizing he was misunderstood he laughed and then repeated his name much slower. "My name is MAR-CHELLO," he replied.

"Do you live near here?" I asked.

"Yes," he replied. "I live across the street from you!"

His response came as a surprise. Apparently, he had noticed me long before I had noticed him. Who was this man? I was now intrigued. "Do you play for the soccer team?" I asked. I remembered that the team rented the building across the street from our house.

"Yes," he replied with a look of whimsy in his eyes. "I am one of the players who make Mendoza look good every week!" After that, we chatted for a moment until he glanced at his watch.

"I need to get going," he remarked. "It's nice finally meeting you. Perhaps we will meet again sometime."

"I would like that," I replied.

I was mesmerized by his broad and welcoming smile. As he jogged away, I watched him disappear. He had made my day. I felt much happier now that I realized I had such a handsome admirer.

After Marcello left, I wandered down into the city, following a steep and winding street. Along the way, I passed several small one-room dwellings hidden within the cliff. Beside one of them sat a blind man with a tin cup.

"Is this where you live?" I asked, as I dropped a five hundred lire coin into his cup.

"Si'" he replied, giving me a Neapolitan blessing.

At the bottom of the hill, I entered a narrow alleyway walking past two more cave-like dwellings under the road. One was a flower stand and the other a magazine stand. I stopped to look at a Newspaper entitled "Il Mattino" but could not understand what it said. After the newsstand, I emerged into the busy Piazza Sannazaro. I now knew where I was. I had come out near the pizzeria, that Robbie had taken me to during our first day in Naples.

That morning, I walked along the waterfront and then wandered the Spanish Quarter, exploring the alleys and markets. Everywhere I went, there were people, young and old, going about their lives. There were mothers hanging their laundry, fishermen selling live fish in pans, men busily working in little shops, children kicking soccer balls, young couples kissing, and old women gossiping. For the first time, I saw Naples, the real Naples. Despite the graffiti, crumbling building facades, and trashcans, there was a beautiful city full of life.

When lunchtime arrived, I took the funicular up to the top of Vomero Hill for a nice lunch at a trattoria near Piazza Vanvitelli. After lunch, I went window shopping, looking for Antonella's dress shop.

I remembered Elsa telling me that Antonella worked in a shop on Via Giordano, and I hoped to find it. Most of the shops were closed for the Mezzogiorno (Siesta). However, a few were still open, including the dress shop where Antonella worked. As it turned out, the shop was easy to find.

When I entered, Antonella was busy helping a young woman trying on wedding dresses. The dresses were beautiful. Each dress was a custom work of art. They were much nicer than the mass-produced dresses I had seen in the United States. The shop was small, barely three or four rooms, but very elegant inside. As I waited for Antonella to finish what she was doing, I looked at several of the dresses on display, until Antonella approached me.

"Did you design these?" I asked.

"Some of them," Antonella replied. "Would you like to try one on?"

I had not come to try on dresses but to speak with Antonella, to tell her to stay away from Robbie. My reasons for coming were petty, and I knew it. In the end, I could not confront her. As soon as I started trying on dresses, I forgot the purpose of my visit.

Antonella was so wonderful, so gracious, and so friendly. It was hard to be jealous. If it were not for Robbie, we might be best friends. After trying on several dresses, I asked Antonella's opinion.

"Which dress do you like?" I asked.

"I like this one," she said, pointing to a particularly unique dress. "This dress compliments your figure best," she said.

I had to admit I agreed with her. The dress was angelic, accentuating my curves while also making my waist look super narrow. It hinted at much but tastefully showed little. It was an unbelievably beautiful dress.

"Did you design this one?" I asked.

"No," she replied. "This dress is made by a dressmaker in Milano."

"How much does it cost?" I asked. I feared the answer.

"Thirty million lire," Antonella replied.

I could not believe the price. That was nearly $20,000. No wonder I liked it! I always picked the most expensive dress! "Does it come with a mortgage?" I asked.

Antonella laughed. "I agree it is a bit pricey," she said, "but it's also definitely you!" I had to admit she was right; I was worth the money, if only I could afford it.

"Perhaps another day," I replied. "First, I need to get Robbie to ask me!"

Antonella smiled. "Good luck," she said! "That boy has wandering eyes, just like my boyfriend, Tony!" Hearing Antonella says that was music to my ears. Not the part about Robbie's wandering eyes, but the part about Antonella having a boyfriend.

"Are you engaged?" I asked, hoping she was off the market.

"I wish," Antonella replied. "I have been dating Tony for three years. He promises the moon and the stars, but when it comes time to offer me an engagement ring, he always has an excuse. I am being strung along just like you!"

"What does he do?" I asked.

"He races motorcycles," Antonella replied. "His name is Tony Russo. You may have heard of him." She then pulled a picture out of her purse. It was a picture of a handsome man with long wavy black hair wearing a red and white leather racing suit. "We met at the university" Antonella explained. "My mother despises him, but I adore him."

"So, do you like "bad boys?" I asked.

"No" replied Antonella. "I like boys who LOOK like bad boys but who are really mama's boys. A woman needs a man she can control, not a man who controls her. The last thing I want is a man who abuses me."

"I agree with you on that," I replied. "We let the men think they are in control, but we know who is really in control." Antonella laughed. Despite our cultural differences, we understood each other exactly.

Changing the subject, I asked Antonella another question. "Julie tells me you are from New York."

"Yes," Antonella replied. "I was born in New York City. My parents lived in an apartment on the west side, somewhere between Hell's Kitchen and Lincoln Center. It was a tough neighborhood when we lived there, but I hear it is much better now. We moved to Italy when I was seven. We now live in my grandfather's old house on the Posillipo hill."

"What do your parents do?" I asked.

"My father is an engineer, and my mother runs my grandfather's fashion magazine," Antonella replied. "Where are you from?" Antonella asked.

" I am from New York, also," I replied. "I was born in Greenwich Village and grew up in Scarsdale."

"So, we are both New Yorkers at heart," Antonella exclaimed! She leaned over and gave me a hug. "It's a small world. Welcome to Naples! Would you like a cup of espresso?"

After the espresso, I left the dress shop, hailing a taxi to take me back to the house. I now had a better appreciation for Antonella. She was not so bad after all. Under different circumstances, we could be best of friends. I realized Antonella was not my challenge. My challenge was Robbie. For some reason, he always thought the grass was greener somewhere else.

That day, I decided to stay for a few more months and give up the job at the World Trade Center. Perhaps Robbie was right. Perhaps I needed to go with the flow and stop pushing him so hard. My career in New York would have to wait! I owed it to Robbie and to myself to give our life together a chance. If it did not work out, there were always other fish in the sea, men like Marcello.

I remembered something my Italian grandmother once told me. "Sometimes you have to be willing to lose your life to find it," she said. Perhaps she was right. In the meantime, I would try to have fun and enjoy living in Italy.

CHAPTER 16:

CONVERSATION BETWEEN ELSA AND ANTONELLA (EARLY NOVEMBER)

ELSA'S NARRATIVE

I awoke to sunlight streaming into the bedroom window. The past week had been cold and rainy; however, it seemed the weather had changed, just in time for the weekend. Pulling on my bathrobe, I stepped into our small kitchen, finding Antonella by the stove. She was making something that smelled delicious. "What are you baking?" I asked. "It smells wonderful."

"I am baking cinnamon rolls," Antonella replied. "Would you like one? They are almost ready to take out of the oven."

"Certainly," I replied! "Would you like to sit on the balcony?" I asked. "It seems like it is going to be a beautiful day!"

Pouring myself a cup of coffee, I proceeded onto the balcony, followed by Antonella, who was now carrying a plate of rolls, two small plates and a stick of butter. "What is the butter for?" I asked.

"To put on the rolls," Antonella replied, smiling. "The rolls by themselves are good, but with butter, they are even better!"

"No thanks," I replied. "I don't need an additional layer of fat on top of my already fattening cinnamon roll. I am already looking a little pudgy as it is."

"So, what are you doing today on this beautiful Saturday?" Antonella asked.

"David and I are supposed to go to Positano today," I replied. "He wants me to take him to Chez Black for lunch. Do you want to come with us?"

"Thanks for inviting me," Antonella responded, "but I am driving over to Benevento today to watch Tony's race."

Changing the subject, I asked Antonella her opinion about an upcoming modeling gig. "I have been meaning to ask you about a photoshoot opportunity next week. Donato Malatesta wants me to pose for another perfume advertisement. Do you think I should accept?" I knew Antonella did not like Donato.

"I don't know," Antonella replied. "Mother does not like to work with Donato. He has shady friends. What is he asking you to do?"

"I am supposed to pose in a nightgown in front of an open window," I replied. "The shoot is in the Santa Lucia Quarter."

"Is that all?" Antonella asked.

"No, he also wants to introduce me to an independent film director named Bruto Cativo, who wants me to do a screen test," I replied.

"His name is really Bruto Cativo?" Antonella asked, laughing.

"Yes," I replied. "What's so funny?"

"His name means "ugly bad,"" Antonella laughed. "Be careful," she added. "I would stay away from anyone with a name like that! What is the name of his film company?"

"Amore produzioni," I replied.

Antonella laughed again. "Really, Love Productions?" she said. "This Bruto sounds like a bad character! How much money are they paying?"

"Donato's paying two million Lire," I replied.

When I mentioned the amount, Antonella's opinion changed. "That's good money," she said. "Perhaps it's okay to go. If you don't like the looks of Bruto, you can leave after the perfume shoot. Make sure you take someone with you, however."

"Are you available to come with me?" I asked.

"What day is it?" Antonella replied.

"It's next Wednesday," I answered.

"I can't," Antonella replied. "I have a dentist appointment that day. Why don't you ask David?"

For Antonella, that would be easy. However, I wasn't ready to tell David more details about my modeling career. He knew I modeled, but that was the extent. I wasn't ready to tell him about the billboard.

"So, how are things going with David?" Antonella asked as she spread a large helping of butter onto her cinnamon roll.

"How can you eat that?" I asked. "I am gaining weight just watching you!"

"The secret is not to care," Antonella replied, "that and to work out!"

Clearly, Antonella did not have a problem with weight. If she spent any time near a camera, it was behind it, not in front of it. Of course, Antonella could eat anything and not gain weight. Working out was not her secret; it was her genes. She had the metabolism of a bird.

"David and I are doing great," I replied, not wanting to share more. I was still trying to figure David out.

"How are things going between you and Tony?" I asked.

"Tony is still Tony," Antonella replied, giving me a non-answer answer. "As usual, he is avoiding the subject of marriage!"

"Are you planning to spend the holidays together?" I asked.

"No, he never takes me to see his family," Antonella replied. "As usual, he is going to Milan to visit his parents, leaving me here in Naples."

"Don't you find that strange?" I asked.

"How is it strange?" Antonella replied.

"It's strange that you have been dating for three years and have never met his family. Has he ever taken you to his apartment?"

"No," Antonella replied.

"Don't you find that weird?" I asked. "Have you ever considered he might be married?"

"Don't be silly," Antonella replied. "I met Tony in college. He wasn't married then, and I don't think he has gotten married since." Clearly, Antonella did not want to talk more about Tony.

"Tell me about Robbie," she asked. "Do you think he looks like Harrison Ford?"

"I do," I replied. "I don't know, Robbie. I only met him last Saturday. He seems nice enough. You realize Kimmy is his girlfriend, don't you?"

"Yes," Antonella replied. "She came by the shop last Monday to try on wedding dresses. It seemed strange to see her. I do not think it was an accident."

"Did you have a chance to talk with her?" I asked.

"Yes, I did," Antonella replied. "She was genuinely nice. I was surprised. I thought she had come to tell me to stay away from her boyfriend, but instead, she seemed genuinely interested in shopping for a wedding dress."

"Julie told her that you design wedding dresses," I replied.

"I must have missed that conversation," Antonella replied.

"Did she tell you that she is returning to the States this week?" I asked.

"No," Antonella replied.

"David told me that she was offered a job in New York," I replied. "David said that Robbie has been stringing her along for years now and that Kimmy and Robbie may be breaking up."

"Really," Antonella replied. She was now smiling from ear to ear. "No, she did not tell me that little tidbit! You and I should invite David and his friends to a party sometime."

"What sort of party do you have in mind?" I asked.

"I have always wanted to have a costume party," Antonella replied.

"We need a good theme," I replied, "something that we can either make or buy costumes for. How about a Toga party?" I asked. "We can all dress up like Romans!" I could see the wheels turning in Antonella's mind as she thought about costumes.

"That's a promising idea," Antonella replied. "Mother's been wanting to shoot a period photo shoot at the house. Perhaps we can tie the two things together. I will talk to her about the idea. Maybe she will pay for the party."

After we finished our breakfast, Antonella and I took turns in the shower and then dressed for the day. Antonella left the house for Benevento around 9:00 AM. David arrived to pick me up at 10:00.

That day, as we dined in Positano, I thought about asking David to come with me to the photoshoot but decided not to. I was not ready to spoil our beautiful day together by telling him my secret. That would have to wait for another day. I decided to go to the photoshoot alone. I told myself that I would just leave if I didn't like Bruto. Amore Productions, what a stupid name for a film company, I thought!

CHAPTER 17:

THE PHOTO SHOOT

ELSA'S NARRATIVE

When the day of the photoshoot arrived, I was extremely nervous. I thought several times about calling Donato and canceling, but each time got cold feet. Donato had, after all, paid me very well for the billboard photos. I didn't want to burn a bridge that had previously proved lucrative. I wasn't, however, comfortable. There was something about this day that filled me with dread, something I couldn't put my finger on. Your acting silly, I thought. You're afraid of shadows.

I arrived at the photoshoot site a half-hour early, at 10:00 am. I thought about parking my motor scooter in front of the building but decided instead to park by the Egg Castle. As I walked towards the building, I took note of my surroundings, making a point to write down a description of the building, as well as the address. You're being silly, I thought. This is going to be an ordinary photoshoot with Donato, nothing more. By noon you will be finished and headed to lunch. Even so, I checked to make sure my cellphone and address book were in my purse.

When I arrived at the entrance to the interior courtyard, I decided to wait rather than go up to the apartment. Better to be fashionably late, I thought, rather than early. To kill time, I walked further up the street towards the Royal Palace, stopping along the way to look in some shop windows. It was a beautiful day. I thought about getting back on my moped and riding home. I could always tell Donato that I forgot about our appointment. Of course, if I did that, he might never call again. After more nervous pacing, I decided to go up. Time to get this over with, I thought.

The ride up the elevator seemed to last forever. When it finally stopped, I stepped out onto the eighth floor, entering a dimly lit corridor. At the far end of the corridor, as far from the elevator as possible, I found the apartment. I asked myself why the apartment was so far from the elevator. I then knocked on the door. Behind the door, I could hear men and women talking. Good, I thought, there are women inside. Then the door opened.

"Ciao Bella," Donato exclaimed. He gave me a hug and kissed me on the cheeks. "Welcome," he said. Then he introduced me to his crew. There were at least eight people in the room, five men and three women, all busily setting up. Everything seemed very professional. Clearly, I was worried about nothing.

The apartment was splendid inside, with white wood-paneled walls which were decorated with gilded patterns. Looking up towards the ceiling, which was also gilded, I saw a large baroque-style painting with dozens of cupids swirling in the air. In the center of the room hung three large chandeliers.

"Where should I change?" I asked.

"The dressing room is at the far end of the room," Donato replied. "Elena will take you there. There is a bathroom as well as a makeup room." Following Elena's lead, I proceeded to the bathroom to prepare for the shoot.

The shoot took two hours, and during that time, we took pictures in many different poses. I liked Donato's attention to detail. He was particularly good at his work. "When will I get to see the pictures?" I asked.

"I should be able to show them to you tomorrow," he replied.

After the shoot, I returned to the dressing room to change back into my street clothes, forgetting about the next shoot. I was hungry and ready to go to lunch. When I came out, Donato's crew had all departed, leaving me alone with Donato and several new men and one woman.

"This is Bruto and his crew," Donato replied. "They are here for the screen test." Suddenly the feeling of comfort that I felt previously evaporated.

"Are you staying?" I asked, begging Donato to stay with my eyes.

"No," Donato replied. "I have another shoot this afternoon in the Vomero. I am going to leave you alone with Bruto and his crew. Do not worry; they will take care of you."

"How much does the screen test pay?" I asked.

"Nothing," Donato replied. "A screen test is like an interview. If they offer you a job, then you can negotiate the price."

Before I could ask more questions, Donato said goodbye and walked out, leaving me with Bruto and his crew. Help, I thought! What do I do now? I didn't have to wait long for my answer. Bruto opened the door allowing another man to enter the room. The man was tall and good-looking. He introduced us and asked us to get acquainted while he set up. I didn't know what to say; my head was swimming. All my alarm bells were going off. Something wasn't right.

After the crew set up, Bruto asked us to disrobe. I was stunned! "Take your clothes off," he repeated! This was not what I expected. For a moment, I felt paralyzed. Then instinct took over. I decided to play the role of a belligerent female. Don't let them see your fear, I thought.

"Donato never mentioned this when I agreed to come here," I exclaimed! "I don't do nude scenes!"

Bruto didn't buy what I was saying. I could tell from his expression that he knew about the billboard. "You are wasting my time and money," he said! "Take your clothes off!" Out of the corner of my eye, I could see one of the other men put his hand into the front of his suitcoat. I wondered if he might have a gun.

Meanwhile, the good-looking man, the actor, began to disrobe in front of me, removing his clothes until he was standing in front of me in only his underwear. I felt completely vulnerable. What should I do? I needed to somehow get out of the room.

Finally, I produced an idea. "I need to freshen up," I said!

"Do what you need to do," Bruto replied, asking the woman to take me towards the restroom.

"Can I help you with anything?" she asked, as she followed me into the room.

"No," I replied. "I can do this myself. Can you please leave the room?"

"Ok," she replied, "but don't take too long."

As soon as she left the room, I locked the door and turned on the shower so she couldn't hear me talking on the phone. I needed to call someone but didn't know who. I looked through my phonebook. I could call Antonella. No, I thought, she was still in the dentist's chair. What about Silvana, I thought? No, that won't work either, I told myself. Silvana might tell my parents. Finally, I decided to call David. I called his office twice, but no one picked up. Where are you, David, I thought? Finally, on the third try, I reached someone. It was a woman named Rosalba.

"Is David there?" I asked.

"Let me see," she replied, walking away from the phone. Seconds later, I heard her voice say, "David, pick up on line 2."

Then I heard his voice. "Pronto," he said.

"David, this is Elsa," I replied.

"What's wrong?" he asked. He could hear the fear in my voice.

"David, I need your help," I whispered. "I'm at a photoshoot. They want me to take my clothes off! I managed to get away from them and have locked myself in the bathroom. I need help! Please, come rescue me!"

For a moment, there was complete silence on the other end of the phone. Then David returned to me with a calm and reassuring voice. "Where are you at?" he asked. I began telling David the address. "Slow down; I am writing this down," he replied. "Where is that?" he asked.

"It's on the street running along the water," I replied, "between the Egg Castle and the Royal Palace. We walked by this building the night of our first date. It's a large eight-story yellow and grey building with many balconies. At present, I am looking at the Royal Palace, which is on the other side of a small green park. Do you remember the place? We stopped to kiss near here."

"I remember," David replied. "I'm on my way."

As I hung up the phone, I could hear the woman banging on the door. "Elsa, are you ok?" She asked.

"Yes," I replied, "I am getting out of the shower."

"This is not very professional," the woman replied. She was now lecturing me on professionalism. I was not about to take opinions from this woman.

"Don't lecture me about the professionalism," I replied! I was starting to get angry. "It's not professional to invite someone to a photoshoot on false pretenses and then demand they take their clothes off!"

She either did not hear me or didn't care. "You are costing us money," she replied!

She was now shouting at me angrily through the door. Hearing her screaming reminded me of the precariousness of my situation. Thinking quickly, I opened the closet door to wedge it against the bathroom door. I then looked for the nearest object to hit someone with. The only thing I could find was a used plastic toilet bowl brush. I thought of Antonella. She would love this scene. I pictured the newspaper headline. "Woman defends her honor with a dirty toilet bowl brush, film at 11:00".

For thirty minutes, I stayed in the bathroom, waiting for David to arrive, expecting someone to break through the door at any minute. No one did. Twice, I walked out onto the balcony to see if there was another escape route. Unfortunately, no other route existed. Finally, after waiting for what seemed an eternity, I heard the apartment doorbell ring. It was David. I could hear words and then a knock at the door.

"Elsa, it is David, please open the door," he replied.

"Are you alone?" I asked, fearing that the others might enter the room.

"Yes," David replied, "everyone is in the other room."

Quickly I opened the door and let David in, locking the door behind him. David was a dashing spectacle. He was my knight in shining armor, wearing his white choker uniform with the big black shoulder boards. "You didn't need to dress up just for me;" I smiled.

"You are lucky you reached me," he replied. "I was at a change of command all morning."

"Is that a real sword?" I asked, looking at the long scabbard hanging from his side.

"Yes," he replied, returning my smile. "Let's get out of here," David replied, eager to leave. "Follow me," he said. "Let me do the talking!"

After several minutes of gathering my things, we emerged from the restroom. "Elsa's not feeling well," David exclaimed. "She's called me to take her home." I could see the tense look on everyone's face and wondered if the uglier men had guns. I hoped not. David, however, was noticeably confident, showing no fear whatsoever. I think the long sword hanging by his side had a chilling effect.

Within seconds, we were out of the room, into the elevator and back on the street. As we emerged into the light, I could now see sweat streaming down David's face. "Where are you parked?" he asked.

"I parked over by the Egg castle," I replied.

"Let's get lunch," David suggested. "I'm starving."

That afternoon, David and I dined beside the Egg Castle for a second time. David never asked me about how I got into such a dire situation. Instead, we talked about pleasant things. We talked about what we might do on the weekend and about our plans for the holidays. During the conversation, I invited David to the Toga party planned for the end of the month and encouraged him to bring his roommates. By 4:00 pm, it seemed as if my dreadful day were just a distant dream. I would give Donato a piece of my mind in the morning. When the meal was finished, David walked me to my motor scooter to wish me goodbye.

"David, thank you so much," I replied. "You are my hero. How can I ever repay you for your kindness?"

"Don't worry about it," he replied. "I don't get to play the role of "knight in shining armor" that often." Before he could say another word, I gave him a long kiss. He deserved this one. What would I do without you, I thought!

CHAPTER 18:

THE TOGA PARTY

I first learned about the Toga party from Elsa. I had been thinking about traveling home for Thanksgiving but decided to stay. As usual the Stork's Nest was full, and it seemed a poor time to take vacation.

Kimmy was an irresistible ball of energy preparing for the party. While the boys were content to wear bedsheets, viewing the party would be something like the scene from "National Lampoon's Animal House," Kimmy was determined that she and I should get into character.

We started our preparations by watching Roman epic movies on the VCR on a rainy Tuesday afternoon. I had watched these movies a hundred times, but never with the intention to imitate the costumes. First, we watched "Quo Vadis," starring Deborah Kerr, and then afterward, we watched "Cleopatra," starring Elizabeth Taylor and Richard Burton. Throughout each film, Kimmy kept hitting the pause button, so we could study what the women were wearing. Kimmy was really getting into this. Her attention to detail was extraordinary.

"Are you always like this?" I asked.

"Yes," Kimmy replied, blushing. "Robbie thinks I'm too anal, but I have always found attention to detail to be the key to success. When I do something, I want to do it right!"

In the end, Kimmy's diligence paid off. By the time of the party, she had created beautiful costumes for both of us. For her costume, Kimmy wore a long white gown with a deep royal blue cape which she could wear as a scarf over her hair. She also wore a thin brown leather belt around her waist which accentuated her narrow waist, as well as two leather straps across her chest to highlight her figure. The effect was stunning.

Kimmy created a royal costume for me, befitting an Empress. It included a long white gown with a royal purple silk cape fringed with a gold-colored thread. We purchased our costumes at a store. Kimmy embroidered the cape herself. She was quite talented with a needle and thread.

The night of the party, Harry and Robbie departed early in a separate car while David waited for us to finish our makeup. When we arrived at the party, we found a street filled with cars. There was nowhere to park near the house. We ended up parking at the bottom of the hill in front of the restaurants, leaving our keys with a parking attendant, who was busily shuffling cars. As we walked away, we could see him moving cars until our car was parked deep within the lot, nearest the back wall. "I hope you're not planning to leave early," I remarked to David. "It looks like we are parked in for the duration."

As we walked back up the hill towards the entrance to Antonella's family house, we noticed many people walking towards the same entrance. "How big is this party?" I asked David.

"I don't know;" he replied, smiling. "It appears all of Naples has been invited."

As we walked down the long driveway, Kimmy and I noticed many people adorned in elaborate costumes. This was no ordinary Toga party. As we stood in line waiting to enter, Kimmy and I teased David about his simple bedsheet. He didn't own a white bedsheet, so he was wearing a bedsheet with little yellow flowers instead.

"Did you wear anything under that?" we asked.

"Yes, but not much," David replied. I could see he was freezing, as goosebumps were appearing on his arms. "I hope this party is indoors;" he remarked, smiling. David was headed for a long cold evening.

When at last, we came to the gate, we were greeted by two men dressed in Roman Praetorian Guard Uniforms. Both wore black legionnaire tunics with black breastplates and black plumed helmets. They were quite an impressive pair. They checked our names against an extensive list and then opened the gate for us to enter.

When we stepped past the gate, we entered a large outdoor terrace with a swimming pool in the center. Around the pool stood hundreds of people, all elaborately dressed, sipping cocktails, and talking in Italian, while a band played music at the far end of the terrace. Along the railing, I could see a camera crew busily taking pictures of the guests.

As we stood there, a man dressed as a Roman Senator stretched out his hand to greet us. He had a broad face with a Roman nose (i.e., a nose which roamed all over his face). He had a balding head encircled by a laurel wreath.

"This is Charles Scipione," David remarked, introducing us to the host, "and behind him is his wife, Silvana."

David then introduced us. "Charles and Silvana, these are two of my roommates, Julie Steinman and Kimberly DeGennaro."

"We have heard so much about you," Charles and Silvana replied. "Julie, is it true you are from Chicago?" Charles asked. "I grew up in Detroit," he added.

"Yes," I replied. "I grew up in Evanston. My father works for an engineering firm there."

"Interesting," Charles replied. "Did he work on the design of the Sears Tower?" he asked.

"No," I replied, "but he did work on the design of the John Hancock Building."

"Excellent!" Charles replied. "You must be so proud of your father. The Hancock has always been my favorite Chicago building." I was impressed that Charles knew so much about Chicago.

"Kimberly, is it true that you are from New York?" Silvana asked.

"Yes," Kimmy replied.

"Charles and I once lived in Manhattan," Silvana replied. "We still consider New York our second home, after, of course, Naples."

It seemed remarkable that our hosts knew something about both Kimmy & me. After engaging in minutes of pleasant conversation, Charles and Silvana bid our leave to greet their other incoming guests.

"What do you think?" remarked David.

"It is quite impressive," I replied! "Do you see Harry and Robbie?" I asked.

"I see Harry over there," David replied, pointing towards a group of people standing by a fountain. Harry looked handsome in his bedsheet, more like a Roman god than a stodgy Navy Lawyer.

"Excuse me," I replied. "I am going to join Harry." When I reached Harry, now standing alone by the fountain, he smiled, complimented me on my costume and asked me a question.

"Where are Kimmy and David?" he asked.

"I thought they were behind me," I replied. It seems I had lost them in the crowd. After several moments of standing next to Harry, I found them. David was now standing next to the bar, and Kimmy was standing next to a small elevator inside the living room. She then stepped into the elevator and disappeared.

"Seems we're all alone," Harry remarked. "Let's go inside; I'm freezing," he added.

We proceeded inside into the crowded living room, hoping to find David at the bar, but we could not find him. He had gone off to look for Elsa. "Let's get some drinks," Harry suggested, "and then find a place to stand." After another ten minutes, we came to rest at a piano, sitting on a platform overlooking the living room. "Don't look down," Harry remarked. "The floor is made of glass, and we are standing over the hot tub."

It was too late; I looked down. Below me were several couples in the hot tub wearing tiny swimsuits, leaving little to the imagination. "Let's sit on the piano bench," I remarked, realizing that the people below might be able to see us just as easily as we could see them.

Once we were safely seated, Harry looked at me and smiled. "You can't make this up," Harry remarked. "Care to join them in the hot tub?" he teased.

"If one more person steps up here on this glass floor, we will join them soon enough," I replied. "Let's find a place less dangerous to sit!" It was then we noticed the office. "Let's go stand in there," I replied, directing Harry towards the crowded office.

Minutes later, we found ourselves leaning against a large desk, surrounded by many people all chattering away in Italian, gesticulating wildly. In the corner, I could see a woman making a gesture as if she were praying, while the man opposite her was responding by biting his hand. "What are they saying," I asked?

"I have no idea," Harry replied, "but they are clearly animated about it."

"Do you think they could talk if they had to sit on their hands?" I asked.

"No," Harry replied, laughing.

"I think we are the only Americans here," I remarked!

"It seems so," Harry replied.

We now, both understood what it meant to feel completely alone in a crowded room. At least we had each other. I wondered at that moment what Kimmy was doing. "Where is Robbie?" I asked.

"I have no idea," Harry replied. "He disappeared shortly after we arrived."

ANTONELLA'S NARRATIVE

Preparing for a major party was a significant undertaking that consumed my entire day. It wasn't until the guests began to arrive that Elsa and I returned to our apartment to change into our costumes. When I finally returned to the party, I entered the terrace, now full of guests. Where are Robbie and his friends, I thought? After wandering through the growing crowd, I found Robbie standing by the railing, looking out towards the water. As I approached, he saw me and smiled.

"I was just admiring your view," he said.

"Are you alone?" I asked.

"Yes," he replied. "Harry is over there with Julie," he replied, pointing towards the office.

"What about David?" I asked.

"He's gone off to find Elsa," Robbie replied.

I didn't think to ask about Kimmy, as I assumed she had already returned to the States.

"Does your father's property extend down to the water?" Robbie asked.

"Yes," I replied. "Father, owns the entire cove, including the disco & beach club next door on the right. Our property extends around that point on the left. There is a small rocky beach around the point where Elsa and I go to sunbathe." It seemed Robbie was mesmerized by the waterfront cove in front of us. "Would you like to see father's boats?" I asked.

"Certainly," Robbie replied! "How do we get down there?" he asked.

"Follow me," I replied. "There is an elevator in the house that goes down to the grotto."

Within moments we arrived at the elevator, pushed the button, and walked out into the grotto. We entered a cave with a paved walkway leading to a metal dock in the center. The path continued beyond the dock into a tunnel on the other side. On the left side of the dock were two small boats. A fiberglass speed boat and a small sailboat. On the right side was a wooden speed boat. Father had left the gate open, looking out towards the sea.

"This is amazing," Robbie replied! "Your father has beautiful boats," he exclaimed!

"The boats once belonged to my grandfather," I explained.

"Can we take one out?" Robbie asked. He was admiring the wooden speed boat.

"Yes," I replied. "Let me find the keys."

Within minutes, I retrieved the keys from father's key cabinet and motioned for Robbie to join me in the wooden speed boat. "Let me back the boat out," I offered. "Once we clear the rocks, we can take turns driving it."

Backing the boat out of the grotto was always difficult for me. Fortunately, tonight the water was exceedingly calm. There was no way I would have tried backing the boat out in rough water.

The speed boat was my father's pride and joy. I hoped he didn't see us borrowing it. The last thing I wanted to do was damage it as I would never hear the end of it. It took me a solid 10 minutes to back the boat out into the cove and then turn it around.

It was now dark. However, the sky was brilliantly lit by the full moon and a vast sea of stars. As we entered the bay, we could see many other boats out enjoying the evening sky. Far to the left was the usual party boat, anchored off the city, blaring loud Italian disco music. Further offshore were the twinkling lights of hundreds of fishing boats between our location and the brilliantly lit towns on the other side of the bay. In the distance, at the mouth of the bay loomed the giant rock of Capri, emerging from the black waters. I could see that Robbie was anxious to drive the boat. "Let me get further offshore," I replied, "away from the other boats and then I will let you drive."

That night, Robbie and I crisscrossed the water, taking turns driving the boat. Even though it was chilly, we didn't seem to mind, forgetting about the time. It wasn't until 10:00 pm that I realized it was getting late. "Let's return to the party," I suggested. I could tell Robbie was disappointed. He could have stayed on the water all night.

KIMMY'S PARTY EXPERIENCE

After David, Julie and I entered the party; we split up to find our significant others. Julie walked across the terrace towards Harry, who was standing by the railing. David went into the house to look for Elsa, and I went to a corner of the terrace to take in the entire view, searching the party for Robbie. Where was Robbie?

After a few minutes, I walked towards the other side of the terrace, looking into the living room through the large windows. There were several people in the large hot tub on the far side of the pool. The water was bubbling vigorously. I could see some of the people in the hot tub had swimsuits, and some perhaps did not. Fortunately, Robbie was not in the hot tub.

After scanning the terrace, I proceeded into the house, wandering the living room as well as the upstairs balcony but not finding Robbie. Where was he? Perhaps I missed him, I thought. I returned to the lower pool level. I still couldn't find Robbie. Perhaps we keep missing each other, I thought. Maybe if I stand by the railing for a while, he will find me?

The sky that night was beautiful, with a million stars all twinkling. As I looked across the bay, the moonlight shimmering off the water, I could see the lights of Sorrento on the other side. Somewhere to the right of those lights, I thought, is the little beach that we visited the other day. Antonella's parent's home was magnificent that night.

As I stood transfixed, gazing at the Mediterranean Sea, reality interrupted my reverie. Below in the cove, I heard the low grumble of a boat engine starting up. Looking down towards the waters below the terrace, I saw a wooden speed boat begin backing out of the cliff. There must be a boat garage under the terrace, I thought. Seated in the back of the boat was a man, while at the controls driving the boat was a woman. Although it was dark, I recognized the man. It was Robbie. Who was the woman? After cleaning off my glasses, fogged by the sea air, I recognized the woman as well. It was Antonella.

Seeing the two of them together caused me to feel faint. I suddenly felt terribly ill, all alone and far from home. Words cannot describe how badly I felt at that moment. I felt betrayed. As I stood there wallowing in self-pity, David approached me from behind.

"You look like you have seen a ghost," he replied!

"Perhaps I have," I replied. "I feel sick. I haven't eaten all day. David let's go inside." I didn't want David to see Robbie in the boat below. I was embarrassed enough as is. What I really wanted to do was crawl under a rock and die.

Wrapping his arm around my shoulders, David led me inside to the buffet table, where we loaded up a plate of hors devours to share and then proceeded to the bar. "Can I get you a drink?" David offered.

"Yes," I replied. "Please get me a glass of Champagne." That night I wanted to get drunk, very drunk, anything to blot out what I had just seen. I was ready to leave, I wanted to leave the party, as well as Italy.

The day before yesterday, I had given up my new job at the World Trade Center for Robbie, and this is how he had repaid me. It seemed he would never change. Then, as I sat stewing in my anger, I got an idea, an evil, ugly idea. Elsa was the reason that Robbie had met Antonella. If I could break up Elsa and David, it might also keep Robbie away from Antonella. I knew just how to do it. It was time to tell David Elsa's secret.

As we sat next to each other, sipping our drinks, and eating our food, I leaned over to David and asked him a question. "Would you like to know a secret?" I asked.

"Do I want to know?" David replied, smiling back at me. He had no idea of the bombshell I was about to lay upon him.

Leaning over more closely, I whispered the secret in his ear. "Elsa is the woman on the car stereo billboard."

His immediate reaction was silence. Then after a long pause, he asked me a question, deliberately drawing out his words to comprehend them himself. "How do you know that?" he asked.

"Antonella told Julie and me; when we were at the beach," I replied.

"Does anybody else know?" he asked.

"No," I replied. "I don't think Robbie or Harry know yet."

"Please don't tell anyone," David replied.

"Why are you smiling?" I asked. It seemed to me that the news would have shocked David, but it seemed he wasn't shocked.

"I wondered," he replied. "Perhaps it was just a hunch, but I wondered."

Hearing his reply was another disappointment, which made me more depressed. It seemed David already knew. So much for my latest idea, I thought. "Can you buy me another drink?" I asked. I was starting to feel tipsy from the previous drink. It didn't take much to make me feel drunk.

"Why aren't you with Robbie?" he asked.

"Robbie, who?" I replied. "Robbie has deserted me. He and Antonella are currently riding around the bay in a speedboat!" I had not meant to tell anyone about what I saw, but at this point, the Champagne was doing the talking.

"I am sorry to hear that," David replied. "I mean that. You deserve better than that!"

"Thank you," I replied, now feeling a little better inside. I thought about giving David a thank you kiss but decided against it, telling myself I had done enough damage for one night.

DAVID'S NARRATIVE

As Kimmy was relating the latest development in her ongoing saga with Robbie, Elsa joined us at the bar. She was looking very pretty that night in her light green gown. It was as if she had stepped out of a Pompeian fresco. We had spoken earlier in the evening; however, she had been busy all evening assisting Silvana, making it difficult for us to spend time alone. "Are you finished with your duties?" I asked.

"Yes," Elsa replied. "It has been a long time since I hosted a party. I forgot the amount of work involved. I much prefer attending other people's parties. Would you like to see the beach?" she asked. "Before Silvana asks me to help with something else?"

"Yes," I replied. I then turned toward Kimmy and asked her if she wanted to join us.

"No, thank you," she replied. "Thank you for asking, however."

After we bid Kimmy goodbye, Elsa and I proceeded to the grotto below the house. I had seen the boats before but had not walked through the tunnel from the grotto to the beach. Following Elsa through the tunnel, we entered a large underground chamber. "Did you wear your swimsuit under your Toga?" she asked.

"Yes," I replied. "We're not going swimming in the sea, are we? It's the end of November and much too cold."

"No," she replied. "I want to show you the natural hot spring."

We continued walking down the tunnel until we reached a large room. "What is this room?" I asked.

"It is an ancient nymphaeum," Elsa replied. "The Romans built these at natural springs as shrines for the local water nymphs. They used them for recreation and sometimes for weddings," she replied. "This room is quite ancient. The fountain and statues are new, however the paving on the floor is original Roman, restored, of course, by Silvana and Charles."

The room was quite dark, illuminated only by the pool of water in the center of the room. The water was a deep iridescent blue color. "Where is the light coming from?" I asked.

"There are some small lava tubes deep in the pool, connecting the pool to the sea," Elsa replied. "The tubes bring water and moonlight into the pool. Isn't it beautiful?"

"Yes," I replied. "It is dazzling."

"Let me turn on the light and show you the total effect," Elsa replied.

She then flipped a switch, flooding the room with a soft indirect light which suddenly enhanced the color of the water. In an instant, the other features of the room were revealed. On the far side of the pool stood a small fountain with three streams of water entering the pool. The fountain was flanked by two Roman busts sitting within niches in the wall. In the far corner of the room stood a beautiful statue of a naked woman pouring water from a jar. It was the Roman Goddess Venus.

As I stood there admiring the room, Elsa removed her Toga, revealing her yellow bathing suit underneath. She was incredibly beautiful as she stepped into the water, the very embodiment of the Goddess Venus herself.

"Come in," she replied, beckoning me to join her. "The water is nice and warm."

Removing my Toga, revealing my swimsuit, I followed her into the pool, sitting beside her on a small stone seat. Just as I did so, a small fish jumped in front of us. Seeing the fish brought a whole new dimension to the experience.

"Is there anything else in this pool with us?" I asked. For a moment I thought I saw squid swimming below.

"Perhaps," Elsa replied, "the pool is quite deep."

"How deep?" I asked.

"Fifteen to twenty feet," Elsa replied, now smiling. I loved her refreshing smile and knew my next question would erase it.

Turning towards Elsa, I could see her body below the water. She was like a dream. This didn't seem like the right time to ask my question, but I really needed an answer.

"Elsa, I heard something tonight which is troubling me," I began. "I need to ask you a question." As I said that, I could see Elsa visibly change.

"What's your question?" Elsa replied.

"Are you the woman on the car stereo billboard?" I asked.
Elsa paused and looked at me intently, probing my eyes. I could tell she was trying to think of something to say. Her eyes told me everything I needed to know. "How did you find out about that?" she asked.

"Kimmy told me," I replied. "She's terribly upset tonight. Robbie abandoned her at the party and ran off with Antonella."

I could see far-off lightning bolts begin to flash in Elsa's eyes as her anger began to build towards Kimmy. Then her eyes softened, and she looked again towards me. "Yes," Elsa replied, answering my question. "I meant to tell you, David. Honestly, I should have told you earlier, but I didn't know how to do it. I didn't know how you would react."

"David, I'm falling in love with you," she said. It was the first time I had ever heard Elsa say that. I wondered if she really meant it or was just using it as an excuse for failing to tell me something so important.

"Why did you do it?" I asked.

"I was out of money," Elsa replied. "Living in the city with Antonella burned up all my savings. I needed money to pay the tuition bill."

As I watched her reply, I could tell she was lying to me. She wouldn't look me in the eyes. Why was she lying to me? I thought back to the scene two weeks before when I had rescued her from the photographer. He had wanted her to take her clothes off. Why? Had she taken her clothes off before? Who was this woman sitting next to me? I needed to know the answer, so I asked a second question. A stupid question I should not have asked.

"What else have you done for money?" I asked.

In an instant, Elsa's face changed. She was reading more into my question than I had intended. My Venus was turning into a Medusa. It was then that she did something I didn't expect. She slapped me hard across the face!

"How dare you judge me," she exclaimed! "You have no right to judge me! You do not own me, David Moore! I am not a prostitute if that's what your dirty mind is thinking. I made the mistake of posing once for a topless picture, but that is all!"

At last, I had the truth. However, it had come with a terrible price. Before I could respond, she stepped out of the water & began drying off.

"I've had enough of this conversation," she said! "You can show yourself out!"

She then tossed my toga into the water, turned out the light and departed, leaving me sitting in a now blackened room. I had opened Pandora's box and had released a fury. We had had our first fight, and it now seemed our relationship was at an end. As I sat there in the dark, I wondered how to approach her. Like my conversation with Dana months before, I could not find an answer.

After Elsa departed, I sat in the room for another half hour. The only clothes I had were now wet. I wondered how to return to the party. Clearly, it was time to go home. I was not looking forward to the cold ride back to our house in a wet bathing suit.

When I finally returned to the party, I proceeded towards the bar, where I had left Kimmy. She was still at the bar, now seated next to Harry and Julie.

"What happened to you?" Harry asked.

"Elsa and I had a fight," I replied. "She threw my toga into the water!" Harry and Julie were laughing at my misfortune. "Can I borrow your car?" I asked. "My car is blocked in at the restaurants down the street. I need to go home before I catch cold."

"We figured something happened," Julie replied. "Elsa came by here a few minutes ago in her bathing suit. She was crying. We tried to ask her what happened but could only hear part of what she said before she wandered off sobbing. How bad was it?" Julie asked.

"It was bad," I replied. "We said things we shouldn't have said."

"Is it over?" Julie asked.

"I don't know," I replied. "I hope not. I'm still trying to figure out a way to put the toothpaste back in the tube. Are you ready to go home?" I asked. My goosebumps had goosebumps, and I was beginning to shiver.

"Not yet," Harry replied. "We're still waiting for Robbie to return from his boat ride."

"So, you heard that story?" I replied.

"Yes, Kimmy filled us in," Harry replied. Looking toward Kimmy, I could see that her eyes were red. She had been crying. As we exchanged car keys, I asked Kimmy if she wanted to come home with me. She replied yes. The party was over for both of us.

CHAPTER 19:

TOGA PARTY AFTERMATH

DAVID'S DRIVE HOME

The drive home from the Toga party should have been simple and straightforward; however, like everything else in Naples, it was not. As we stepped into the chilly night air, Kimmy removed her dark blue cape and wrapped it around my shoulders. "You look cold," she said. "I think you need this more than I."

After leaving the party, Kimmy and I walked up the hill towards Harry's car, which was parked on the right side of the road adjacent to a stone wall. When I had passed his car earlier that evening, the car was parked by itself, however, now the situation had changed. As we approached Harry's green machine, I felt a knot grow in my stomach. Harry's car was firmly wedged between two other cars. Behind his car, barely three inches from his rear bumper, sat an Alfa Romeo 164, and in front of his car was a tiny Fiat barely two inches from his front bumper.

Kimmy saw the same problem I saw. "What do we do?" Kimmy asked.

"We need to move one of the cars," I replied.

When we approached the Alfa Romeo, I tried to open the car door, setting off the car alarm. "Maybe the owner will come," Kimmy commented optimistically. I doubted it, however. Car alarms were like birds chirping in Naples. They were constantly going off, and no one ever responded.

After my disappointing venture with the Alfa Romeo, I tried opening the Fiat front door. This time I met with success. The car door was unlocked. "Kimmy, I have an idea," I remarked. "I need you to steer the Fiat while I push from behind with Harry's car. We need to be careful not to push the Fiat into the wall." Kimmy understood my concern. The last thing I wanted to do was push the Fiat into the nearby stone wall.

"Ok," Kimmy replied as she climbed into the front seat of the Fiat.

"Release the clutch," I replied, "so that the Fiat rolls back into the car." Kimmy did, as I requested, letting the Fiat begin to roll. Bump, the Fiat rear bumper gently touched Harry's front bumper. "Now turn the steering wheel towards the left," I instructed. I will start up Harry's car and begin to push. My idea worked. Within a few moments, we were on the road, enjoying the warm air now blasting from Harry's car heater.

After a few minutes of driving, we reached the busy intersection of Via Posillipo and Via Boccaccio. All of Naples was out that night. Despite the chilly weather, the gelaterias were doing a brisk business. Even in November, Neapolitans still loved their ice cream.

We waited a minute for the traffic to pass and then proceeded further up the road towards Via Manzoni. On the left, we could see a large crowd waiting to enter a disco, all puffing away on their cigarettes. The woman wore high heels, tight leather pants, and sweaters, while the men stood next to them in blue jeans and very wrinkled checked sport coats. Many had sunglasses perched on their foreheads even though it was night. Many were also carrying their pull-out car stereos. Kimmy laughed at the scene. She understood how silly they looked. Then she asked me a question. "Why is everyone carrying their stereos?" she asked.

I tried not to laugh. "They are all afraid their stereos may be stolen," I replied.

Italian Discos were a phenomenon by themselves. They opened late, usually after 10:00 pm, were small, and often very crowded. Some people went to the disco just to be seen standing in line. The cover charges to enter were enormous, and the drinks were miniature. The most memorable sight, however, was watching hundreds of immaculately dressed young people bouncing up and down, tightly packed together, holding their car stereos in one hand and their cigarettes in the other.

As we drove past the disco, I diverted Kimmy's attention to the right side of the road. On the right sat hundreds of tiny cars parked on the sidewalk, their windows completely covered with newspapers. Kimmy giggled as we drove by the cars, commenting that some of the cars were rocking. She understood what was happening. Then she smiled at me and asked a question.

"Have you and Elsa gone parking yet?"

"Not yet," I replied. "How about you?"

"Not yet," Kimmy replied. "Robbie's worried someone might recognize his AFI plates." It was nice to see that her mood was improving from earlier that evening. She was much prettier when she was laughing.

"I'm sorry about what happened tonight," Kimmy remarked. "I should have never told you Elsa's secret."

"It's ok," I replied. "If you hadn't told me, someone else would have."

I could tell Kimmy was not satisfied with my response. Clearly, she now felt guilt for what happened. "Did you see Elsa when she returned from the grotto?" I asked.

"Yes," Kimmy replied. "She was crying."

"Crying?" I asked, somewhat puzzled by Kimmy's response.

"Yes, she was sobbing," Kimmy replied. "Elsa tried to tell Julie what had happened, but we couldn't tell what she was saying. She stayed with us for only a minute and then disappeared."

As I listened to Kimmy's account, I was surprised by Elsa's behavior. Elsa had left the grotto angry, and yet a few minutes later, she was crying. Perhaps, our relationship was not over, I thought. This didn't mean I was ready to forgive her, however. She still needed to be honest with me about the nature of her modeling career. I couldn't forget that she lied to me and wondered what she was still hiding.

Changing the subject, I asked Kimmy what she intended to do about Robbie. "I'm not sure" she replied. "Robbie really hurt me tonight. Part of me wants to go home tomorrow, while the other part wants to remain and forgive him. What should I do?" she asked.

"I would wait a few days," I replied. "Let the dust settle. Perhaps there is a misunderstanding?"

Glancing toward Kimmy, I could see she didn't agree with me. "I've known Robbie for a long time," Kimmy replied. "I can tell when he's cheating. He doesn't hide it well. If he's cheating, I will probably go home." I noticed as she spoke, that she used the word "probably." This meant she wasn't certain. Perhaps, Robbie still had a chance.

Just as we finished the conversation, we pulled up in front of the green gate. We were finally home. "Can we sit in the car for a few more minutes?" Kimmy remarked. "I dread entering our cold house." For a few minutes, we sat in the car until the smell of burning oil began to get to us.

"Let's go inside," I remarked. "I will start a fire in the fireplace."

Within minutes after entering the house, we settled in on the sofa in front of the fire. I at my end of the couch, and Kimmy at the other end, each of us now wrapped in a pile of blankets. It was not long before we both fell asleep.

KIMMY'S ACCOUNT LATER THAN NIGHT

At 2:00 am, I awoke to the sound of people entering the hallway. Robbie, Julie, and Harry were now home from the party. As I sat on the sofa pretending to sleep, I could hear the three of them laughing. It seemed all three were tipsy. Clearly, they had had a lot to drink. I wondered if I should confront Robbie or pretend nothing happened. I decided to do the latter, remembering advice my grandmother had given me.

My British grandmother (mother's mother) had always been right. After all, she had survived the London Blitz. I couldn't imagine living through such an awful time. The secret to a long marriage, she said, was to "treat every catastrophe as if it were an incident, and to treat every incident as if it never happened." I decided to follow her advice and pretend I wasn't hurt. "Keep a stiff upper lip," I thought.

Wearing one of my blankets now as a robe, I joined the party sitting around the dining room table. "We're having a shot of Amaro," Harry replied. "Would you like one?"

"No thanks," I replied. "I would prefer something warm. Would any of you like a coffee?" I asked.

"Yes," Julie replied, "that sounds delicious!" Robbie and Harry agreed also.

As I proceeded into the kitchen to make coffee, Robbie followed, offering to help. Once we were safely in the kitchen, away from the others, Robbie apologized to me. "I'm sorry I left you alone at the party," he began. "We should have gone together, rather than in separate cars."

Robbie continued. "When I arrived, Antonella offered to show me her father's boats. Antonella's father has some amazing classic boats! You would love them," Robbie exclaimed with delight! "Charles has this beautiful wooden speedboat from the 1950s. When Antonella offered to let me drive it, I couldn't turn her down. It was an amazing boat with a huge inboard engine. At one point, we were traveling at 50 mph! I'm sorry I stayed out so long. I guess I lost track of time."

Hearing Robbie wax poetic about boats was reassuring. Robbie & I loved boats. This was one of the shared interests we had in common. I remembered the weekend we spent in San Diego after graduation. Robbie rented a thirty-five-foot sailboat that day, which we took out into the Pacific Ocean.

It was a gorgeous and memorable day. I will never forget when we sailed alongside an enormous aircraft carrier approaching the harbor. We were traveling fast; however, it was traveling faster. That day I understood why Robbie loved the Navy. It wasn't because he wanted to serve on a ship, but rather because he loved being part of something much bigger than himself. The sight of a ten-story tall, Nimitz-class aircraft carrier from the water level was amazing! It was a sight I would never forget.

As Robbie continued with his description of the wonderful speedboat, I realized that Robbie had not deserted me for another woman but rather for a boat. I felt much better inside. I could live with that type of rejection. I only wished he had remembered to take me with him.

That night, after our nice hot toddy, Robbie and I went to bed. It was wonderful to lay next to him. He was so warm and cuddly. We slept in late the next morning until 11:00 am. It was nice and warm in the bed, and neither of us wanted to get up.

ANTONELLA'S PARTY AFTERMATH

After our night of partying, Elsa & I were awoken at 8:00 am by the urgent ringing of our apartment doorbell. "Do you want to get it, or do you want me to get it?" I asked. Elsa did not reply. Putting on my bathrobe and slippers, I went to the front door, knowing who it would be. Sure enough, it was father.

"Time to get up," he said. "You two need to help your mother & I clean up from last night." As I looked out on the terrace, it seemed as if a trash bomb had gone off. There were hundreds of plastic plates and cups with half-eaten food lying everywhere, some of it floating in the swimming pool. I had not had much to drink the night before, but suddenly I felt terribly hungover.

It seemed that father and mother had drafted the army to help clean up. Everyone was busy at work. There was our gardener Enzo, the cook Pasquale, and our maid Maria all busily cleaning up. Father had even drafted the entire crew from his beach club next door. Even so, it was clear it would take hours to clean up the mess. Why did we do this, I thought? What was I thinking? I had forgotten how much work a party could be.

This is not to say we didn't have parties. Mother loved parties and tended to host them often. For mother, parties were part of her business. Something to feature in the next edition of her magazine.

"Let me change," I replied, "and I will be out shortly." "Get up, Elsa," I exclaimed as I returned to the bedroom! "We have work to do!"

I could see she was still upset. Her eyes were still puffy from a night spent crying. I didn't know what happened but could guess. Something happened with David. The party had been a bust for me as well. I had hoped to spend time with Elsa's American friends but instead spent the entire evening riding around the cold, freezing bay with Robbie. Before the party, I had fancied Robbie. However, afterward, I was not so sure. "Get up lazy bum," I cried, throwing a pillow at her. "This was your idea!"

Within a few minutes, we reemerged on the terrace, reporting for duty, and examining the disaster area. Where to begin, I thought. The task seemed insurmountable. Perhaps the best answer was to go back to bed. Elsa immediately claimed the pool skimmer, going after the items floating in the pool, leaving the more disgusting job of cleaning up the terrace to me. As I stood there hoping the mess would clean up itself, Enzo offered me two rolling trash cans.

"Empty the food in this one," he remarked "and put the trash in that one." The task seemed simple enough, provided I didn't look too closely at what I was dumping. It seemed there were hundreds of cups filled with cigarette butts and ashes swimming in liquid. It took everything I could muster not to gag.

By the time we finished, both Elsa and I were famished. We had forgotten to eat breakfast. "What's for lunch?" I asked.

"Left-overs," mother replied. I wondered about eating food that had set out for hours but decided to risk getting sick. I was hungry.

"Stay away from the turkey tetrazzini;" I warned Elsa. "That was a leftover from <u>before</u> the party."

After five minutes of foraging through the refrigerator, we sat down at a counter in the kitchen to eat. "So, what happened last night?" I asked Elsa. "Why did you spend half the night crying?"

"David & I had a fight," she replied, not seeming to want to say more.

"About what?" I probed further.

"David found out about the billboard" Elsa replied. "Kimmy told him."

As I heard those words, I felt a twinge inside. I had seen Kimmy standing by the railing when I pulled the boat out of the garage the previous evening. It must have broken her heart to see Robbie and me departing in the boat. All night long, I had tried to get Robbie to go back in, but he only wanted to ride around in the moonlight. It was a selfish, heartless thing to do, leaving his pretty girlfriend all alone at a party with strangers. I couldn't blame Kimmy for taking a small bit of revenge. It was I, after all, who had told her Elsa's secret, to begin with.

As I returned to Elsa, I could see she was deep in her own thoughts. "I told you to tell him," I replied. "Sooner or later, he was going to find out."

"I know," Elsa replied. "I was going to tell him, but I couldn't bring myself to do it."

"What else happened?" I asked. Surely the billboard was not the only thing that happened. I could tell there was more that Elsa wanted to share. Something worse than the billboard.

"Do you remember that photo shoot you told me not to go to?" Elsa replied. "The photoshoot with Donato and Bruto?"

"Yes," I replied.

"I went to the shoot by myself," Elsa responded. "It was as bad as you said it might be. Donato left me alone with Bruto."

"What happened?" I asked. I could see the look of sadness in Elsa's eyes. Something terrible must have happened.

Elsa began her story. "After Donato left, a male porn star came into the room and began undressing in front of me. Then Bruto demanded I take my clothes off. The situation was awful. Bruto was accompanied by two men who seemed they might have guns and an abusive woman who yelled. I think they wanted me to have sex in front of them while they filmed me."

"What did you do?" I asked.

"I ran to the bathroom and locked myself in," Elsa replied. "Then I called David and asked him to come to rescue me."

"I take it David rescued you," I replied.

"Yes, he did," Elsa replied. "David was quite heroic that day. He was my knight in shining armor. He showed up in his dress uniform, complete with his sword." As Elsa described the scene, I pictured Robert Redford coming to her rescue.

"So, what caused the fight?" I asked.

"I told him I did the billboard shoot for money. Then I lied to him about what I spent the money on. I told him I used it to pay for tuition rather than to purchase the motor scooter."

"Why did you lie to him about something like that?" I asked.

"I don't know," Elsa replied. "It was stupid. I could tell by his eyes he knew I was lying. Afterward, he asked me the question that set me off. He asked me what else I did for money."

"That's a bold question," I remarked. "What happened?"

"I lost my composure and slapped him hard across the face. Then I threw his toga in the water and left him sitting in the dark." "What am I going to do, Antonella?" Elsa asked now sobbing. "David now thinks I'm a porn star or perhaps a prostitute! I can't believe this situation. I wish I had never posed for that billboard. I hate that damn thing! I have seen at least six of them driving around Naples. They are springing up like weeds! It's like I posed topless on TV."

Listening to Elsa's lament reminded me why I didn't model. Mother wanted me to model, but I always declined. Now I was glad I did. "Elsa, calm down," I replied. I could see she was getting very worked up. "The billboard's not the problem. Frankly, it's a beautiful picture. Someday you will wish you still looked that good. The problem is you didn't tell David. Remember the only people who know it's you are David, Julie, Kimmy, and me. Do you think David will tell anyone?"

"No," Elsa replied. "I think he is ashamed of me."

"Is he ashamed, or are you ashamed?" I asked. Elsa did not respond to my question. However, it was clear she was ashamed.

"How do I convince him that I haven't done worse?" Elsa asked. "Antonella, I'm falling in love with David. I adore every day we spend together. How do I win him back?" I didn't know the answer to Elsa's question. It was a hard question to answer.

PART III. RELATIONSHIP CHALLENGES

CHAPTER 20:

MIRACLE OF THE BLOOD

Ever since our fight at the party, David and I had not spoken. I expected David to call but he never did. Instead, we failed to communicate altogether. As days turned into weeks, I realized David was slipping away. If I wanted to continue our relationship, I needed to do something.

Deep inside, I knew I had wronged David, although it was difficult to admit it. I knew the morning after the party. It was I who had hidden my past, who had lost my temper and who walked away from a difficult conversation. It was I who had behaved badly. It was easy to blame others, to blame Kimmy for disclosing my secret, or to blame David for confronting me with an uncomfortable truth. I had done things for money. We all do that, but I had crossed a line. The mere fact I was embarrassed by the billboard told me I had crossed a line.

For days afterward, I was depressed, replaying in my mind the events of that evening, trying to understand what went wrong and how to reverse the damage. I knew I needed to apologize, but I also knew it might not be enough. How does one regain respect after it has been lost? I didn't know the answer to that question. All I knew was that I needed to find an answer. I realized I had fallen in love with David and wasn't ready to give up on him.

Several times, I attempted to phone David, but each time I lost my nerve. I had even ridden by his house but then left without ringing the doorbell. I knew I only had one chance to get this right. Somehow, I needed to know what he thought before I apologized. I needed to know how he would receive the apology. Somehow, I needed to regain his respect.

It was then that I had an idea. I remembered that Julie and Kimmy had expressed interest in seeing the Miracle of San Gennaro, which occurred three times per year. The first occurrence was on September 19 on the Saint's Feast Day. The second opportunity would be on December 19, and the third on the first Sunday in May. I would offer to take them to the December 19 event and seek their advice on how to approach David. After several phone call attempts, I was able to reach Kimmy. She was interested in joining me. However, Julie could not attend, having to work.

I woke up early that day to the sound of rain hitting the bedroom window. It seemed the day was not starting well. Please make the rain stop, I thought, whispering a silent prayer. At 9:00 am, the rain stopped for a moment, enabling me to travel to the Villa Maria to pick up Kimmy. It was a cold and cloudy day. Another winter day befitting my mood. When I arrived at the Villa Maria, I found Kimmy sitting by the fireplace, still in her pajamas, trying to keep warm. Kimmy wasn't ready yet. "Let me take a quick shower first," she exclaimed, as she ran upstairs, leaving me alone by the fire. The warm house I had visited only a few weeks before was now terribly cold. Walking over to the radiator, I confirmed my assumption. The radiator was cold. The heat was not working. By 10:00 am, Kimmy was ready. However, the weather was not. Rain was now coming down again in buckets. "Do you have a raincoat?" I asked.

"No," Kimmy replied. "All I have is an umbrella."

The thought of Kimmy holding an umbrella during our ride brought a smile to my face. "We should wait until the rain stops," I offered.

"Would you like a cup of coffee?" Kimmy asked as she disappeared into the kitchen. "All we have is instant American coffee."

"That's fine," I replied. The house was bone-chilling cold, and I was ready to drink something warm.

"What's wrong with the heating system?" I asked. There was no response. Apparently, Kimmy could not hear my question over the humming of the microwave. A few minutes later, Kimmy reappeared, carrying two cups of hot water that she had heated in the microwave oven. She also carried a jar of instant coffee.

"Do you have any cream and sugar?" I asked.

"We have some milk," Kimmy replied, "however, it's rather old. You're welcome to try it." I could tell from the grimace on her face that she did not recommend it, however.

"The refrigerator is old," Kimmy added. "Sometimes it works, and sometimes it doesn't. There seems to be no rhyme or reason to it. I've learned to consider everything in it as a suspect." Taking the hint, I decided to drink my coffee black. Within a few minutes, between drinking the coffee and holding the warm cup, I began to feel warm again.

As we sat in silence, sipping our coffee, I pondered how to start the conversation. Kimmy was not my favorite person for obvious reasons; however, she was the only person I had. "How is David?" I asked.

"I don't know," Kimmy replied. "I haven't seen much of him lately. He seems preoccupied with work. He tends to leave the house early and return home late. Like Robbie, he is showering at the gym every morning rather than here."

I could tell by her tone of voice that she wished she could shower there as well. "Are you able to go on the base?" I asked.

"No," Kimmy replied. "I can only go if Robbie escorts me. I'm not a dependent and, therefore, cannot get a badge." It seemed she was very unhappy with that status.

"How are things going with Robbie?" I asked.

"Ok I guess," Kimmy replied. "It's nice when he is around. However, he's gone much of the day. I spend most of my time alone here in this cold house. My only company is Maria, Rosa, and Bari. We try to communicate; however, they only speak Italian, and I only speak English. Most of the time, we just smile at each other."

"What do you do all day?" I asked.

"Mostly, I read and watch television," Kimmy replied. "I do go out when the weather is nice. There are some lovely viewpoints in this neighborhood. I also enjoy watching "The Young and the Restless" every afternoon with Maria & Rosa. The show is dubbed in Italian. However, I can tell what they are saying. It's funny sometimes to watch the people move their mouths, uncoordinated with the audio."

"Do they have any heat?" I asked.

"No, the heating system doesn't work," Kimmy replied. "Maria says it will cost thirty million lire to fix. She doesn't have that much money."

"How do they stay warm?" I asked.

"Maria and Rosa spend their days in the kitchen, using the oven for heat," Kimmy replied. "It's not terribly safe, but it does take the chill off."

Changing the subject back to David, I asked Kimmy a question. "Has David said anything to you about me since the party?" I asked.

"No," Kimmy replied. "He's quiet and keeps to himself. I think he misses you. He seems very depressed." Hearing that David was depressed brought a glimmer of hope to my prospects. Perhaps I had a chance.

During the conversation, we periodically stopped to look out the dining room windows. The rain was still coming down in sheets, bouncing off the solid surface of the terrace. I had never seen it rain so hard. This was my first winter in Naples, and so far, I had witnessed first-hand the torrential downpours common during a Neapolitan winter. The downpours could literally last all day.

I had been caught in such a downpour the day before riding my motor scooter to class. Even with my raincoat, I arrived at the university completely soaked. Raincoats keep the rain off but do nothing to protect from the splashes caused by city buses.

As we waited for the rain to subside, I asked Kimmy if she had heard the story of San Gennaro (St Januarius). Of course, she had, I thought. Her last name means "of Gennaro."

"Yes," Kimmy replied, she had grown up attending the annual San Gennaro festival in New York. She then related to me how she loved attending the festival each year in New York's Little Italy. Every year they would eat dinner outdoors on Mulberry Street, and then afterward would buy cannoli for dessert. Listening to her describe the food reminded me I had not eaten yet today.

"Did you ever see the procession?" I asked.

"Once," Kimmy replied, "when I was little. For the most part, we went for the food," she added. "Little Italy has the best Italian food in the city. You look hungry," she added. "Would you like some cookies?"

A few minutes later, she reappeared from the kitchen with a package of shortbread cookies. "I love these things," she said! "Would you like another cup of coffee?"

"Yes," I replied, sampling the American-made biscuits. "Where do you buy these?" I asked, thinking I might buy some myself.

"At the commissary store on base," Kimmy replied. "You won't find them at the local Italian grocers."

After digressing into the subject of cookies, we returned to the subject of the day. "San Gennaro is big in Naples," I explained. "Since the 14th century, San Gennaro has been an important part of the life of the city. According to one story, he is said to have saved the city during an eruption of Vesuvius. His blood usually liquefies. However, when it does not, dreadful things can happen."

"What happens?" Kimmy asked.

"Mostly your basic cataclysm type stuff, plagues, earthquakes, or volcanic eruptions," I replied. "The most recent event occurred in 1980. The saint's blood failed to liquefy, and later that year, a major earthquake hit the city, killing several thousand people." As I said this, I thought of the apartment in the Spanish Quarter, feeling relieved that Antonella and I no longer lived there. The 1980 earthquake had been less than 6.0, however, it didn't take much to bring the buildings down.

As I continued my story, I noticed that the rain had stopped. Looking at my watch, it was now 10:30 am. "Do you still want to go to the Cathedral?" I asked. "It's likely the service will be over by the time we arrive."

"Yes," Kimmy replied. "Even if we miss the service, it will be nice to get out. I haven't seen the oldest part of the city yet. Will we be near the Christmas market?" Kimmy asked.

"Yes," I replied, "we can stop there on the way back from the church."

Within a few minutes, the sun came out. It seemed it might be a lovely day. As we rode into the city, Kimmy shared with me her San Gennaro Festival experiences growing up in New York. It turned out she was a firm believer, knowing more about San Gennaro than I did.

The traffic into the city was congested as always. However, the motor scooter gave us an advantage, as we could ride between the lanes of traffic to our destination. I hope no one changes lanes; I thought as we sped through the city, weaving in and out of traffic.

When we reached the university, I decided to park the scooter in one of the interior courtyards rather than park closer to the Duomo (Cathedral). My motor scooter was still new & I wanted to make sure it would still be there when I returned.

As I locked up, Kimmy admired my collection of padlocks. I had one lock to secure the motor scooter to a pole and then another lock for each tire to make it so that no one could ride, even if they could remove it from the pole. We would walk from the University to the Duomo. It would give me a chance to show Kimmy the historic heart of the city.

We exited the University onto the Via Palladino, one of the many narrow Greco-Roman streets forming a grid in the city center. The street was narrow, barely one car width wide, with tall seven-story buildings towering overhead on both sides. This part of the city seldom saw the sun. Everywhere the walls were covered with graffiti, political posters, and handbills. Grit was part of Naples' charm.

As we proceeded north up the narrow alley, it began to rain again. However, we were able to stay dry by walking close to the wall. We kept dry until we reached the intersection of a major cross street. The street was somewhat wider, although not a wide street. Ducking into a doorway to get out of the rain, we watched the parade of umbrellas pass by. Across from us, in a tiny square, we could see an ancient reclining statue covered with bird droppings, sitting next to an overflowing trashcan.

"What is that?" Kimmy asked, pointing towards the statue.

"That is a statue of the Nile god," I replied. "It's been sitting in that spot for at least two thousand years. It was originally commissioned during Roman times by merchants from Alexandria, Egypt. At some point, the statue lost its head. The head you see was later added in the 16th century."

Kimmy nodded her head. "Perhaps the original head fell off from the weight of the bird poop," Kimmy suggested. For a moment, I laughed. I was thinking perhaps he lost his head to vandalism (by real fifth-century Vandals); however, Kimmy's theory also seemed plausible.

Then I continued my narration. "The street in front of us is known as the Spaccanapoli. (The street that splits Naples), I continued. This was the main street of the ancient Greco-Roman city." It was hard to believe the Spaccanapoli could have ever been the main street. It was barely wide enough for a single lane of traffic and two narrow sidewalks on either side. The main street in Pompeii was wider.

As we stood in our doorway, we watched the parade of people, all carrying umbrellas, bumping into each other. After a few minutes, the rain stopped enabling us to cross the street. The name of the north-bound street had changed. We were now on the Via Nilo. Up ahead, I could see the next intersection. "The next street, the Via Tribunale, is a more direct route to the cathedral," I remarked. When we arrived at the corner, the rain began to drizzle again as we turned right and proceeded towards the cathedral.

We walked along the narrow Via Tribunale for several blocks until the Duomo came into view. The Cathedral was a stunning sight, the tall white marble façade now decorated with crimson banners for the day's activities. Across the busy Via Duomo, we could see streams of people coming out of the cathedral. It was clear the service was over.

"This street is the main street in town to buy wedding dresses," I remarked. Kimmy stopped for a moment to look inside a shop window to admire the dresses.

"Do you still want to go in?" I asked.

"Yes," Kimmy replied. "We might as well, while we are here."

As we entered the cathedral, we encountered a mass of joyous people coming out. Clearly, the miracle had occurred as expected. The city was safe for another year.

As we entered the church, the air was thick with mixed odors, the smell of burning incense mixed with dampness from the rain and body odors from the crowd. It seemed clear that several of the people coming out had not bathed in weeks. "Let's move inside," I recommended, as we watched the mass of humanity exiting the church. There were young and old, rich, and poor, all crowded together, moving towards the giant doors.

Immediately inside the church, towards the right side of the church, we could see the chapel where the Patron Saint's remains were kept. There was a large crowd gathered in front of the chapel, making it impossible to see anything inside. Seeing that the center of the church remained congested, we decided to move towards the altar on the left, more open side of the church.

As we moved to the left, I noticed an ancient and empty chapel. Motioning to go inside, Kimmy and I left the crowd to wander the chapel. As we entered, I noticed that several sections of the floor were made of glass, enabling us to see beneath the floor. I had been in this room once before. Below us stood the remains of an earlier church built in the fifth century during the reign of the first Christian Emperor, Constantine. I pointed out the walls below to Kimmy, who responded with a smile. This site had always been a church.

We stayed in the chapel for 20 minutes to allow the crowd in the nave to dissipate. "Would you like to see something else interesting?" I asked.

"Yes," Kimmy replied, enjoying the tour.

I then led Kimmy into one of the side aisles and proceeded towards the back, entering a small room with a basin in the center of the floor. "This is the oldest baptistry in the Western world," I exclaimed, proud of myself for remembering this small fact. I had been studying Neapolitan history for months and was beginning to develop a deep knowledge of my adopted city.

When we emerged from the chapel, the situation changed dramatically. The large crowds had departed, leaving a smaller line of people remaining. The line was moving slowly towards the altar. Sensing the purpose of the line, Kimmy grabbed my hand and pulled me towards it. I would have preferred to get lunch, being skeptical of the miracle, thinking it was some sort of medieval trick. However, Kimmy wanted to see for herself, so I joined her.

Up ahead, we could see the archbishop tilting the reliquary containing the blood from side to side in front of each person. He would make the sign of the cross and then give each person a blessing. Some would kiss the glass containing the blood, and some would not.

When it became our turn, Kimmy stepped up to receive the blessing. At last, I could see the reliquary for myself. The bishop, held in his hand a large silver and gold scepter-like object surmounted by an ornate crown. In the center was the transparent section containing two sealed vials said to be the blood of San Gennaro.

Was it really the saint's blood, kept since his martyrdom in the fourth century? Who knew for sure? One of the vials was small, while the other was larger. As the archbishop turned the reliquary from side to side, it was clear the contents had turned to liquid. After receiving the blessing from the priest, Kimmy leaned over and kissed the glass, exposing herself to all the combined germs of the city. She then turned towards me, smiling, with tears streaming down her face. Clearly, she was moved by the experience. I suddenly felt very warm inside. I had made Kimmy's day.

When my turn came to stand in front of the reliquary, I saw for myself the reddish substance within the vials slosh from side to side as the bishop turned the object in front of me. For a moment, my past scientific rationalizations and skepticism ended as I, too, leaned over in a leap of faith and kissed the glass. As I touched the sacred object to my lips, I closed my eyes and whispered a prayer for David and me.

After our religious experience, Kimmy and I wandered the church for another thirty minutes, taking in the sights. Behind the Bishop sat the gilded head of San Gennaro wearing a tall red bishop's miter. The gold reliquary was said to contain his skull.

There was something almost pagan in the Christian symbolism. It seemed everyone was worshipping gilded heads, jeweled crowns, and saintly bones. I remembered for a moment the colossal head of the Greek god Zeus from the acropolis of Cumae. One side of me was repulsed by the macabre medieval display, and yet part of me was also drawn to the mystery. Clearly, there was something to the miracle of San Gennaro, both when it occurred as well as when it didn't. Could the spirit of a dead saint really hold the fate of the city in his hands? After minutes of pondering the impenetrable, I was ready for lunch. It was now 1:00 pm.

When we exited the church, we emerged into a transformed world. The dark rainy skies were gone, replaced by warm sunshine and blue skies. It seemed the storm was over. It was still not warm enough to remove my winter raincoat, however. "What would you like for lunch?" I asked.

"Pizza," Kimmy replied.

After crossing the busy street, we returned to the heart of the city by a different route, the Spaccanapoli. The mezzogiorno (afternoon siesta) was beginning. Shops were beginning to close for the afternoon. "Why does everything close in the afternoon?" Kimmy asked.

"I have no idea," I replied. "I guess the Neapolitans work to live rather than live to work." It was a mindset completely foreign to either Kimmy or me, having grown up in northern European & American cultures.

As we walked down the street, we passed a building courtyard containing the large statue of a horse's head. For a moment, we stopped to gaze at the magnificent sculpture. "Do you think anyone will mind if we step inside to have a closer look?" Kimmy asked.

"No," I replied.

As we entered the courtyard, we could now see the sculpture, fully surrounded by mopeds and the ever-ubiquitous trashcans. "This should be in a museum," Kimmy remarked, touching the sculpture with her hand! Knowing something of the sculpture's history, I began my dissertation.

"That sculpture was given to the original building owner by Lorenzo De Medici," I replied. "It dates to the Italian Renaissance." Listening closely, Kimmy stopped to take a picture.

"What is this place?" Kimmy asked.

"The Palazzo Carafa," I replied.

Kimmy understood the significance of that name. It was the same last name as Antonella's mother.

Following our detour into the Renaissance-era courtyard, we returned to the street to visit a nearby pizzeria. After a few minutes of waiting, we departed with our pizza. The restaurant was full, given the hour of the day, so we decided to get our pizza to go. I expected to receive our lunch in a box. However, it was delivered to us folded, wrapped in a piece of paper. It was a simple Margherita pizza with tomatoes and mozzarella. It was extremely hot.

Eating a hot and sloppy pizza while walking was an impossible task, so we decided to sit on some nearby church steps to enjoy our lunch. How do we eat this thing, I thought? Kimmy was one step ahead of me.

She retrieved a slightly used cardboard pizza box from one of the nearby trash dumpsters and set it on the steps creating a table for our pizza. It was slightly better than laying our pizza on the dirty paving stones. Not content with this arrangement, however, Kimmy pulled a handkerchief from her purse and laid it on the box, giving us a tablecloth. It was none too soon, as my hand was burning from the sauce now leaking through the paper.

Eating pizza with Kimmy on the steps of a church was an experience I won't soon forget. The pizza was warm and delicious. We had no silverware or napkins but instead used our fingers to tear off small pieces. By the time we finished, our hands and faces were a mess, but we were happy.

"Do you have anything in that purse we can use to clean up?" I asked. Kimmy did not respond but instead opened her purse producing several handkerchiefs. Kimmy's small purse contained a universe of essential items. Within minutes we were good as new, ready to set off on our next adventure.

After our lunch, Kimmy and I wandered the city center. Even though most of the shops were closed, we found things to do. We visited the nearby Capella San Severo, where we saw one of the most beautiful sculptures in the world, The "Veiled Christ," by the 18th century Neapolitan Sculptor Giuseppe Sanmartino.

The sculpture, carved from a single block of white marble, depicts Christ after the crucifixion, laying on a cushion covered with a shroud. The work is so exquisitely carved that it appears as if a real person were transformed into marble. One of the myths concerning the work was that a medieval and infamous alchemist had created the sculpture by turning a real person into stone.

After visiting the small, exquisite chapel, we visited the busy Christmas market on the Via San Gregorio Armeno. Situated in a narrow alley next to the famous monastery and in front of an ancient city gate tower stood the Christmas market. It was the main place in the city to buy Christmas figurines. Kimmy and I enjoyed looking at the many detailed figurines, eventually buying several. I bought a wise man to hang on the Christmas tree. Kimmy bought a small baby Jesus and a cradle.

When we finished our shopping, it was late in the afternoon and time to return to the Villa Maria. The day which had begun rainy was now beautiful and warm. As we made our way back, through the busy streets towards the house, I asked Kimmy about her plans for Christmas.

"Robbie and I are going to New York for Christmas," Kimmy replied.

"What are Julie and Harry doing?" I asked.

"Julie is going to Chicago, and Harry is going to Boston," Kimmy explained.

"What is David doing?" I asked.

"I'm not sure," Kimmy replied. "He was talking about going to Chicago until he learned his parents were going to Hawaii for Christmas. I think he's planning to stay in Naples," Kimmy replied.

Within a few minutes, we arrived at the villa. Looking at my watch, it was now 5:00 pm. As Kimmy unlocked the gate, I peered into the driveway taking stock of the cars behind the gate. In front of Harry's green car sat Robbie's car, and in front of that sat David's car. All the roommates were home from work. Seeing David's car gave me a knot in my stomach. It was time to talk with David. What would I say?

As we walked down the driveway, I could hear voices on the terrace above. It seemed Harry and Robbie were on the terrace, but not David. Where was David? Just then, I was knocked to the ground by a large animal. I forgot about Bari, but he had not forgotten about me. Getting an unexpected wet kiss from a St Bernard is not an experience I will soon forget; fortunately, Rosa came to my rescue with her broomstick, sending Bari scurrying.

Overhead I could hear the men laughing at my misfortune. Looking up, I could see the smiles on their faces. "Where's David?" I asked.

"I think he's on the roof;" Harry replied, quite amused by my appearance. "We're cooking out tonight," Harry added. "Would you like us to throw a burger on the grill for you?" I wasn't sure what to say. I didn't know how long I would be there. Thinking positive, however, I decided to accept Harry's offer, figuring he would eat the hamburger if I didn't.

When I entered the house, I proceeded up the stairs to the second floor and then out onto the back terrace to climb the spiral stair to the roof. When I emerged onto the roof, I was greeted by David, who was coming down to see me.

"Are you staying for dinner?" He asked. This seemed a strange icebreaker, but I decided to go with the flow.

"Do you want to stay for burgers?" I asked.

"I would rather go to a restaurant," David replied. "Someplace where it is warm." Following his lead, I agreed. It was then that David did something unpredictable. He sat on the parapet and bade me sit beside him.

"I'm sorry I hurt your feelings" David whispered softly.

"I'm sorry also," I replied. "I should have told you about the picture. Can you forgive me?" I asked.

"I already have," David replied.

That night we ate dinner together, David and I, at my favorite restaurant in the city. We ate dinner at Fenestella (the little window), which was located near my house, in the romantic fishing village of Marechiaro. It was wonderful to dine again with David. The location was so romantic. It reminded me of a Neapolitan folk song about Marechiaro. It was said that Marechiaro was so romantic that even the fish made love there.

After dinner, we returned to the scene of our argument, enjoying a warm swim in the nymphaeum grotto together. My prayer to San Gennaro had been answered.

201

CHAPTER 21:

THE HOLIDAY SEASON 1989-1990

JULIE'S HOLIDAY

The 1989 holiday season began with disappointment as usual. Ever since I started my medical career, I had always had to work through the holidays. It was an aspect of my career choice that I had not anticipated when I decided to pursue medicine. My parents wanted me to return to Evanston for the holiday season; however, as usual, I couldn't. I had to work. The stork's nest was full again, with expectant mothers waiting to deliver.

When I returned home from work that Monday, I looked and felt depressed. It was impossible to plan anything with my family. It seemed I would be spending Christmas alone again for another year. Harry planned to travel to Boston. Kimmy and Robbie had already left for New York, and David was spending his time with Elsa.

When I walked in the door, Harry could immediately sense that something was troubling me. He always seemed to sense my moods. Harry asked me what was wrong. "My plans have fallen through, as usual," I replied. "I need to work over Christmas." Harry peered at me over his glasses and smiled.

"Would you like company for Christmas?" Harry asked.

"I thought you were going to Boston," I replied.

Harry looked at me and smiled once again. "I can always go to Boston," he replied. "This year I would prefer to stay in Naples with you." For a moment, I was touched. Once again, Harry had done something unexpectedly nice for me.

After Harry's offer to spend the holidays with me, I recommitted myself to spending more time with Harry. I had been taking him for granted. Up until that point, I have viewed Harry as a roommate, not as a love interest. Perhaps Harry wanted to be more than a roommate, I thought.

When Christmas Eve arrived, I invited Harry to visit the hospital for a little impromptu party. Harry arrived wearing a Santa hat, with a small bottle of whiskey hidden under his winter coat. He was ready for some fun. Soon thereafter, we spiked our coffee, enjoying the holiday season together.

That evening, Harry decided to stay at the hospital rather than return home. I couldn't blame him. It was freezing cold in the house. It was a slow night at the hospital, and I was able to set up Harry with blankets and a pillow on the sofa in my office.

Later in the evening, after I finished my rounds, I returned to the office to find Harry sound asleep. Soon I joined him under the blanket for some shuteye. During the wee hours of the morning, perhaps around 4:00 am, Harry rolled over, woke me up and gave me a Christmas kiss. As he did this, we both fell off the sofa onto the floor. It was an auspicious first kiss. Harry and I just laughed.

Later that morning, after my shift ended, we returned home and continued our evening sleep together in Harry's king-size bed, sharing his electric blanket for the first time. It was wonderful to sleep in a warm bed again. Perhaps Harry would let me borrow his blanket, I thought? We were, after all, living on different shifts from one another.

THE CHRISTMAS CAKE

On Christmas Day, Maria paid us a visit to wish us a Merry Christmas. She brought a Christmas present, a traditional boxed Italian Christmas Cake. I had seen these cakes everywhere during the weeks before Christmas. They sold them at the supermarket, the coffee bars, and the salumerias. They even sold them at the gas stations.

Opening the box, Harry pulled the cake out and removed it from its plastic wrapper. The cake was tall, round, and crusty. It resembled a twelve-inch-tall muffin. "Perhaps it's like an angel food cake," he remarked. After he opened the box, I cut two slices, one for Harry and the other for me and placed them on plates.

"What do you think?" Harry asked, after we had eaten several bites. The cake was exceedingly dry, with a strange aftertaste, which I attributed to the mysterious candied fruit inside. Perhaps, it might be better with ice cream, I thought.

"Maybe we are supposed to dip it in something," I offered, remembering the Italian almond flavored cookies we shared the week before. Then I asked Harry a question. "How old is the cake?" Harry picked up the box and began to look for the expiration date.

For a few minutes, he said nothing. "The date is in Roman numerals," Harry replied. "They don't want to make this easy. Can you guess how old the cake is?" Harry asked.

I offered a number. I was wrong. "How old is it?" I asked. Harry smiled at me.

"It's three years old," Harry replied. Hearing this, I spit the cake out of my mouth. No wonder it tasted so awful! Harry was now laughing.

"This reminds me of the cookies we tried last week," Harry replied. He continued chewing his cake, cataloging the taste in his mind. Harry had a cast-iron stomach. He could eat anything and often did. The more creepy-crawly, the better. I could not stomach eating octopus. However, Harry loved them.

As Harry continued to eat his cake, enjoying the potential protein crawling within, I asked him if he ate bugs as a kid? "Of course," Harry replied. "Didn't you?" He asked. I had to admit; that I tried chocolate-covered grasshoppers once. I drew a line in the sand, however, when it came to eating anything moving.

Harry was always a kidder. The first time he cooked Italian for me, I asked him what he was making? His response was classic. "Topo Testa al Forno, con Insalata Gatto Misto," he replied. His Italian accent was excellent. I had no idea what he said, however. The food sounded delicious.

"What's that?" I asked, playing along.

"Baked rat head with a mixed cat salad," Harry replied.

For a moment, I laughed, enjoying his repartee. "I wondered what happened to all the stray cats," I replied. "Thanks, but no, thanks," I replied. "I already had topo today." This was perhaps true. I had eaten the usual mystery meat in grey-brown gravy at the hospital.

"Can you make me a salad?" I asked. "Do you know the one with mummy meat?"

"Sure," Harry replied. "Would you like the motor oil dressing on the salad or on the side?" By this point, Harry was laughing so hard that he could barely contain himself.

Back to the story of the cookies. The previous week, Harry had purchased a bag of small donut-shaped cookies near the waterfront. The cookies resembled Italian Christmas cookies but tasted dreadful. They were hard, like rocks, with an awful taste. They tasted like black licorice mixed with black pepper.

"Perhaps they are dog biscuits," Harry offered? When we returned home, we offered a biscuit to Bari. Bari would eat anything, we thought. Bari picked up the biscuit in his mouth, then dropped it on the ground and began licking his butt. Even Bari hated the cookies.

Back to the story of the cake. "What should we do with the cake?" I asked.

"Let us see if Bari will eat it," Harry replied, smiling.

I felt awful giving Maria's Christmas present to the dog. "Shouldn't we at least wait a few days?" I asked. Harry didn't wait for me to reply. He had already begun to offer the cake to Bari. Bari did not hesitate. He grabbed the cake and disappeared into the garden. Apparently, he liked it.

Several days later, Rosa visited us and asked us for help getting something away from Bari. We couldn't tell what she was saying. However, I did recognize two words, "topo," which meant rat, and "schifo," which meant disgusting.

Following Rosa into the garden, we found Bari chewing on something which resembled a deflated soccer ball. The object was covered with dog slobber, hair, and dirt. Was it a dead animal or something else? I looked for a stick. I didn't want to touch the object; however, Harry dived in and began to extricate the object from Bari's mouth. For a moment, they played tug of war together. Then Bari let go. The object was gross but looked familiar. It was the Christmas cake.

We never told Maria about the Christmas cake. As far as she knew, we ate it. By the way, I finally learned how to eat a Christmas cake. The secret was to scoop out the center of the cake and fill it with ice cream.

KIMMY'S CHRISTMAS IN NEW YORK

The thought of returning to New York for Christmas was both a blessing and a curse. It might present more opportunities for Robbie to propose. However, it would also subject us both to parental pressures. I knew my father was unhappy that I turned down the job in New York, and I expected both mother and father to be worried that Robbie and I were living together. I was not looking forward to the awkward silences around the dining room table or the expected discussion with my parents about money. The truth was I was out of money. It was a condition I could not disclose to Robbie.

The holiday plan was for us to divide our time evenly between both sets of parents. We would spend the days before Christmas with Robbie's parents in Manhattan (to facilitate shopping), and then on Christmas Eve, we would move to Connecticut to spend Christmas and several days thereafter with my parents in Greenwich.

We would return to Naples before New Year's Eve. I knew from one of my mother's letter's that Robbie's parents were invited for Christmas dinner. If Robbie were to propose, it seemed to me that he would do so before Christmas. I was hoping he might ask on Christmas Eve.

We flew from Rome to JFK via TWA on an aged 747 jet. During the flight across "the pond" (as U.S. military personnel referred to it), the airline played the movie "When Harry Met Sally." I found the movie delightful. However, Robbie closed his eyes and pretended to fall asleep.

I knew he preferred action movies and that he hated "chick flicks." When the movie ended, I tested Robbie by asking him if men and women could be friends?

"No," he replied, winking at me; "the sex always gets in the way." He had been listening, after all.

He then gave me a kiss, promising this would be our best Christmas ever. Was he planning to propose? I was not sure. Robbie often dangled a proposal in front of me, only to jerk it away at the last minute.

We were met at JFK airport by Robbie's younger brother Frank Jr., who drove us into the city. The traffic crawled the entire trip. New York had not changed. We took the Belt Parkway to the Brooklyn Queens Expressway and then traveled across the Brooklyn Bridge to the FDR, exiting onto 42nd Street by the United Nations. It was a typical New York winter day, cold and cloudy with a hint of potential snow in the air.

Within a few short minutes, we parked the car and proceeded to Robbie's parent's apartment. I liked Frank and Marjorie's top-floor apartment. On one side, we could see the United Nations Building, and on the other side, we could see the forest of skyscrapers in Mid-town Manhattan. I could almost reach out and touch the Chrysler Building. I loved the look of the Chrysler building at night; its pointed top lit up like the Statue of Liberty's crown. It was a wonderful place to stay for Christmas shopping in New York.

On our first night in New York, Robbie & I both had large American cheeseburgers with French fries. It was nice to eat American food again. The only taste of Italy I included in the meal was mayonnaise for the fries instead of ketchup. Mayonnaise was better, in my opinion. Later that evening, back at the apartment, Robbie's mother made sure to assign us separate bedrooms. There would be no hanky-panky under her roof. It seemed Robbie's mother, Marjorie did not approve of our living arrangement.

The next day, during our first full day in New York, Robbie and I walked the length of Midtown Manhattan's shopping area, from the New York Public Library to Bloomingdales. Along the way we stopped to peer into the many brightly decorated store windows. My favorite windows, as usual, were at the Saks Fifth Avenue store, across from Rockefeller Center.

When we reached Saks, I insisted we walk into the store to buy a small bottle of the perfume I loved. The aroma of perfume in the ground floor air was intoxicating! For me, it was the smell of Christmas. That day the sidewalks were filled to overflowing with holiday shoppers, making progress up the street slow. The smell of chestnuts roasting on every corner filled the air.

When we reached the park, we stopped for lunch at a hot dog cart across from the Plaza Hotel. It was the only lunch we could afford that day. My small bottle of perfume had emptied Robbie's wallet, leaving little behind for lunch. Robbie wanted to eat our hot dogs near the cart. However, I insisted we sit beside the Statue of General Sherman away from the smell of the horses. I like horse carriages. I think they are romantic. However, I can't stand the smell where they park. At least it was winter and not summer when the smells could be truly awful.

That day we only bought a small bottle of perfume and two hot dogs. We couldn't afford anything else. Christmas was not Christmas without a walk down Fifth Avenue, unfortunately we could afford nothing. I hated being poor. I had been poor for six years of college and was ready to get a job. Instead, I was chasing after "Peter Pan." I wondered for a minute if I should have stayed in New York.

The following day we embarked on a real shopping trip, now armed with parental credit cards. We borrowed Robbie's parent's car and drove to the shopping malls in Edison, New Jersey. Robbie grew up in Edison, graduating from high school there. He lived in a neighborhood where everyone had the last name Singh, and they all watched the Indian movie channel on cable TV. His parents moved to Manhattan while Robbie was in college. Robbie's father accepted an appointment as a judge at one of the city's many courthouses and had to move into the city.

During our shopping day in Edison, I managed to finish all my shopping. I felt quite proud of myself. I bought gifts for everyone and spent less than two hundred dollars doing it. That day we ate lunch in the food court of the Menlo Park Mall. I enjoyed a mixture of Chinese food, and Robbie ate a Philly cheesesteak sandwich. The last thing either of us wanted to eat was Italian food.

During our walk through the double-deck mall, I tried to get Robbie interested in looking at rings, but he would not take the bait. Instead, he kept wandering away from me to sit in the mall. Once I even saw him step into a candle store. My god, Robbie in a candle store! He clearly had no interest in buying a ring that day!

On Christmas Eve-day, we returned to shopping in Manhattan with Robbie's parents. It was a good day for Robbie as they showered him with gifts. It was a lousy day for me. I was the unwanted, invisible girlfriend trying to take Robbie away from them. Robbie's parents never liked me.

I held out against hope that Robbie might take me ring shopping, but nothing like that occurred. Instead, we went to lunch next to the Rockefeller Center ice rink. Afterwards Robbie wanted to go skating on a full stomach. Robbie was good at skating, whereas I was not. I was good at dancing but turned into a total klutz on ice skates. That afternoon, after lunch, we went skating. Twice, I landed on my rear end when someone ran into me. By the end of the twenty-minute skate, I was ready for traction. I also felt sick to my stomach.

CHRISTMAS DINNER WITH THE PARENTS

On Christmas Day, we rode with Robbie's parents, Frank, and Marjorie, out to my parent's house in Connecticut for dinner. Mother went all out cooking a giant feast, determined to impress Robbie's parents. She couldn't decide whether to cook our traditional Italian family Christmas dinner or a turkey dinner for Robbie's parents, so she cooked both.

The table and sideboard were overflowing with food. By the end of the meal, I felt as big as a house. One more bite, and I would explode, I thought. During dinner, Robbie and I remained quiet while our parents chattered endlessly about sports, the weather, and politics. They were having an enjoyable dinner, whereas we were not. Thank goodness father didn't say anything awkward; however, grandmother did.

"So, when are you two getting married?" Grandmother asked. For a moment everyone stopped talking. Leave it to my Italian grandmother to ask the question on everyone's mind! Robbie looked like a deer caught in headlights, losing control of his motor skills. When he finally spoke, gibberish came out.

"We have not discussed it yet," Robbie stuttered. Robbie was acting like a weasel! We had discussed getting married many times. Turning towards me, grandma redirected her question, putting me on the hot seat.

"We have not decided yet;" I replied. My answer insinuated we had decided to get married but had not decided on a date. Grandma's question was, after all, "When are you getting married? Not are you getting married?" I could tell by the look on grandma's face that she misunderstood my answer.

"You should get married in June," she replied. "June weddings are the best!" Robbie gave me a priceless look. He was not a happy camper.

As grandma spoke, she stopped short in mid-sentence and looked at my hand lying on the table. Instantly her demeanor changed when she saw there was no ring. Mother followed grandmother's eyes and, seeing my predicament, quickly changed the subject. "Fiddle-dee-dee," mother replied. She then invited grandmother and I into the kitchen.

Once we were safely behind the kitchen door, the questions began. "So, he hasn't asked you to marry him yet," mother asked? "No," I replied, "not yet. He wants us to live together for a while first." I could tell from my mother's look that she was concerned.

"Are you ok with birth control pills?" she asked, "or should we plan to visit the doctor while you are here?" As usual, Mother was worried I might get pregnant. Mother had been worried about that possibility since I hit puberty.

"I'm ok," I replied. I wasn't ready to share with her my plan to get pregnant. The truth was I only had thirty days' supply remaining. After that, something was going to happen. As my mother and I talked, I could see my grandmother smiling out of the corner of my eye. She understood I was lying.

"Don't be so old fashion," she remarked, chastising my mother. "Kimmy is a modern woman! If she wants to live with Robbie for a while, good for her! Remember your father and I lived together first also." I could see a gleam in grandma's eye as she related her story. There was clearly more to her story than she was telling. Had grandma been a wild woman, perhaps a flapper in a previous life? Grandmother had, after all, lived through the roaring twenties in New York.

Mother changed the subject. "How are you doing for money?" She asked.

"I am out," I replied. "My savings from my college internship at the bank are all gone."

For a moment mother gave me a serious look, then she smiled. "Don't worry," mother replied. "I will give you some money before you leave. Don't tell your father, however."

It was nice to have a mother who made more money than father. Mother let father think he was in charge however it was clear to me who was really in charge. It was my mother, the bank executive.

"Have you set up a bank account yet in Italy?" Mother asked.

"Yes," I replied.

"Give me name of the bank and the account number before you leave so that I can wire you more money later if you need it," mother continued. "Whatever you do, don't ask Robbie for money," she added. "You need to remain independent; that way, you can always leave!"

"How long are you allowed to remain in Italy?" Mother asked. I hadn't thought about that question and didn't know the answer.

"I think six months," I replied, not sure of the answer.

"That sounds too long," mother replied. "I think tourists can only stay for three months," she replied. "You might be able to stay longer if you can claim you are visiting family in the country." I had not considered the fact that I might be returning to Italy as an undocumented immigrant. Mother, however, had.

"Do we have any family in Italy?" I asked.

"Yes," mother replied. "Your father has several distant cousins who live somewhere around Naples. I don't have their addresses but will give you their names before you leave."

"How does this help?" I asked.

"Italy is a special place," mother replied. "Your name itself can make you Italian, even if you have never lived there before."

As we walked out of the kitchen back into the dining room carrying two pies, grandmother slipped a Christmas present into my apron pocket. 'Buon Natale," she said, as she gave me a kiss on the cheek. "You asked me about this earlier," she replied.

At this, I remembered I had asked her if we had ancestors from Naples. When we re-entered the dining room, we found the room empty. The men were now sitting in the living room watching a football game through their eyelids. The Christmas turkey overdose had taken effect. So much for the pie, I thought. We would eat the pies later after the game when the men woke up.

Later that evening, I opened the envelope grandmother had placed in my pocket. Included in the envelope was a $100 bill as well as a picture of my great grandparents on their wedding day. At the bottom of the worn and faded black and white picture was the name of the photo studio and the words Napoli, Italia. On the back of the picture were their names and wedding date. The caption read, "Giovanni De Gennaro et Clarice Brancaccio, sposata 27 Septembre 1898." It turns out I had ancestors from Naples, after all.

DAVID'S CHRISTMAS NARRATIVE

The year 1989 brought tremendous changes across Eastern Europe. Everywhere borders that had been closed since the construction of the Berlin Wall were suddenly opened, allowing a flood of tourists to enter Western Europe. This tide, which began in May before my arrival, accelerated during the first week in November when the people of Berlin spontaneously demolished the Berlin Wall. Within months the Soviet-backed governments of Eastern Europe fell like so many dominos. It was a remarkable and unexpected year.

During the fall of 1989, we saw many East German cars driving around Naples. The flood of tourists would increase during the coming year. They drove little cars, known as Trabants, which were filled to overflowing. The cars often had piles of suitcases strapped to their roofs.

During December, shortly before Christmas, I stopped to help an East German family change a flat tire on the coast highway near Lago Patria. I remember all their tires were bald with no tread remaining. Even the spare tire was completely worn out. They didn't seem to mind, however, and seemed to be having the time of their lives. When we finished changing the tire, I watched them climb back into their tiny car and drive away in a cloud of blue smoke. This was what the end of Communism looked like.

After Christmas, Elsa and I decided to see for ourselves the changes sweeping across central Europe. On the first day, we drove the length of Italy from Naples to Innsbruck, Austria, arriving late in the afternoon after an eight-hour drive.

It was my first exhilarating experience driving the Italian Autostrada, a modern marvel of high-speed toll roads running the length of the Italian boot. It was Italy's equivalent of the German Autobahn, only with more tunnels. For the first time in its four-year existence, my BMW ran as its German makers intended, gliding down the road effortlessly at speeds exceeding ninety miles per hour.

Elsa and I experienced our first winter snow of the season, crossing the Brenner Pass into Austria, just south of Innsbruck. It finally felt like Christmas. During our first night in Innsbruck, we stayed at a hotel in the city center, only a short walk from the main square and the Little Golden Roof balcony.

That evening we ate at a nearby restaurant, splitting a large helping of a local specialty known as Bauernshmaus. It was a pile of sausages arranged on a large plate, like an Indian teepee leaning against a large potato dumpling. The pile was surrounded by a sea of sauerkraut and gravy. We washed down our Germanic feast with liter-sized steins of the local beer brewed by Augustinian monks and afterwards finished our meal with a heaping helping of tasty apple strudel.

By evening's end, we were feeling light on our feet, the high alcohol content beer working its magic. As we stumbled back to our hotel room through the snow, we gazed into the many shop windows selling cuckoo clocks. Several times we stopped to kiss. Elsa looked beautiful that evening in her fur hat and new loden coat.

The night we spent in Innsbruck, was the first night we slept together in the same bed. We kept our pajamas on, of course. We were not ready yet to have sex. Elsa may have been more than willing to remove her top for a fashion photographer, but she was still shy when it came to removing it for me.

Since our reunion earlier in the month, Elsa and I had spent considerable time together at her apartment. We had still not shared a bed, but we had slept under the same roof. Elsa would sleep in the lower-level bedroom on her mattress, which lay on the floor, while I slept upstairs on Antonella's bean bag chair. It was better than sleeping in my freezing cold bed at the Villa Maria

I needed desperately to buy an electric blanket, but there were no blankets for sale at the Navy Exchange. The Navy Exchange always had an ample stock of things that no one needed but often lacked basic things everyone bought, such as size thirty-four waist blue jeans or electric blankets. I found I had to buy what I needed, when I first saw it in the store. If I didn't, it would not be there the next day.

After my initial disappointment at the Exchange, I attempted to find what I needed in town. In doing so, I learned that Naples offered few options. Naples had thousands of small stores but did not have large department stores like in the States. Finding an item could often take months. Instead, Naples had small family-owned shops, many only one room in size. Each shop specialized in a particular type of item. I learned if it was not hanging in the window, it often was not in the store. Shopping in Naples was not like shopping in Chicago. It was more like shopping in ancient Pompeii.

Our whirlwind trip to Central Europe lasted eight days, and during that time, we visited Innsbruck, Salzburg, Prague, and Munich.

The trip to Prague was the most memorable of all, however. We arrived on December 30th, the day after Václav Havel became President of Czechoslovakia. We stayed at an old Communist-era hotel on Wenceslaus Square, the site of the 1968 Soviet crackdown. That night there would be no Russian tanks, however, to spoil the dawn of a new era. As we walked about the city center for hours, mingling with the crowds, we witnessed history in the making. It was the aftermath of an event historians would later refer to as "The Velvet Revolution."

Communism in Czechoslovakia was finally gone. At the stroke of midnight, Elsa and I embraced and kissed in the old town square in front of the dark gothic towers of the Our Lady of Tyn Church, as fireworks went off all over the city. It was the perfect way to begin the 1990s. The Cold War was finally over.

ROBBIE'S RETURN TO NAPLES FROM NEW YORK

Kimmy and I returned from our Christmas vacation, taking the red-eye flight from New York to Rome. We arrived at Rome's Leonardo De Vinci airport at 10:00 am on New Year's Eve-day. The flight home had been long and quiet. There was nothing more left to say. Both of us were exhausted from our holiday ordeal.

The last three days at Kimmy's parent's house seemed to drag on for weeks, the hostility towards me palpable in the air. In retrospect, we should have left the day after Christmas. It was good to finally return home, back to a more comfortable world without parents.

Returning to warm Italian weather was also a joy after two weeks of frigid near-zero weather in New York. As we stepped off the plane and boarded our bus to the terminal, it felt like sixty-five degrees outside. It was much too warm to wear our heavy winter coats.

That morning, we drove back to Naples, following the coast road through Terracina, and Gaeta, rather than driving the Autostrada. It felt wonderful to drive with the windows open again.

We stopped for lunch at a roadside sandwich shop between Sperlonga and Gaeta, where we split a prosciutto and mozzarella sandwich. As we sat at the picnic table sharing our sandwich and can of soda, Kimmy barely spoke a word. Kimmy, who was normally boisterous, stayed silent most of the trip home. I couldn't tell if she was angry with me or just exhausted.

When we finally arrived home around 1:30 pm, Kimmy went upstairs to bed. So much for spending New Year's Eve together (the entire reason we came back early), I thought. I knew Kimmy was disappointed. She had been expecting me to propose, and I had not delivered. Sometimes, she was not subtle about what she wanted.

The truth for me, however, was more complex. I didn't know what I wanted. Kimmy had been out of my life for two years and was now suddenly back in it. I loved being around her, but I also loved my newfound single life. I hated the thought of giving up one to have the other. It seemed much easier not to decide.

Marrying Kimmy would, of course, have its benefits; however, it would also bring with it high costs. Kimmy was accustomed to expensive things, to always having money. I could not afford the life she wanted on Navy pay. I could not even afford the ring she wanted.

I had trouble wrapping my head around the idea of spending $10,000 on a diamond engagement ring. The truth was I had saved very little, barely $5,000 during my first two years in San Diego and had spent half of that buying a car when I arrived in Naples. Working for the Navy was fun, but it didn't pay as well as the private sector.

Kimmy had expensive tastes. The rings Kimmy wanted ran from $15,000 to $20,000. I didn't have that kind of money, nor did I want to borrow it. I was still trying to pay off my student loans.

Kimmy was fortunate she had no student debt. She had rich parents, whereas I did not. We were both now adults, but when it came to money, Kimmy was still a child, unable to accept reality. She expected me to give her the fairy tale, which she felt entitled to, but which I could not afford. Our life together would be so much easier if she did not have such lofty expectations.

That afternoon, after we returned home, I took a long walk into the city to collect my thoughts. Naples was beautiful that day. The sun was shining, and the water was its usual deep blue. I thought about breaking up, sending Kimmy back to New York. It seemed a simpler solution than trying to make our relationship work.

Was I wrong to like my single life? I had a great life! Did I really need a woman to somehow make it better? I didn't have the answer to that question. I suppose I wasn't ready to give Kimmy up. I was still addicted, and so I chose to have it both ways.

When I returned to the house, Kimmy was finally out of bed and now sitting with Maria and Rosa in the garden sipping coffee. The twinkle in her eyes had returned. Maybe she wasn't mad at me after all.

"I was wondering where you went?" She replied. I thought about telling her the reason for my walk but instead decided to lie.

"I went to buy some of your favorite cheese;" I responded, pulling two small Scamorza cheeses from a plastic bag. Kimmy liked Scamorza, particularly the smoked variety. In the States, Scamorza is known as Provolone. They often hung from the ceiling in the salumeria, resembling tiny little sacks.

They were particularly good when roasted slightly on the grill. It would make the cheese inside the sack melt, making it good to spread on crackers. "I bought these for the party tonight," I exclaimed, proud of my purchase.

"Why wait until the party?" Kimmy replied. Soon we shifted from coffee to wine and cheese, sharing our afternoon snack with Maria, Rosa, and their St Bernard dog, Bari.

"Do you know that we are related?" Kimmy asked.

"Who is related?" I answered.

"Maria and I," Kimmy replied. "It turns out that Maria's husband was a 2nd cousin of my grandmother." This was interesting news.

"Does this mean your visa issues are resolved?" I asked.

"Perhaps," Kimmy replied. "It certainly offers us more options."

I had looked at the possibility of obtaining a Sojourner's Permit for Kimmy and had determined it was not possible. There was no category available for live-in girlfriend or common-law wife. It seemed to me that Italy, the "land of amore," should have been more accommodating. I couldn't be the only man with this problem, I thought. The only way I could obtain a permit for Kimmy was to marry her. It was the one thing I wasn't ready to do. If she could solve her immigration problems on her own, it would remove that thorny issue as a pressure point in our relationship.

ROBBIE'S NEW YEAR'S EVE

Harry, Kimmy & I left for the Navy Legal Service Office New Year's Eve party around 8:00 pm. Kimmy really looked nice in her red cocktail dress. She was especially hot looking that night. It was only a short distance to Captain Simpson's apartment on Via Manzoni, but we decided to drive anyway. In retrospect, we should have walked the two miles, but I was worried Kimmy would catch a cold.

Finding a place to park near the apartment was exceedingly difficult, as all the available spots were under balconies. Both Harry & I had been warned beforehand not to park under a balcony. The last lawyer who did so the previous year had returned to find a sofa lying on the hood of his car.

In the end, after much searching, the only empty parking space we could find was a spot next to a trash receptacle. It was not the typical metal trash receptacle but one of the new green plastic models. As I parked the car, this seemed an ill omen.

Ever since the city had changed the trash contractor, the new green cans had been catching fire. It was a predictable outcome. The new Mayor had pledged to clean up the city by removing the local crime lords from the trash collection business.

Ever since the contract change, chaos had ensued. Sanitation workers went on strike, and trash cans caught fire. Whoever had the idea of buying flammable plastic cans needed to have their head examined. Not only did they burn, but they left behind molten globs of green plastic stuck to the pavement, creating axle-breaking speedbumps across the city.

When we arrived at the party, we found the penthouse apartment full of people. It seemed the entire military community in Naples had crashed the party. As we walked out onto the roof terrace, it became clear why. Captain Simpson's apartment enjoyed one of the best views of Naples.

On the north side of the roof, we could see the densely packed Fuorigrotta quarter, a literal sea of high-rise apartment buildings housing 70,000 people surrounding the soccer stadium.

Towards the west of Fuorigrotta stood the now abandoned wasteland of the steel mill, its many rusting blast furnace towers blocking our view of the NATO base in Bagnoli on the opposite side. Beyond the steel mill, we could view the Agnano volcanic crater, (Where the U.S. Navy base was located), as well as the city of Pozzuoli and the islands of Procida and Ischia.

On the south side of the roof, we could see the grandest spectacle of all, a sweeping vista of the Bay of Naples from the Island of Capri to the slopes of Vesuvius. We were now ready for the fireworks. Unfortunately, we would have to wait another three hours.

After taking in the view, we returned inside. It was too cold and windy to spend three hours standing on the roof. I could see that Kimmy was shivering, her bare arms covered with goosebumps. Once inside, we joined a poker game, drinking beer and smoking big cigars. Even Kimmy joined the fun, lighting up a stogey.

Soon she was whipping our asses as usual. Kimmy had always been a great poker player. She seemed eternally lucky in cards, constantly beating my roommates and me in college. Who would think that my girly-girl could hold her own with the boys in a poker game? That was part of her charm. Kimmy could be a chameleon.

As I watched her bluffing her way through yet another bad hand, I couldn't help admiring her beauty. I certainly knew how to pick them. I could not wait to get her home to remove that little red dress.

Once I lost my last dollar in poker to Kimmy, we changed games, proceeding to the quarter bounce table, where we took turns bouncing quarters into glasses of beer. Kimmy, as usual, kept winning. She was a champion at this game, too. Every time she bounced the quarter into the glass, she made me drink. By the time the fireworks began, I was no longer in any shape to drive. Kimmy would have to drive us home. Looking at my watch, I saw it was now 11:40 pm.

Walking back out onto the roof, we watched the fireworks begin. First, there were random pops here and there as Roman candles went off sporadically around the city. As we counted down the clock till midnight, the fireworks grew in intensity filling the night sky on all sides until great clouds of smoke obscured our view. It seemed the entire city was ablaze with Roman candles. Looking below, we could see fireworks shooting off balconies below us like salvos from a battleship. This must be an awful night for the fire department, I thought.

New Year's Eve fireworks in Naples were not like in New York. It was not a structured municipal event supervised by the fire department. Instead, it was complete chaos without regard to life, limb, or property. The fireworks were both amazing and scary to watch. The celebration continued for an hour as the citizens of the city disposed of millions of fireworks all at once in an uncontrolled roar. In the distance, I could see similar celebrations across the bay and on the islands. Everyone was celebrating the New Year, even boats out on the bay.

It was not until 1:30 in the morning before it was safe to venture from our rooftop to the street. When we stepped out of the building, we entered a world of honking cars. Everyone was now driving home, and the city was hopelessly gridlocked. As we walked towards the car, we saw sofas and chairs lying in the street, as well as the spent remains of thousands of fireworks. At one point, we passed a car that had caught fire. A Roman candle had landed between the car and the nearby stone wall, setting it ablaze.

Seeing the car, I had a sinking feeling in the pit of my stomach. I wondered what my car might look like, parked as it was, next to the flammable trash can.

Five hundred yards later, down the road we rounded a bend, and I got my answer. In front of us sat the blackened, smoldering remains of my car. The once ugly car was now a smoking ruin. Even the tires had burned.

Turning towards Kimmy, I asked the question most important on my mind. "Did you remove the new electric blanket from the trunk? I asked.

"Yes," Kimmy replied! Kimmy smiled. I felt awful but also good at the same time. At least the new electric blanket was saved, I thought! So much for the ring, however. I would now need to spend the remainder of my life savings to buy a new car.

That night we walked home from the New Year's party, arriving back at the house by 2:30 am. We arrived home quicker by walking than had we driven in the car.

The personal party I had dreamed of earlier in the evening no longer mattered to me. Kimmy slept upstairs under the new electric blanket while I sat downstairs on the sofa staring into the fireplace. I could not sleep; the thought of my burned-out car was freshly seared into my brain. The 1990s were not off to a great start.

CHAPTER 22:

SLEEPING ARRANGEMENTS

DAVID'S WINTER

After our New Year's Eve in Prague, my relationship with Elsa entered a new phase. Like all relationships, ours could not remain on the emotional mountain top forever. Following our return to Naples, we decided to spend more time apart. It was not that we decided to break up, but rather that we mutually agreed to give our relationship "breathing room." I suppose we each needed our privacy.

Living together in Elsa's apartment had been challenging. The apartment was tiny, less than four hundred square feet total, on two floors. It was not sufficient space for three people. While I was not an official resident, I was spending a lot of time there.

I enjoyed Elsa's company. We were natural together, but I didn't necessarily enjoy living with Elsa's roommate Antonella. Antonella thought mostly of Antonella and not of anyone else. From the start, she made it clear; I was living in her house and at her pleasure.

Separately Elsa and Antonella were tidy; however, living together, they were slobs. One seemed to rub off on the other. I could see that Elsa was frustrated, however, there was little she could do. Antonella was a best friend from childhood, a person whose friendship Elsa needed. Antonella's family was Elsa's ticket to a life in Naples. I was still a luxury.

When Elsa confided she needed her privacy, hinting my occasional overnight presence was creating problems with her roommate, she didn't need to ask twice. I went home.

I had come to realize why Antonella chose to live in the pool house rather than the main house. The answer, of course, lay with Antonella's boyfriend, Tony. Antonella lived separately from her parents for one reason and one reason only, so she could sleep with Tony.

When Tony came to visit, Elsa and I were expected to retire to Elsa's bedroom. This was the unwritten rule adopted when Elsa and Antonella first became roommates. At first, it was an inconvenience, but as time went by, it became a major annoyance as Tony would show up unannounced at any hour of the day or night.

Elsa would later confide that Antonella's relationship with Tony made life in the one room Spanish Quarter apartment untenable. There was simply no place to go when Elsa needed to leave. In those days, Tony often came to visit, sometimes in the middle of the night after both girls had gone to bed.

When Tony arrived, Elsa was obliged to leave the apartment until Tony and Antonella finished. Elsa hated walking the streets of the Spanish Quarter after dark. She would check into the small one-star pensione nearby for 35,000 lire per night. Doing so ate up a lot of her money. She could not afford to purchase a proper hotel room at one of the better hotels. Once, in late July, Elsa spent the night sleeping on a park bench in the Villa Comunale Park. She was out of money. It was the last straw.

"Why did you put up with that arrangement?" I asked. "Why didn't Antonella go to Tony's house?"

"I don't know," Elsa replied. "He always came to her."

It sounded to me as if Tony might be married. "Do you think he is married?" I asked.

"Yes," Elsa replied. "I have shared this concern with Antonella often. She, however, is in denial, unwilling to accept that possibility."

It was during the sleepless night on the park bench that Elsa decided to move out. "I had enough," Elsa confided. "I stood up to Antonella, forcing her to take her relationship with Tony on the road. If she wanted to sleep with Tony, she would have to do so in his car up on Via Manzoni, like so many other Neapolitans."

"Did she take the show on the road?" I asked.

"No," Elsa replied. "She was afraid of her parents. Via Manzoni was too close to their house."

"Was she afraid that someone might recognize her car?" I asked.

"No," Elsa replied. "Charles and Silvana know Antonella is having sex with Tony. They don't seem to care. Antonella was afraid she might embarrass her parents. She was afraid one of their friends might see her there."

"So, what happened?" I asked.

"We compromised" Elsa replied. "We moved to Antonella's parents' pool house. Its' much cheaper to live there than in the apartment. Antonella's father is letting us live there for free until he rents it. I now have my own bedroom. We no longer need to share a bedroom. When Tony arrives, they go to Antonella's bedroom. If the noise gets too loud, I simply retire to my bedroom, shut the door, and insert my earplugs." It was a strange existence.

Returning to my home was refreshing. We still had our occasional drama, but it was nothing compared to the continuous drama of living with Antonella. It was nice to sleep in my own bed again. Sleeping in the bean bag chair was giving me a backache.

Returning home also solved another growing problem, the conflict-of-interest problem caused by sleeping in a house owned by one of my contractors. Charles and Silvana were nice people, but I did not feel comfortable accepting their hospitality on a regular basis. Perhaps it was his deep raspy voice, but Charles reminded me too much of "The Godfather."

Sleeping in my own bed in an unheated house brought new challenges, however. I reminded myself that people had lived for centuries in colder climates than in Italy. Most of my ancestors came from Great Britain. Certainly, I could figure this out, I thought.

I would learn to rediscover old techniques for keeping warm in a house without heat. First, I covered the bed with every blanket I owned. I even unzipped my old sleeping bag and laid that on top as well. The sheer weight of the blankets kept me from moving during the night. However, I was still cold.

To keep my head warm, I added a winter stocking cap to my already considerable apparel, looking like a character from a Charles Dickens novel. I even wore gloves to bed, but still, I was cold.

Then I rediscovered a trick from the past. I purchased a bed warming pan from a local antique market. It was made of brass and had a long wooden handle. I would fill the pan with warm coals from Robbie's charcoal grill and then slip the pan between the bedsheets before going to bed. The trick was to move the closed pan quickly between the sheets like an electric iron (so as not to scorch anything). Afterward, I would empty the contents back into the charcoal grill.

Preheating the bed was the answer. The effect did not last all night, of course, but it did ease the initial shock I felt when sliding into a freezing cold bed. The real solution was to sleep with someone. However, that solution was still not possible.

Once I figured out how to get the bed warm, getting up in the morning became the hardest task. From the moment I pulled back the covers, I raced to get dressed and out of the house into the warm car as soon as possible. I tried taking a shower in the freezing cold bathroom once and resolved never to make that mistake again. Someone had turned the water heater off. The experience was like jumping into Lake Michigan in the winter. It was one of the coldest experiences of my life. I learned my lesson. Thereafter I showered and shaved at the gym on base.

JULIE'S ELECTRICAL PROBLEMS

Following the Christmas Holiday, Harry agreed to let me use his electric blanket. I was still working the night shift, and the blanket allowed me to sleep with comfort during the morning hours after my shift. Unfortunately, it also sometimes tripped the main electric panel, revealing a problem with the house.

While the house was large, the electrical service was not. This was not a problem unique to our house but rather a problem faced by many Neapolitan households. The standard electrical service for any house or apartment was 3 kW. Our house had an upgraded 6 Kw service, but that was not enough given the size of the house and the many constantly humming transformers installed by previous residents.

Somehow, they had rewired the house, transforming the normal 220v Italian house into a partial 110v American firetrap. They didn't, however, change or label the outlets, which all had 220v receptacles. We were just supposed to know which was which.

The power to our house was often erratic. The voltage constantly fluctuated, causing anything digital to constantly reset. My 220v electric bedroom alarm clock proved useless. Soon I replaced it with a tiny battery-powered alarm clock.

Sometimes, we could see the power fluctuations at night. The lights would brighten and then dim often. Somewhere far away, I pictured a nuclear reactor control panel with red lights flashing, abandoned by its operators, while they watched a soccer match on TV.

Armed with a box of adapters, freely available at the "Country store," the Navy Exchange's equivalent of a hardware store, I experimented with the outlets in my bedroom. I had a transformer in my room but didn't know which outlets it served. I should have bought an electrical tester but instead decided to conduct the test with something I cared about, my new boombox stereo. When I plugged the stereo into the outlet, sparks flew, transforming my new stereo into a boat anchor. After that, I was much more careful.

During the day, we could only run four items at once, not five. For instance, we could run the two water heaters, the refrigerator, and the TV all at the same time. We could not, however, also run the microwave. This meant we would have to turn something off to turn something else on. There were additional caveats that kicked in when the blanket was in use. The rule of four turned into the rule of three.

This led to unexpected, sometimes comical results. One particular result was that Kimmy kept the water heaters off, creating unexpected surprises for anyone wanting to take a shower in the morning. More than once, I heard someone let loose a string of expletives when they turned on the shower only to be unexpectedly doused with freezing water. Fortunately, Kimmy sometimes caught herself by surprise, causing the rest of us to laugh. If you wanted to take a shower, you needed to turn on the small 10-liter water heater a half-hour beforehand.

During the winter, the rule of four was further reduced to the rule of two when running the two electric blankets at the same time. This meant the water heaters were always turned off at night, as well as the refrigerator. I wish we could have figured out how to turn the transformers off, but we were never able to solve that puzzle. Harry tried to navigate the tumbleweed of wires above the kitchen cabinet (where the main transformer was installed) but was unable to decipher it. It seemed there was no main switch controlling the transformers. They seemed to be connected directly to the main breaker.

Thursday mornings were the most difficult. This was the day that the washer and iron were in use. Fausta, our maid, would arrive at 8:00 am and take over the house. She would clean the kitchen, do the laundry, and mop the floors. The weekly ritual would end in the afternoon by 2:00 pm. Fausta's services were not cheap, costing the boys 200,000 lire per week, but they were essential. Without Fausta's services, the house would quickly become very dirty.

The problem was the air. The air in Naples was dirty. It wasn't just the auto exhaust causing the problem. It was also the volcanic ash soil itself. Once it got on your clothes, it was difficult to remove. The air proved to be a problem for many American servicemembers living in Naples. Children who never had respiratory problems at home sometimes developed asthma while living in Naples.

Between the washing, ironing, and cleaning, Fausta took complete control of the electricity, running it like she was running a railroad. No one got to turn anything on without Fausta's permission. If you did, you got "the look." From the moment she arrived until the moment she left Fausta was a perpetual motion machine. She was also a condition of the lease and, of course, not included in the rent.

As Harry would learn, there were many lease conditions not spelled out in the contract. These tended to change whenever Maria wanted to change them. The additional unwritten clauses included Christmas bonuses for Rosa (who swept the garden), Mario, the gardener who serenaded us once a week with O Sole Mio, Luigi, who parked his vegetable cart in front of the driveway (because he was a nice man) and Pasquale who guarded the Italian soccer team across the street. There was also the annual "parking tax" of two million lire per year (sometimes paid more than once per year) which went to who knows who.

Fortunately, we did not have to pay someone to fill the oil tank, as I heard horror stories about that experience from other people working at the hospital. Nothing ruined Christmas more than an unexpected four million lire bill to fill the heating oil tank.

From the beginning, Fausta made sure Kimmy and I knew the terms of her unwritten contract (i.e., what was not included). She only cleaned for the three roommates, not "the guests." We had to pay extra if we wanted service. I agreed to pay the additional 50,000 lire per week. It seemed a small price to pay to avoid spending an afternoon sitting at the base laundromat. Kimmy, however, refused to pay, as she never had any money. Instead, she slipped her laundry into my laundry basket before Fausta arrived. I caught her once doing this but decided not to press the issue. If Fausta did not object, I would not object either. Fausta never figured out that Kimmy was not my size.

Back to our electrical constraints. As I said before, on the coldest winter nights, the rule of four turned into the rule of two and a half. Apparently, electric blankets use a lot of juice. We could only run two electric blankets at night. If we even turned on the lights, the circuit breaker would pop. Kimmy learned this condition one particularly chilly night and made a command decision for everyone, deciding to turn off the refrigerator. She reasoned that the refrigerator didn't need to run when it was 40 degrees in the house.

Unfortunately, she forgot to plug the frig in the next morning, leading Harry, Robbie, and David to think the refrigerator was broken. I will never forget the look I received when I showed them how to fix the refrigerator. I reached behind the refrigerator, pulled it away from the wall, and plugged it in, as they stood there dumbfounded. I never told them that Kimmy was the gremlin that kept turning things off. That would be our little secret.

SHARING THE BLANKET WITH HARRY

Beginning in February, my relationship with Harry changed. I stopped working shifts in the emergency room and began working days. During the first week, I tried to sleep in my bed alone, following the strategies David used. I even borrowed his bed warmer, which unfortunately scorched my bedsheets. I did not realize that I needed to move the warmer around.

After my attempt to burn down the bed, I resolved to buy myself a kerosene heater. That option, unfortunately, did little to heat the room, as I needed to keep the bedroom window open all night to vent the heater.

As an aside, there is no way to open a French door onto a balcony just a little. It's either all the way open or all the way closed. I learned this the hard way one night when the door closed on its own. Apparently, the wind picked up outside. After nearly killing myself with carbon monoxide, I decided to retire the heater. I needed another solution.

As usual, Harry offered a remedy. He offered to let me sleep with him in his king-size bed. We had tried this before on Christmas day; however, sleeping together every day seemed a bridge too far.

"What's the big deal?" Harry replied. "My bed is enormous, large enough for a family of four."

Harry did have a point. His king-size bed was larger than the dorm room I shared with a roommate in college. In the end, I relented. My desire to stay warm trumped my fears of sharing a bed with Harry. I agreed to the arrangement, provided Harry kept his body parts on his side of the bed. Harry agreed.

We agreed to share the bed without having sex. We agreed that men and women could be friends. We even adopted an additional rule. Namely that having sex might ruin our friendship. We could sleep together without "sleeping together." We hadn't seen the scene from "Seinfeld" yet, where Jerry and Elaine decide that they need to have sex for the sake of their friendship.

Remaining on my side of the bed, however, proved a challenge, not for Harry but for me. I love to constantly turn over (like a rotisserie chicken, as Harry says) when I sleep. While my brain agreed to our division of the real estate, my limbs were not a party to the agreement. They had a mind of their own.

After two nights of trying to keep to our bargain, we dispensed with the notion that there was an invisible wall within the bed. Harry kept his third while I claimed the remaining two-thirds and sometimes all the covers. Harry did not seem to mind. Our relationship was evolving.

CHAPTER 23:

SNOWS ON VESUVIUS

KIMMY'S STORY

It was still dark outside when I awoke; my toes were so cold they were beginning to go numb. The electric blanket was off again. The power must have tripped again! Climbing out of bed, I groped in the dark for my winter coat and slippers. I hated having to go outside to the electrical closet to press the reset button. However, it was my turn. Robbie had pressed the reset button the last time the power tripped.

Looking over towards Robbie, I saw he was still asleep. My personal Harrison Ford looked so cute in his Santa hat. Seeing that hat always brought a smile to my face. He had his choice of stocking caps to wear to bed, and yet he always chose the red and white Santa hat.

As I fumbled in the dark looking for my glasses, I heard the noise of voices downstairs in the living room. The lights were on, and the T.V. was blaring. It seemed the problem wasn't the power; it was our blanket. Turning on the bedroom light, I peered under the covers at the end of the bed, finding the source of my cold feet. The blanket was unplugged again. Thank goodness it was not broken, I thought. I felt relieved.

"What's wrong?" Robbie asked, rubbing his eyes.

"Did you do this?" I asked, holding up the plug.

"Yes," Robbie replied sheepishly, "the bed was too warm."

Robbie and I were always doing this to each other. When I was cold, he was hot, and when I was hot, he was cold. Our internal thermostats were out of sync.

"Can I plug it back in?" I asked.

"Sure," Robbie replied. "It is a bit nippy."

Soon we were back in bed snuggling. That is until Robbie tried to kiss me. His breath almost melted my stocking cap. He had eaten too much garlic the night before.

"No thanks," I replied, "go brush your teeth first."

"Your loss," he replied, mumbling to himself as he rolled over on his side, showing me his back. Glancing at the tiny alarm clock on the nightstand, I saw it was 6:00 am. It was too early to get up.

When I awoke again, it was 8:30 am, Sunday morning and time to get up. I dressed, ready to begin the day, while Robbie continued to saw wood.

"Get up, lazy head," I remarked as I jerked back the covers to let in the cold.

"Why did you do that?" Robbie exclaimed, grabbing them back. He didn't seem to want to get up.

"I'm hungry" I exclaimed! "Let's go to the base for breakfast. I need to get out of this cold house!" The last thing I wanted to do was spend all day sitting around the cold house. We needed to get out and do something, anything, besides sit in front of the T.V. and watch football!

It took some further prodding to get Robbie up, but once he got dressed, he was eager to depart. Soon we were on our way to the base in our new little car.

After our dreadful New Year's Eve, Robby and I bought the only car for sale on the base, a 1960s dark blue Fiat Five Hundred. It was what the Italians referred to as a Cinquecento.

Our little Fiat was the smallest, cutest car I had ever seen. I had no problem fitting in the car, however Robbie looked rather comical driving it. He had to place his knees on either side of the steering wheel because they would not fit under it.

I had no problem driving the car myself. It was fun however to watch Robbie drive the car. His head kept hitting the ceiling every time we hit a bump. Fortunately, the car had a sunroof we could open if the road got too bumpy. It was also easy to park. I could park it anywhere.

We bought the car for $1500. Robbie only had $500 left to his name, so I contributed the rest. It was our first major purchase together as a couple.

That morning, we joined a dozen other American families at the base for breakfast, eating our usual cinnamon rolls with jumbo cups of American coffee.

"What do you want to do today?" Robbie asked. Delightfully, he had forgotten it was football day.

"Let's see the snow," I replied.

I noticed that Vesuvius was covered with snow that morning and wanted to see it. It was supposed to be a rare event that only occurred perhaps once a year. Winter was not winter without a little snow.

Soon we were on our way, still sipping our coffee as we departed the base. The Tangenziale, which was normally crowded, was empty that morning.

That morning, we gave our little four-wheeled baby the mountain climbing test. As we drove up the mountain through the barren landscape, I learned for the first time that Vesuvius was a mountain within a larger crater known as Monte Somma. Monte Somma was the original mountain blown apart in 79 A.D. during the eruption which destroyed Pompeii. Vesuvius was its child.

After we left the crowded towns surrounding the base of the mountain, we passed through vineyards until we reached the floor of the Monte Somma crater. Suddenly the landscape changed from one of lush greenery to barren rock.

Robbie focused on the road ahead while I read from the travel book. "This lava flow dates to 1944," I explained, pointing towards the bleak, blackened, barren rock beside us. The rock was not flat but instead looked like twisted ropes with chunks of rock embedded within. There was no plant life, only small patches of lichen attempting to gain a foothold.

Stopping beside the road, we got out to take a closer look and take pictures while walking on the lava flow. It was bitter cold, but we had still not reached the snow, which was now clearly visible nearby, on the slopes of the taller Vesuvius.

I needed to tell Robbie something that day, something I dreaded discussing but needed to deal with. My birth control pills were almost gone. I needed to know Robbie's intentions but did not know how to ask. I was having second thoughts about my plan to become pregnant. Trapping Robbie into marriage no longer seemed like a clever idea.

"I wonder how far this road goes?" Robbie inquired, as we started back up the mountain.

"I hope it goes to the top," I replied.

Soon we discovered the answer to our question. The road ended at a parking lot, one thousand feet below the summit. We would need to walk the rest of the way to reach the summit.

Gazing up towards the mountain, for the first time, we saw steam rising from the crater. Somewhere beneath our feet lay a pool of molten rock. Vesuvius may be sleeping, but she was still alive.

The climb to the top took thirty to forty-five minutes, the trail appearing steeper from the parking lot than it was in real life. We were now walking up a gentle slope covered with reddish-brown volcanic ash. I thought the trail might be slippery however it was not. It felt good to stretch my legs. We climbed the mountain in silence, stopping several times to take pictures, admiring the view.

I thought it would be windy and cold, but remarkably the air was calm and warming. Soon we opened our coats and removed our stocking caps. It was beginning to get warm. The sun was shining bright. The snow would soon melt and disappear.

We expected a coating of heavy snow on the ground but found only a light dusting instead. It was less than a half inch thick. The white blanket of snow that I saw from our balcony was more like a veil. It was a soon to disappear illusion.

At one point, I smiled at Robby, picked up a handful of snow and made a snowball while he did the same. I threw the snowball at him. It was not as fun as I remembered. When we reached the summit, we found that the trail continued for another mile along the rim.

"Do you want to keep going?" I asked.

"Yes," Robbie replied.

The view from this height was extraordinary. Below us sprawled the city, stretching far north, towards the horizon. This was not the sight that captured our attention, however. Beside us, far below, we could see the steam rising from the floor of the crater. Vesuvius was no ordinary mountain. It was a deep and impressive volcano. We had entered the realm of the gods.

Looking deep into the throat of the volcano, we could, at last, see the source of the steam. There were hundreds of fumaroles on the sides of the crater, venting their heated air into the wintry morning sky. Vesuvius was sleeping. We dared not wake it up.

"I hope this thing never erupts while we live here," Robbie remarked.

"I agree," I replied. It was an awesome sight.

I thought of broaching the topic I needed to discuss but decided not to, while we stood on the edge of an eight-hundred-foot cliff. Better to discuss on the way down, I thought. As we walked back to the car, I finally mustered the nerve to begin the conversation I had avoided for weeks.

"Robbie, do you love me?" I asked. Robbie stopped walking and turned to face me.

"Why are you bringing this up?" He replied. "Of course," he replied. He dismissed my question out of hand.

I noticed, as usual, that he didn't use the "L" word. He never did. Not once in the six and a half years that I had known Robbie did he ever tell me that he loved me. It seemed as if his whole suit of armor might fall off if he said the word. Why was it so hard for Robbie to admit he loved me?

For the next several minutes, we were completely silent as we walked down the mountain. Then he asked a question. "What is this about?" He asked. "I can tell that something is bothering you. You've been giving me the silent treatment since New Year's. What's eating you? Are you still angry about the ring? I told you I cannot afford an engagement ring right now!"

I was sick of the ring conversation. It was an excuse that drove me crazy. It was time to take the ring off the table. "Screw the ring, I exclaimed! We don't need a ring. I would marry you today without the ring." For a moment, Robbie stared at me with a puzzled expression on his face.

"I love you, Robbie," I said! "I want to spend my life with you. I want to have children with you. This is not about the ring! Do you love me!"

There was more silence as Robbie searched for words. I had just offered him my entire life, without condition, and yet it didn't seem enough. At last, he finally spoke honestly with me, or so it seemed.

"I don't know," Robbie replied. "All of this is moving too fast. You tell me you are not ready to get married, we live apart for two years while you go to graduate school, and then you reappear and suddenly want to pick up where we left off. The world doesn't work that way, Kimmy!" He was clearly worked up; his face was now turning red. "I cannot turn it on and off, like a switch," Robbie replied.

"Is there someone else?" I asked.

"No," Robbie replied. "You know the answer to that question. Why do you even ask it?"

"Is there something wrong with me?" I asked.

"No," Robbie replied, "it's not about you. It is about me!" Robbie was losing me. I didn't understand where this was going, but I sensed he was not telling me the real reason. He was holding something back.

"Robbie, what would you say, If I told you I am pregnant?" I asked.

There it was, I dropped the hypothetical bombshell. The question I needed to ask. I wasn't, of course, pregnant, but I needed to know the answer to that question before I got pregnant. Would our child have a father, or would Robbie abandon us?

Robbie did not respond to my question but instead looked at the ground as we continued our walk down the mountain. I had hit him squarely between the eyes. After about twenty minutes of walking, we stopped at a bench and sat down. Robbie was finally able to respond to my question.

"Are you pregnant?" Robbie asked.

"No," I replied. "I just wanted to know what you might say."

For a moment, Robbie looked relieved. "Good," Robbie replied!

I had hoped he might show a little excitement at the news, but instead, he did not. It was incredibly disappointing. We had been playing house now for four months, having sex every day. Eventually, it would happen, even if we tried to prevent it. We couldn't keep lighting matches without eventually starting a fire.

For a moment, we sat on the bench incredibly quiet. Then I asked my next question. "Don't you want children?" I asked.

"I don't know," Robbie replied. "I'm not ready to be tied down yet. I thought you wanted to see the world first."

"I do," I replied, "but we can do that with children. This base is full of young couples just like us. Many have children. Having a child doesn't mean we have to give up our dreams."

"I know," Robbie replied. "I'm just not sure I'm ready. I'm not sure I am ready for the responsibility."

I wondered as he said this whether he didn't want children at all or whether he really meant he didn't want children with me. I suspected the answer to that question was the latter. Maybe I wasn't good enough for Robbie. Perhaps I had a fundamental flaw that prevented Robbie from loving me. As I sat there pondering, I tried to hold back the tears. It was a pointless gesture, however, as soon the waterworks were flowing.

"What's wrong?" Robbie asked. He reached into his pocket to find a tissue. Sometimes Robbie could be very supportive. I couldn't tell Robbie the real reason I was crying, so I told him something else.

"Robbie, I am almost out of birth control pills," I replied. "I forgot to get more while we were in New York."

"How many pills do you have left?" Robbie asked.

"One," I replied. "Tomorrow we will run out."

For a moment, he sat in stunned silence, realizing his playground was about to close. Robbie loved having sex.

"Can't you get more?" He asked.

"Perhaps," I replied, "but I don't know any Italian doctors. Can you get me an appointment at the base hospital?"

"No," Robby replied firmly. "The hospital is for DoD service members and their families only. Can't you ask Julie?" He asked. "She is a doctor." I hadn't thought about asking Julie.

"This problem seems solvable," Robbie replied. He was now acting quite sure of himself. "Ask Julie to get you more pills," he exclaimed! His voice was now commanding as if somehow, he owned me.

At that moment, I suddenly found Robbie very ugly. I wasn't sure anymore that I wanted to get more pills. He was talking about my body. I had the right to close the playground at any time for any reason.

"Dammit, Robbie," I exclaimed! "This is not about the pills. I am tired of being your sex object. I'm a flesh and blood real person, just like you. Do you want to marry me, yes or no?"

For a moment, Robbie stopped talking, thunderstruck. I was forcing him to finally decide. It was clearly a decision he was not ready to make. Instead, he punted. "Do we really need to discuss this right now?" He asked, changing the subject. "I am hungry; let's drive to Ravello for lunch!"

Robbie knew my soft spot. I loved eating Sunday dinner in Ravello. It was hard to resist his smile when he turned on the charm. "I guess not," I replied, my stomach reminding me that it needed to be fed. "We can discuss this some other day." What a stupid thing to say! I lost my nerve. I guess I was not ready to walk away after all.

As we climbed into the car and began to drive down the mountain, I remembered a piece of advice my grandmother had given me back at Christmas. It was a piece of advice I had forgotten. "Don't ever show your hand," she said, "unless you are willing to play it. Marriage is for keeps," she said. "It is not a game. The course of your entire life will change based on the marriage decisions you make."

As we drove down the mountain and onto Ravello, I finally realized Robbie, and I might never get married. I was not ready to accept it yet, but the realization had finally begun to take root, like the lichen growing on the lava flow. I would never again allow myself to be so vulnerable with Robbie. I would never again give him an ultimatum. Instead, I began the process of letting go.

CHAPTER 24:

WEEKEND IN ROME

It was an ordinary Friday afternoon in February when Elsa phoned me at work, inviting me to spend a weekend with her in Rome. Elsa had the opportunity to visit the Necropolis under the Vatican with one of her professors and wanted some company. I wasn't necessarily interested in touring another underground cemetery; however, when Elsa mentioned we might see St Peter's bones, it perked my interest. "Please invite your roommates," Elsa added, just before she hung up the phone.

After our phone call, I proceeded up the stairs to the next floor to find Harry and Robbie. Robbie declined to attend. He planned to spend the weekend in Siena with Kimmy. Harry seemed interested but decided to call Julie first to confirm she would be off work. Within a few minutes, all was confirmed. Julie was available.

"Do you know a place to stay near the Vatican?" I asked.

"No," Harry replied, "but I have heard of a pensione nearby, frequented by Americans from the base. It's not really a pensione per se, but a hostel for religious pilgrims."

"That sounds ok to me," I replied.

Harry looked in his telephone book for the number and gave the pensione a call. On the other end of the line, I could hear someone pick up the phone. "Pronto, this is Sister Mary Margaret," a woman replied.

"I am calling to see if you have some rooms for tomorrow night," Harry responded.

"Yes," the woman replied. "How many rooms do you need?"

Harry looked at me for a command decision. Did we need two rooms or four?" He asked. I decided on two rooms, figuring four rooms might be hard to get on such short notice.

"I need two rooms to sleep two people each," Harry replied.

"Married or single?" The voice asked.

Holding his hand over the receiver, Harry sought my opinion. "Why should it matter?" I replied.

"Single," Harry replied. It seemed bad form to lie to a nun.

After Harry's reply, there was a moment of silence; then, the cheery voice returned to the phone. "We can accommodate that," the sister responded.

"How much will the rooms cost?" Harry asked.

"Fifty thousand lire per night, per room," the voice responded. It seemed to me the price was acceptable. I gave Harry a thumbs up sign.

"What about the beer?" Harry asked. This seemed an odd question.

"Can you bring us a six-pack of American beer?" The voice responded.

"Certainly," Harry replied. After the call ended, I asked Harry a question.

"What's with the beer?" I asked.

"The sisters are from Detroit," Harry replied. "The note on my phone directory said to offer them beer."

Later that afternoon, before we left for the club, I called Elsa to confirm our plans for the weekend. "Harry and I made reservations for tomorrow night at a pensione near Vatican City," I said. "Do you mind sharing a room?"

"You and me, or You, me, Harry and Julie?" Elsa replied.

It was cute; she thought all four of us might share a room. "No," I replied, "just you and me. Harry and Julie will have their own room." I could hear Elsa giggle on the other end of the phone. "Don't get any ideas," I responded. "There is one other catch."

"What is it?" Elsa asked.

"The hotel is a convent," I replied.

For a moment, there was silence on the end of the phone. Then Elsa replied, "That's ok". She sounded disappointed.

The next morning, we picked Elsa up early and proceeded to drive to Rome via the Autostrada. It was a beautiful day when we left Naples. As we drove north however, it began to rain.

Up ahead, we could see the Benedictine Abbey of Montecasino, perched on a mountaintop. It wasn't just a building on top of the mountain. The enormous structure completely covered the top of the mountain. I had read the story of the abbey in my travel book, about how there had been a major World War II battle there; but had never visited it. Perhaps some other day, I thought. I knew Harry wouldn't want to tour a monastery.

As we drove by the abbey in the pouring rain, Elsa suggested we rearrange our plans for the day. When the weather was sunny, we had planned to spend the day touring the Forum, the ruins on the Palatine Hill and the Colosseum. This is what Harry wanted to do. Instead, Elsa suggested we spend the day visiting churches and museums.

In the back seat I could hear Harry groan. Harry didn't necessarily have his own plan. Instead, he preferred to criticize Elsa's plan. This was the downside of travelling with a group. Reaching consensus on the plan was always difficult. We planned to visit the Vatican Museum and St Peter's Basilica on Sunday before our appointment with the professor at 4:00 pm. Following the tour, we would drive back to Naples.

Elsa liked to plan things. She was good at planning things. I didn't mind her planning things. She didn't however necessarily consider the opinions of others. Elsa believed, as keeper of the travel books, that she got to decide what we did.

That day Elsa was my navigator, the keeper of the maps and travel books. I would have preferred to be more spontaneous. All of Rome was a museum to me. Let's just roam around Rome, I thought. Big deal that it was raining. We had umbrellas. We wouldn't melt. Of course, we might freeze. It was cold that day.

Looking in the rearview mirror, I could see Harry and Julie looking out the windows, expressing no opinions whatsoever during the discussion between Elsa and me. They had given up trying to influence the discussion. "Do you have an opinion?" I asked.

"Any day away from the hospital is a good day for me," Julie replied. Harry pretended not to hear me.

After traveling around Rome on the G.R.A, Rome's version of a beltway, we entered the city, following the only route I was familiar with, the Via Cristoforo Columbo. The goal of our day was to reach the city center, not wander aimlessly through the suburbs.

As we drove down the wide boulevard through the modern part of the city, I asked Elsa if we were on the map yet.

"Not yet," she replied.

I had learned from a previous trip to Mexico City that maps were only helpful if you were driving roads on them. As we passed through an area of Rome known as the E.U.R. Elsa informed me we were now on the map. By this point, the rain was blowing horizontal. It seemed we had picked a dreadful day to visit Rome.

"Would you like to see something interesting?" Elsa asked.

"Sure," I replied. I was tired of driving.

"Turn left at the next light," Elsa remarked. As usual Elsa's directions came seconds after I needed them.

"You need to give me a little more warning," I replied.

"That's ok," Elsa responded. "Turn right at the next street, and we will double back."

Making any turns on the broad boulevard was difficult as the road was more of an expressway than a city street. First, I needed to get out of the main roadway onto the frontage road and then I needed to double-back around the block. For a moment I felt like I was in Mexico City again.

After looping around a block of apartment buildings, we, at last, entered the cross-street we missed previously. We were now driving east on the Via Alessandro Severo.

"Where are we going?" I asked.

"We are going to the Basilica San Paolo Fuori le Mura," Elsa replied. In the back seat I could hear Harry groan again. As she said this, the street we were traveling on ended at another busy street.

"Now what?" I asked.

"Turn right, go one block, and then turn left," Elsa replied.

A few blocks later, we found ourselves passing a hospital. "Where is the church?" I asked.

"It's behind the hospital," Elsa replied. "Turn right at the next street."

As we entered the Viale San Paolo, I could see that Elsa was correct. Behind the hospital stood a giant church. It was nice to know my new girlfriend could read a map, as my last girlfriend could not. The church was more a complex of buildings, rather than a church, and unlike many cathedrals, this church was not tightly constrained within a dense urban area but instead located within a green park.

Turning into the empty parking lot, we parked the car, turned off the engine and waited for the rain to stop. Outside, the rain was coming down in buckets while the wind buffeted our car. After several minutes waiting, Harry expressed his impatience.

"Let's get this over with," Harry exclaimed! "We all have umbrellas. How bad can this be?"

We found out soon enough. Within less than 30 seconds, three of our four umbrellas turned inside out. Giving up on the umbrella, Elsa and I ran for the entrance, using her rain poncho to cover our heads. Harry and Julie followed soon thereafter, clutching the one remaining umbrella.

When we entered the church, we entered an outdoor courtyard. In the center of the courtyard stood a tall statue of a bearded man with a sword, flanked by two tall palm trees. It was a statue of St Paul. Behind stood a pillared entrance and above the entrance rose the gilded façade of the church with the images of four saints between the three large windows. Above the windows sat a pediment with an image of Christ. Below the Christ we could see the image of a lamb with waters flowing in opposite directions from a spring. It was a beautiful sight in the pouring rain.

We walked around the portico and into the church. When we stepped inside, we entered an enormous church. It had five aisles and a high, coffered, and gilded ceiling. At the far end, we could see gilded mosaics behind the altar canopy covering St Paul's final resting place. As we stared at the great empty hall, Elsa began to relate the churches' story.

"The Basilica of St Paul's Outside the Walls is one of the four ancient Papal Basilicas in Rome," she said. "This church was founded by the Roman Emperor Constantine over the burial place of St Paul. It was dedicated in the year 324 AD. For fifteen hundred years, this church survived barbarian invasions, wars, and plagues. Unfortunately, it did not survive a catastrophic fire in 1823. Most of the ancient Basilica was destroyed. The only part of the ancient church which remains is some of the mosaics in the apse. The rest of the church is a restoration completed in the 19th century."

Marveling at the beauty of the interior, we walked slowly down the center of the nave towards the tomb of St Paul. Behind the tomb, we could now fully see the ancient, gilded mosaics restored after the fire. Elsa continued her narration.

"The mosaics were first commissioned by the Empress Gala Placida in the fifth century A.D. Portrayed in the center of the mosaics, above the main altar, is the gilded image of a hallowed Christ seated on a throne, flanked by his saints."

As I stared at the magnificent image, I remembered the story of Gala Placida, which I had read in a book previously. The woman who commissioned this art witnessed the end of the Roman world, the defeat of the armies of Atilla the Hun by the Roman General Aetius, and the sacking of Rome in 410 A.D. by Alaric, the Visigoth.

As a young woman, she had been forced to marry a barbarian chieftain. Somehow, she survived to rule the empire herself through her son. Despite everything that happened to her in her tumultuous life, she had survived to commission this beautiful work of art. I made a mental note to visit her tomb if I ever found myself in Ravenna.

When we departed the church, we found the rain had stopped. After our visit to the Church of St Paul, we proceeded into the city, passing through the ancient city walls near the ruins of the Baths of Caracalla. The gale had now reduced to a gentle drizzle.

I was now driving on a familiar route, the route that Harry and I had followed last fall, the first time we visited Rome. Up ahead loomed the Colosseum. We were now in the ancient heart of the city.

"Do we still want to visit museums or go back to the original plan?" I asked.

"Let's do the original plan," Harry replied. "It's not raining that hard anymore," he said.

Turning onto the wide Via Foro Imperiale linking the Colosseum to Rome's central square, the Piazza Venezia, I began to look for a parking place. Soon I found a space next to a statue in the small park across from the entrance to the Roman Forum. It had finally stopped raining.

As we exited the car, I marveled at the sights around us. We had parked in a field of ruins surrounding us on all sides. Near the Piazza Venezia stood the massive pile of white marble, known as the Vittoriano, a giant monument to the glory of Italy's 19th-century reunification. The structure had many nicknames. Some Italians referred to it as the "wedding cake," while others called it "Mussolini's typewriter." Nearby stood an earlier monument to past Roman military glories, Trajan's column, a structure that once stood tall but now looked like a dwarf compared to its nearby, more modern cousin.

Behind us, below the level of the street, stood the steps and columns of Augustus's Temple of Mars, a once magnificent marble temple dedicated to the Roman god of war. It was ironic that it did not survive centuries of warfare. Behind the temple of Mars sat ancient Rome's equivalent of a modern shopping mall, Trajan's market. That structure had survived virtually intact.

Across the street, we could now see a panoramic view. On the right stood an intact building that once housed the Roman Senate, a magnificent triumphal arch, the Rostrum speaker's platform where many a great speech was delivered, and the remains of temples climbing the Capitoline Hill.

Atop the hill stood the back of the Capitoline Museums. Hiding behind the museums, on the other side, stood Michelangelo's magnificent square. Towards the center and left stood the remains of the Roman Forum, seated at the base of the Palatine hill. Further towards the far left, at the end of the street, stood the Colosseum.

That morning, we toured the Roman Forum, walking amidst the ruins of the ancient city center. We admired the triumphal arches and the remaining pillars of the ancient temples. Then we walked the length of the Via Sacra under the Arch of Titus, towards the Palatine Hill.

Stopping within the arch, we could see the image of Roman soldiers carrying a Jewish[1] Menorah. The arch was commissioned in 81 A.D. to commemorate the Roman victory over the Jewish Rebellion. We were looking at history, a monument celebrating the destruction of the City of Jerusalem. It was the war that ended with the siege of the fortress Masada.

The Palatine Hill, where Rome was first settled three thousand years ago, had once been an entire neighborhood housing the most important residents of the city. Over the centuries, it had been transformed by the many emperors into a vast palace complex that covered the entire hill. The very word "palace" itself was derived from the name of this hill.

It was difficult to envision just how big the palace really was until we stood in the gardens of a small Renaissance villa on the top. It was then that we realized we were not standing on a hill but rather on the roof of the palace. As we looked over the edge, we could see a street running below through a maze of tall brick arches. This was the part of the palace built by the Roman Emperor, Tiberius.

After admiring the view from our lofty perch, we proceeded toward the other side of the hill. We had now entered the side that contained most of the palace. At the far west end sat the remains of the small house once belonging to the first Emperor, Augustus. He had lived in a modest house compared to his successors.

In the center of the hill sat the ruins of the great throne room first built by the Flavian Emperor, Vespasian, the man who commissioned the Colosseum. The only thing remaining was some brick walls and some pavements.

At the Far East end of the hill sat what looked like the remains of a large stadium, but which was more likely a large garden. As we wandered through the ruins, we noticed that the structure we were standing on was not the hill but rather another roof. Below us, we could see brick vaults, courtyards that once contained fountains, and the remains of the Circus Maximus.

I imagined what it must have been like to stand there seventeen hundred years before, watching the chariot races. We were standing somewhere near the emperors' box. It had not dawned on me that he could watch the races from inside his palace. We ended our tour of the ruins, as all tourists do, with a visit to the Colosseum.

After our tour of the Colosseum, we piled into the car and headed to the area around the Pantheon and Piazza Navona for lunch. Finding a place to park in the heart of Renaissance City was an impossible task. We got lucky, however, finding a place to park beside the river, behind the Palazzo Farnese. It was now 2:00 pm, and our stomachs were reminding us we had forgotten about them.

We ate lunch at a small outdoor café in the Piazza Navona, across the square from Bernini's Fountain of the Four Rivers. The piazza, which was one of the largest in Rome, was a long rectangular square with semi-circular ends and three magnificent fountains.

I had read previously that the square followed the outline of a stadium, built by the Emperor, Domitian, which once occupied the same spot. Many of the buildings rested on the original foundations of the stadium.

As we waited for our food to arrive, Elsa related to us the story of the fountain in front of us. The sculpture Gian Lorenzo Bernini (the same man who designed St. Peter's Square) disliked the design of the church opposite his sculpture, a church designed by his rival Borromini. To show his displeasure, he carved his sculptures so that all the faces faced away from the church. Like the sculptures, Bernini was horrified by the architecture of Borromini's church.

Elsa's Impressions of the Convent

When David told me Harry had made reservations at a convent, I was disappointed. The main reason I had invited David to accompany me had been to spend the night with him at a hotel. David and I had been dating now for seven months, and not once during that time had he shown any interest in sex.

After "the pause" in our relationship, following our trip to Prague, we hadn't spent the night together. I wasn't necessarily ready to get naked but was becoming concerned that David hadn't at least tried.

Since high school, men had always wanted to get in my pants. It had been my task to keep them out. With Sven, I had known his intentions on our second date. As my sister Kristina would say, he had "Roman hands and Russian fingers." Sven was preoccupied with sex. David, however, only seemed interested in kissing. What was his problem?

During our week together at New Year's, I had expected him to try something, but he never did. My biggest fear, of course, was that David only wanted to be "friends" and that he had no sexual interest in me. I didn't want a "friend." What I wanted was a boyfriend.

When I discussed my problem with Antonella, she suggested that David might be gay. What a horrible waste, I thought. Why were the best-looking men always gay? I hoped David was not gay. I couldn't bear the thought. Perhaps I just needed to give Mother Nature a nudge, to somehow signal to him that I was willing.

This brought me to a unique problem, a problem of my own creation. He already knew I had posed topless. Did he think I was too easy? How did I signal I was interested without signaling I was easy? I didn't want him to think badly of me and possibly break up.

Finding the convent proved challenging. When we found the street, it was, in fact, a staircase, not a street. We were somewhere near the Vatican wall; however, it was not clear how to get to the top of the stair by car. Pulling out the map, I began to study it to find a way around the stair. Within a few minutes, I found a path, a very circuitous route of one-way streets climbing up the Vatican Hill which would bring us to the top of the stair. Rome, like Naples, was created before cars.

When we finally arrived at the hotel after unintentionally exploring an entire quarter of the city, we parked behind the building, as there were no spaces near the front door. Across the street loomed the wall of Vatican City. Nearby stood a giant round tower with a large radio transmitting antenna mounted on the top. We had parked next to the Vatican radio station.

Walking back around to the front door, we knocked on the door. There were no markings indicating either a convent or a hotel was inside. I wondered if we had the right address. The only decoration on the door was the triple crown with crossed keys. We were about to enter a Vatican-owned building.

After several knocks, the door opened, revealing a woman wearing a black and white habit. "Is this the St Mary of Mercy Convent?" Harry asked.

"Yes," the woman replied, "I am Sister Mary Agnes, Buono Sera."

"I am Harry Beeman," Harry replied. "I made a reservation for tonight with Sister Mary Margaret."

Motioning for us to step inside, the sister consulted her reservation book. "Yes, I see it," she replied. "We show you reserved two rooms for one night. Are you married?" She asked.

"No," Harry replied. "We reserved the non-married rooms."

"Oh yes, I see that" the sister replied. "Follow me, and I will show you to your rooms."

We picked up our suitcases and followed the sister into the convent. It seemed like an ordinary apartment building, not anything particularly religious. Perhaps this was just a hotel, I thought.

"Are you here to see the Vatican?" She asked.

"Yes," Harry replied, "we have an appointment with the superintendent for archaeology tomorrow. He's offered to show us the Necropolis under the church."

"That sounds fascinating," the sister replied. "I have always wanted to tour under the crypt, ever since the existence of the Necropolis was first disclosed by the Pope in 1968."

We stopped in front of two doors across the hall from each other, marked Rooms 201 and 202. "Here you are," she replied. "Here are your keys." She handed us each two long skeleton keys attached to large metal medallions. "Breakfast is from 6:00 am to 8:00 am," she replied. "There is a T.V. room on the first floor if you would like to join us later."

As we stood in the hallway, Harry asked what time we should meet for dinner. "Let's meet at 7:30 pm," David replied. The restaurants did not open until 8:00 pm. We then entered the room. We had three hours to kill until dinner.

Our room was a spartan affair with a bare tile floor and beige painted walls. On either side of the room sat two narrow single beds separated by a small table with an alarm clock. The beds had no blankets, only sheets and deflated pillows. On the wall hanging over one bed was a simple cross. Behind the entrance door stood a doorway into a tiny bathroom with the smallest sink I had ever seen.

On the opposite side of the entrance door stood a small table with a large statue of the Virgin Mary. It was the most prominent fixture in the room. What a waste, I thought. The décor completely killed any chance for romance. Sitting on the bed, David and I gazed around the room. We then turned towards each other and smiled.

"Can you believe this?" David asked.

For a minute, we just absorbed the moment, and then we laughed. "What do you want to do until dinner?" David asked.

"Let's visit St Peters," I replied. The last thing either of us wanted to do was sit in the room and stare at the four walls.

"Sorry," David exclaimed; "I had no idea our room would look like this. Perhaps we can move the beds together."

I looked under the beds. Both were attached to the wall. "I'm afraid not," I replied. "The beds are attached to the wall." I was beginning to understand what came with the "unmarried" room.

Locking the door behind us, David and I left the building to find the entrance to the Vatican. It was now raining again. We retrieved David's new large umbrella from the car trunk and began our walk to the front of St Peter's Square, sharing the umbrella to keep dry. It was only a short distance from our hotel.

Walking down the stair and then around the block, we passed under Bernini's colonnade and entered the square. The piazza, which before, was filled with people, was now entirely empty. All the barricades had been removed. Walking across the square in the rain was a solitary person, a woman holding a black umbrella. I had never seen St Peter's square so empty. It was sublimely beautiful.

In front of us stood the façade of St Peter's Basilica, with Michelangelo's magnificent dome shrouded in the mist. The pavement of the square glistened in the rain, its millions of gray cobblestones now shining black. Rome was an enchanting city, especially in the rain.

On opposite sides of the piazza stood the tall Doric colonnades symbolizing the outstretched arms of the church, beckoning all to enter the great Basilica. In the center of the square stood the tall Egyptian Obelisk, which once adorned the central spine of Caligula's circus. Flanking the Obelisk on either side of the square stood two large fountains adding their gentle spray to the rain-soaked pavement.

I knew some of the history of the obelisk, which I shared with David. "The obelisk was brought to Rome from Egypt by the Emperor Caligula in 40 A.D. to adorn the Vatican Circus," I explained. "It later witnessed the terrible persecution of Christians during the reign of the Emperor, Nero. He blamed the Christians for burning Rome. It was during this persecution that St Peter was executed at the base of the obelisk. He was crucified upside-down. Before he was put to death, he is said to have made a prophecy that someday Christ would rule in that same spot forever. His prophecy came true.

"The obelisk once stood on the left side of the church in its original location. It was moved to its current location in front of the church in 1586, one hundred years before this square was built. The cross on top of the obelisk was added to symbolize Christianity's triumph over the pagan world."

As we stood there under our umbrella, David put his arms around me and gave me a kiss. "Thank you for inviting me to accompany you on this trip," David said. David had a way of making me feel warm and cozy inside. There would be other opportunities for us to "get acquainted," I thought. It was enough to just be with him.

That afternoon, we visited the church, wandering the nave, gazing up into the great dome, and then listening to the choir. The church was filled with people, and yet it seemed the church was quiet. Even the sound of the choir seemed lost in the great expanse of space. Neither of us understood a word, as the mass was in Latin, but it didn't matter. All that mattered was that we shared the moment together.

Later that evening, David and I joined Harry and Julie for dinner at a nearby restaurant. We both enjoyed discussing our interesting rooms. Our room had a statue of the Virgin Mary, their room had a statue of John the Baptist.

David ordered the house specialty, and I ordered a pizza. I should have ordered what David ordered. My pizza tasted like cardboard with red paint.

After dinner we retired to our hotel rooms. The Madonna sitting on the end table was now lit up like a giant three-foot-tall nightlight, fully illuminating the room. To make matters worse, there was no way to turn it off. It seemed the light was hardwired into the wall. That night David and I had difficulty sleeping.

In the morning, we met Julie and Harry for breakfast. "Did you figure out how to turn off the nightlight?" I asked.
"No" Julie replied, "but we did figure out how to cover it up."

"How did you do that?" David asked.

"I put my winter coat over it," Harry replied with a smile. Why hadn't we thought of that?

That morning, we ate food suitable for a convent bed and breakfast. The nuns served angel food cake with coffee. After breakfast, we checked out of our hotel, offered the nuns a six pack of beer, loaded our bags into the car trunk and set off on foot for the Vatican Museum. It was raining again.

We decided not to drive to the museum, reasoning the entrance must not be far from the hotel. We should have consulted our maps first. The entrance was far away on the opposite side of Vatican City.

Crossing through the square, we passed through the colonnade, following the signs to the museum. We passed under the ancient wall leading from the Papal Palace to the Castle San Angelo.

Above us ran the corridor once used by Popes to escape from their palace to the castle in times of trouble. As we walked along the walls of Vatican City, the rain began to pour harder. Then within about one hundred meters of the entrance, we met the end of the line. Glancing at my watch, it was still ten minutes until opening time. Fortunately, the line began to move.

Elsa Describes Exploring the Vatican Museum

When we entered the museum, the small crowd which had been in front of us dispersed into the giant museum, leaving us entirely alone. Obviously, the heavy rain was discouraging other tourists from leaving their hotels. I knew the museum would fill up once the rain stopped.

That morning we wandered the halls of the Vatican palace, all alone, exploring one of the largest museums on earth. It was not one museum but rather a collection of museums with names such as the Pio Clementino, the Chiaramonti, the Gregorio, and the Pinacoteca.

As we wandered upstairs through rooms filled with art, we entered a room with a beautiful mosaic floor and an enormous red stone basin in the center. Behind the basin, which resembled a giant birdbath, stood a monumental sculpture of a Roman emperor, the Emperor, Claudius. Reading the inscription beside the stone basin, I read that it came from Emperor Nero's palace, the Domus Aurea, "the Golden House."

After admiring Nero's birdbath, we exited the room and entered a long gallery lined with sculptures. The floor was covered once again with Roman mosaic floors, and overhead a series of windows let light into the gallery. Ahead of us, I could see Harry standing in front of a statue, a statue that looked remarkedly like Harry.

"Do you think I look like this man?" He asked. I stared at him intently, shifting my gaze back and forth between Harry and the statue. The statue was a statue of Augustus.

"Maybe if you hold your arm up like his," I suggested. No, that was not it. "Stop smiling," I suggested! "Yes, that was it." As Harry held his pose, I took a picture.

"What's his name?" Harry asked. I forgot to bring my reading glasses. There was no label on the statue, but there were some labels on the wall. Leaning over, I read the label silently to myself.

"Harry, you're in some good company here," I replied.

"Who is it?" Harry asked. Leaning over, I whispered the name in his ear.

Turning towards Julie, I asked her a question. "Do you think Harry looks like the statue?" She looked at me puzzled and then walked over towards Harry, who was still gazing up at the statue.

"Harry, turn around and look at me so that I can take your picture," Julie exclaimed!

Harry turned towards Julie, who then snapped a picture. When Julie returned to me afterward, she smiled, fanning herself with her hand. "I think he does," she replied! "I knew he was handsome; now I know why." The statue was a statue of the Emperor, Augustus, known as the Augustus of Prima Porta. We later saw copies of the statue all over Rome.

After we wandered the endless sculpture gallery past the Egyptian statues, we proceeded upstairs to the papal apartments and the Sistine Chapel. It was now getting close to lunchtime.

"Is there anything after this?" Harry asked.

"No," Julie replied, consulting her guidebook; "I think the Chapel is towards the end of the tour. According to the map, we can exit afterward between the chapel and the church."

"Good," Harry replied. "I'm starting to get hungry. A person can only absorb so much art in one day!"

As we entered the chapel, we could now see the ceiling high above us. The Sistine Chapel was empty, with only a dozen other people wandering within the vast room.

"Follow me; I have an idea," Harry instructed. Harry led us to the center of the room and bade us join him lying on the floor. Soon all four of us were lying on our backs, staring up at the ceiling. It was much better than trying to break our necks looking upward.

Above us spread the vast expanse of Michelangelo's ceiling. It was not one painting, but in fact, hundreds of paintings all woven together. My favorite was the fresco directly above us, depicting the birth of Adam. I had seen that image a thousand times before in books, but seeing it in person, made the entire trip worthwhile. It was a magnificent, breathtaking sight.

As we lay there for 10 minutes, we noticed a tour group entering the room. Soon the room was filled with people. It was time to get up before someone accidentally stepped on us. Our fun was over.

When we emerged from the museum, the rain had stopped, and the sun had come out. We lingered for a few minutes in the square, admiring the church and then decided to get some lunch. Surprisingly, there were no places to eat near the front of the church. We ended up having to walk halfway to the Tiber River to find a place to eat.

That afternoon we ate pizza-to-go at a cafeteria. Once again, my pizza resembled cardboard covered with red paint. I suppose I had become spoiled living in Naples.

After lunch, we walked back towards the church, stopping several times to visit the many religious gift shops lining the Via Della Conciliazione. The gift shops, which were owned by the Vatican, all sold the same merchandise.

There were pictures and small statues of saints, rosary beads of all shapes and sizes, crosses to hang on walls and around the neck and of course, my personal favorite, small bars of soap attached to ropes. Harry got a good laugh when I showed him the "Pope on a Rope." He bought several for friends and family.

Julie's personal favorite was the pictures of saints. She searched the entire display until she found the picture she wanted. "Is that your favorite saint?" I asked.

"Yes," Julie replied. "This is a picture of Santa Benzine, the patron saint of "gas pump jockeys.""

She then related to me a story. Once a week, she filled up her gas tank at a small gas station below the villa on Via Orazio. The gas station was not a station per se; it was more a gas pump standing beside the road, in front of the local Catholic Church.

Every time she stopped, she would be greeted by the same gas station attendant, a man named Giacomo, who would be smoking a cigarette. One day, Julie asked him how he was able to smoke while pumping gas. The man pointed towards the picture of a saint displayed in his booth, next to the no-smoking sign. "Santa Benzine protects me," he replied!

After loading up on our trinkets, we returned to the car, deposited our loot in the trunk and proceeded back to the church to meet our guide, Professor Curcio, for our afternoon tour of the catacombs. It was now approaching 4:00 pm.

Julie's Account of the Tour of the Necropolis

Harry, Elsa, David, and I, met Elsa's professor at the base of St Peter's statue at 4:00 pm, as planned. Within a few minutes thereafter, the professor escorted us past the Swiss guards and into Vatican City. As we walked towards the parking lot beyond the entrance, I could now see the new, modern Papal Audience Hall on our left. On our right stood the massive stone wall of St Peter's Basilica. In front of us stood a rusting metal walled fence. We were about to enter the excavations.

First, we entered through a metal gateway, and once inside, we stepped around a portable cement mixer and other equipment randomly scattered about. "Be careful of the mud;" I cautioned after stepping in it myself. It was too late. Elsa stepped in the mud. "Sorry about that," I said, as we waited for the professor to open the next door.

After trying several keys, he found the key to the door and pulled it open, beckoning us to follow him inside. We were now at the top of a set of concrete steps, obviously recently constructed. At the bottom of the steps was another door.

We followed the professor down the steps and waited once again for him to find the keys to the next door. After several minutes of fumbling in his pockets, he found the key he was looking for, opening the door to reveal a pitch-black space beyond.

For several seconds, the professor searched the wall beyond the door with his hand feeling for the light switch. Flicking on the switch, we then saw an ancient brick wall. "Follow me," the professor replied.

Inside the door, we entered another world, stepping back in time two thousand years. We were now under the church, walking down a narrow path between ancient brick buildings. We had entered an ancient Roman cemetery, the same type of cemetery I had seen outside the walls of Pompeii. We were not, however, on a Roman road but walking on a path between tombs. The road which once ran beside the circus had not yet, been excavated.

On either side of the path stood family tombs, which had been filled in with earth during the construction of Constantine's Basilica. Ironically, the earthen fill had preserved the tombs. I tried to imagine what this place might have been like in Roman times. The sun would have shown down on the tombs then, and we would have heard the roar of the crowds inside the nearby stadium.

Following the professor, we entered each of the tombs to hear his descriptions of what was discovered therein. Elsa and David were listening to his every word, whereas Harry and I were enjoying the tour as it was meant to be enjoyed, absorbing the sights in front of us.

The Necropolis reminded me of the excavations we had visited at Pompeii and Ercolano. In several tombs, we saw mosaic floors, which were like the floors we saw at Pompeii. We also saw the small pediment-covered altars, known as "larium," common to many Roman homes, which were used by Roman families to remember their ancestors. People would have come here to remember their dead relatives, their parents, their grandparents and even their children. They would have come here to shed tears and leave flowers.

In one of the tombs, we saw the mosaic of a man with sunbeams emerging from his head. "Is that Christ," I asked, believing we had entered an early Christian tomb.

"No," the professor replied. We think that is a depiction of the sun god Helios.

At the end of the long corridor, we entered another chamber, which in turn led to a room with a red wall. We were now under the main altar of the church. Pointing towards the wall, the professor began his dissertation.

"This is what we think remains of an early Christian tomb of St Peter," the professor replied, "and besides this wall behind the graffiti-covered wall is where the bones of St Peter were found." Staring at the wall, I could make out various symbols. I had seen some of these symbols before.

"We think people came here to visit St Peter's tomb" the professor explained. "We found many people buried near the apostles' tomb." I tried to picture this place in ancient times, having considerable difficulty, as the place had been altered significantly during the years before the first Basilica was constructed.

"Will we be able to see the bones?" Elsa asked.

"No," the professor replied. "The church has locked them away for safekeeping. I can, however, describe to you what was found." He then pointed to a niche in the graffiti-covered wall. "Do you see this writing?" He asked, pointing towards some scratches on the wall.

"Yes," Elsa replied.

"That writing indicates that Peter was buried here," the professor replied. "Within the niche behind the wall, we found the bones of a man who died in the first century A.D. He was a strong, robust man about sixty-five years of age who may have been crucified. In addition, his head was missing. This is consistent with the church tradition that St Peter's head was moved to the church of St John Lateran during the fourth century."

"Do you think the bones belonged to Peter?" I asked.

"We do not know for sure," the professor replied. "There are many differing opinions."

"What is behind the wall?" I asked.

"The well below the main altar within the church," the professor replied. "The tomb is located exactly where it should be."

As we prepared to depart, I touched the graffiti-covered wall near the place where the bones were first discovered, as thousands of people had done centuries before me. It seemed to me this was the last resting place of the fisherman called Peter. For a fleeting moment, the girl from Evanston felt a connection with the divine.

CHAPTER 25

THE BREAKUP – MARCH 1990

ELSA'S NARRATIVE

I awoke to the sun streaming through the bedroom window. It was Saturday, a day to sleep in. Glancing at my alarm clock, I saw it was 8:00 am. Upstairs I could hear noise in the kitchen. Antonella was busy making breakfast.

It was my first Saturday without David in four months. David had returned to the States for seven days to attend a training course in Florida and would not be home until tomorrow afternoon.

Donning my robe and slippers, I proceeded upstairs, finding Antonella seated in front of the T.V. eating her breakfast. "What's for breakfast?" I asked.

"I made an egg sandwich," Antonella replied. "There's one more egg if you want one."

"Is there any bread left?" I asked.

"Just one slice," Antonella replied. Our cupboard was bare again.

"I think I'm just going to have a piece of toast and a coffee," I replied. Making an egg seemed like too much work. Ten minutes later, I sat on the bean bag chair next to Antonella, watching R.A.I. Uno News, while eating my toast.

"Is there anything happening today?" I asked.

"No," Antonella replied. "It's just the usual news. There's a nationwide general strike planned for Monday." Just what we needed, another general strike, I thought. Italy always had general strikes.

"Who is it this time?" I asked.

"The truck drivers again," Antonella replied.

Wonderful, I thought; I remembered what happened the last time the truck drivers went on strike. They blocked the highway for hours forcing everyone onto the city streets. My usual twenty-minute commute to the university turned into a two-hour ordeal.

"Are you doing anything tonight?" I asked. "David's out of town, and I'm looking for something to do."

"No," Antonella replied. "Tony canceled our date again. He's gone to Milano again to visit his sick mother."

"Would you like to check out the new disco?" I asked.

"Which one?" Antonella replied, "there are several."

"I was thinking of the new disco near the Mergelina," I replied. "You know, the one with the "Texas" theme." I had ridden by the new disco several times and had been intrigued by the fancy sign at the entrance.

For a moment, Antonella didn't reply. "Mother's having another party again tonight," Antonella finally responded. "Would you rather go to that?"

"No, thank you," I replied. "The last time we attended one of your mother's parties, I had to play waitress all night. Let's leave before the party starts," I suggested. "What time do you get off work?"

"The shop closes at 9:00 pm," Antonella replied. "I should be home by 10:00 pm." It was a little bit late. I would have to hide in the apartment for an hour to avoid impressment into server duty.

"Do you want to go out?" I asked. It was not clear Antonella wanted to go to the disco.

"Sure," Antonella replied. "I guess so, but I'm not wearing a cowboy hat!"

"How about wearing the Mexican Sombrero?" I asked.

"No way," Antonella replied, sticking out her tongue at me. "I'm not wearing the Mexican Sombrero either!" It was settled; we would check out the Texas disco.

David had bought me a new "Cowboy" hat for Christmas from a catalog, and Antonella loved to make fun of my hat. I, however, loved it. David referred to the hat as a fedora. It was the perfect hat for days spent doing archaeology work in the field. I loved hats and had several, but my favorite by far was the fedora.

"What are you doing today?" Antonella asked.

"Not much," I replied. "I need to catch up on schoolwork and study for a test next week."

"What are you doing today?" I asked.

"The same as always," Antonella replied. "It's my weekend to work at the dress shop."

Poor Antonella, her life revolved around work and her boyfriend. Occasionally our paths crossed, but for the most part, I had our apartment to myself. She had no time to enjoy the simple pleasures of life.

After Antonella departed for work, I poured myself another cup of coffee and proceeded to the back balcony to begin my work for the day, donning my new hat. It was a perfect day to sit in the sun, not too hot nor too cold. It was perfect weather for wearing a sweater and blue jeans.

Sitting on the balcony looking out towards the sea while drafting my field notes seemed a much better way to spend my day than working in a dress shop.

For the past year (before I moved to Naples), ever since I graduated from college, my boyfriend Sven had insisted I get a job rather than continue my education. Why incur more debt, he thought, if it doesn't increase your earning potential? He wasn't paying for my education, but he seemed to think he might someday be stuck paying my debts.

Sven wanted to get married and settle down. Anything which interfered with that plan was something he opposed. At the time, I was working in a dress shop while modeling on the side. I enjoyed the modeling but hated working in the dress shop as the hours were awful. I hated working evenings and weekends. It felt as if I were running on a treadmill, which went nowhere I wanted to go.

Making money was the only thing that mattered to Sven, whereas for me, it was a means to an end and not the end itself. Sven, like many people in our generation, always wanted more. He was never satisfied.

At first, my infatuation for Sven tended to render me blind to his selfishness, but as time went by, I began to see the entire person. Sven could be a sweetheart when he wanted to be, but he also could be controlling and super jealous, two qualities that felt increasingly threatening.

In our relationship, there was only one person who mattered, and that person was Sven. I was just a passenger, a possession in his life, a necessary accessory. I was not a person in my own right.

For months we muddled along, trying to make our relationship work, as our love for each other slowly died. I don't think Sven realized it, but he was slowly draining the life from me. By the end, I dreaded our time together and often felt as if I couldn't breathe.

Marrying Sven meant giving up my dreams. I suppose that is why I broke our engagement. It was the reason Sven put his fist through the wall. Besides our mutual physical attraction, we had little in common.

As I stared out to sea, lost in my thoughts, a seagull landed on the balcony railing, interrupting my trance. It was clear he wanted the crust of bread on my plate. Soon he was joined by several friends, all now staring at the remains of my breakfast. "Here you go," I exclaimed, tossing my bread crust off the balcony. It never touched the ground. A small sparrow swept in from below and grabbed it before the others knew what happened.

That morning I sat collecting my thoughts from the previous week, typing up my field notes. The past week had been an exciting week. For three days, I had worked on my first archeological dig, and thanks to my lucky hat, I found something, my first archeological find.

I first became interested in archaeology as a teenage girl, watching Harrison Ford on the big screen. "Raiders of the Lost Ark" was my favorite film. It made me dream of a glamorous life flying around the world, searching for lost buried treasures.

The reality of the profession was, of course, more literally down to earth but not without its joys. It involved spending weeks researching in libraries, followed by days digging in the earth with small brooms and toothbrushes, looking for pieces of the past, discarded garbage, broken pots, remains of houses, and human remains if we were lucky.

This past week I was lucky. For several days I had been assisting Professor Balsamo and my classmates in clearing a site for the construction of a new elementary school north of the city. The first day on-site was spent setting up, surveying the site, and laying out a grid to record the location of anything we found. We managed to dig a little bit that first day but found nothing. We needed to dig below the levels impacted by farming before we would find anything.

On the second day, I decided to dig in an area believed to contain a buried Roman road. Our research showed that two Roman Roads crossed at one of the corners of the site. Confirming the location of the road was the first step in implementing our excavation plan. The roads were not the traditional paved Roman roads linking cities but instead a grid of dirt roads subdividing farming plots.

The presence of these roads could still be detected from aerial photographs. However, most of the roads lay below the surface. We were not sure if the roads were paved or just packed earth. Nearby I could see a line of umbrella pine trees stretching into the distance across the horizon. The pines marked the route of the nearby Appian Way.

The road grid, which covered broad areas of the Campania plain, was constructed around 80 B.C. during the Dictatorship of the Roman General Lucius Cornelius Sulla. While the roads are now buried under more modern roads, their basic layout remains and is clearly visible from the sky.

The cities of Campania had rebelled against Rome in a war later known as the Social Wars. It was a war about the rights of citizenship, and while the rebels lost the war, they did obtain the one concession they wanted, equality as citizens under Roman Law.

Following the defeat of the rebels, General Sulla subdivided the captured lands to create farm plots for his soldiers. It was a means to reward the soldiers for their service, as well as a prudent measure to prevent future rebellion.

As I was digging in the vicinity of the road, I found the road surface. The road was composed of several feet of compacted earth mixed with gravel. It was deeply rutted from centuries of use but did not have paving stones. If there were stones originally, they had been removed a long time ago. Within the roadbed, I found my first find of the day. It was a Roman coin in the middle layer of packed earth. Perhaps it had fallen out of someone's pocket and had gotten lost in the mud.

The coin was about one inch in diameter and greenish in color, indicating it was made of bronze. It was not a rare or particularly valuable coin. On one side, it had the raised image of a man's face. The other side was very worn, the image no longer legible. Showing the coin to my teacher, we searched his books to identify it. After several minutes we found a similar coin in the book.

It was an image of the Roman Emperor Antoninus Pius, the emperor who reigned between Hadrian and Marcus Aurelius. The coin dated somewhere between the years 138 AD and 161 AD. As I washed the coin in a coffee can filled with water, I admired my prize. It was the first archeological find of my career.

During the afternoon, we began excavating another grid square further from the road, following the random sampling plan agreed to with the municipal school authority. When we reached six feet below the surface, one of my colleagues found a small intact piece of pottery containing valuables. We had stumbled upon a burial.

Switching from small shovels to brooms, we began looking for more. Soon we uncovered leg bones and then hips. We had found a skeleton. Switching to toothbrushes, we slowly and carefully brushed away more of the volcanic earth surrounding the body, noting, and recording what we uncovered. Most of the small bones had deteriorated completely, leaving behind only the largest bones and the skull. My teacher indicated this was not unusual given the composition of the soil. It indicated the burial was incredibly old.

It seemed from the person's positioning that the person may have once been buried in a wooden box, but that the box had completely decomposed, leaving only the skeleton behind. We assume the person was once fully dressed when they were buried. However, we found no traces of clothing. The person was small in stature and appeared to be a young woman, as her bones showed no signs of advanced aging.

We could tell from her hips that she had had at least one child. On her wrist, she wore a beautiful gold bracelet, and on her fingers, she wore several rings, one of which had a red stone. She had obviously been a person of importance who had once been loved.

Beside her feet, we found a clay pot now filled with earth that may have once contained food. Next to her head, we found several pots, one of which contained more jewelry and a necklace made of colored stones. One of the stones was blue, lapis lazuli from far off Persia. In the pot next to her head, we found a small silver coin. It was a Greek coin minted in the nearby city of Cumae.

It would be several weeks before we knew the age of the burial. The woman had died sometime between 750 and 800 B.C.E. She would be the first of two dozen skeletons we would eventually find nearby. We had stumbled upon a graveyard of Italic peoples, Samnites, who had once traded with the Greeks at nearby Cumae.

At last, I was living my dream and was sublimely happy. I had not found a golden idol or the lost Ark of the Covenant, but I had made a discovery. It was a beginning. David's Christmas gift had brought me good luck.

Drive to the Disco

Antonella arrived home from work at 10:00 pm, just as she promised, rescuing me from server duty. Charles and Silvana's party was now well underway. The pool-side terrace was full of people, and the street was filled with cars.

Before we left for the disco, Antonella and I had a bite to eat from the buffet table and then returned to the apartment to dress. I put on my disco outfit, a pair of brown leather pants, brown leather boots, a white sweater, and a brown leather jacket. I decided to leave my fedora at home and instead wear sunglasses on my forehead, as the sunglasses accentuated my blond hair. Why cover my best asset under a hat, I thought.

Antonella wore clothes bought by her boyfriend Tony; clothes emblazoned with the word Ferrari. She wore a pair of black leather pants, black boots, and a Ferrari logo leather jacket. "Are you going to a race or the disco?" I asked, teasing her about her outfit. Antonella smiled and asked me to fetch the Sombrero. She was ready to go full Cowboy, "Italian style," of course.

When we emerged to leave, Antonella's car was now parked in. The driveway was full of cars. Seeing Antonella was parked in, her father offered to let her use his SUV, which was parked on the street. We were soon back on our way.

We decided to take Via Petrarca to the disco rather than Via Posillipo, as the traffic on Via Posillipo looked heavy. Clearly, there was an accident up ahead. As we drove up the hill, we saw a long line of people standing at the entrance to the Inferno disco. All of Naples was going to the discos that night.

On the opposite side of the road, we saw hundreds of cars parked on the sidewalk under the tall umbrella pine trees with newspapers covering their windows. It was a typical Saturday night in Naples.

Glancing away from the parked cars, I asked Antonella a question. "Have you ever been to Inferno?" Antonella did not reply. I asked my question again, and once again, Antonella did not respond. Something had caught her attention on the opposite side of the road.

"Did you see the red car?" She asked.

"No," I replied, "why do you ask?"

"I just passed a car that looks like Tony's new car," Antonella replied. "It was parked on the sidewalk under the trees."

"You don't think it was Tony?" I asked.

"It can't be," Antonella replied. "Tony's on his way to Milan tonight. It must be someone who has a similar car." I could tell Antonella was not sure. She had caught Tony in lies before.

When we arrived at the Texas disco, we found the line exceptionally long. We stood in line for 30 minutes, waiting to get it, but the line did not move. The disco was full. Walking up to the front of the line, we confirmed our assumption. The disco was, in fact, full.

"Do you want to go back to Inferno?" I asked.

"We might as well," Antonella replied. Soon we were back on the road. "Let's drive by Porto Nero," Antonella suggested.

The "Black Door" was another new Neapolitan disco on Via Manzoni, close to the High School. When we arrived at the Black Door, it too was full. Outside of the disco, we could see hundreds of people waiting in an extensive line on the street. They were dressed just like us, wearing the latest leather disco clothes and holding their car stereos. They looked so silly wearing sunglasses and holding their car stereos.
"Do we really look that awful?" I asked.

"Speak for yourself," Antonella replied, winking at me. "You may look awful, but I look hot!" Antonella was right. She did look hot!
After several minutes of driving on the crest of the hill past apartment buildings and small shops, we reached the roundabout where Via Manzoni joins with Via Petrarca.

"Do you want to go to Inferno or ride into the city?" Antonella asked. "We could go to the Café Gambrinus or the McDonalds inside the Galleria."

"Let's go to Inferno," I replied. I didn't get all dressed up to sit in a McDonald's.

Within a few minutes, we drove past Inferno and began looking for a parking spot. The line seemed to be moving and was shorter. We might get in. As we looked for a place to park, Antonella pulled up alongside the red car still parked on the sidewalk.
In the back window, I could see a large decal that said, "Tony Russo Motocross Team." Antonella saw the decal too. It was Tony's car.

Looking over towards Antonella, I could see anger building in her eyes. She was about to do something rash. No sooner than the thought crossed my mind, Antonella pressed on the car horn. She didn't just beep the horn; she laid on the horn for a solid minute to provoke a response from the nearby car.

Nothing happened. The couple in the car were ignoring us. As we sat there staring, I noticed the car was bouncing up and down. Someone inside was having sex. Antonella was now quite angry and beside herself.

She backed up our car, the SUV and then drove forward up onto the sidewalk behind Tony's car. Once again, she pressed on the horn, flashing her high beam headlights. Once again, no one responded.

"Don't do anything rash;" I offered; however, it was too late.

Antonella's blood was now boiling. It was then that Antonella took matters into her own hands. She began hitting the back bumper of Tony's car with the front bumper of her father's new SUV. She had lost control.

It only took a few taps before both people emerged from the car, partially dressed. One person was clearly Tony, and the other was a woman we had not seen before. Tony's shirt was wide open, and his pants were unbuttoned, revealing a hint of his underwear underneath. The woman emerged in a state of undress. She was buttoning her pants, wearing only a bra, when she emerged from the car.

It was clear Tony did not recognize the SUV we were driving. As I sat there looking at the couple, Antonella opened the door and stepped out onto the sidewalk, rendering Tony speechless. The look on his face was priceless. Listening to Antonella through the open car door, I could hear her let loose a barrage of Neapolitan curse words. She was really letting him have it. On the other side of the car stood the woman straightening her sweater.

Tony was trying to apologize to both women at the same time, succeeding with neither. As he tried to lie his way out of the situation, I could see the other woman pulling at a ring on her finger. It looked like a wedding ring. Was the other woman Tony's wife?

After a few minutes of tense conversation followed by a slap across Tony's face, Antonella returned to the car, exchanging places with the other woman who was now cursing at Tony. Tears were streaming down Antonella's face.

"Who is the other woman?" I asked.

"It's Tony's wife," Antonella replied. "The bastard is married!"

That night, Antonella's three-year relationship with Tony ended. We never visited the disco "Inferno" that night, opting for a night of hell, instead.

CHAPTER 26:

GIRLS WINETASTING WEEKEND IN TUSCANY

JULIE'S ACCOUNT OF THE TRIP

It was April 1990 when I invited Elsa and Kimmy to join me for a wine-tasting weekend in Tuscany. I had been working six-day weeks at the hospital since Valentine's Day and finally had an entire weekend off. It would be our first trip together without the men.

On our first night together, we stayed at a cute hotel overlooking the medieval city of Siena. The hotel, which sat in a leafy residential neighborhood, looked more like a house than a hotel; however, once inside, it offered a spectacular view of the city.

We shared a room on the top floor with three small single-size beds. It was more like an attic than a hotel room, but it did have a nice walk-out balcony on one side, overlooking the city. Below our balcony spread the medieval city of Siena, filling the valley floor below, its red-tiled roofs hiding the narrow streets, lanes and alleyways hidden within. Nothing had changed in this vista in over seven hundred years.

On the opposite side of the valley stood a beautiful cathedral. The tall, magnificent structure had a striped appearance with alternating layers of black and white stone. It towered above the roofs of the city. It was an exquisite jewelry box of thirteenth-century art, which, in my opinion, had the most beautiful floors of any church in Italy. Unfortunately, it was also an unfinished work. A fourteenth-century effort to expand the cathedral was never completed.

Beneath the city's beautiful appearance lay a terrible secret. There was a reason Siena looked as it did, frozen in time. The once-proud city had lost two-thirds of its population at the very zenith of its power during the Black Death. When the plague swept across Italy like an enveloping fog, it ravaged some cities while sparing others. Siena experienced the worst possible outcome. Its misfortune, like all tragedies, however, created an opportunity for its nearby smaller neighbors to flourish. Florence became the dominant city in the region, and as you say, the rest was history.

That night, the three of us dined in the Piazza Del Campo, the main square of the city, opposite the magnificent medieval city hall. The town hall, also known as the Palazzo Publico, had beautiful tall gothic windows which glowed a soft orange color under the floodlights.

As I admired the building, I attempted to imagine in my mind this same square filled with people watching the twice-annual horserace, known as the Palio. The race was on my list of things to see. Perhaps some other day, I thought. There would be no Palio this weekend.

During our first night in Tuscany, I splurged and bought the Florentine Steak, a porterhouse steak grilled to perfection and served artistically with green vegetables and roasted potatoes. It cost me 50,000 lire but was worth every penny. I had read stories of the famed steak and was not disappointed. It was big as a house but tender and tasty.

Kimmy decided to try the pasta with pesto and pine nuts, a choice which she lived to regret after seeing my steak. Elsa, meanwhile, ordered the Veal Marsala. It was one of the few times I witnessed her eat something other than chicken. We accompanied our meal with a bottle of dry red wine from nearby Montepulciano as minstrels serenaded us.

Unfortunately, the minstrels would not go away. Don't bother to waste your time here, I thought. We are all poor, especially after buying the steak. Go play for the rich couple nearby. My mental telepathy, however, did not work, as the trio lingered by us all evening, playing O Sol O Mio, over and over. Eventually, Kimmy offered them 5,000 lire to make them go away.

After dinner, we enjoyed our choice of desserts from the dessert cart. I selected profiteroles, small little creampuffs swimming in a chocolate sauce. Elsa selected Crème Brulé, which the waiter lit on fire at our table, and Kimmy chose the Tiramisu. We followed dinner with a shot of espresso and a good walk before bed.

After dinner, we wandered the city streets, trying to find our way back to the hotel. At night, all the streets looked the same. Just like during the afternoon, we found ourselves looping, each time returning to the same small square in front of the same gothic palace.

On the facade above a gothic doorway was a sign which read "Monte Dei Paschi." I would learn the next day that it was the world's oldest bank, the Monte Dei Paschi di Siena founded in 1472.

During our second day, we spent the morning exploring Siena, visiting the Cathedral and the City Hall. We even climbed to the top of the clock tower to take in the panorama of the city below. Afterward, we proceeded to the next stop on our itinerary, the lovely village of San Gimignano.

Driving across the Tuscan countryside was an experience in and of itself. The rolling green hills were dotted with distant stone houses surrounded by green vineyards. Everywhere we saw long lines of tall cypress trees standing in rows marking the location of roads, entrance driveways or farm paths. It was the quintessential postcard-perfect picture of Tuscany. In the distance, we could see ancient hilltop towns dating back to Etruscan times. It was a landscape that had not changed in hundreds of years.

While my passengers enjoyed the view, I found the driving to be maddening. At every intersection, I was presented with a plethora of signs, offering me a multitude of routes to reach our destination. Trying to read a dozen signs, at thirty miles per hour however was very difficult. When I stopped to read them, everyone behind me honked their horns. Apparently, they knew where they were going and were annoyed with the fact that I didn't.

We were going in circles and were lost. Kimmy however did not agree. "How could we be lost," she said, "if we had never been here before?" Being lost implied we knew where we were going. Little miss sunshine did have a point.

Every road we chose seemed to take us back to a town named Poggibonsi. At one such intersection, which we kept passing, I found three possible routes to Rome. One route said, "Rome 227 km", the second option said "Rome 290km", and the third option read "Rome 320km". Why would anyone traveling to Rome choose the 320km option, I thought? If I were driving to Rome, I certainly wouldn't start from here, as all roads led back to Poggibonsi.

After passing the same place three times, we decided to park on the side of the road and consult our maps. Across a valley, I could see our destination, the village of San Gimignano, perched on top of a hill. How the hell do we get there, I wondered? After several minutes of studying the map, we decided to take a break. Our map was worthless. It might as well have been a map of Bulgaria.

As we sat on a stone wall enjoying the view. Elsa pulled out her travel book and turned to the section describing San Gimignano. There on the page in front of us was a map showing how to reach the town. It turns out one of the road signs at the corner was pointed in the wrong direction. No sooner did we find the map than we found the town.

Within a few minutes, we were back on the road and standing outside the city gate of San Gimignano. Just as I thought, we had been going in circles. Parking the car under a tall umbrella pine, we walked into the city to find our hotel. Little did I know that parking under an umbrella pine was a no-no. The next morning, I returned to find my car completely covered with bird poop.

We entered the city through a stone gate, the Porta San Giovanni, pulling our rolling suitcases behind us. I tried not to laugh as Kimmy tried to walk up the cobblestone street in her high-heeled shoes. She had been wearing her tennis shoes earlier but had decided to change shoes thinking we might go somewhere nice for dinner.

It was hard not to laugh at her misfortune. Several times she stopped to retrieve her shoe from the cracks between the cobblestones. Eventually she gave up, opened her suitcase, and put her tennis shoes back on. Who the hell wears high heels in Italy, I thought? Then I remembered that Italy was the home of high fashion. Once again, another contradiction presented itself. Italy was full of humorous contradictions.

Eventually we reached the first of two main squares, the Piazza Cisterna. In front of us stood one of the city's many distinctive tower houses, the towers which gave the town its nickname "The Manhattan of Tuscany." In front of the tower stood an ancient well atop several steps. It was the centerpiece of the square. Our hotel must be close, I remarked. We were looking for the "Hotel Cisterna." Of course, we were looking in the wrong direction as the hotel was now behind us.

Our choice of hotels proved perfect for the occasion. Our hotel sat both in the center of the town as well as on the edge of town. That's how small the town was.

San Gimignano had three main squares, which were all interlinked. One was known as the Piazza Della Cisterna, the second was known as the Piazza del Duomo, and the third was Piazza Delle Erbe.

Each of the squares was flanked by tall stone towers, which once served as the homes of the city's most powerful families. The towers give the city its charm. It was difficult to picture a world where families needed to build tall windowless stone towers to protect themselves from their neighbors. That was the world that created San Gimignano. It wasn't created that way for the tourists.

On our second evening together, we dined sumptuously at a local Osteria. We ordered the roasted meat platter enjoying our fill of grilled meats, including chicken, pork, and beef, accompanied by an assortment of antipasti. By evening's end, we were stuffed. After coffee, we decided to sit in the square beside the well and eat ice cream cones. It was a beautiful evening for people-watching.

Conversation Between Julie and Kimmy

After an hour, Elsa bid us goodnight, leaving me alone with Kimmy. She was tired and beginning to yawn. It was another beautiful Tuscan evening. As we sat on the steps beside the well, I attempted to start a conversation with Kimmy. All day, she had been quiet, barely saying a word. "How are you doing?" I asked.

"Fine," she replied. Getting Kimmy to talk could sometimes be like pulling teeth.

"I've been meaning to ask you a question," I began. "Has Robbie asked you to pay any rent?"

"No," Kimmy replied. "He hasn't. Has Harry asked you to pay rent?"

"No," I replied. "I asked him how much the rent was, and he said I owed him nothing. Do you know how much the boys pay for the house per month?"

"Two million lire," Kimmy replied. "They pay four hundred dollars each per month," Kimmy added.

"My last place cost me 1.5 million lire per month. I wonder why the rent is so low," I replied.

Kimmy just smiled. "I suppose we're fortunate," she replied.

I then asked her another question. "I understand you've known Harry for a long time."

"Yes," Kimmy replied. "Harry and I go way back. I've known him longer than I've known Robbie."

"Is Harry the type of guy who expects something in return?" I asked.

"What do you mean?" Kimmy replied.

"Do you think he will expect me to sleep with him?" For a moment, Kimmy paused to think, then she replied.

"I don't think so," Kimmy replied. "Harry's not like that."

"Is he gay?" I asked.

"No," Kimmy replied. "Harry's not gay. He's just generous, I suppose. "

Kimmy's response increased my interest, begging another question, as I knew they had previously dated. "If Harry's so wonderful, why did you break up with him?"

Kimmy smiled. "There's something you should know about me," Kimmy replied. "I like danger. Harry is too safe for me. He's like a lovable golden retriever. He's a genuinely friendly guy, willing to overlook any fault. He's almost too nice if you know what I mean. I prefer the guys who are slightly bad, like Robbie."

"Do you remember the movie "Star Wars"?" Kimmy asked.

"Yes," I replied.

"In the movie, "Han Solo," the bad guy, gets the girl, not "Luke Skywalker", even though "Luke" is much prettier," Kimmy continued.

"That could be because the girl is his sister," I replied.

"True," Kimmy replied, "however, we don't know that until later movies. The point is that the bad guy always gets the girl."

"What about Luke?" I asked. "Shouldn't he get a girl also?"

Kimmy shrugged her shoulders. "He never gets the girl," Kimmy replied. "I don't know why, but he never does. Of course, if you want Luke, that's ok with me."

"Do you mean Harry?"

"Yes, that's what I mean," Kimmy replied. "There is something else you should know about Harry, however."

"What's that?" I asked.

"Harry is hairy," Kimmy replied.

For a moment I could not contain my laughter. "What's wrong with that?" I asked.

Kimmy smiled. "I don't mind a hairy chest" she replied, "but I can't stand a hairy back." She then continued her story. "I think I misjudged Harry," she said. "Harry is a great guy. Sometimes I think I picked the wrong guy. Robbie is cute, but he can be a pain in the ass. Do you want to know something else?"

"What," I replied.

"I think Harry likes you," Kimmy replied. For a moment she stopped talking to let her words sink in. Then she added more to her statement. "I think Harry may be falling in love with you."

"How can you tell?" I asked.

"It's just a hunch," Kimmy replied. "He treats you different than I have seen him treat other women. He clearly likes you." For a moment I felt warm inside. I decided to change the subject.

"You seem like something's bothering you," I offered. Kimmy's demeanor had changed since I first met her. The once talkative, perpetually happy chatterbox had become a quiet little mouse.

"I've got a lot on my mind," she replied.

"How are things with Robbie?" I asked.

"Not good at present," Kimmy replied. "We're going through a rough patch." At last, she was beginning to reveal her secrets.

"What's the problem?" I asked, trying to be helpful.

"Robbie and I have stopped sleeping together," Kimmy replied. "Robbie thinks I have cut him off. However, the truth is I am out of pills."

"How did that happen?" I asked.

"I was thinking about getting pregnant," Kimmy replied. "I thought perhaps; it might inspire Robbie to make a commitment."

"So, I take it you decided not to move forward with that plan?" I asked.

"Exactly" Kimmy replied. "I realized it wouldn't work. Robbie says he doesn't want children. Since our day trip to Vesuvius, I tried to get my doctor to send me more pills. However, she wants me to come in first. She's not willing to give me a new prescription."

"Have you tried to find an Italian doctor?" I asked.

"No," Kimmy replied. "I've looked but haven't been able to find a woman doctor that speaks English. Do you happen to know any?" she asked.

"No," I replied.

"Could you give me a prescription?" Kimmy asked.

"I am afraid not," I replied. "My license is only valid at the American Hospital. I only have the authority to give prescriptions to military personnel and their dependents."

"That's what I thought," Kimmy replied, "but I thought I would ask anyway."

"What about going back to the States?" I asked. "You could visit your family for a couple of weeks, get a new prescription and then come back."

"I've thought of that," Kimmy replied. "Flying back would be easy; returning to Italy would be the problem. You see, I've overstayed my visa. According to my mother, I would need to remain outside Italy for six months before I could return."

After ten minutes of silence, I asked another question. "Do you want children?" I asked. Kimmy did not respond immediately.

"I suppose I do," Kimmy replied. "However, Robby says he doesn't."

As I looked toward Kimmy, I could see tears forming in her eyes. She was struggling with insecurity, a feeling she was not good enough. Perhaps the truth was Robbie wanted children but didn't want children with her.

"I've fallen in love with "Peter Pan,"" she whispered.

I understood how she felt. My last boyfriend had been a "Peter Pan" also. What is it with men, I thought? Why are they so afraid of commitment? I didn't know the answer to that question. I suppose the answer depended on the man.

"Have you considered returning to New York?" I asked.

"Yes," Kimmy replied. "However, I'm not ready to give up just yet. I've invested six years into my relationship with Robbie. Besides, I'm not ready to leave Italy. I love it here. Italy gets under your skin." I understood what Kimmy meant. I had fallen in love with Italy also.

"You know this is the first time in my life that I feel totally free," Kimmy continued. "I don't have to work or attend school. I have no responsibilities whatsoever. Every day I wake up and do whatever I want. It's wonderful. It's like being retired without being old. I always wondered what it would be like to take a year off."

The thought of not working seemed alien to me. Someday I thought. Perhaps when I am 80 years old and have finally paid off my medical school loans.

"Don't you miss not having money?" I asked.

"No," Kimmy replied. "I have some money of my own. However, Robbie pays for everything. It's amazing how well a person can live without money. Whenever we go somewhere, Robbie pays for everything. He even gave me money for this trip." By this point in the conversation, Kimmy was smiling again. It was good to see her smile. The old Kimmy had returned.

Kimmy changed the subject back to Harry. "How are you and Harry doing?" Kimmy asked.

For a moment, I didn't reply. I needed to capture my thoughts. I was becoming very fond of Harry. Should I tell Kimmy? I decided to confide in her. She had confided in me.

"Harry and I are great together," I replied. "He's nothing like my last boyfriend. I think I am starting to fall for him. Harry is a real marshmallow," I replied.

"That reminds me," Kimmy responded changing the subject. "Speaking of marshmallows, have you met our neighbor across the street?"

"No," I replied. "I only see the soccer players when they drive their cars in and out of the underground garage."

"I've met one of them," Kimmy replied. "We sometimes run into each other walking down into the city. He goes running a lot to stay in shape. His name is Marcello; however, I call him "marshmallow." He doesn't seem to mind."

"Is he handsome?" I asked.

"Yes, quite handsome," Kimmy replied. "He plays soccer for the Naples Team. Everyone who lives in the building across the street plays soccer for the Naples team."

"Do you think he might be able to get us some tickets?" I asked. Harry was dying to go to a soccer game.

"I'll ask next time I see him," Kimmy replied. "Perhaps he can get us some seats near the field. Robbie wants to go also. You and Harry could come with us."

Harry wanted to attend one of the upcoming World Cup games. Perhaps Kimmy's new friend could help us get tickets.

CHAPTER 27:

KIMMY'S VISITOR (EARLY APRIL 90)

The day after I returned from Tuscany, I received an unexpected visitor. Maria, Rosa, and I were enjoying a cup of tea in the garden when a man in uniform rang the buzzer at the main gate. "It's Signore Piccolo," Maria exclaimed! "Rosa, can you please let him in?"

While Maria and Rosa were both in their eighties, it was clear that the years had not been as good to Maria as they had been to Rosa. Rosa remained active, able to walk but often misdirected by her poor eyesight. Maria by contrast could still see without glasses but could only walk with difficulty. Theirs was a symbiotic relationship that enabled both to retain their independence.

As Rosa disappeared up the driveway, I asked Maria about our guest. "Signore Piccolo is a long-time friend of the family," Maria replied. I could tell she was lying. "I asked him to come here today to answer your visa questions."

I had spoken to Maria about my need to obtain a resident Visa several weeks before and had forgotten the conversation, as Maria did not seem interested in helping me.

Meeting with a policeman sent a chill up my spine, changing the expression on my face. I suddenly felt extremely nervous. "Don't worry, my child," Maria replied, smiling. "Signore Piccolo is my friend. Don't be troubled by the expression on his face. He seldom smiles."

Perhaps Maria had not been lying, I thought. Maybe she always looks that way. I then remembered what Robbie had told me during my first week in Italy. Maria had married a man twenty years her senior. From the beginning of her marriage, she had been a "General's Wife." She had even lived in the large Villa next door, the Villa Nike, now occupied by the CINC. What type of woman marries a general, I asked myself? I had not yet figured out Maria.

A few minutes later, Rosa reappeared with our guest, a dapper, middle-aged gentlemen with thick black hair. He had a pencil-thin mustache with sideburns to match and wore an immaculately pressed greenish-gray uniform. There was something menacing about the man, however. He made my skin crawl. As he sat next to me, he gave me a look, gazing at my body from head to toe. For a moment his gaze paused on my chest. It seemed he might also be a pervert.

Maria's dog growled. Even Bari knew the man was evil. Sensing trouble, Rosa, reached for her broomstick, sending Bari scurrying for safety. Maria and I tried to suppress our laughter, but it was difficult.

"Excuse me;" Maria exclaimed, laughing! "Bari does that to all my guests. If it's any consolation we like you, even if my dog does not."

I could tell the officer was not amused. Maria began her introductions. "This is my niece "Keeemee" DeGennaro from America," Maria explained. "She is distantly related to my dearly departed husband Giovanni, "may he rest in peace." Kimmy is interested in obtaining a residency permit. Unfortunately, she has overstayed her Visa." Why did Maria need to mention I overstayed my Visa?

As she said this, the man's expression changed. His scowl changed to a thin, yet evil, smile. "How long have you been in Italy?" He asked.

"I arrived last September," I replied.

There was no point in lying. He probably knew when I arrived. "So, you've been here seven months?" he asked slowly, drawing out his words for effect.

"Yes, I replied," avoiding his gaze. I knew I was in some trouble.

"Why are you here?" he asked.

"I came here to visit my boyfriend Robbie," I explained. "He's in the U.S. Navy and works as a lawyer at the base in Agnano. He invited me to come. I expected him to marry me, but he has been slow to get around to it."

"Are you engaged yet?" The man asked.

"No," I replied, "not yet."

"I am sorry to hear that," the man replied. "Such a beautiful woman; she should have a man to love her, but unfortunately love is always difficult." He seemed to be laying it on a bit thick.

He then began to relate a story. "I recently worked with a Navy lawyer from the base named Harry Beeman, on an adoption case. An American teenage girl living in the country without papers gave birth to a baby boy at the Navy hospital. The mother died during childbirth, and afterwards, the boy's father, a Greek officer at the NATO base, refused to acknowledge the child. The poor bambino was born without a country. Harry helped us find an American couple on the base willing to adopt the child."

I had heard this story before from Harry and Julie. Julie had been the doctor in attendance at the delivery. I related this fact to the policeman, who responded with a broad smile. Perhaps he wasn't so bad after all.

"Do you want to become a resident?" He asked.

"Yes," I replied, "if that is possible. What do I need to do?"

"You have several options," the police officer replied. "The easiest path, of course, is to marry your fiancé. Once you marry, he can obtain a Sogiorno Permit for you, enabling you to stay in the country with him." He could tell from the expression on my face this was not a viable option.

"Do I have any other options?" I asked.

For a moment he stopped to look in his book. Then he responded. "A second route is to obtain a student visa. Are you currently enrolled somewhere?"

"No," I replied. "I recently finished my master's degree at the University of Pennsylvania."

"That's too bad," the policeman replied. "The last route is to apply for residency leading to citizenship," he continued. "There are three paths you can take to become an Italian citizen. The first path and perhaps easiest, is to marry an Italian. Your boyfriend is not Italian, is he?"

"No," I replied.

"Too bad" he smiled. The he continued. "The second path is to apply for citizenship using the "Italian Citizenship by Descent" process. This is the best process for Italian Americans like yourself to use. You would need to obtain documents from the Italian Government showing that you are a direct descendant of an Italian Citizen. The relationship can go back several generations. This process may sound difficult, but it is not. The Italian State keeps particularly good records. Are your ancestors from Naples?"

"Yes," I replied. "My great-grandmother was a Brancaccio."

For a moment, the man stopped talking, then he continued. "That is a very noble Neapolitan family, the policeman replied with a smile. Perhaps you are a duchess?" It seemed like he was poking fun at me. Then he continued. "Documents should exist for your family, either in the State Archives or in the Kingdom of Naples files. Those records go back hundreds of years and should contain considerable records concerning the genealogy of the Brancaccio family. I think your family had several Cardinals."

"What is the last process?" I asked. "You mentioned there are three processes."

"The last method for obtaining citizenship is through the Naturalization process," he replied. "This is the most complicated process. I would not recommend you try that process."

"Would I need to give up my U.S Citizenship?" I asked.

"No," Signore Piccolo replied. "Italy allows for dual citizenship status. I don't know, however, what the U.S. Government might require."

That last news was troubling. I loved the idea of living in Italy, but not at the expense of losing my U.S. Citizenship.

"How do I start the process?" I asked.

"You need to start the process in the United States," the policeman replied! "You cannot start it here. First, you must go home!"

I knew this conversation would eventually end badly. The hammer had finally dropped. For a moment, the tension in the air was palpable.

The policeman studied me as if he were studying a bug. Then he replied with a sickly voice. "I will be lenient," he replied. "I will give you until the end of April. After that we will of course come to arrest you and expel you from Italy." My instincts had been correct. The man was evil. As he said the words, I could hear Bari growling again in the bushes.

The news was bad but not as bad as I originally thought. At least I had four weeks to buy a plane ticket. "Thank you for your most generous assistance," I replied. I was determined not to show this man what I was really thinking. "I will discuss this with my boyfriend and will let you know what I decide."

"No problem," the officer replied. He then handed me his business card. "If you need any help starting the process, please give me a call. I know several historians who can help you research your ancestry." With that, he bid us adieu, kissing Maria's hand as he departed. Afterward, I finished my tea with Maria and Rosa as if nothing had happened.

Evening Conversation with Robbie

That evening, when Robbie returned home from work, I asked him to take a walk with me. I had something to tell him in private and didn't want others to eavesdrop. As we walked down the hill towards the bend in the road overlooking the Hotel Paradiso, we passed Marcello walking up the hill. As usual, Marcello said hello, and smiled at me.

"Who was that?" Robbie asked.

"That's Marcello," I replied. "He and I often cross paths on our morning walks. He lives across the street from us."

"Does he play for the soccer team?" Robbie asked.

"Yes," I replied. "He is a close friend of Savio Mendoza."

When I mentioned the name Mendoza, Robbie's eyes lit up. "We should invite Marcello and Mendoza over sometime for a drink," he suggested. Robbie had wanted to meet Mendoza ever since we moved into the Villa.

"Let's walk to the Piazzetta," I suggested. "Do you know the one over the top of the tunnel entrance?" Robbie nodded his head in the affirmative. The Piazzetta was our favorite place to visit on our evening walks together. When we reached the Piazzetta, we stopped to look out over the city. Naples looked splendid that evening.

"I have something to tell you," I confided. The look on Robbie's face suddenly turned serious.

"Are you pregnant?" he asked.

"No," I replied, laughing. "That's not it! An immigration officer visited me today. They know about our situation," I replied. "He gave me until the end of the month to leave the country."

For a moment, Robbie stared at me in silence, fumbling for words. "What are you going to do?" Robbie asked.

"I suppose I'm going to go home," I replied. "I need to go back to New York anyway. Grandmother hasn't been doing well lately. I need to visit the doctor and the dentist and take care of other matters."

"When do you plan to return?" Robbie asked.

"I don't know," I replied. "I need to stay away for at least six months." I could see Robbie counting the months on his fingers.

"So, you will be gone until October?"

"At least until October," I replied. "The officer gave me several options to apply for residency status. I'm not sure which, if any, I want to pursue."

The easiest course of action was for us to get married. However, I decided not to mention that to Robbie. Better to leave that option unsaid, I figured. If Robbie was serious about marriage, he would reach that conclusion on his own.

Afterward, we stared out over the city for a prolonged period. Then Robbie offered a reply. "I will miss you," he said. "We have had some good times here."

That was all he could say. What a waste, I thought! He was not ready to take the plunge. Perhaps he never would be ready. When we returned to the Villa, I felt numb inside. Tomorrow I will visit the airport to buy a plane ticket home, I thought. It seemed our life together might finally be at an end.

Robbie's Conversation with Harry

After my conversation with Kimmy, I had difficulty sleeping. I kept replaying over in my head Kimmy's decision to return to New York. She never once mentioned the "M" word, even though we both knew getting married would be the easiest way to solve our problem. Instead, she seemed to be giving up on us. What had I missed? What had I done wrong?

Beside me, Kimmy lay sound asleep in the bed, her thoughts apparently not troubled by the events of the day. For the first time in seven months, I realized I was losing her. I needed to do something before she walked out of my life forever.

That evening I decided to go downstairs and start a fire. Perhaps sitting by the fire would help me gather my thoughts. As I sat in front of the fireplace, my mind wandered back to the start of our relationship.

I was not opposed to the idea of getting married, nor to the institution of marriage itself. What I dreaded was the thought of being "institutionalized," of becoming trapped in a loveless marriage like my parents.

My earliest memories growing up were of my mother and father fighting. They were always fighting and then making up. After my little brother was born, the fights got worse. In those years, my father was struggling to start his law practice, working long hours at the office. Sometimes he didn't come home from work, causing mother to fear the worst, that he might be having an affair.

My mother worked when I was young, sending my brother Jake and me to a variety of babysitters during the day. Growing up in the sixties, this is what mothers did. Childcare centers were rare and expensive in those days. To make a little money on the side, women in the neighborhood would take in kids for the day. I particularly liked staying at Mrs. Smith's apartment. She would take us to the park, where my brother and I would play for hours.

After my brother Frankie was born, my mother gave up her job to take care of us. She couldn't work anymore, having to care for three children. To earn some money on the side, she began taking in kids. That was when my brother first met his future wife, Lucy.

At the time, I did not understand what was happening with my parents; I only saw the slow unraveling of their marriage. Mother began drinking and smoking, and father always came home late. There were many nights when I awoke to them fighting. Many times, I saw my mother cry.

When I reached age seven, my father moved out of the apartment to live in another apartment with his new girlfriend, Melanie. I would later learn she was his secretary. Like every other kid in our neighborhood, mother and father decided to get a divorce. It seemed to be a contagious disease spreading down our street.

Later that same year, the divorce plague reached a climax when Mrs. Bancroft, our neighbor on the second floor, shot Mr. Bancroft in the leg. I remember the ambulance arriving at the building and feared the same thing might happen to my parents. After the shooting, our mother sold father's gun.

Then something remarkable and unexpected happened. After a year of living apart, mother and father suddenly got back together. It happened the day they met in the lawyer's office to sign the divorce papers. The two great superpowers in my life, my mother and father, reached a détente.

Many years later, I asked my father what had happened. His reply was interesting. "We stared into the abyss," he said. "We realized our lives would never be better, that breaking up would be worse than staying together," he said. "Don't ever get divorced," he said. "It's expensive, and no matter what you do, both you and your wife will be poor for the rest of your lives."

The problem they had, was us children. Even if they wanted to separate permanently, they couldn't. So, they decided to make it work. After the reconciliation, my parents adopted new rules. Both continued to have affairs on the side, which were now allowed, provided they didn't cause embarrassment to the other party, and both went to work. Never again would the checkbook be shared, as fighting over money had been the root cause of most of their problems.

In addition, both gave up smoking and drinking.
Once the peace was restored, my teenage years were uneventful. It seemed the truce was holding, then a second crisis occurred after my brothers and I, finished college. Mother and father flirted with the idea of getting divorced again. Then they decided to remain married. I would later learn, many years later, that they decided to remain married so that they wouldn't have to split their pensions.

Several months ago, I shared this story with Kimmy. I told her this was the reason I wanted to wait to get married. It was the reason I wanted us to hold off having children. I needed to know that we would never let this happen to us. The conversation seemed to go way over Kimmy's head. She didn't want to understand. Instead, she thought something was wrong with her.

As I sat by the fire contemplating my situation, Harry joined me. "Having trouble sleeping?" He asked.

"Yes," I replied. "Did you hear what happened today?"

"Yes," Harry replied. "Maria told me Kimmy's going home." He then paused and said something I didn't expect to hear. "Maria's in some hot water right now," he said. "Turns out she never filled out the paperwork telling Immigration that Kimmy was living in the house."

"Did she do that with us?" I asked.

"Not exactly," Harry replied. "The attorney at the housing office did it for her. He's been doing the paperwork for Maria every year that she's been renting to Americans. She didn't realize she needed to do anything."

"How did Immigration find out about Kimmy?" I asked.

"You made them angry," Harry replied! "Remember that pain-in-the-ass immigration officer we dealt with on the adoption case, Signore Piccolo?"

I remembered Piccolo; he was an ass! He pushed his work off on us. He automatically assumed the woman who died in childbirth was an American, when in fact, all that was known, was that she spoke English. The woman died in our hospital without papers leaving behind a beautiful baby girl.

Instead of acknowledging the situation, Piccolo demanded that we find a solution, as the baby was delivered in our hospital. It didn't matter that the mother had been brought there by an Italian ambulance. I was angry at how he handled the matter. I wanted to tell him to "pound sand"; however, Harry worked to diffuse the crisis. Eventually, Harry found an American couple willing to adopt the child.

Harry continued what he was saying. "After you offended Piccolo, he began watching our house," Harry continued. "That is how he learned about Kimmy. Now Maria has a problem. She may face a fine."

"Do you think she will have to pay?" I asked.

"I don't know," Harry replied. "Maria has lots of well-connected friends. I think she will figure out a way to take care of herself."

Harry then changed the subject. "What are you going to do about Kimmy?" He asked.

I paused for a minute to collect my thoughts. It seemed time to take the plunge. "I'm going to ask her to marry me," I replied! "Do you know where I can get a nice ring for a low price?" I had looked previously in the Navy Exchange. The rings were all expensive and much too small to satisfy Kimmy. I needed something worthy, something she could show off to her friends.

"Talk to David," Harry replied. "He has a ring he might sell."

Robbie Takes Kimmy to Dinner

Four days after Kimmy's decision to return to New York, Kimmy & I visited her favorite restaurant for dinner. We discovered the restaurant several months earlier during one of our exploratory drives on the Posillipo Hill.

Kimmy and I loved to visit the many view spots on the hill and look down at the beautiful houses below. The Posillipo hill was an enchanting place covered with enormous villas, many of which were hundreds of years old. They dwarfed in size the mansions of Long Island. These were once the palaces of counts and kings, not the type of houses built by modern-day millionaires.

Every house was suitable for a villain in a movie. One of our favorite houses stood on a rock surrounded by water on three sides. It was white with green windows and stood three stories tall from the back. Its name was the Villa Elisa. One night Kimmy and I decided to try and find the house in the car.

We drove up and down several dead-end roads, but each time ran into ornate locked gates, blocking our view of the houses within. During one of these forays, we emerged at the bottom of the hill beside the sea, opposite a large house with crenelated castle towers. We had discovered the Villa Volpicelli, another beautiful mansion on our list. Beside the villa was a restaurant. That night we ate dinner at Giuseppone a Mare for the first time. It became our place to go for special occasions.

This night Kimmy wore her pretty red dress, the same one she wore on New Year's Eve. I wore my best blue suit. Inside my coat pocket, I carried a small blue velvet-covered box containing a ring, the ring I had bought from David.

Kimmy looked positively gorgeous that night, more lovely than I could have imagined. She seemed to glide across the floor, her feet barely touching the ground.

That night we ate well. Kimmy ordered her favorite meal, the Spaghetti Frutti De Mare, and I ordered my favorite dish, the swordfish. Both meals resembled works of art. Kimmy's spaghetti was adorned with clams, mussels, and calamari and topped with two large prawns. It was too beautiful to eat.

After dinner, after our table was cleared, I reached into my coat pocket, pulled out the small blue velvet box and set it on the white tablecloth. As I did so, Kimmy's eyes widened like two saucers. She had such beautiful eyes.

"Is that what I think it is?" She asked.

"I don't know," I replied. "Why don't you look inside?"

Kimmy reached for the box and gently opened it, revealing the diamond ring within. As she did so, tears began to fill her eyes.

"Kimberly DeGennaro, will you marry me?" I asked.

For a moment she sat in silence, pondering the ring, then she slipped it on her finger. It fit a little loosely, but at least it fit. "I think we can make it smaller," I offered. She didn't say a word. Then she smiled, the biggest, most radiant smile I had ever seen. It was a smile worth every penny of the $4000 I had paid David for the ring.

"Yes," she replied, "yes, yes, yes!"

By this point, everyone in the restaurant was looking at us. I leaned over to kiss her, and everyone started clapping. Our private moment had become a public event. Kimmy and I stood up and thanked the crowd. Then we kissed again.

After dinner, we took a walk along the water past fishing boats parked along the quay. "When should we get married?" Kimmy asked. It seemed she was ready to set a date.

"It's up to you," I replied. "We can get married tomorrow in a simple ceremony at the base chapel, or we can have a big wedding at home. Which do you prefer?"

She thought for a moment and then replied. "I would like the big wedding back home," she said. "Somehow it seems wrong for us to get married without our families. This is as big a day for them as it is for us."

"When shall we do it?" I asked.

"Let's do it next spring," Kimmy offered, "so that I have time to plan."

For a moment I wondered at her response. "What about this summer?" I asked.

"That's not enough time," Kimmy replied. "I expect the best places are already reserved for this summer. We will have better luck finding a good place on Long Island next spring."

"Ok," I replied, "this will be your show." Kimmy smiled at me with a questioning look.

"Hardly," she replied, "my mother has been planning my wedding since I was born." Both of us laughed at the thought of our parents taking charge of the whole affair. Like all weddings, this would be more about the parents than about the children.

"Where would you like to go on our honeymoon?" I asked. Kimmy stopped to think for a moment.

"I don't know," she finally replied. "Let's first figure out the wedding. "

When we got home, we walked into a dark house and were greeted by our roommates with noise makers and party hats. That night, we toasted our future around the dining room table and made plans for an even bigger party before the end of the month. Kimmy still planned to return to New York, but now it wasn't to avoid deportation. It was to plan our wedding.

CHAPTER 28:

DAVID & ELSA'S WEEKEND IN CAPRI

ELSA'S ACCOUNT

I awoke to bright light streaming through the hotel room windows. Looking towards the terrace, I could see the blue sky beyond. It was another beautiful day on Capri. For the first time, I could see our hotel room in the bright light of day. The walls and ceilings were painted a brilliant white as if we were in heaven. Gazing at the floor, I saw that it too was white, with a beautiful, elegant royal blue scroll pattern. At the foot of the bed lay our crumpled gold and blue bedspread, removed the night before.

Beside me lay, David, sleeping soundly, his handsome chest exposed to my gaze. I remembered the first night I saw him like this, back at the Spanish quarter apartment. He was still my personal Robert Redford, looking more handsome than ever.

I couldn't remember much about our night before. We had arrived just before nightfall, had eaten a light dinner, and had then retired to the main square for drinks. Sometime around midnight, we returned to the hotel and had perhaps made love. I wasn't entirely certain. I didn't remember the details much, only the warm glow I felt afterward, lying in his arms. Even now, I could feel his warm body beside mine.

Gazing beneath the bedsheets, the mystery deepened. I was topless but still had on my panties, while David appeared to be wearing only his underwear. As I emerged from under the covers, David looked at me intently. "Do you see anything you like?" He asked.

"Perhaps," I replied coyly. "Perhaps, I was also looking for my socks." I then dropped the covers to reveal a hint of breasts beneath. "Care for a peek?" David nodded his head and lifted the covers to look beneath.

When he emerged, he said nothing, only staring at me intently. "What are you thinking?" I asked.

David smiled and then replied. "I feel this sudden urge to buy a car stereo," he said. For a moment, I giggled, and then I began to laugh. David had started tickling me under the covers.

"Stop," I replied weakly. However, he kept tickling. "No, seriously, stop," I whispered again, giving him a kiss. I didn't really want him to stop.

"Do you think we did it?" David asked.

"I don't remember," I replied.

"Care to have another go?" David asked. "It seems a waste not to know."

"What time is it?" I asked.

David turned over and looked at the clock. "It's 8:00 AM," he replied.

"What time does the breakfast buffet close?" I asked.

"I think 10:00 AM," David replied. He kissed me once again.

After a few minutes, we shed the covers as it became too warm. David had his reply. Our fun was short, less than thirty minutes. When it was over, we lay back on the bed, staring up at the ceiling. David looked at me and then puffed on an imaginary cigarette, offering me a drag when he was finished. I suddenly felt the desire to smoke a cigarette, even though I had never smoked before. After several minutes of catching our breath, I turned again towards David. "That was incredible," I remarked! "Why did we wait so long?"

"I don't know," David replied. "Care to do it again?"

Just then, we heard a knock on the door. Behind the door, we heard a woman say, "housekeeping." As we raced to cover up, I noticed the "Do not disturb sign" was hanging on our side of the door." David saw it too and laughed.

When the door opened, a young woman entered the room. "Mi scusi," she said with a gasp!

"No problem," David replied, "Buon Giorno!"

After she left, David and I had a hearty laugh. "Next time, we need to remember to post the sign," I suggested with a grin. "Let's take a shower and get some breakfast." We then retired to the bathroom for another round of fun, making sure to post the sign first on the exterior of our hotel room door.

Afterward, as David shaved, I slipped into a thick plush hotel bathrobe and stepped out onto the balcony. Below me, I could see the hotel's lush green lawn and swimming pool. Beyond in the distance, I could see the Faraglioni Rocks rising from the Tyrrhenian Sea.

We emerged from the hotel room just before 10:00 AM to partake of the hotel's sumptuous breakfast buffet. After breakfast, as we sipped our morning champagne, we consulted the travel book contained in my backpack.

"What do you want to do today?" David asked.

"Besides a return to bed?" I replied.

David smiled. "You're insatiable," he replied. "I like the new you!"

"Let's hike up to the Villa Jovis," I suggested. "According to the map, the route to the Villa starts in the main square."

David took one last swig from his champagne glass, and then we departed, passing through the elegant lobby into the village's main street. The village of Capri was now awake, the designer shops opening their doors for the day. We turned back to look at our hotel in the full light of day. The Grand Hotel Quisisana towered above the street, its pastel yellow and white façade looking magnificent in the morning sun. On the second level above the entrance fluttered dozens of flags, their bright colors providing a vivid contrast to the front of the hotel.

Searching the flags, I saw the flag of Sweden, my flag, fluttering in the breeze next to the United States Flag. "How did you discover this place?" David asked.

I turned and smiled. "My parents stayed here on their honeymoon," I replied.

David's Account of the Hike to the House of Jupiter

The walk to the main square was short, barely a hundred yards up a small hill. On either side, the main street was coming to life as a flood of tourists, recently arrived from the marina, walking past us. I liked this part of the Island, as there were no cars. Several times, Elsa stopped to look in shop windows at the latest hats and jewelry.

After a few short minutes, we passed into the main piazza, the Piazza Umberto. In front of us stood the village clocktower, the same tower where Clark Gable stayed in a movie co-starring Sophia Loren. Towards our left sat the village church, perched at the top of a stone staircase and to our right sat the village square, its coffee bars now filled with patrons. Piazza Umberto was the living beating heart of Capri, the living room of the Mediterranean's most beautiful Island.

Elsa and I had each visited Capri before but had never visited the island together. That morning, we stopped in the square to people watch and sip a morning café. Afterwards, we continued our hike to the summit of Monte Tiberio.

Capri has three towns, the Marina Grande, where the hydrofoils arrive, the village of Capri, the main town in the center of the Island; and the village of Anacapri, which sits on the highest part of the Island, high on the flanks of Monte Solaro.

Capri has been a resort since ancient times, as well as the vacation home of Emperors since the time of Augustus. The name most associated with Capri, however, is that of the Emperor, Tiberius, who is said to have built twelve palaces on the island.

The largest palace, the Villa Jovis (house of Jupiter), served as his main residence during the final years of his reign. It was once eight levels tall, composed of several wings, and covered an area of 1.7 hectares in size. It must have been enormous, gleaming white, perched atop its mountain.

Tiberius came to Capri to escape palace intrigues in Rome. It was from this island that he ruled the Roman world for the last eleven years of his life. After his death, in 37 A.D. at the age of seventy-eight, lurid tales were told of his life on the island, about the many perversions committed at his villa, as well as his penchant for murder.

One of the more lurid rumors was that he enjoyed throwing people who displeased him from the thousand-foot cliff within his villa into the sea. Whether or not these stories are true is anybody's guess. What seemed clear was that Tiberius was universally disliked by the time he died.

For twenty-three years, Tiberius was the most powerful man in the world, and yet it was a power he never wanted and seldom used. Instead, he left the governing of the Empire to the Senate and to the state bureaucracy created by his predecessor.

After finishing our morning café, we exited the main square under the Municipio arch and entered another world, the whitewashed narrow covered alleyways of Capri. I had explored these alleys on a previous trip to the island and found them more like an Arab souk than an Italian resort. Capri was like this in many places, providing a vivid reminder of the island's connections to the Arab World.

One such connection occurred in 1534, when the feared Ottoman Pirate, Hayreddin Barbarossa, sacked the island. Barbarossa was remembered by history for his ruthlessness. He drove the Knights of St John out of Rhodes and murdered all the inhabitants of the Italian city of Otranto. I wondered what terrors might have befallen the inhabitants of Capri.

Of course, that was centuries before, when Capri was a poor backwater island guarding the entrance to the Bay of Naples. Today's Capri was much different. It had become a playground for the rich and famous, an island famous for its celebrities and for its authors. It had become a place where nothing could ever go wrong, a place of endless sunny days and perpetual happiness.

We wandered the alley, passing restaurants and shops, until it came to a dead-end and abruptly turned right, passing a small butcher shop. Soon we were walking up a hill, beginning our ascent up the mountain. As we walked up the narrow Via Sopramonte, a street more like a sidewalk than a street, we gazed out over the village below. The roofs of Capri were gleaming white in the morning sun.

We followed this route for a kilometer, passing a stone wall with gated entrances to villas. We could not see the houses which sat above us, only the purple bougainvillea flowers which enveloped their entrances. From this vantage point, Capri was an island of white roofs, interesting chimneys, and flowers.

In front of us walked a woman pulling a rolling cart, the type used to carry a single bag of groceries. In front of her, chugged one of the battery-powered pallet carts used by hotels to deliver luggage. I wondered what it must be like to live on the island.

As we continued up the narrow street, we came to a fork in the road. Towards our left ran the route to the top of the mountain, and towards our right, a path back to the village. We chose to turn left and began the steep ascent to the ruins. Soon a panoramic image of the island emerged. In the distance, we could now see the cliff face of Monte Solaro, the highest mountain on the Island.

Capri is an island of cliffs, giant cliffs plunging into the sea. In ancient mythology, this was the Island of the Sirens, A place of extraordinary beauty which beckoned sailors to their doom.

On our right, Elsa and I passed an enchanting house looking out over the Island. It was painted white and had green windows. It had a low domed roof with an interesting chimney. The chimney caps of Capri were an interesting attraction in and of themselves. Each was a unique work of art.

After we passed the house, the road turned towards the left and began a slow ascent to the Villa Jovis, presenting more enchanting views of Anacapri. We could now see the cliffside road to Anacapri and the famous stairway. The stairway is known as the Scala Fenicia and is said to be incredibly old. Its name suggests it may have been built by the Phoenicians sometime in remote antiquity. At the top of the stairway, we could now see the Villa San Michelle, the famous home of the 19th Century Swedish Author Axel Munthe. I remembered reading his book, "The Villa San Michelle" as a young boy.

A few steps later, we arrived at the entrance to the Villa Jovis. Ahead of us stood a red brick wall containing a relieving arch. At one time, this wall must have once been higher, I thought. The bricks were ancient, the type used by Romans during the first century. We had entered a place once guarded by the emperor's Praetorian Guard.

Imagining what the Villa once looked like was difficult for Elsa and me, as the apartments were now gone. Instead, we gazed into three large rooms, deep holes in the ground, which once housed the Villa's water cisterns. The Villa's commanding position on top of a mountain created a problem, which the Roman Engineers solved with their usual flair. They constructed an elaborate system to capture the rainwater from the Villa's roof to fill the cisterns. The roof was now gone. Only the cisterns remained.

As we walked along the metal catwalks gazing into the cisterns, we entered a palace corridor paved with mosaic stone. It was the corridor that once linked imperial apartments above to the loggia overlooking the sea. For a moment, we walked on the same path trod by the Emperor, Tiberius himself.

After fifty meters, we arrived at the loggia, which was now no more than a dirt path. We had reached the edge of the notorious thousand-foot cliff known as the Salto Tiberio (Tiberius's leap). Across the water stood the Sorrentine Peninsula.

"Come sit next to me," Elsa whispered as she beckoned me to join her on a nearby wooden bench. For several minutes, we sat in awed silence, gazing at the beautiful view in front of us. Elsa was beautiful that morning, as beautiful as the view itself. In her hair, tucked behind her ear, she wore a purple flower she had picked on our walk to the Villa. She seemed the very embodiment of spring itself.

"I have something I need to tell you." She replied.

"What is it?" I asked.

"I need to find a place to live," Elsa replied. "Charles and Silvana have rented the pool house again. Antonella and I have until the end of April to move out."

"To whom?" I asked, wondering if they paid the full asking price.

"To the State Department," Elsa replied. She then turned towards me and smiled. "Can you believe they paid six million lire per month?" We had a good laugh. The house was scarcely worth one million lire as a house.

After a few minutes, I asked Elsa the question on my mind. "Where will you live?" I asked.

"I don't know," Elsa replied. "Antonella is talking about moving back in with her parents. She has been terribly depressed since her breakup with Tony. We seldom talk anymore."

"I'm sorry to hear that," I replied. I didn't really know Antonella well. However, the woman Elsa described seemed incompatible with the Antonella I knew.

"Where do you plan to live?" I asked.

"I don't know," Elsa replied. "I need to find a roommate to share the rent."

It was interesting she didn't mention moving in with me. I wondered if this was on her mind. "Would you like to move in with me?" I suggested.

For a moment, Elsa was silent, contemplating my suggestion. "That's a big step," Elsa replied. "Are you sure we are ready? I would hate to move in too early and have it wreck the good thing we have."

Elsa did have a valid point. Living with someone could be much different than dating them. However, it was a useful next step to understanding if we wanted to get married. I wondered what secrets about Elsa the experience might reveal. I had already met the messy Elsa, the woman whose bathroom looked like a swamp, so I decided to take the plunge.

"Why not," I replied. "Let's do it!" Soon we were kissing. It seemed I had my reply. "Do you have much to move?" I asked.

"Not much," Elsa replied. "I only have my clothes and motor scooter. Everything else in the apartment belongs to Antonella." It was settled. Elsa would move in the following weekend. We had entered a new phase in our relationship.

Elsa's Account of the Afternoon in Anacapri

After our morning walk to the Villa Jovis, David and I returned to the village of Capri to catch the minibus to Anacapri. By the time we arrived in Anacapri, it was 2:00 PM, and we were quite hungry. I hadn't been to Anacapri before and didn't know any places to eat, however, David did. Soon we were seated at an outdoor restaurant gazing at the menu.

"What do you plan to order?" David asked.

I was very hungry and ready for something filling but instead decided to eat something light. "Do you want to split a Caprese salad?" I asked.

"Ok," David replied. "What else are you going to have?" David liked to kid me that I sometimes ate like a bird. I did; however, I didn't appreciate the jab.

Maintaining a figure for modeling meant giving up eating sometimes. David appreciated the results but didn't necessarily understand the hardships involved in maintaining a slim figure. I looked forward to the day I would not have to model anymore. I yearned for the day I would teach college, like my parents, and no longer need to pose for magazines. Modeling was not a career for me. It was a way to make some quick money to pay for school.

"Would you care to split a pasta?" David asked.

"Sure," I replied, "let's get the Pasta Amatriciana." I loved the pasta with bacon and onions in a tomato sauce. At home, I even threw in a shot of Cognac for added flavor. "Do you think they will add some Cognac?" I asked.

"We can ask," David, replied. The waiter consented to my request. He understood the difference it made.

Our salad arrived first. It was the typical salad of the island, a salad composed of layers of fresh ripe tomatoes and buffalo mozzarella cheese, all covered with olive oil and basil. It was wonderful. After we finished our salad, the pasta arrived on two plates. It was also excellent. Soon we were quite content, sipping the last of our white wine.

"What do you want to do next?" David asked.

"Let's take the chairlift to the top of Monte Solaro," I replied. "After that, we can visit the Villa San Michelle."

The entrance to the chairlift was only a few steps away from the restaurant. Soon we were seated, in our individual chairs, traveling up the mountain, our feet dangling in the air. Looking down, I noticed my shoe was untied again. It was always coming untied.

Below us, perhaps less than 10 feet, passed the vineyards of Anacapri, rising in terraces up the side of the mountain. Monte Solaro had a gentle slope on this side of the mountain, much different than the thousand-foot cliff facing the village of Capri.

Within fifteen minutes, we arrived at the top of the mountain, stepping out onto a broad stone-paved terrace, now thronged with other tourists. As we wandered about the busy plaza, two thousand feet above the sea, we took in the sights.

Towards the west stretched the deep blue waters of the Mediterranean Sea. Somewhere over the horizon, hidden behind the curvature of the earth, stood the Island of Sardinia and beyond that, Spain. Peering over the edge of a two-thousand-foot cliff was unnerving. Below swirled clouds of mist from the crashing waves. "Let us go to the other side of the terrace," I suggested.

David and I wandered over to the north edge of the terrace. In the distance, we could now see the bay's largest island, the Isle of Ischia, rising out of the waters. In the center of the island stood a large volcano, standing slightly taller than our own. It was Mount Epomeo. As we scanned the horizon towards the east, we could see Capo Miseno, another smaller volcanic cone, which marked the entrance to the bay of Pozzuoli.

Looking towards the east, the flanks of Mount Vesuvius came into view. In the distance, somewhere to the left of Vesuvius, hidden within the air pollution, lay the city of Naples, the home of two million people. It was difficult to see the outline of the city. All we could see was the cloud of dirty air above it. I imagined a million vehicles all idling, stuck in traffic. David pictured the scene as well.

"Do you want to go back to that?" He asked.

"Let's just stay here forever," I replied, wrapping my arm around his waist.

Our reverie was soon interrupted by a group of Chinese tourists, led by a man holding an umbrella aloft. "Let's go where it's less crowded," I suggested. David nodded his agreement.

We walked towards the opposite side of the terrace, passing a line of people waiting in front of the snack stand. Clearly, they were not Neapolitans, as no self-respecting native would stand in a queue. Behind the counter, I saw several granita machines swirling. I loved the shaved ice, especially the lemon-flavored. David loved the coffee flavored ice. "Let's stop there before we go back down the mountain, I suggested." David smiled and agreed.

A few seconds later, we reached the other side of the plaza. Below us stretched the island. At the far end, we could now see the Villa Jovis. Beyond stood the mountains of the Amalfi Coast. In the saddle below, between the two mountains, sat the gleaming white village of Capri, its central square hidden within the town behind the clocktower. Towards the right stood three large sea stacks rising from the water. These were the Faraglioni Rocks, I had seen back at the hotel.

"Let us walk further down the hill," I suggested. "Perhaps, there is a lovely place to sit away from all the people." Soon we found our spot. Hidden behind a stone wall, some bushes, and some trees, lay a large meadow covered with thick green grass. We were now all alone, far from the crowd. Somewhere at the edge of that meadow was the thousand-foot cliff face, and towards our left sat the remains of the Turkish pirate's fort.

Guiding David towards a spot in the sun, I pulled a hotel towel from my backpack and laid it on the ground. I had brought it, thinking we might go swimming later, however soon discovered it was too cold for swimming. Seeing the towel, David smiled and winked at me.

"Did you plan to go skinny dipping?" He asked.

"Maybe later," I replied with a smile. "In the meanwhile, come sit next to me on the towel." The truth was I didn't want my white pants to get grass stained.

"So, David," I began. "Can I ask you a question?"

"Certainly," David replied.

"Did we really do it last night?"

David looked at me and smiled, brushing the hair back from my eyes. "No," he replied, "you were really drunk. I could have, but it didn't seem right."

"How did I end up with my top off?" I asked.

"You took it off," David replied. His eyes were dancing.

"What else did I do?" I asked. I could tell there was a story I was missing.

"You don't remember?" David asked.

"No," I replied. "I really don't remember."

"You took it off after you got sick in the bathroom," David replied.

At last, I was beginning to remember. I got sick and then must have passed out on the bed. "David, I am sorry, I had too much to drink. Now you know it doesn't take much to get me drunk. I hope I didn't gross you out."

"I'm fine," David replied, smiling. "I had too much to drink also. Those things happen sometimes. I guess we were both too nervous, and we overdid it." David was right. I was extremely nervous.

"So, what are we going to do for an encore tonight?" I asked. David leaned over and kissed me. "Let's not overthink this," he replied. David was right about that. I had been worried about nothing. "Let's just take this as it goes," David replied. "We're in no hurry."

That afternoon, David and I had a wonderful time lying beside each other in the meadow. God was in his heaven, and all was right in the world. We would have plenty of time to get to know each other. For the first time in my life, I was finally sure of one thing. I didn't know where I was going, but I did know one thing for certain. I wanted to go there with David.

CHAPTER 29:

THE BIG PARTY

HARRY AND JULIE GO TO THE COMMISSARY

It was finally spring and time to celebrate. The house still felt like an icebox inside, but at least the outdoor temperatures were moving in the right direction. Eventually, the three-foot thick walls of our house would warm-up (I hoped). For weeks, Julie and I had wanted to host a party, a big blowout event to christen our house, so when Robbie and Kimmy announced their engagement, it seemed a perfect opportunity.

Julie and I suggested a belated Saint Patrick's Day party which everyone else universally disapproved. No one wanted to drink green beer. Eventually, we settled on a Cinco De Mayo party, as Kimmy knew where to buy avocados for the guacamole. Mexican food won the day.

We extended invitations to a wide audience. Robbie and I tried to keep the work invitation narrow to just our friends but eventually we had to invite the entire NLSO office to avoid hurt feelings. Julie invited her friends from the hospital. David invited his co-workers at the housing office, and Kimmy invited the soccer team from across the street. The bigger, the better, we thought. I forgot the lessons I learned during my frat house days. Elsa's guest would prove the most controversial, however. Elsa invited her best friend, Antonella.

The morning of the party, Julie and I decided to visit the base to pick up the beer kegs we had ordered from the Enlisted Club bar. When we left the house at 9:00 am, Robbie was hard at work cleaning the grill, about to begin smoking the three large pieces of meat he had purchased for the tacos. Kimmy sat on the living room sofa watching TV and pouting as usual, following her latest fight with Robbie.

"Do you think they will ever get married?" I whispered.

"The question is not will they get married," Julie replied. "The proper question should be, should they get married?" Julie was right, of course, as usual. However, Robbie and Kimmy could not see what was obvious to everyone else. They were incompatible.

Meanwhile, David & Elsa were upstairs doing whatever it was they did, behind closed bedroom doors. They did not seem to notice that the rolling shutter in front of their bedroom window was stuck in the up position. I discovered that fact the night before when Julie and I went to sit on the balcony. I made the mistake of walking too close to David's room and caught a glimpse of someone's naked bum. "Don't go over there," I cautioned Julie. Unfortunately, or fortunately, depending on your point of view, she did, returning with a smile.

It was Saturday morning, the morning when every American went to the base to shop. As we sat in traffic inching our way through Bagnoli, I saw up ahead the train crossing gate descend. Hopefully, it was a fast-moving passenger train, I thought. The type that moves through quickly before the horns begin to honk. It wasn't, however. It was a slow-moving freight. Things were not starting out well.

We decided to drive to the base by the back route to avoid the construction in front of the soccer stadium. Italy and Naples were going all-out in preparation for the World Cup, spending like drunken sailors to repair years of neglect. The efforts to improve the city's appearance, unfortunately, caused the city to look worse temporarily. I wondered if the construction would be completed before the World Cup. It was amazing that the government was spending so much money only to host a single game.

As we sat at the railroad crossing, waiting for the train to pass, Julie pointed out something I had missed in my daydreaming. Cars were beginning to accumulate on our left in the oncoming traffic lane. A "Sicilian Standoff" was about to begin. When the last train car passed and the gate went up, we saw what awaited us on the other side of the tracks. In front of us stood an extensive line of cars blocking our path forward. The lead car in front had AFI plates. It was an American.

What was it about this place, which turned law-abiding Americans into lawless bandits? Was it our inherent distaste for rules or the "wild-west" in our genes? I wasn't sure. I only knew that something about Southern Italy turned puritan law-abiding Americans into rogue Italians in less than two months. Even Julie was beginning to drive like a maniac.

Julie was now laughing. She understood the joke. "Only in Naples," she exclaimed! "Did you notice who is driving the car facing us on the other side of the tracks?" She asked.

"No," I replied. "Who is it?"

"It's the head nurse at the hospital," Julie exclaimed, reaching for my car horn.

Within seconds everyone else responded by honking their horns. The side that made the most noise would win the day. Honking achieved nothing, of course, except run down the car battery. It did, however, make us feel better.

"What now?" I asked. No one was moving after five minutes of honking. I wondered how long this scene of bedlam would continue. Soon I had my answer. A man in need of a shave, wearing a rumpled plaid sport coat, began directing traffic. Soon he was joined by others until a small crowd emerged. Great I thought, we will never move forward if everyone gets out of their car. Everyone was waving their hands in the air as people engaged in earnest discussions about the best path forward.

"Can you tell what they are saying?" I asked Julie.

"No," she replied. "Isn't it wonderful?"

Julie loved Neapolitan chaos. For her it was a spectator sport. She seemed to thrive on it. There was no point in getting frustrated.

We waited patiently for another five minutes as the situation began to sort itself out. Sidewalks became streets, transforming two lanes into four. Of course, a large orange bus had to complicate the plan. For reasons surpassing understanding, bedlam was not bedlam unless it involved a bus. Within minutes, the traffic began to move again. We left the house at 9:00 am to drive ten miles to the base. When we arrived, it was 11:00 am. It was another typical Saturday in Naples.

Kimmy's Party Story

The party began for Robbie and me at 2:00 pm, when he and I began to drink martinis. Robbie liked his martinis very "dry," whereas I liked mine "not so dry" with only a mere hint of gin. I never could get past the smell of gin. It reminded me too much of perfume. For me, martinis were a good excuse to eat an olive.

By 4:00 pm, as the meat began to come off the grill, we switched to margaritas. This was, of course, a Cinco De Mayo party. Funny, it seemed, that Americans living in Italy would celebrate Mexican Independence Day, but Robbie had come to love Cinco De Mayo from his years living in San Diego. He also loved Guacamole. I liked guacamole too and wondered if there would be any left for our guests.

By the afternoon, the causes of our morning fight had been set aside. The truth was I enjoyed fighting with Robbie. It gave our relationship zest. Make-up sex was not the same, without a heavy dose of conflict first.

"What do you think of the margaritas?" I asked.

Robbie looked at me with his characteristic smile and shook his head. "Needs more salt on the rim," he said.

I handed him the saltshaker, which made him laugh. "Not in the drink," he said, "on the rim." I didn't understand the whole salt thing myself.

"Doesn't the salt end up in the glass anyway," I replied.

At 5:00 pm, our guests began to arrive. By 6:00 pm, the house was full, the music blaring on the stereo. Harry loved the B-52s, particularly their latest song, "Dry Country." By 7:00 pm, I had already heard that song three times. Robbie agreed it was time for something different and so he broke out his collection of Irish folk music.

What would our Italian guests think about us Americans? We celebrate Mexican Independence Day by listening to Irish folk music. Still, it was better than Italian disco music. I loathed Italian disco music.

At 8:00 pm, my friend, Marcello, arrived with several teammates and their girlfriends. He brought a bottle of Cinzano to add to our liquor collection. "Where is Mendoza?" I asked. Robbie so wanted to meet him.

"He's on his way," Marcello replied. Just then, a man with black curly hair and serious razor stubble appeared at the bottom of the terrace stairs. It was Mendoza.

"Should we tell him?" I asked Marcello.

"No," he replied. "Let's see if Robbie recognizes him." Robbie did not, filling the great soccer star's tortilla with burnt ends from the grill. As soccer's undisputed king disappeared into the living room, I whispered his name in Robbie's ear. Robbie smiled his broadest, widest grin. I had made his day.

Later that evening, as Marcello and I danced, he asked me about the ring on my finger. "I see you are engaged," he said. I blushed and smiled.

"Yes," I replied. "Robbie gave me a ring last week." I still wasn't used to wearing the ring. It seemed too good to be true. Better to have it on my finger, I thought, than upstairs in a box. This was our engagement party, after all.

"I also hear you are returning to America next weekend. Is that so?" Marcello continued.

"Yes," I replied. "My grandmother is not doing well, and I want to see her."

"When do you plan to return to Italy?" Marcello asked.

"Next October," I replied. It seemed a shame to miss summer in Italy. I really wanted to return sooner.

"Why so long?" He asked. "Italy will miss you!"

I wondered if this meant "he" would miss me? Urging Marcello to stoop down to my level, I whispered the real reason in his ear.

"You're Italian, no?" He asked.

"No, I just look Italian, I replied. I am an American from New York City."

Marcello stared at me intently for a moment and then smiled. I wondered what he was thinking. Finally, he replied. "I can help you with your visa problem," he said.

"How?" I asked.

"I know someone at the Prater's office," he responded. "She and I used to play soccer together on Capri when we were children. She might be able to find records related to your family."

It sounded tempting, much more so than calling the immigration officer. "If you could do that, that would be great," I replied. I might be able to return earlier than October.

"It is not a problem, don't worry," Marcello replied with a gracious flourish. Then he asked another question. "Is there anything you haven't seen that you would like to see before you go?" He asked.

"I haven't been to Capri yet," I replied. "I was planning to go next week by myself."

"That is an interesting coincidence," Marcello replied. "I need to go there Monday to sign documents. Perhaps we could go together?" I wondered about taking a day trip with Marcello without Robbie. Would he mind? Marcello seemed able to read my mind. "We can invite Robbie to come with us," he suggested.

For a moment, I stopped to think, then I replied. "I will invite him," I responded. I then added another question. "What documents do you need to sign?"

"I recently bought a house on Capri," Marcello replied. "I can show you if we have time."

"I would like that," I replied.

"The house needs much work," Marcello added. "It will keep me busy in retirement."

"Do you plan to retire soon?" I asked.

"Not immediately," Marcello replied. "I have several more years on my contract."

"How long have you played?" I asked.

"Thirteen years," Marcello replied. "That is a lifetime in the football world."

Elsa's Account of the Party

By 11:00 pm, the house downstairs was overflowing with guests. The first two kegs lay empty on the bathroom floor. Harry had been right about the beverages. Our guests had brought beer, bottles of wine and spirits to replenish our depleted liquor cabinet. Harry's ice tubs on the porch had found clever use, now filled with beverages brought by who knows who.

The party flowed out into the garden and up the driveway, and still, people kept arriving. "Do you know all these people?" I asked David.

"I only know the people," I invited, David explained. "I don't know everyone." That was the problem. No one knew everyone. I suspected we had many party crashers.

"Let's go upstairs," I suggested, "and see what is happening up there."

The hall at the top of the stairs was less crowded than below. When we reached the top of the stairs, we encountered a couple sitting on the sofa. It was one of David's friends, a man named Jim, kissing his girlfriend, Debbie. Looking about the house, the bedroom doors were all open. We could hear noise coming from the back terrace.

"Did you lock up anything you care about?" I asked David.

"Yes," he replied. "I followed your advice and locked everything in the wardrobe earlier tonight."

Walking into our bedroom, I saw an interesting sight. At least three couples I had never met were using our room. On the balcony, I could see a couple taking in the view. There was also another couple sitting in the chair kissing and a third lying on our bed. Fortunately, all were still fully dressed.

"Excuse me," David remarked as he entered the room to retrieve warm clothes from the wardrobe. "Would you like Michigan State or Northwestern?" He asked.

I wasn't following his question, too preoccupied with the couple on our bed. David pushed a Michigan State sweatshirt into my hand, reminding me it was starting to get chilly outside.

"Who are all these people?" I asked.

David said nothing, only raising his eyebrows. "Let us look in the other rooms," he suggested, smiling, then he turned towards our guests and remarked, "Continue, as you were."

The same sight greeted us in the other rooms. Harry and Julie's room had one couple, a middle-aged man in a suit and a woman in a bridesmaid dress. "Excuse me, I remarked," closing the door. David smiled. It was clear the wedding party from the restaurant next door had crashed our party.

When we entered the bathroom through the open doorway, we found a couple standing in front of the mirror kissing. It was David's friend Mark and Antonella's friend, Concetta. I wondered who invited Concetta. Certainly, Antonella had not. Later I learned she learned about the party from a friend of a friend.

"Fancy meeting you here," David remarked. "I didn't know you were a couple." The two just smiled. Obviously, they had just met. David shook their hands, welcoming them to the party, and then closed the door bidding them to "carry on."

Walking through the back bedroom, we entered the back terrace, entering a crowd surrounding the guest of honor. Mendoza seemed the very embodiment of the "Neapolitan Man," I thought. He needed a shave and wore a rumpled olive plaid sport coat with a sweatshirt underneath. Who would ever guess he was from South America, I thought?

As I gazed about the terrace trying to identify our other soccer star guests, David pointed out an important truth I was missing. On every piece of furniture, there were half-filled cups filled with cigarette butts. There were even cigarette butts on the bedroom floor. My God, I thought, this is going to be an awful mess to clean up tomorrow!

Then David & I did something we should not have done. We climbed the spiral staircase to the roof. As we neared the top of the stairs, I saw two familiar people seated on the parapet on the opposite side of the roof. It was Robbie and Antonella. They were sitting close together, with Antonella's back facing me. Were they kissing?

Stepping out onto the roof, David walked up to Robbie and broke the ice. "Did you meet Mendoza?" He asked, pretending we had not seen what we had just seen.

"No," Robbie replied. "I saw him earlier but haven't had a chance yet to introduce myself."

"Right now, he is on the back porch," David remarked.

"Antonella, have you met Mendoza?" Robbie asked. Antonella did not reply. "Let's go say hello to the soccer king," Robbie suggested, as he grabbed Antonella by the hand, leading her towards the stairs. As they climbed down, Antonella turned back towards me and held an imaginary telephone receiver to her ear. The message was clear. She wanted me to call her later. Then she and Robbie disappeared below the parapet railing.

Antonella's Account

I arrived at the party at about half-past nine. The street was full of parked cars that night, making it difficult to find a parking space. The nearby restaurant was holding a wedding reception the same night as Elsa's big party. As I walked through the open gate to the Villa Maria, I followed two couples coming from the nearby wedding reception. I would not be the only unwelcome stranger at the party.

When I arrived on the terrace, I found Robbie standing beside the grill, assisting the guests in filling their tacos. On the grill sat a large platter of meat on a metal cookie sheet.

"I'm keeping it warm," he said, as he motioned for me to pick up a paper plate and tortilla. Soon I was eating the taco, the juice from the meat running down my arm.

"Where are the napkins?" I asked.

"We're out," Robbie replied, handing me a towel hanging from the side of the grill. The towel was moist but better than nothing. Wiping off, I spread barbecue sauce on my arm. I was now worse off than I was before.

"I understand you are engaged," I replied, as I wiped my arm with the towel.

"Yes and no," Robbie replied.

What a strange answer, I thought. "Why yes and no?" I asked. "Aren't you sure?"

"I needed to do something," Robbie replied, "as Kimmy was about to break up and return to the States."

"Was it time to go or get off the pot?" I asked.

"That's one way to frame it," Robbie replied. "Have you tried the refried beans?" Robbie asked with a grin.

"No thanks," I replied, handing Robbie another tortilla to fill with meat. "This is exceptionally good," I added. I then doubled back to our previous conversation. "So, are you really getting married?" I asked.

"Should I?" Robbie asked.

For a moment I stared at him wondering what to think of his response. There was still something between Robbie and me, something I could not put my finger on. I knew I felt it the first time we kissed. The unfortunate truth was that I did not want him to marry Kimmy. I wanted him to marry me.

"I hear you have broken up with your boyfriend," Robbie mused.

"Yes," I replied. "Tony was a Cesso!"

"What's that?" Robbie asked.

"A toilet full of shit," I replied.

It was hardly a phrase to be using standing next to the food. "You really should try the beans," Robbie replied. "I made them myself." I decided to take the cue. The beans did taste good, even if they did not look so good.

"Try them in a tortilla," he added, "with cheese." Robbie could tell I did not know what I was doing. "Like this," he replied, creating a bean burrito for me. It was excellent once I added peppers, taco sauce and sour cream on top. Folding the white tortilla around the beans also made them less visible and, therefore, more appealing.

"Have you ever had Mexican food before?" Robbie asked.

"Yes," I replied, "but not since I was little. My parents used to take me to a Mexican restaurant in Tribeca, I replied, a place they called "Maria's.""

"I know the place," Robbie replied. "I used to like to go there myself."

Perhaps it was our New York connection, I thought, that made me attracted to Robbie. Or perhaps, it was because he looked like Harrison Ford. "Would you like to see the view from the roof later?" Robbie asked.

"Ok," I replied. "I'll see you later." I wanted to find Elsa and the others to say hello.

Robbie and Antonella Go to the Roof

It was hours before I ran into Robbie again. This time he was drunk. "Would you like to see the roof?" He asked.

"Ok," I replied. I was ready to go home but decided to humor him. Following Robbie onto the back terrace and up the stairs, we emerged on the roof all alone. Motioning to Robbie, I bade him sit with me in the middle of the roof rather than venture near the parapet rail. I didn't want him to fall off. He did not join me, however, but instead walked to the far side of the roof overlooking the city and sat on the parapet.

"Come over here," he chided. "I won't bite you." Soon I joined him on the parapet, making sure he did not lean too close to the edge. "What do you think of the view?" He asked.

"Are you referring to the city or you?" I asked. Robbie smiled. I then asked him a question. "Why does a man recently engaged bring a beautiful woman to such a secluded place?" I asked.

"You don't trust me?" He asked.

"Not exactly," I replied. "You are, after all, a man!" I then asked a more provocative question. "Do you want to sleep with me?" I asked.

Robbie did not blink; his eyes were too glazed from alcohol. "No," he replied, protesting! "I just wanted to come here and sit with you!"

"Good," I replied, "otherwise, I might have to slap you around."

Robbie smiled. "I hear you are not so bad with a SUV," he replied. Someone had told him that story. "Have you been seeing anyone since your breakup?" He asked.

"No," I replied. "I have been too depressed to even leave the house. Tonight, is my first night out."

Robbie looked into my eyes intently. "You have such beautiful eyes," he remarked. "If I were Tony, I would have left my wife for you," he added. Was Robbie trying to send me a signal?

"I don't do threesomes anymore," I remarked.

"Why not?" He asked. "It might be fun. You know we owe it to ourselves to understand this thing between us." He then leaned over and gave me a kiss on the cheek. Inside I felt like I was melting. I couldn't do this again. I pulled away and then slid away on the parapet, outside Robbie's reach.

"Robbie, I admit I like you," I offered. "But I cannot go through this again. I cannot allow myself to fall in love with a married man."

"I'm not married yet," Robbie replied. "Seems Kimmy would rather wait a year and have a big wedding rather than marry me now. I'm wondering if she really wants to get married or just wants to play the part of getting married."

"Every woman wants a big wedding," I replied. "Why should Kimmy be any different? I know; I sell wedding dresses for a living," I added. "It's ingrained in our souls from childhood."

Robbie didn't seem to follow me. "What is the big deal?" He asked. "It is just a big fancy dress-up party!"

"Robbie, do you love her?" I asked.

He sat for a minute in silence before replying. "I don't know," he replied. "Sometimes I do, and then sometimes I do not." I understood what he meant. I felt the same way about Tony. "Do you think we ever know for certain?" He asked.

"I do not know," I replied. Then I let slip what I was really thinking. "Maybe, she is not the right person for you," I suggested. "Just maybe, I am the right person."

Robbie looked at me and smiled. Then, I leaned over and gave him a kiss on the lips, just before David interrupted us.

CHAPTER 30:

MARCELLO AND KIMMY VISIT CAPRI.

KIMMY'S BOAT RIDE TO CAPRI

Marcello arrived early at 8:00 am Monday morning to take me to Capri. He was dressed in a short-sleeve yellow shirt, white pants, and deck shoes, looking particularly charming, as usual, that day. Over his shoulders draped a red sweater, and on his forehead sat a pair of designer sunglasses atop his black curly hair. He wore a fine watch on his wrist. One of those expensive nautical watches made by Breitling.

"Are you ready?" He asked.

"Yes," I replied.

"You look stunning," Marcello remarked, admiring my outfit. I did look the part, I admit. The previous fall, I had bought a pair of white Capri-style pants with a blue and white sweater at a local clothing store. It was a copy of the same outfit I had seen Elsa wear. It was the perfect clothes to wear for a day trip to Capri.

"You missed the fun yesterday," I remarked.

"Do you mean the cleanup?" Marcello replied. "I saw you making frequent trips to the trash can yesterday. You know you could be fined for leaving trash bags on the street," he added. "How bad was it?"

"Let us just say we will not be having a party again anytime soon," I replied.

"How did Maria take it? Marcello asked.

"Not well," I replied. "She must have been up all night. Yesterday she drove Rosa crazy, sweeping up the garden. There were cigarette butts everywhere."

"Did she have an enjoyable time?" Marcello asked. "She seemed quite "lubricated" when I left."

"I think so," I replied. "I have never seen an eighty-year-old woman drunk before. At one point, we thought she had a stroke."

Marcello smiled. "I have known Maria for ten years now. She does like to drink. Does she still make her homemade strawberry liquor?"

"Yes," I replied. Then I changed the subject. "Do you know what happened to my shortbread cookies?" I asked. "Yesterday morning, when I woke up, I found the pantry empty. Someone stole our American food, the things that cannot be purchased in any Italian food store. Harry lost his breakfast cereal, Julie lost her peanut butter, and Robbie lost his last unopened bottle of steak sauce. And, of course, I lost my shortbread cookies."

Marcello smiled at me. It was a guilty smile. "You offered me the box, he said, don't you remember?" I did remember something; however, it was a bit hazy.

"Were they good?" I asked.

"I do not know," Marcello replied, "but I did include them in my backpack for the trip to Capri today." Thank goodness Marcello had my shortbread cookies!

"Are we walking or driving to the port?" I asked.

"Let us walk," Marcello replied. "It is a beautiful day; besides, there is no place to park at the bottom of the hill."

As we walked to the end of the street, Marcello reached into his backpack and pulled out my cookies. You read my mind, I thought. I hadn't had any breakfast yet.

When we arrived at the Mergelina harbor, Marcello bought me a ticket and then flashed his monthly pass as we walked out onto the pier. I had been unsure about spending the day with a man I had just met, but Robbie had convinced me to go. He wanted to begin a friendship with Mendoza and thought my day with Marcello might help in that regard. He even gave me 100,000 lire to spend, inviting me to enjoy myself. Sometimes Robbie seemed more like my father than my lover.

Beside the pier sat a slender, low-profile boat with small fins sticking out of the bow. On the side was written the word "SNAV," in dark blue letters. It was the hydrofoil to Capri. On the deck strolled burly men in need of a shave, all wearing heavy blue sweaters, the uniform of the company. I had seen these boats from the roof of our house, gliding effortlessly across the water. They would move slowly into and out of the harbor, and then once they cleared the breakwater, they would accelerate rapidly, rising out of the water on their curved wings. It was one of the modern things about Italy that I liked. So much about the country was ancient, and yet, they also had these graceful modern ships that rode above the water on airplane-like wings.

"How long does it take to get to Capri?" I asked.

"Forty-five minutes to an hour," Marcello replied. "The ferry takes much longer, a full two hours, he added. I prefer the hydrofoil when the weather is good. However, the ferry is best when the weather is rough.

We stood in line with hundreds of people as the crew set up for the day. "Is the boat always this full?" I asked.

"No," Marcello replied, smiling. "In summer there are more people. This is the commuter boat," he added. "Many of these people live in Naples and commute every day to the island for work." It seemed an expensive commute to me. Fifty thousand lire for a roundtrip ticket would add up fast. Just then, the line began to move.

When we stepped onto the boat, handing our tickets to the purser, Marcello bade me follow him to the upper level rather than following the herd of the passengers to the lower level. "I always sit on the top," Marcello remarked, "in the back row, so that I am the first to exit the boat."

As we departed the harbor and began our journey, I turned toward Marcello to ask him more questions. "How did you come to live on Capri?" I asked.

Marcello put down his newspaper and turned in my direction. "I came to Capri when I was eight," he remarked. "Before that, I lived in Virginia Beach with my parents."

I had not realized Marcello might be American. 'Were you born in America?" I asked.

"Yes," Marcello replied. "I am a dual citizen, both Italian and American. My father and mother met in Naples back in 1954, when father was stationed at the NATO base. You see my father was an officer in the Navy."

"What did he do?" I asked.

"He was a lawyer," Marcello replied. "He worked as an advisor to an Admiral." He then continued his story. "Father and mother married in 1955, nine months before I was born. We lived in America for eight years until my parents decided to move back to Italy to care for my mother's parents, who lived on Capri. Mother hated Virginia and missed Italy. For a year mother and I lived alone on Capri. Then father joined us."

"Were your parents considering divorce?"

"I think so," Marcello replied. "As mother has told me, father made the mistake that many Americans make. He took the woman out of Italy but found out the hard way that he could not take the Italy out of the woman."

"So, what happened after you moved back to Italy," I asked.

Marcello smiled. "I fell in love with Capri," Marcello replied. "Once I moved to Capri, I never wanted to go back to Virginia."
Capri was a fun place to grow up. During the day, after school, I had my run of the island. Taking care of myself suited me fine. In those days, I hated school. It seemed a waste to spend every day sitting inside a classroom, while the island beckoned me. What I enjoyed most was making money from the tourists. I would shine their shoes, sell them flowers, and even work the tables in the main square. I also loved to play soccer."

"Do you have any siblings?" I asked.

"Yes," Marcello replied. "I have a younger brother named Vincenzo and a sister named Cinzia. You will meet them when we reach the island. Vinny drives a taxi, and Cinzia helps mother with the family business."

"Are your parents still alive?" I asked.

"My mother, Donatella is," Marcello replied. "My father, Bruce passed away back in 1983. He was much older than Donatella."

"What is the family business?" I asked.

"Donatella and Bruce purchased a coffee bar in the village square back in 1964," Marcello replied. "Since then, we also purchased a restaurant. Coffee is a good business," he added. "We make eighteen hundred lire per cup, plus tips!"

Listening to Marcello talk was sweet music to my ears. He had a way about him, difficult to describe, a sense of confidence that permeated his entire being. I suspected he was always that way. He was comfortable like a bowl of spaghetti and yet incredibly handsome. As his hands gesticulated and his eyes danced, I pictured in my mind a cute little boy, eight years old, shining shoes for tips.

Arrival at the Island

After feeling the power of the engines beneath my feet for fifty minutes, I began to feel the boat suddenly slow down. "We have arrived," Marcello remarked. "Let us go on deck!" Before the others could respond, Marcello and I sprang to our feet and walked out onto the back of the boat into the warm morning air. In front of us stood the Isle of Capri, the fabled land of the sirens, its tall cliffs gleaming in the morning sun.

We had entered the main harbor for the island. It was a fabricated structure built in the middle-ages. "What is the name of that town in front of us?" I asked.

"That is the Marina Grande," Marcello replied, waving his arm in a gesture toward the waterfront. He then pointed to one of the many buildings lining the waterfront. "That building is where my mother and I lived when I first arrived," he said. "We lived there for a year, until father arrived. After father arrived, we moved up to the main village."

The line of buildings in front of us seemed continuous, like one long structure. Towards the right end sat a curious arched sign. It was the entrance to the funicular railway.

The boat took several minutes to park as the crew furiously scampered about tying up the ship to the jetty. Then they pulled the gangway into place, and we stepped off the boat. The molo was constructed of massive lava stone blocks and one thousand feet in length. At the end of the molo sat several taxis and horse-drawn carts in front of sidewalk cafes and tourist shops. On our left sat the entrance to a separate dock. The dock where the tours to the Blue Grotto departed.

"Have you been to the Blue Grotto?" I asked.

"Yes, many times," Marcello replied, "although never by tour boat. I used to go swimming there with friends," he added, "after the tours ended for the day. That is where I met my wife, Mina."

Mina, Marcello had not mentioned that name before. I thought he was single. Was Marcello married?

"Where do we go to meet your lawyer?" I asked.

"His office is near the clocktower in the main village square," Marcello replied. He pointed towards the top of the hill. At the top I could see a clocktower standing beside the funicular station.

When we reached the end of the molo, we were greeted by a man with a white cap driving a tiny Fiat convertible. "This is my brother Vinny," Marcello remarked. "He will take us up to the village." Vinny doffed his cap and then opened the car door bidding me enter.

"Ciao Bella," he exclaimed, noticing my engagement ring! Vinny turned to Marcello, congratulating him. "Molto Bravo," he exclaimed! "Is this your new fiancé?"

"No," Marcello replied, drawing his words out slowly. "Unfortunately, Kimmy is engaged to an American lawyer. She is just my guest for the day." I could see something in Marcello's eyes when he said those words, something dreamy and far away. It was an "only if." What did he mean by "unfortunately"? Perhaps, he wasn't married after all? I wondered what might have happened to Mina. Was Marcello divorced? It was the first I realized Marcello might fancy me.

The drive up to the village was short, less than ten minutes. When we arrived at the end of the road, in front of the mini-bus stand, we proceeded the remainder of the way on foot, entering the village square. This was not an impersonal imperial square like the piazzas in Naples, but rather a small and intimate place. It was a comfortable living room in which to sip coffee, soak up the sun, and read a newspaper while the world walked by. It was a quintessential Italian place, like walking onto a film set.

The square was encircled on three sides by yellow and white buildings containing cafes and shops. On the second floor sat the community offices and apartments of the shop owners, including Marcello's mother. In the center of the square ran a narrow and circuitous path between tables and chairs already filled with people. On the right, beside the square, perched atop a small flight of stairs, sat the side of the whitewashed baroque village church. Behind us stood the clocktower, a place I had seen once before in a movie starring Clark Gable and Sophia Loren.

"Is this where you worked shining shoes?" I asked.

"Yes," Marcello replied. "This is the family business."
Just then, I saw another little boy moving between tables, shining shoes. "There are at least three coffee bars in this square," Marcello continued. "Mother's, however, is the largest."

"Where is the restaurant?" I asked.

Marcello pointed to an archway at the side of the square leading into a narrow and covered street. "It's beyond that arch," he said. "Our restaurant is small, but it has a fabulous view of Anacapri." He then changed the subject. "Would you like a café?" Marcello asked.

Glancing at my watch, I saw it was 10:30 am. "Certainly," I replied, "what time is your appointment with the lawyer?"

"11:00 am," Marcello replied. "However, time here is not so important. We are now on island time."

Within ten minutes, a beautiful young woman appeared at our table. "Marcello, is this the woman you told me about?" She asked.

"This is my sister Cinzia," Marcello remarked. "Cinzia, this is my friend Kimmy." Cinzia turned towards her brother and whispered in his ear. After she departed with our orders, I asked Marcello what she said. "She thinks we make a cute couple," he replied. Marcello's family liked me.

After we finished our coffee, Marcello and I walked across the square, no more than fifty feet, and entered a staircase leading to the upper level. Soon we were seated in the lawyer's office overlooking the square. No doubt he saw us enjoying our coffee, I thought.

Marcello's lawyer sat at his desk, slowly puffing on his large Sherlock Holmes-style pipe, gently blowing smoke rings about his head. "This is Luciano Carrillo," Marcello remarked, introducing us. After introductions, Luciano reached into his desk drawer and pulled out a cigar box.

"Would you like a cigar?" He asked in a deep voice. I assumed he was offering Marcello a cigar, but he was, in fact, offering both of us cigars. "Marcello, is this your wife?" He asked, smiling in my direction.

Marcello smiled and blushed. "Not yet," he replied, laughing. "Kimmy's engaged to someone else, a lawyer from America."

"I once knew a lawyer from America," Luciano replied. "Marcello's father, Bruce and I were partners."

Marcello continued, "I brought Kimmy here today to show her Capri before she returns to America next week."

"Bellissima," the lawyer, replied, "Capri, is a beautiful island. Once you see Capri, you will never want to leave! When are you getting married?" The lawyer inquired, noticing my ring.

"We have not set a date yet," I replied. "We have decided to wait a year before marrying. My fiancé, Robbie, only proposed last week."

"Mi Dispiace," he replied. "That is a tragedy. Marcello, you must try harder," he said! "Alas, another goddess is no longer available!" It seemed Luciano had a personal mission to get Marcello married. "There is still hope for you;" he replied, turning towards Marcello. As he said this, Marcello reached into the box and pulled out two cigars.

"Would you join me?" He asked, offering a cigar to me. "It's for good luck." I had smoked a cigar before but didn't wish to admit it. Still, it was not every day that I was mistaken for someone's wife. Soon we were puffing away. The cigar tasted good. I even enjoyed it.

The transaction took an hour or two, as we sat beside the phone listening to men talk on the other side. I had no idea what they were saying, only that they spoke loudly. It was a comedy to watch as Luciano and Marcello waived their hands in the air. Several times Marcello signed documents which Luciano then sent through the fax machine. The people on the other end of the phone were missing half the show.

When it was over, Luciano's secretary, a pretty woman named Elena entered the room with four tall champagne glasses and a bottle of champagne which we shared.

Lunch

After concluding our business, Marcello and I proceeded to the restaurant next door, the family business with the view of Anacapri. We were accompanied by Luciano and his assistant Elena, who turned out to also be Luciano's wife. She was young enough to be his granddaughter.

As we sat at our window-side table, in the distance, I could see a small white house perched high on the edge of the cliff. "Can we see your house from here?" I asked.

"No," Marcello replied, "my house is above the village of Capri facing the Faraglioni rocks. The small white building you see in front of you is the chapel of St Michael. Behind the chapel sits the Villa San Michelle. I must take you there sometime. It is quite beautiful."

The view from the restaurant was enchanting, something out of a romance novel, not a place in the real world. "If you would like, I can take you there after lunch," Marcello offered. "After we visit my house of course."

"I would like that very much;" I replied, gazing into his eyes. Marcello had the most beautiful brown eyes. There was so much promise in those eyes. There were hidden secrets as well. Who was Mina?

That afternoon we dined on local island favorites, tomato, and mozzarella salad, followed by heaping plates of spaghetti with clams. During the meal, Marcello's mother Donatella came to sit with us briefly, taking a break from commanding her restaurant. Despite her age, she still retained her beauty. She had beautifully tan skin and immaculately coifed hair surmounted tastefully by a pair of designer sunglasses on her forehead.

From her ears dangled golden-hooped earrings, and on her wrists, she wore several gold bracelets. This graceful businesswoman did not fit my mental image of Donatella. I had pictured Marcello's mother might look like a woman at the fish market. Instead, she looked like a Hollywood actress.

We finished our meal with tiny cups of espresso followed by ice-cold shots of the island's famous liquor, limoncello. When it came time to pay the check, Luciano treated us to lunch. "It is the least I can do," he exclaimed, "enjoy your tour of the house!" Then we bid farewell to our guests and proceeded on foot to the mini-bus stop.

Marcello's New House

After lunch, Marcello and I began the walk to his new house. We passed the mini-bus stand and continued down the main street until we turned left through an archway and began our walk up a winding road. We had entered the Via del Castiglione, the road which led to a castle. It felt good to stretch my legs after a morning spent sitting.

After twenty minutes walking up the steep and winding street, we arrived at a gentle sloping part of the road. We were now high above the island, perhaps eight hundred feet in the air. Below sprawled the west side of the island. In the distance stood several tall rocks standing in the sea.

"What are those rocks?" I asked.

"Those are the Faraglioni," Marcello replied. Far below I could see a speedboat passing between two of the rocks. Looking further below I noticed a winding path descending the face of the cliff.

"What is the name of that road?" I asked, pointing below.

"That is the Via Krupp," Marcello replied.

We were now walking down a beautiful tree lined lane. On either side of the street stood walls, partially blocking the view of the houses within. Several times I stopped to look inside as we passed iron gates. The street was beautiful, the scent of flowers hung heavy in the air.

"Do you see that wall?" he asked, pointing towards a wall.

"Yes," I replied. The wall was composed of volcanic tufa stone set in an interesting diamond pattern with layers of thin red brick. At the bottom stood a portion of the wall covered with a thick coating of plaster, painted red. I had seen that type of construction in Maria's garden, as well as at Pompeii. "How old is that?" I asked, pointing towards the wall.

"At least two thousand years," Marcello replied. "That style of construction was popular during the first century B.C. It is known as opus reticulatum. I have a wall like that on my property."
We then came to a pretty, white house. "This is my new house," Marcello exclaimed.

The house stood two stories tall facing the street. (It was three stories tall facing the garden.) Along the roofline ran little crenelations like a castle, which gave the house a middle eastern appearance. "What style is this?" I asked.

"It is Saracen," Marcello replied. "The type of architecture is typical to Capri, the Amalfi Coast and Tunisia." Marcello then began his story of the island. "Capri was once part of a small independent Duchy, the Republic of Amalfi. Amalfi retained its independence for two centuries, before losing its independence to the Norman kings of Sicily in 1073 A.D. This area has deep trading roots with coastal North Africa and the Middle East," Marcello continued.

"At one time, Amalfi was one of Italy's four great maritime republics, an equal to Venice, Genoa, and Pisa. It reached its zenith during the time of the first crusade when the knights of Amalfi brought the bones of St Andrew back to this region from Constantinople.

"This house is believed to have been built by an Amalfi merchant after the first crusade on the remains of a much older imperial villa." As Marcello said these words, I pictured a world long vanished, a world of men who wore togas, and a world of knights on horseback. Gazing up at one of the delicate windows, I pictured a maiden leaning out the window, greeting her lover returning from crusade. For a moment I sensed the timelessness of the place.

The first level of the house contained an elaborate arched doorway surrounded by a delicate border of carved white marble. The bottom floor facade contained several small windows covered with elaborate black metal bars. On the second level ran a line of large and small arched windows. Each window contained within it two small arched windows, divided by slender twisted stone columns.

"This is my house," Marcello exclaimed with pride! "The house I bought this morning."

Reaching into his pocket, he pulled out an ancient-looking skeleton key and inserted it into the lockset on the thick wooden door. Inside I could hear the ancient metal tumblers click as the door unlocked.

"Andiamo," Marcello remarked, smiling as he bid me enter his home. We entered a corridor leading into an atrium bathed in sunlight. For a moment, I was temporarily blinded by the brightness of the room. Once my eyes adjusted, I saw in the center of the atrium an ancient stone well.

"Does your well work?" I asked.

"No," Marcello replied. "The house sits high on rock. Below the courtyard is a large cistern. Here on Capri, in olden times, every house had a cistern which was used to catch water when it rains. They used the water for drinking water. Today however we get our water from pipes."

"Does the cistern still collect water?" I asked.

"No" Marcello replied. "Today the cistern functions as my wine cellar. I will show to you during the tour."

Glancing upwards towards the second level, I beheld a covered loggia with three white arches and two slender twisting stone columns. In the center, within a niche in the wall, stood a small bronze statue of a woman, another reminder of the antiquity of the house. It was a backdrop fitting for a William Shakespeare play.

"Do you like the sculpture?" Marcello asked.

"Yes," I replied. "Does the house have more sculptures like this?"

"Yes," Marcello replied, "many more. The prior owners of the house, wanted to sell the sculptures separately at auction. Luciano and I prevailed in convincing them to include them in the sale of the house. I paid dearly for the sculptures, but the house is not complete without them."

"How much did this cost?" I asked pointing towards the house.

"Five billion lire," Marcello replied. The amount was stunning, but of course, all prices in Lire were stunning to me. There were so many zeros they could hardly be contained on a check.

"How much is that in U.S. Dollars?" I asked.

"About three and a half million dollars," Marcello replied. That did not seem so much to me, I thought. My parent's house cost more than that. It seemed to me Marcello had found a bargain.

"Let me show you the rest of the house," Marcello replied. He guided me into the first floor through another room, and into the dining room. In the center of the room stood a large inlaid wooden table surrounded by high-backed highly carved wooden chairs.

"Does the furniture come with the house?" I asked. "It is magnificent!"

"Yes," Marcello replied. "The prior owners had many houses and did not want the furniture. I bought the house as-is with the furniture."

Marcello bid me follow him further as we toured the house's many rooms. There was a large room with a fireplace, another room with rows of ancient books on shelves and a kitchen not changed since the 19th century. On the second floor were four enormous bedrooms, each with lofty ceilings. The third floor had a billiard room leading onto a terrace, and several other rooms.

The rooms were connected not by an interior corridor but by a row of doors beside the windows. It was a type of construction I had seen at the Royal Palace in Naples, a type of construction commonly used before electricity.

"Does the house have heat and electricity?" I asked.

"In places," Marcello replied, "but much work is still needed. My first task is to replace the roof, then wade into the 1920's electrical system. I also plan to turn one of the unused ground floor rooms into a modern kitchen," Marcello continued. "What do you think I should do with the old kitchen?" Marcello asked.

"I would leave it as-is," I remarked. "It is charming, even if not used. I would leave it as a museum piece of the house's past."

"That was my thoughts also," Marcello smiled. We thought alike. "Let me show you the garden, he continued. The outdoor spaces are the best parts of the house."

As we exited the living room through a broad set of doors, we entered the garden facing the sea. The view was truly magnificent. Below I could now see the Faraglioni Rocks, each rising several hundred feet above the sea. Despite the house's age, it also had its modern features. In front of me stood a small but very elegant swimming pool. Looking backwards I could now see the façade of the house. From the back, the house was three stories tall with many windows. Each of the beautiful arched windows contained striped yellow and white fabric awnings. For a moment the house reminded me of houses I had seen in Palm Beach, Florida.

On the other side of the pool ran a long stone balustrade. On the top of the railing sat a row of stone busts. Some of the busts looked familiar.

"Is that a bust of the Emperor, Tiberius?" I asked pointing towards one of the busts.

"No," Marcello replied. "I think it is the Emperor Marcus Aurelius."

"Is it original?" I asked, "or a copy?"

"It's a copy" Marcello replied.

Hearing this, I walked over to the bust and touched the bearded face. Italy was full of such treasures as this. Below I could now see the garden. Marcello had several beautiful fruit trees, a pretty, green lawn, and a magnificent palm tree. I then turned my gaze back towards the pool.

At the far end of the terrace, under a loggia, sat a bronze copy of a famous sculpture from Herculaneum. I had seen the original in the Museum in Naples. It was a statue of a woman. It was my favorite sculpture in the collection.

"This must be the most expensive piece?" I remarked.

"It was," Marcello replied. "That piece cost me $50,000 by itself!" It was beautiful.

At the opposite end of the garden, overlooking the sea stood a small round white wrought iron table with two chairs. Marcello beckoned me to have a seat.

"Would you like something to drink?" Marcello asked. "The realtor said he left lemonade in the refrigerator for us."

"That sounds terrific," I replied.

As Marcello disappeared into the house, I stood up and looked about the terrace. In front of me on the railing sat a sculpture of an Egyptian sphinx. Stretching out my hand, I pretended to pet the stone cat, begging it to reveal its secrets. How long have you been sitting here?" I asked. There was no reply.

Minutes later, Marcello returned, carrying two glasses and a ceramic pitcher. "Here we go," he said, placing the glasses on the table. When he returned, I continued our conversation where I had left off.

"While you were gone, I was admiring your sphinx," I said. "Is it Egyptian?" I asked.

"No," Marcello replied, "it is a copy of a sculpture displayed at the Villa San Michelle."

As he said this, I pictured the Emperor, Tiberius seated on the parapet, petting the sphinx. Then as we sat by the sea, drinking our lemonade, I admired my host. If I ever won the lottery, I thought, I would want to live in a place just like this. Marcello was an extremely fortunate man.

"This house seems so large for one person," I remarked. "Do you have a girlfriend?" I asked, "someone to share it with?"

"No," Marcello replied. "I was married up until three years ago. However, now I am single." As he said that, I noticed that his face changed. A look of sadness filled his eyes.

"What happened? I asked."

"My wife Mina died in an auto accident" Marcello replied.

"I am sorry to hear that," I replied. "I really mean that!"

I felt sorry for this beautiful gentleman. I then reached for his hand to comfort him. For a moment, we sat in silence. Then I asked my next question. "What was she like?" I asked.

"She was a little like you," Marcello replied, "pretty and petite with beautiful blue eyes. We met when we were young. I was ten years old. We used to go swimming together in the Blue Grotto at night."

"Do you have any children?" I asked.

"Alas no," Marcello replied. "The first time Mina became pregnant she lost the baby. I wish we had time to have children, but unfortunately, our time together was cut short. If I had it to do over again, we would have married sooner," Marcello continued. "We courted for seven years and were married for only a year and a half. I would reverse that now if I could," he added. "I would give anything just to spend one more day with Mina."

Listening to Marcello describe his wife was eye-opening. They were clearly in love. I wondered if Robbie would ever say the same thing about me.

"Have you dated since?" I asked.

"No," Marcello replied. "I tried once but found I was only going through the motions. I am still not ready. Perhaps this house will inspire me to try again."

Marcello had revealed a side of himself to me that few people ever show. It was amazing how he spoke about his wife. It was so tender and so loving. I squeezed his hand gently. "You will find someone," I reassured him with a smile. Afterward, we sipped our lemonade in silence, enjoying the gentle breeze.

"So, Kimmy, tell me about yourself," he began. "You know so much about me. However, I know so little of you."

"There is not much to tell," I replied. "I am just starting my life." I then began to relate my story as Marcello listened intently. He did not try to interject or comment but instead just sat and listened. It was refreshing and so unlike Robbie, who was always prone to interrupting me. It seemed as if Marcello was genuinely interested in what I had to say.

When I finished, he stared at me intently, his hands folded in front of him on the table as he formulated his thoughts. "That is quite a story," he remarked. "I had no idea you were so educated. You said your mother is a vice-president at a major international bank," he repeated.

"Yes," I replied. "She heads up their global securities group. I planned to go to work on Wall Street after graduation, for a brokerage firm but then decided to put my plans on hold for a few months to pursue Robbie."

"Have you found what you are looking for?" Marcello asked. This seemed a bold question to ask.

"What do you mean?" I replied.

"Have you found your one true love?" He asked. For a moment, I sat stunned by his question. He had seen directly into my soul. For a moment, I searched for words to explain my thoughts.

"Why do you ask?" I replied.

"I wondered why a woman who has dated a man for six years would wait yet another year before getting married?" Marcello replied.

The conversation was becoming difficult. I was not sure where this was going. Marcello saw my discomfort and smiled. "I am sorry," he said. "I was simply curious. Excuse me for my directness. Too often, I say what I think when I should be more circumspect. Would you like another glass of lemonade?"

"Yes," I replied, feeling less tense.

"Could you do me a favor?" Marcello asked.

"What sort of favor?" I replied.

"I need to find an investment manager in America," Marcello replied. "My mother thinks I am too heavily invested here and that I should shelter a portion of my assets in America. There is talk here in Europe of creating a single European currency, a move which my mother thinks may result in a loss of value in the Lire. She thinks I should begin investing outside of Europe to protect my assets. What do you think?"

I thought for a moment to formulate a reply. "I would tend to agree," I replied. "Do not rush into anything, however. Every market has its issues. America can be volatile also. I would invest slowly in the American market until you become comfortable with it."

"Would you like to help me?" He asked.

"Certainly, if I can," I replied. "I am not a broker yet; however, I know a few good brokers. Last year, I worked in an internship for a New York investment bank. I may be able to connect you with someone there. I will speak to my mother next week about the best path forward and then get back to you. Do you have a phone number I can reach you at?"

Marcello handed me his business card. The card was simple. It had a Naples Soccer team logo, included his name, Marcello DeCarlo, and had a phone number underneath. Our business relationship had begun.

Later that evening, as we rode the ferry back to Naples, I watched him as he slept. Marcello had become a gorgeous, wealthy, and famous man. Was my dream too small? Had I aimed too low when I accepted Robbie's proposal?

I quickly dispelled the thought from my mind. I was good as married, I thought. Even so, Marcello's question continued to nag at my heart. Why did I, the person always pushing to get married, suddenly want to postpone the big event? Why was I suddenly having cold feet? Marcello had seen something deep inside me. Something I had not even seen myself.

PART IV. SERENDIPITY
FINDING THE UNEXPECTED

CHAPTER 31:

COMMUNAL LIFE IN THE VILLA

(MAY & JUNE 1990)

ELSA DESCRIBES LIFE WITH DAVID

Living with David was quite different than dating him. It was, in fact, much better. I was supremely happy, happy like I had never been before. I had only lived with a boyfriend once, and it had been awful. Sven was a slob, a real Neanderthal, when it came to his apartment. He never cleaned up anything, not even the toilet. David, by contrast, was neat and tidy. Nothing was ever out of place. He even picked up after me.

But the best part of our relationship was the time we spent in bed. That was until we broke the rolling shutter on the balcony doors. I do not know what I did wrong for sure. One day I was turning the crank, and then suddenly, I heard a noise as if a spring had let go. Something broke; unfortunately, I kept turning the crank, moving the right side of the shutter upward but not the left. David tried to stop me before I made the fatal error but arrived too late. The shutter was now stuck in the up position, firmly wedged at a cockeyed angle.

"Has this ever happened before?" I asked.

"Once," David replied. "It got stuck in the down position. Harry and I managed to straighten the shutter working both inside and outside. However, at that time, the spring did not break. This time I think the spring is broken."

I did not fully comprehend our situation, however, that morning. This was just another problem to fix, one more thing in the house that was broken. The house had many things that did not work.

There was the bedroom outlet that occasionally tried to electrocute me and the toilet flush button that always got stuck in the "in" position. I hated Italian toilets with their tanks embedded in the wall. The man who invented such a contraption clearly never had to fix it.

The first time the button got stuck, David and I spent an entire Saturday playing "repairman." In the end, we failed and had to call a plumber. Now the button was stuck again, requiring us to pay another 200,000 lire to fix it.

What would it cost to fix the shutter, I thought? A million lire, perhaps? Somehow none of these repairs were included in the rent. It was what the lease referred to as "ordinary maintenance," which was a tenant's responsibility. There was nothing "ordinary" about it.

This brings me to our second challenge as a couple; money. Living with Antonella and her family had been cheap. We lived for free. We even ate for free. The only expenses I had were gas for the moped, social activities, and personal items. Once I moved in with David, all of that changed. David was gracious in paying for the rent, but I did not feel comfortable having him pay for everything else. He was not my father. He was my lover. I needed to somehow find a way to make money.

Since the photoshoot fiasco, my modeling gigs had dried up. I suppose it was because I lost my temper with Donato Malatesta. I should not have yelled at him for setting me up with that dreadful film director Bruto Cativo, but unfortunately, I lost my cool. After the "screaming incident," as Donato referred to it, Donato stopped calling me. Even worse, he told others in the industry that I was not "professional" in my behavior. My modeling career was over, even though my pictures were still posted all over town.

For weeks, I had noticed deliverymen arriving daily at the villa. Maria and Rosa never left the house. Instead, they had everything brought to them. I had never noticed this part of the economy before. Maria had a delivery person for everything. There was the gas bottle guy, the young man from the butcher shop, the woman from the Salumeria and the high school-aged boy from the local grocery store. One day as I was preparing to leave the house, the boy from the grocery shop arrived to make a delivery. He stopped me in the driveway to admire my motor scooter & start a conversation.

I asked him if he made much money delivering groceries and he said he did. This gained my interest. Perhaps I could make some money on the side delivering groceries.

"Do you need more delivery drivers?" I asked.

"We do", the boy replied.

"My sister recently had a baby and has decided to stop working. I need someone to help me. My mother and father have asked me to recruit my friends to help, but I cannot find anyone willing. They would rather play soccer and chase girls."

"How much do you make?" I asked, intrigued by the offer.

"Five thousand lire per trip," he replied, "plus tips."

I was not sure I was interested, as the pay seemed low. "How much do you make in a day?" I asked.

"One to two hundred thousand lire per day," he replied.

Hearing him say that got my attention. "Can I set my own hours?" I asked. "I am going to school at the University and don't want to be on call all the time. Also, I have no cell phone." I had canceled the cellphone contract the previous month. The last thing I needed was a monthly cellphone bill again.

"That is ok," the boy replied. "I am going to school also. You can pick the days and times you want to work. Also, my parents will provide you with a radio and will also reimburse you for the gas. Our delivery area is local, mostly Posillipo Hill. Occasionally we make deliveries in Chiaia and sometimes the Vomero, for a larger fee, of course. It is a terrific way to see the city. What do you think?" He asked.

I was sold. During my first week on the job, I earned enough money to fix the toilet and pay the shutter repairman. Unfortunately, the shutter turned out to be unfixable.

This led David and I to our second dilemma. Could someone see us while we were having sex? I had nightmares of the Admiral below watching us through our bedroom window. (It never occurred to me that our roommates might take a stroll by our window on the balcony).

David reassured me the Admiral's bedroom looked towards the sea, not towards our bedroom, but even so, I was worried. He might go to the kitchen for a sandwich at night, I thought. He might look through the staircase window facing our room. At night, our room would look like a lighthouse. Certainly, everything would be visible, I thought.

David had fun laughing at my paranoia. "The Admiral has more important things on his mind than looking at your cute little bottom," he exclaimed, flicking me with his bath towel! Even so, I insisted on turning out the lights while we had sex. Then, I remembered the Admiral might have night vision goggles? Didn't all military commanders have night vision goggles? When I suggested this to David. He almost died laughing.

The next day, David took me to scout Villa Nike and meet our neighbors. The Admiral, it turns out, was off somewhere on an exercise. Mrs. Admiral was home and gave us a tour. When we walked down the back staircase towards the kitchen, I looked out the window facing our bedroom. I couldn't see our bed. I could only see the ceiling. It turns out I had been worried about nothing.

I was a host of contradictions, not worried about posing nude for a billboard but worried to death that someone might see us in bed. As David remarked much later, I had exposed the "Woody Allen" side of my personality. David never did fix the shutter. He did however buy us a set of drapes.

Julie Describes Water Rationing (Summer 1990)

The summer brought new challenges for Harry and me when the city began to ration water. The exact cause of the problem was not clear. It never was in Naples. One news station reported that an aqueduct had broken, another said that the shortage was caused by a lack of rain, and a third attributed the shortage to the World Cup construction.

Whatever the reason was, we suddenly found ourselves without water. Officially the water was supposed to be out only two to three hours a day. Unofficially, the water was out most of the time. When I called the water company, I received a curious answer. "We have a lot of water," the man on the phone replied. "Unfortunately, it is like a lake."

What did that mean, I thought? Harry understood. After the call ended, Harry turned to me and explained. "They have no pressure," he replied.

One day when I returned from work, I found something particularly interesting. Rosa was watering the garden, and yet we had no water upstairs. It turns out Maria's house had a small valve in the back of the gardening shed, beside the house, which controlled water stored in the rooftop water tank. Whoever controlled the valve could also control where the water went. When I showed this valve to Harry, the water wars began, as we fought for control of the house water tank.

Harry would go out to the garden in the early morning hours to divert the water so we could take showers. After we finished, he would turn the valve back before Maria woke up. Eventually, Maria discovered what we were doing and installed a padlock on the cabinet, forcing us to take our showers at the base.

Each of us found a solution to the water problem. Elsa began doing laundry in the middle of the night. David showed initiative and established a system for tracking the number of times each toilet was flushed. Once a particular toilet hit its two-flush limit, the amount of water in the tank, we had to stop using it. Harry and I also began doing dishes at 2:00 am.

Harry and I had our own little bathroom ritual as well. We had our little secret, a separate bathroom off our bedroom. We began filling buckets at night whenever the water started running. We used these to flush the toilet. Soon we had a veritable bouquet of buckets covering the bathroom floor.

Harry & Robbie's Conversation at the Bar

It was less than four weeks after Kimmy's departure that I began to hear rumors at the office that Robbie was chasing another woman. What did it matter to me, I thought? Robbie had always chased women; besides, his relationship with Kimmy was his affair, not mine. Still, it bothered me. I had seen them together the day Kimmy departed. Kimmy looked radiant that day, as did Robbie. It was the happiest I had ever seen them together. Their world was full of promise. What had happened in two short weeks to change all of that?

The problem was not just that Robbie cheated; it was also his lack of discretion. I was tired of picking up the pieces, constantly playing the intermediary between Robbie and his girlfriend. The only way the office gossip would have found out was if Robbie somehow told her. It was time to have a talk with my old friend and find out what was going on.

That night, which was a Tuesday, I decided to take Robbie to the NATO Officer Club to watch the Soccer match on the big TV there. Getting him to talk always required a drink first. When we arrived at the bar, I offered to buy him a drink. "What is your poison?" I asked. Gazing at the sign behind the bar offering half-price mixed drinks, Robbie turned to the bartender and ordered a Manhattan. "Make that two," I replied. After we finished two half-price drinks, I started our conversation.

"Have you been following the World Cup?" I asked. Overhead at the bar, on the television, Italy was playing Czechoslovakia. They were ahead 2-1.

"Is Mendoza's team still in the tournament," Robbie asked?

"Yes, I think so," I replied. "His team tied their game last night against Romania here in Naples. I think they are still in the race." Talking soccer seemed to take Robbie's mind off whatever was bothering him. "Were you able to get tickets for the quarterfinals in Naples?" I asked. "You know, the game is scheduled for July 1st."

"No," Robbie replied. He sounded disappointed. "Everything was sold out," he replied. "Napoli has become soccer-crazy between the Italian team and their favorite son, now playing for the Argentine team."

"When is the final?" I asked.

"July 8th," Robbie replied. "The game is being played at the Olympic Stadium in Rome."

It seemed our dreams of attending a World Cup Game were going up in smoke. We would be watching the tournament like the rest of the world on TV, even though we lived in Naples.

As we watched the match, sipping our drinks, I turned to another subject, the real reason I had brought Robbie to the bar. "Today, I heard an interesting rumor at the office" I began. "I overheard Loredana tell Fabrizio that you are seeing another woman. Is there any truth to this?" I asked.

Robbie looked down into his drink. "Loredana?" He asked.

"Yes, Loredana," I replied.

I could see Robbie's wheels turning. "I wonder how she found out?" He replied.

"Who did you tell?" I asked.

"Maurizio," he replied.

It was true; Robbie was seeing another woman. "Who is she?" I asked.

Robbie stared at the TV in silence, seeming to be absorbed again in the match. There were loud cheers in the bar, followed by groans. Italy had just missed a goal. Then Robbie turned to the bartender and ordered another drink, a double this time. After his drink arrived, he turned to me and began to explain.

"Let me tell you a story" he began. "A long time ago, back in the second grade, when I attended PS 111 in New York, I helped a little Italian girl on the playground. The other girls were picking on her because she could not speak good English. One of the bad girls had even knocked her down, causing her to fall into the mud. When I saw the fight, I felt sorry for the little girl and decided to help her. I went over and broke up the fight and then helped the little girl get up, wiping the mud off her pretty face with my lunch napkin. It seemed the right thing to do. I even tied her shoelaces.

"Afterward, she stooped down and picked a dandelion growing between the cracks in the playground and offered it to me as a gift. Then she stood on her tiptoes and kissed me on the cheek. It was the first time that a girl had ever kissed me. That small little kiss was the only thing I still remember from the second grade. I only attended PS 111 in Hell's kitchen for one year and never saw the girl again, that is until our last party."

"Who is the little girl?" I asked.

"Antonella," Robbie replied. "Antonella me that story at the party while we were alone together on the roof. It brought back a flood of memories. I had no idea she was that little girl!" For a moment, we stopped talking, absorbing what Robbie had just said.

"So, what happened?" I asked. I was eager to hear more.

"She kissed me and told me she was in love with me, that she had been in love with me since the first grade," Robbie replied. "She thinks we should see each other and figure out "this thing" between us."

"What do you plan to do?" I asked.

"I don't know," Robbie replied. "Antonella is so beautiful. Just being around her makes me turn into jelly. It is the same feeling I felt when I was eight. There is something about her, something almost magical. How is it that a girl I met, halfway around the world, when I was eight, suddenly reenters my life now? This is more than a coincidence; it is creepy."

"What should I do?" He asked.

Once again, I was being asked to play referee in Robbie's love life. It was a position I never asked for and did not particularly enjoy. Even so, he was my best friend. The one person with whom I could share secrets. We trusted each other implicitly, and now he needed my advice.

"Robbie," I began. "I can't decide this for you. You need to follow your heart wherever it takes you."

It was time for honesty. Robbie needed to know what everyone could see except for him. I decided to tell him the truth. "I have witnessed you and Kimmy together for seven years," I continued. "Sometimes you are good together, but oftentimes you are not good. Frankly, I wonder how you have made it this far as a couple. I realize you are too close to this thing, so I am offering you a bit of candid advice. You need to think long and hard before marrying Kimmy."

Robby looked at me thoughtfully and paused. My words had sunk in. "You are right," he replied. "I am too close to this thing. Sometimes love blinds us to reality." Then he continued. "Do you want to hear something interesting?" Robbie asked.

"Ok," I replied.

Robbie then continued. "The night I asked Kimmy to marry me, we had a long talk afterward. I offered to marry her the next day. I gave her everything she said she wanted. She never had to go home. She could have stayed in Italy as a married woman."

"Why didn't she marry you there and then?" I asked.

"I do not know," Robbie replied. "She backed away and asked to postpone the wedding for a year. She claimed she wanted time to prepare for a big wedding back home, but I could tell in her eyes that there was another reason. A reason she did not want to tell me."

"Do you think she had second thoughts?" I asked.

"That could be," Robbie replied. "There is something missing between us." Robbie continued. "Sometimes I feel like I am competing with a phantom, an image she formed in her mind when she was seven. I am competing against an image of the man she should marry. Somehow, I am not that man in her mind."

"Maybe, she doesn't know what she wants," I offered. "Maybe, that is her problem."

"For sure, it is a problem," Robbie replied. "It is the same problem I have. Neither of us knows what we want. We are groping in the dark, chasing dreams."

As I heard Robbie say those words, something twinged in my heart. Did I have the same problem? Was I constantly looking for the next better thing? Robbie had hit a raw nerve.

CHAPTER 32:

KIMMY'S LONG GOODBYE

It seemed as if time stood still, the day I returned to New York. After riding in the crowded plane for ten hours, time on the ground had only advanced by three hours. It was 3:00 pm now and raining hard when I finally stepped out of the TWA terminal doors at JFK. Outside, I was greeted by the sight of cars and buses, weaving in and out of traffic, picking up and discharging passengers. Where was the taxi stand, I thought?

The day before, I had spoken to my mother on the phone. She would not be able to pick me up at the airport, she said. She had an important meeting to attend. When I asked if my father could pick me up, she did not hear my question. You will need to take a taxi home, she replied, seeming to think I had hundreds of dollars. I did not. All I had was thirty dollars to my name. I hope the cab accepts credit cards, I thought. Otherwise, I am going to have to take the train.

Traveling from the airport to Greenwich, Connecticut, was always a challenge. I had taken this trip many times before. There were no direct links but instead a network of trains and buses that had to be navigated like a board game. It could take hours. Fortunately, that afternoon I found a taxi that accepted my credit card. The ride cost me $200, but at least I did not have to play the board game.

When at last I arrived home, I found a surprise sitting in the front yard. It was a "For Sale" sign. Mother and I had spoken twice during the past month, and not once did she mention selling the house. What was going on? When I opened the front door, I found a realtor showing the house to a couple.

"Can I help you?" She asked.

"No," I replied. "This is my parent's house. I just arrived home from Italy." She smiled and offered me a welcome. "How long has the house been on the market?" I asked.

"It came on the market at the beginning of March," the woman replied. I then went upstairs to my bedroom to unpack.

When I entered my bedroom, I found it just as I had left it seven years before, only now it was neat and tidy. On the pink bedspread sat my collection of stuffed animals, things that had not decorated my bed since eighth grade. Mother had turned my bedroom into a shrine. It was too cute to sleep in.

Once I heard the realtor leave, I proceeded down the stair to the kitchen. As I walked past my father's bedroom, I looked inside. The closet doors were open, and the closet was empty. Where were all his suits? When I arrived at the kitchen, I peered into the refrigerator, looking for something to eat. On the door sat the usual collection of expired condiments and salad dressings, unchanged since last Christmas. The shelves, however, were empty, except for a collection of takeout Chinese leftovers and a bottle of orange juice. It felt like I had entered a parallel universe.

It was not until 9:00 pm that I heard the garage door open, signaling someone was home. Then mother emerged and entered the kitchen, depositing her purse on the island in the center.

"I see you made it home fine," she began. "I am sorry I could not pick you up at the airport. How was your flight?" She asked.

"It was long," I replied. "Has the rain stopped?"

"Not yet," mother replied. "It is still raining hard. The drive back from Manhattan was awful tonight." For a moment, we sat at the kitchen counter in silence as mother sifted through her mail.

"When did you decide to sell the house?" I asked.

"Your father and I decided to sell the house back in January," mother replied. "I told you in a letter. Did you get my letter?"

"No," I replied. "The Italian mail does not work so well."

"There is something else you should know," mother continued.

"What is that?" I asked.

"Your father and I are getting a divorce."

Hearing those words rendered me speechless. It was like hitting my thumb with a hammer. For a moment, I sat there stunned. Then I began to speak. It seemed like someone else was talking as if I were standing beside myself watching. "What happened?" I asked.

Mother continued looking down at her mail as she spoke. "Your father and I have been drifting apart for years," mother replied, "ever since you all moved out of the house. We seldom see each other anymore. I am always on the road, and father is as well. We want different things. Your father moved to Washington D.C. last month to accept a position with the Bush Administration at the Justice Department. It is a job he has always wanted. I have decided to move to London. I have been traveling there twice a month for work for the past year. It seemed a suitable time to just move there."

As my mother spoke, in her usual business-like voice, each word demolished my preconceived notions of my parent's marriage. They had created an illusion of stability, just for me. The truth, however, was not what I thought. The world had moved on without me. My home was no longer my home, and there was no way to get it back.

"Where will you be staying?" I asked.

"With your grandmother in Belgravia," mother replied. "You are welcome to join me for the summer if you want. How long do you plan to be home?" She asked.

"The Italian government invited me to leave," I replied. "I need to stay away from Italy for at least six months."

"Were you deported?" Mother asked.

"No," I replied. "I left voluntarily," then I reached for my purse. "Mother, I have something to show you," I continued.

After minutes of searching in the bottom of the purse, I found the box containing my engagement ring and set it on the counter. Mother smiled her biggest smile. "Did Robbie finally propose?" She asked.

"Yes," I replied. "He proposed two weeks ago!"

Mother opened the box to look inside. "It's beautiful" she exclaimed! Then she asked a curious question. "Why aren't you wearing it? Did you accept?" I continued looking down at the kitchen counter.

"I did accept," I replied, and then I added, "the ring is too big for my finger. Do you know a jeweler who can fix it?" Mother reached into her purse and handed me a business card. Written on the card was the name of a jeweler in Greenwich.

"Have you decided on a date for the wedding?" Mother asked.

"I was thinking here in New York, a year from now," I replied. "However, I am not sure now. Everyone is leaving. What do you suggest?"

"It's up to you," mother replied. Then she offered a suggestion. "Italy would be nice," she said. "It would give us all a good excuse to visit you. Your father and I went to Italy for our honeymoon." I had heard this story before about how they spent their honeymoon in Portofino.

"I would not want to impose on you," I replied. "An Italian wedding could be expensive."

"Nonsense," mother replied. "I really do think that small weddings are much better than large ones," she continued.

"We do not have money," I replied. "Robbie and I are penniless. It would have to be modest."

"Do not worry about the money," mother replied. "Your father and I would love to spend money on your wedding. You decide where and when, and I promise we will show up!" By this point, mother was beaming, her usual smile having returned.

"How is Grandma Gennaro?" I asked.

"She is not doing well," mother replied. "Ever since we moved her to a nursing home, she has been steadily declining. She has cancer, Kimmy. The doctors discovered it two months ago when grandmother fell and broke her hip. It is bad."

"How bad?" I asked.

"It is inoperable," mother replied. "The doctor gave her two to three months to live. Last week she moved into the hospice unit at the home. You should visit her tomorrow."

Planning the Wedding

The next day and every day thereafter for two weeks, I visited my grandmother at the nursing home. I had hoped we might talk, that I might get to know her better and, in so doing, get to say goodbye. Unfortunately, I was too late.

On the first day, I found her sitting in a stark grey room, seated in front of a TV set, staring into space. On the back of her wheelchair hung an IV bottle and one of those ubiquitous hospital meters administering her medicine. When I went to squeeze her hand, she did not squeeze back. She was now on heavy pain medication and would not return. When the visit finished, I sat outside on the lawn for a prolonged period, staring blankly into space and crying. Is this how life ends, I asked? It was too painful to bear.

I spent the first four weeks at home with my mother in Greenwich until April turned into May. Each day mother left the house early before I awoke and returned after dark. During the day, I watched TV and read old books while realtors showed the house to potential buyers. Everyone seemed interested. However, there were no offers. It was as mother had feared. The high price, coupled with high-interest rates, we're making the house difficult to sell.

During this period, I got to know my mother better, not as my mother, but as a person. It had been seven years since we had spent this much time together. I had left home as a teenage girl to attend college and had returned as a woman. As it turns out, mother could be fun to be with. Behind her sunglasses and sleek business suit was a twenty-something girl that liked to have fun with her daughter.

Three times we met for lunch in the city. Afterwards we spent the afternoon shopping. We visited our favorite stores, Saks, Bloomingdales, and Bergdorf Goodman. She even took me to lunch at her favorite restaurant, the Capital Grill, where we ate large salads while seated beside an enormous picture of the famous banker J.P. Morgan.

Afterwards, we returned to her office, where I observed her in her natural habitat. Mother had an enormous corner office in Lower Manhattan overlooking the Stock Exchange. It was fascinating to watch her work. I had not been to her office since I was nine years old.

During one of my trips to the city with mother, I visited Robbie's parents to discuss wedding plans. I never understood Robbie's parents. His father was cold and taciturn, as cold in real life as he was from behind his bench at the courthouse. I think when he looked at people, he did not see human beings but rather criminals who had not been caught yet.

Robbie's mother was not much better. Robbie had always referred to her as "the ice queen," and now I understood why. The day we met for lunch at the food court under Grand Central Station, she barely spoke three sentences as we ate our food in silence. She never liked me and made a point of showing it that day.

After my experience with Robbie's parents, I lost interest in planning my wedding. No one cared about planning a wedding; not Robbie, nor his parents, nor mother, nor father. Everyone was preoccupied with their own lives. They all said they would come, but no one wanted to help set it up.

After hitting the wall for four weeks, I decided to take a break and drive to D.C. to visit my father at the beginning of May. He might take an interest in my situation, I thought. Mother wanted me to deliver his convertible to him, and this seemed the opportunity I needed. She was not ready to see him. I needed to know what had happened to my parent's marriage.

Father owned a beautiful Mercedes, a 1985 380 SL convertible, painted white with a dark blue top and interior, which he kept covered in the garage. I loved the spinner wheel rims. During college, he let me drive his car occasionally. I was driving the car the day I met Robbie and think it was the reason he noticed me. A car like father's was meant to be driven, not sit in a garage gathering dust.

On my third night in D.C. I met the reason father and mother were getting a divorce. It was not just that father and mother wanted different things or that their careers were going in different directions; it was also because father had found a new love interest, a stunning young woman named Jillian.

I met Jillian at my father's favorite watering hole, The Old Ebbitt Grill on 14th street across from the Treasury building in central Washington. Father and I had visited the same restaurant only two days before when father had treated me to lunch. The Old Ebbitt was a Washington D.C. institution, a place where legislative deals were reached and where White House staffers retired for a drink at the end of the day. I loved its dark and spacious wooden booths with green cushions as well as its old-fashioned bars. There was a large bar in the front, always crowded with people and a separate bar in the back, an after-hours rendezvous place for White House staffers. It was in the back bar that I first met Jillian, my father's new love interest and future wife.

I will never forget seeing my father and Jillian enter the room. Jillian was a majestic blond with a beautiful face and sparkling green eyes. No woman had any right to look that beautiful, I thought. She had a presence about her that could stop traffic on a busy city street. She resembled Grace Kelly in her prime.

It was hard not to like Jillian, although I admit I tried. Father had met her after he came to Washington, while he was preparing for Senate confirmation. She worked at the White House and managed the confirmation process, keeping father out of trouble. She was an expert in the Washington game, the sort of woman who could disarm tigers with a mere smile. She was also only five years my senior.

That night we talked for hours until the bar eventually closed. During the conversation, I learned much about my father, as well as about his new love interest. She was not so bad. I might even eventually like her, I thought. They would certainly have beautiful children.

After Jillian left, at about 11:30 pm, father and I had a long talk until the bar closed at 1:30 am. We talked about our family, our lives, grandmother and about what mattered most in life. Father was in love with Jillian and wanted to start a second family. He wanted to start over. During our conversation, I met the man behind the mask, a man I had never met. I met my father, the real person, and my future friend.

Saying Goodbye

At the beginning of June, while the world watched soccer, we buried grandmother in Brooklyn's Green-Wood cemetery, next to grandfather. It was the first time I realized my grandparents had lost two children during the 1930s before my father was born. Grandmother had never mentioned that tragedy in her life.

I also saw the graves of my great grandparents, my Neapolitan ancestors, Giovanni De Gennaro and Clarice Brancaccio and realized they had also lost children. Giovanni and Clarice had a large family. Unfortunately, only five children survived to adulthood. I found the graves of four children who all perished. Three of them died in 1918. Two died during the Influenza Pandemic and one died serving as a soldier in France. It must have been a terrible year.

As I paused to kneel and remove the moss from their gravestones, I read their names aloud. Did their lives matter? Did my life matter? Would anyone remember me after I was gone? I did not know the answers to my questions. I only knew I had questions.

After my grandmother's funeral, the months of June and July passed quickly. Mother sold the house and then moved to London, leaving me alone to complete my unfinished business. I was present when my parents split the stuff that decorated their lives and was also there when the auctioneer sold the rest. It seemed a shame to see it go, all that stuff that had once seemed so important to me.

In the end, the only thing that mattered, the only thing that I was able to rescue from the auction, was a box of family pictures that had belonged to my grandmother. I let go of everything else. It was like dying.

After the sale, I continued to live in the big empty house for two more weeks, camping on the living room floor in a borrowed sleeping bag. My brother had lent me his blue car to get around. That week, I visited places I had known all my life to say goodbye. I visited the first house our family lived in, the elementary school I attended and the High School from which I graduated. I even drove up to New Haven and walked around the campus where Robbie and I first met in college.

My dreams of a big wedding and of our life together living in New York had turned into dust. There would be no career on Wall Street, no house in Scarsdale and no vacation house in the Hamptons. I had no sense anymore of where my life would go. No one cared about my hopes and dreams, not my parents, not my friends, not even Robbie.

At that moment, I felt homeless, vulnerable, and all alone for the first time in my life. I had one bit of business that I wanted to finish, an effort that began the first day I arrived, and afterward, I would fly to London to join my mother for the remainder of the summer. Perhaps new surroundings would make me feel a little better.

CHAPTER 33:

THE THUNDERSTORM

KIMMY CONTINUES HER STORY

In mid-July, following the World Cup, Marcello came to New York for two days to open his new account at the bank. He had decided to take a two-week vacation in the United States. For two months, my former boss, Megan, and I had been communicating with Marcello to understand his investment goals. We had tried to steer him towards mutual funds with good rates of return, but he was not interested in handing off his money to professional money managers without knowing how it was being invested.

Marcello had definite ideas about how he should invest his money. He wanted it to make a positive difference in people's lives and not just earn a high rate of return. Defense industry stocks were doing well, as were junk bonds, but he was not interested in either of these. Instead, he wanted his money to create jobs, promote the advancement of innovative technologies and make the world a better place. The last thing he wanted to do was fund companies that built weapons of war or fund mergers that put tens of thousands out of work.

He had a definite philosophy that he had learned from his stepfather Bruce, a philosophy that he intended to now put into action. "The world is what we make it," he said. "If we want the world to be a better place, we must make it so." It was refreshing to hear someone speak this way. It was so different from the 1980's ethics of Wall Street I had become accustomed to. I was beginning to fall under Marcello's spell. He was more than just a soccer player with money; he was a mensch with ideas.

The day he arrived, I met him at JFK Airport, driving my brother's car. He looked as handsome as I remembered him. As we proceeded to the parking garage to retrieve my car, he complimented me on my new shoes. He could certainly turn on the charm when he wanted to. For several minutes we walked the aisles of the garage as I tried to remember where I had parked the car.

"What type of car are we looking for?" He asked.

"I am looking for a blue car," I replied.

Marcello looked at me, perplexed. "What make is it?" He asked.

"I don't remember," I replied.

"What does it look like?"

"It is blue and box-like," I replied. I wished it were bright red. At least I might be able to find it better. Marcello smiled. I was describing his first car, a blue Fiat.

When we finally arrived at the car, he thought the car cute and said it reminded him of his old Fiat. I still thought it looked ugly, but still, I was glad I found it.

"What time is our meeting?" he asked, looking at his watch.

"It is not until 2:30 pm," I replied.

"What time is it now?" Marcello asked.

"It is 11:30 am, I think, I replied.

"Do you have time to take me to lunch?" Marcello asked.

"Where do you want to go?" I asked.

"Katz's Deli," Marcello replied! "I want to see the place where Meg Ryan had her famous "fake orgasm scene" in the movie "When Harry Met Sally." Everything Marcello knew about New York he had learned from watching movies.

Our first stop of the day was Katz's Deli, a local New York eatery located on Manhattan's Lower East Side. The deli was famous for its movie connections, its homemade corned beef, and its heaping generous portions. That day we ordered two corned beef sandwiches with mustard on marbled rye bread, two cans of root beer, a uniquely American beverage, and two large locally made dill pickles.

When our food arrived, Marcello could not believe his eyes. He had eaten large sandwiches before but was not prepared for the pile of meat he now confronted.

"How do you eat it?" He asked.

"Very carefully," I replied, smiling at him. "You need to approach it with confidence, like this," I continued, demonstrating my technique. "Do not show any fear!"

Marcello did not wait to listen to me. He had already begun to enjoy his sandwich. "Why don't they toast the bread?" Marcello asked as he struggled to keep his sandwich together.

It was clear he was losing the battle, as mustard was now leaking out of all sides. He was cute to watch. He kept turning the sandwich, eating first on one side and then on the other, trying to keep the mustard from squirting out. By the time he finished, the bread had completely disappeared, leaving only a small pile of meat firmly sandwiched between his fingers and thumbs.

I, meanwhile, had given up trying to keep my sandwich together and had opted to use my knife and fork to finish it. Marcello had triumphed, whereas I had been defeated.

"You did not think I could do it," Marcello smiled, "but I did." He was quite proud of himself. "Do you want your pickle?" He asked.

"No, you can have it," I replied. I was still busy trying to finish my sandwich.

"I love these pickles," Marcello remarked. "They remind me of the movie "Crossing Delancey." We do not have pickles like this in Italy!" I handed him my pickle. Marcello gave me a big toothy grin.

After lunch, I drove Marcello to mid-town Manhattan to sign the papers at Megan's office and then afterward took him to his hotel, the Plaza Hotel on the corner of Fifth Avenue and 59th Street. It was now 4:00 pm. Throughout the journey up Park Avenue, Marcello poked his head out of the open sunroof, looking upward at the buildings. At one point, he even sat on the roof to get a better view, letting his feet dangle into the car below.

"These buildings are magnificent," he exclaimed! "We have nothing like this in Italy! Molto Piu Bella," he exclaimed! It was not the voice of a thirty-something sophisticated Italian man in designer clothes; it was the voice of little Marcello, the shoeshine boy from Capri.

When we arrived at the hotel, he recognized it instantly. "This is where "Crocodile Dundee" stayed," he exclaimed!

"Did you bring your cutlery?" I asked.

Marcello smiled back at me and stuck his tongue out. Then he asked me a question. "Did you see Neal Simon's movie "Plaza Suite,"?" He asked.

"Yes," I replied, remembering the movie.

"I love the scene where Walter Matthau tries to get his daughter to come out of the bathroom," Marcello continued. "The poor girl had cold feet on the day of her wedding. Do you remember the daughter's name?"

As he said this, I tried to picture the scene in my mind. Then I remembered her name. It was a unique name that made the scene memorable. "Mimsy," I replied. "Her name was Mimsy."

Marcello laughed. "Do you know that Mina did the same thing the day we wed?" Marcello continued. "She locked herself in the bathroom of mother's coffee bar and refused to come out."

"Why?" I asked, "did she have cold feet?"

"No," Marcello replied. "She thought her wedding dress made her look too fat!"

"How did you get her to come out?" I asked.

"I offered her cannoli," he replied. "That and I told her that I loved her."

"Did that work?" I asked.

"Sort of," Marcello grinned. "She opened the door to retrieve the cannoli but then told me to get lost. That it was bad luck for the groom to see the bride before meeting in the church."

"Did you see her?" I was amused by his story.

"Only her hand," Marcello replied.

"So, I assume she came out?" I asked.

"Yes," Marcello replied. "She came out. She was the prettiest little cupcake I saw." Then he smiled and winked at me. "Of course, I would have married her, even if she wore nothing at all."

After he checked in at the front desk, Marcello took his luggage to the room and then returned to meet me in the lobby.

"What else would you like to do today?" I asked.

"I would like to see the Empire State Building," Marcello replied, hailing a taxi at the hotel entrance.

The idea of taking a taxi seemed logical to a man steeped in movie scenes but not practical from a transportation point of view. No sooner did we leave the hotel driveway than we became stuck in the traffic moving south on Fifth Avenue. Midtown Manhattan had become a parking lot as usual. I was glad I had parked the car.

"This reminds me of Naples," Marcello remarked, smiling.

We sat in the cab for 30 minutes, marveling at how the lights changed, but no one moved. "What good are these lights?" Marcello asked. "If you had piazzas instead of traffic lights, we would be there by now." He then told me a story of how he had once driven across Rome, from one piazza to another without ever stopping for a light.

When we reached 48th street, we decided to give up on the cab and instead take the train from Grand Central Station. In retrospect, we should have just walked.

When we entered the station, we stopped to look inside the immense hall before proceeding to the subway platforms underneath. Marcello was once again experiencing the movies. He had been in this hall many times before, but only on the silver screen. It was the first time he had seen it in real life.

"The movies do not do it justice," he remarked. Then he noticed a strong smell coming from the level below. "Is that popcorn I smell?" He asked.

"Yes," I replied, "the smell must be coming from the food court below the main hall."

"Can we get some popcorn?" Marcello asked.

"Certainly," I replied.

For several minutes we wandered below in the food court, looking for the popcorn vendor, following our noses until we found him. We bought a small bag to share and then proceeded to the subway platform, which was now crowded with people waiting for the train. It was a typical July afternoon in New York, terribly oppressively hot.

The New York subway could be unbearable in the summer. Someone has left the door open to hell, I thought. The Neapolitans believed the entrance to hell lay under Lago Averno; however, that afternoon, the New York subway was the entrance.

Overhead I could hear an air conditioner struggling to keep the platform cool. "Let us stand under the air conditioner vent" I suggested. It was the only place on the platform where the heat was bearable. Somewhere on the platform, hidden behind the crowds of people, someone was playing the saxophone. It was the song from "South Pacific" entitled "Some Enchanted Evening." Once again, Marcello was in his element.

"Do you believe two people can fall in love at first sight?" He asked.

"I suppose so," I replied, although I had to admit it had never happened to me. "Has it happened to you?" I asked.

"Yes," Marcello replied with a smile; "Cupid's arrow hit me the first time I met Mina, and it has happened again this year as well." Then he leaned over and whispered in my ear. "It happened the first time I met you," he said.

For a moment, I stood there in silence, admiring his beautiful eyes. There was something in those eyes which caused me to melt inside. Perhaps it was just the heat, I thought. It was then that a loud voice came over the PA. The southbound train was delayed due to switching problems at 104th street. For a second, I jumped, sending the bag of popcorn sailing through the air. I had created a popcorn blizzard.

Next to me, an old lady smiled up at me, aware of what had just happened. Marcello smiled at me also and then laughed as he picked the popcorn out of my hair. He looked so irresistible, laughing. I could not help myself. I leaned over and gave him a kiss. It was not a peck on the cheek but instead a long passionate kiss.

That afternoon we never made it to the Empire State Building. Instead, we returned to the street just in time to experience a thunderstorm. When we exited the station onto 42nd street, the skies had changed. The oppressive haze of summer was gone, replaced with dark greyish-green and menacing clouds.

"What do you want to do?" I asked. It was not a suitable time to visit the Empire State Building.

"Let us start walking back towards the hotel," Marcello suggested. By now, the wind was beginning to pick up. We managed to reach 49th street before it began to rain. At first, it only sprinkled. We might make it to the hotel, I thought.

As we stood in the narrow square in front of Rockefeller Center, looking towards the west, we could see the rain cloud approaching. It was like a wall of rain coming toward us. Then we saw the most magnificent sight we had ever seen. A wall of rain completely engulfed the RCA building hiding it from view.

Within seconds we were inundated, soaked to the skin as if we had been dropped into the ocean. The summer heat was gone, the air temperature dropping twenty degrees in a single second.

Holding on tight to Marcello, we embraced becoming one with the rain. It was one of the most intense moments of my life. I could feel his body next to mine, his heart beating strong. I felt more alive at that moment than I had ever felt before.

When the front finally passed, I looked up at his face. He was smiling down at me, the water pouring off his now matted black hair. "Where have you been all my life?" I asked. Marcello did not reply. He only gazed into my eyes.

That afternoon we never saw the city. Instead, we rushed back to Marcello's hotel room. When we entered the room soaking wet, we tore off our clothes and did not even make it to the bed. After it was over, and we were totally spent, we took a shower together, donned our Plaza Hotel bathrobes and ordered room service. It was one of the best days of my life.

Later that night, as Marcello lay beside me, sound asleep in bed, the full impact of what I had done set in. I suddenly felt truly awful. I knew that Robbie had cheated on me before, but up until that moment, I had never cheated on him. Would Robbie forgive me? Could I forgive myself?

As I gazed at Marcello's naked chest, I then asked myself another question. A question I could not answer. Did Marcello really mean all those wonderful things he said? Did he really love me, or did he just say that to get me in bed?

That night, I lay in bed, unable to fall asleep. My mind was racing and would not be quiet. Finally, at 4:30 am, I got up and decided to take a shower. When I emerged from the bathroom, Marcello turned over and gazed at me.

"Are you going somewhere?" He asked.

"I need to get some fresh air," I remarked. "I am going for a walk."

"Are you coming back?" He asked.

"I am," I replied. "I just need time alone to clear my head. I will meet you in the restaurant at 8:00 am," I replied.

"That is ok with me," Marcello replied. "I will meet you in the lobby at 8:00." He then turned over and went back to sleep.

When I stepped out onto the sidewalks of 5th Avenue, the street was deserted. I had never seen Manhattan before at 5:00 am. It was beautiful that morning. The thunderstorm the night before had left the city fresh and clean. That morning I took a nice long walk down Fifth Avenue towards 42nd Street. Several times I stopped to look in department store windows. As I walked by Tiffany's Jewelry store, I stopped to gaze into the display window and thought of Audrey Hepburn.

I was a jumble of emotions that morning. I had fallen for two men, Robbie and Marcello and did not know which one to choose. One had offered me a ring, and the other had not yet. Why do the men get to choose, I thought? Why can't I choose? For the first time in six years, I realized I had options. I was now no longer emotionally dependent on Robbie. I could decide my own future.

This led me to the big unanswerable question, however, the overarching conundrum of my existence. What did I want? I did not yet have an answer. What would grandmother do, I asked myself? Did mother make the right choice in her life? That last question seemed immaterial. Of course, she did, I thought. I would not even be here if she had chosen differently.

I finally understood what grandmother meant. My decisions did have consequences, enormous consequences, not just for me but for everyone after me. An entire universe of people would either exist or not, depending on my decision.

When I returned to the hotel, I found Marcello waiting for me in the lobby. He was seated in a large chair, reading the newspaper. He looked quite handsome in his glasses. I had never seen him wear glasses before. When I arrived, he looked up at me and smiled. "You look radiant today," he said. "The walk must have been good for you."

"It was," I replied. "I really needed that. It's beautiful today."

"Are you hungry yet?" He asked.

"Yes," I replied, "I am starving. Let us get breakfast."

Afterwards we proceeded to the Palm Court breakfast room for our morning brunch. Spread before us on a large table sat a sumptuous buffet, complete with eggs, bacon, sausage, potatoes, fruit, and a wide variety of pastries. It was not a day to start a diet. That could wait until tomorrow.

After breakfast, as we sipped our morning champagne, Marcello handed me an envelope. "What is this?" I asked.

"I asked my friend at the Prater's office to do research for you," he replied. "You are in luck," he continued. "She found several documents related to your family. Look in the envelope," he continued. "I have included copies of the paperwork necessary for you to apply for citizenship if that is what you want. I also included a copy of your great-grandparent's wedding certificate."

"Were you able to figure out where my great grandparents lived?" I asked.

"Yes and no," Marcello replied. "I was able to figure out where they lived, before they married, but not after. Your great grandfather Giovanni lived in a small basso, on Rampe San Antonio Posillipo, just a few steps from Piazza Sannazaro. He lived there with his father and mother. Today his basso is a vegetable stand."

I had seen many bassos in Naples. They were the small one room street level shops where Naples's poorest citizens lived. I also remembered the vegetable stand on Rampe San Antonio Posillipo. I had walked by that stand many times before without realizing its significance. I now understood my great grandfather had once lived there.

Marcello continued talking. "Your great grandmother Clarice lived at the opposite end of the Villa Comunale Park in Piazza Martiri," he said. "She lived in a large palazzo there facing the main square. Today the building has a Salvatore Ferragamo store on the bottom floor. I can show you when you return to Naples." As he spoke, he then added something, which gave me pause. "I think they married for love," he said. "It is the only way I can explain why a woman from a wealthy noble family would marry a poor shoemaker's son."

For a moment I understood something fundamental. Clarice's family had not approved the match. It was the reason Clarice and Giovanni immigrated to America.

"Do you think that is why they came to America?" I asked.

"Perhaps," Marcello replied. For a moment, Marcello had peeled back a curtain into my past, revealing a story no one in our family remembered. Why had he done this for me? Did he want me to stay in Italy with him?

Like Romeo and Juliette, Giovanni married Clarice. They came to America to begin a new life, in a place where a person's station in life did not matter. If they had never married, I would never have been born. Life had come full circle. At that moment, I began to understand what I wanted. Like a shimmering mirage in the distance, I dreamed of returning to Napoli.

CHAPTER 34:

SUMMER YACHTING WITH ANTONELLA

ANTONELLA AND ATHENA, THE YACHT

The first time I visited my grandfather on his yacht was during my first trip to Europe in 1967. I was just six years old at the time. We met my grandparents in Marseille and spent two weeks with them traveling the length of the Riviera. We visited beautiful places with charming names, places like Saint Tropez, Cannes, Monte Carlo, and Portofino. My favorite place was Portofino. It was the world's most beautiful fishing village, a place too cute to be real.

That night at age six, I met my first movie star, Elizabeth Taylor, and her then-husband, Richard Burton. They ate dinner at the table next to ours, besides the harbor, adoring me in my cute little sailor outfit. I even got to sit on Richard Burton's lap.

Every day at sea with my grandparents was a day spent in heaven. Each day we did something different. Sometimes we went ashore to go shopping, while other days we went swimming. In Monte Carlo, grandfather took me to the Casino, and twice we spent the day fishing. I loved fishing with my grandfather.

We did not mess with the small fish. We always went big, chasing swordfish and tuna. One of my favorite pictures from that summer is a picture that my grandmother took of me standing next to a tuna that my grandfather had just caught. The fish was hanging from a crane onshore and was twice as long, as I was tall. Grandfather loved his yacht. It was his pride and joy and his favorite place in the world. He and his grandmother spent every summer on his yacht, for fifteen years, from 1952 until 1967.

The yacht, which he named Athena, was twenty meters long, sleek, and beautiful. It was painted a deep and brilliant blue with white and black stripes running its entire length. Below the waterline, the color was Pompeiian Red, my grandfather's favorite color.

Inside, the boat was luxurious. Everywhere there was polished wood, nautical fixtures, and plush white and blue cushions. It also had all the latest gadgets required for life on the water. It had its own water maker, electrical generator, radio, and fish finder, as well as a beautiful teakwood deck.

The summer of 1967 was the only summer I spent with my grandfather on his yacht, as by 1968, he was gone. After grandfather's passing, the boat did not leave its slip but instead remained moored at the Naples Yacht Club, neglected, and slowly decaying. Grandmother refused to sell it, despite mother's attempts to persuade her.

Mother never liked the boat. She thought it was a waste of money. I remember her and father arguing about it. "Why do we need it?" She said. "We already have three other boats. It is just a hole in the water in which to throw money!" She was right, of course. However, grandmother refused to sell it. It had been an important part of her life she could not bear to part with. Selling the boat was like saying goodbye to her husband of over fifty years.

When grandmother finally passed away, mother again tried to sell the boat. However, this time father refused. He had taken a liking to it. Father loved the boat even though he seldom used it. He kept promising to take us to Monaco as grandfather had done but only made the trip once when I was seventeen. The reality was that both my parents were too busy working to spend summer holidays on the water. Instead, we flew to the South of France and rented houses there. That is where I met Elsa and her family in 1973. We rented a condominium next to theirs at a family resort known as San Rafael. Back at home, Athena sat neglected, abandoned in her new slip beneath the Egg Castle, soaking up money like a sponge.

Antonella and Robbie's Outing to Capri

From the moment Kimmy departed, Robbie and I began spending time together on the water. Robbie loved boats, as did I. During the week, we would meet for dinner on Athena. It was our way to be together without having to explain ourselves to Robbie's roommates. I enjoyed my time with Robbie. He was so much different than Tony, who always seemed preoccupied with sex. Robbie by contrast seemed not to care about sex. Once, I wondered if he might be gay. Elsa reassured me that he was not.

Robbie and I spent many long hours together on the yacht, talking, daydreaming, reading books, sunbathing & cooking simple meals together. I did just enough to keep his interest, but nothing more. He was engaged, after all.

It was during one of those long Sunday afternoons together that he got his idea to take the yacht to Capri for the weekend. "Do you know how much that will cost?" I asked. Robbie did not have a clue. Three to four hundred thousand lire, he guessed. "Try three times that" I replied. It was the reason the yacht never left its slip.

"Maybe if we bring more people," Robbie suggested. It seemed we had a plan. Robbie would invite his roommates and their girlfriends, and together, after passing the collection plate, we might be able to afford the trip.

Robbie's Narrative

We departed for Capri on Saturday, August 4, 1990, with our guests, David, Harry, Julie, and Elsa. I remember the date because it was two days after Saddam Hussein invaded Kuwait. Harry, David, Julie, and I understood what was coming, whereas Elsa and Antonella did not. The coming year would bring war, a war that would transform our charmed existence in Napoli.

Harry and I had already done two cases together in the Persian Gulf. There was always a sailor somewhere who did something stupid during a port call. It was only a matter of time before we would be sent there again.

That day, we departed the little harbor next to the Egg Castle at 7:00 am, gliding out into the open water on a sea as calm as glass, while below in the cabin, the girls prepared breakfast. It took $500 (at $7 per gallon) to fill the fuel tank. Hopefully, it would not take more money to return to Napoli, I thought. I was, of course, wrong.

Our voyage to Capri took three hours, enabling us to arrive by 10:00 am, just in time to disembark the girls and David for their morning cappuccino in the main square. Harry and I decided to stay behind and tend to the boat. "What time do you plan to return?" I asked.

"Let us shoot for two," Antonella replied. "We want to spend the afternoon on the water."

After the girls departed for their adventures, Harry and I retired to the back deck to sip morning margaritas in the shade. Despite the beautiful warm day, I had no interest in getting sunburned as I had gained respect for the Mediterranean summer sun.

Harry's Conversation with Robbie

As we sat on the deck, I began my conversation with Robbie. "Have you heard from Kimmy?" I asked. Robbie was busy coating the rims of our glasses with salt. "Have you heard from Kimmy?" I asked again. Robbie looked up.

"Yes," he replied. "I spoke to her yesterday on the phone."

"How is she doing?" I asked.

"She has been having a difficult summer," Robbie replied. "Her parents have split up. They have sold the house and have both moved away. Kimmy's father is now living in D.C., and Kimmy's mother has moved to London."

"Where's Kimmy?" I asked.

"Currently, she is camping in the old house in Greenwich," Robbie replied, "until the closing date. After that, she plans to stay with her mother in London until the end of September."

"When is she coming back to Naples?" I asked. "I think sometime during the first week in October," Robbie replied. "She still needs to buy her ticket."

"Did you two ever set a wedding date?" I asked.

"No," Robbie replied. "Kimmy kept hitting the wall. Every place she went, they wanted a large deposit. She was really stressed out, as she had no money. I suggested she wait until she comes back to Italy. There seemed to be no point in having a big wedding in New York after everyone moved away."

"Didn't your parents volunteer to help?" I asked. "They still live in New York."

"You do not know my parents very well," Robbie replied. "Mother cannot stand Kimmy. She has never liked her. They are incompatible."

"So, what is happening between you and Antonella?" I asked. "Do you still plan to marry Kimmy?"

Robbie hesitated for a minute to answer. "Antonella is an enigma," he replied. "I am still trying to figure her out. She came on strong to get my interest but now toys with me like a cat playing with a mouse. She gives a little, then plays hard to get. Living with Antonella is like living with a Siamese cat." I noticed Robbie did not answer my question about the wedding. He had not yet decided. He was still juggling two women in his mind.

"Did I tell you what she did last weekend?" Robbie asked.

"No," I replied, "I suppose you are going to tell me."

Robbie continued smiling. "David, Elsa, and I went to dinner with Antonella at this nice restaurant in Gaeta, he began. Anyway, as I was saying, we went to this restaurant after spending the afternoon at the beach. I ordered a steak. David ordered veal. Elsa ordered her usual roasted chicken with French fries, and Antonella ordered a house specialty, spaghetti with seafood cooked in a paper sack. "When the food arrived, everything looked great. My steak was perfect. Unfortunately, Antonella was not happy. Something was wrong with her spaghetti."

"What?" I asked.

"First off, none of the clams were home," Robbie replied with a laugh. "They had apparently taken a vacation."

"Do you mean the shells were empty?" I asked.

"Yes," Robbie replied, "they were quite empty! Seems the restaurant tried to swindle us by reusing old clam shells. That was not all, however."

"What else was wrong," I asked.

"The pasta was overcooked (according to Antonella), Robbie replied.

"Was it really overcooked?" I asked.

"No," Robbie replied. "I thought it was perfect. Antonella was just angry about the clams."

"So, what happened?" I asked. "Did she send the food back?"

"No," Robbie replied. "Sending the food back was not Antonella's style. No, she had to make a statement, a statement so bold it got us kicked out of the restaurant!"

"What did she do?" I asked.

"She stood up in the crowded restaurant and told everyone that the pasta was inedible! She then walked away without paying."

"What did you all do?" I asked.

"I chased after her," Robbie replied "while David and Elsa kept eating.

"Did she ever return to the table?" I asked.

"No," Robbie replied. "She never came back."

"Did you ever get to finish your steak?"

"No," Robbie replied. "David and Elsa eventually joined us, boxing up our food to go. I ended up eating my steak two days later. That night my dinner was an ice cream cone."

I was now beside myself, laughing. "Is there more?" I asked.

"Yes," Robbie replied. "After dinner, we took a walk on the waterfront. Elsa and Antonella walked far in front of us while David and I walked behind. Have you ever heard the story about how Antonella broke up with her last boyfriend?"

"No," I replied.

"According to David, she saw her boyfriend's car parked on Via Manzoni one Saturday night. He was having sex with another woman at the time."

"What did she do?" I asked.

"She rammed his car with her father's new SUV," Robbie replied, smiling.

"Was anyone hurt?" I asked.

"No," Robbie replied. "Turns out the man was having sex with his wife. The wife became pregnant during the process." Robbie was now smiling the biggest smile I had ever seen.

"Go on, continue," I remarked. "What happened?"

"After the incident, the wife left her husband and has now sued for divorce. She did not know about Antonella. The husband has filed a lawsuit against Antonella for child support claiming that she caused him to lose control of his, you know, manhood when she hit his car."

(Note to the reader. A similar story ran in the local newspaper when I lived in Napoli. It got many laughs at the office)

"So, what happened?" I asked.

"The judge refused to hear the case," Robbie replied. "Turns out the man did not have a middle leg to stand on."

By now, we were both in stitches, laughing so hard we had to pee. After taking turns in the tiny ship's bathroom, we continued our conversation inside the cabin. Robbie reached into the pantry, pulling out a bag of corn chips and an unopened jar of salsa, reminding me it was lunchtime.

"So, what is it you see in Antonella?" I asked, "besides her killer body."

Robbie paused and smiled. "Everything," Robbie replied! "Being with Antonella is addictive. Despite all the crazy stuff I cannot seem to get enough of her."

"Is it because she is rich?" I asked.

"No" Robbie replied. "The money is, of course, nice, but it is not the main reason I like her."

"Why do you like her?" I asked.

Robbie smiled. "I suppose it's because she's forbidden fruit" he replied. "That and she is incredibly sexy." Robbie then changed the subject. "Do you want to hear something else interesting?" Robbie asked.

"What?" I replied.

"Antonella's parents once lived in our house. They met while Antonella's father served in Naples. He was in the Navy, like you and me. He worked on the CINC's staff."

The story was getting more interesting by the minute. "Maria introduced them" Robbie continued. "She was a friend of Silvana's mother. Seems Maria and Silvana have known each other from way back. Maria is Silvana's aunt. They share the same maiden name."

"So back to my original question," I asked, "Are you in love with Antonella?"

Robbie smiled. "Not yet," he replied. "At this point, we are in "heavy like." There is something about her. She is mysterious, like the ocean. Maybe it is her deep blue eyes."

"You realize the eye color is an illusion," I replied. "She is wearing tinted contacts."

"I know," Robbie replied. "I figured that out when she took them out. Maybe it is her attitude about the money," he continued. "Antonella does not care. She simply does not care about the money. It is a means to an end, not the end itself."

"What does she care about?" I asked.

"I have no idea," Robbie replied. "That is what I find so attractive. With Kimmy, I can always tell what she wants. She is obsessed with acquiring things, houses, cars, and me. I am just another thing to her. Something she needs to own. I'm another notch in her toolbelt. With Antonella, I can never tell what she wants. She does not need me, but for unknown reasons, something primitive and animal, she wants me, and that makes her the most attractive woman in the world."

As I listened to Robbie talk about Antonella, I realized he had made his choice, although he did not realize it yet. Kimmy did not have a prayer. Robbie had chosen Antonella.

Elsa's Account of Fishing on the Boat

We returned to the Marina Grande beach as planned at 2:00 pm, following lunch above in the village. We expected to see either Harry or Robbie waiting for us on the beach. However, neither was there. Offshore, three hundred yards out sat our boat at anchor. Tied up behind the boat, floating behind it, lay our rubber inflatable boat. Where were Robbie and Harry? They had forgotten all about us.

"Did anyone wear a swimsuit under their clothes?" I asked. David replied no, as did Julie. We had not planned on this contingency.

"Someone needs to swim to the yacht," David suggested. However, no one replied. We must have appeared as a comical group, standing there on the beach with our shopping bags in hand.

It was then that I noticed Antonella begin to undress. Apparently, she had done this before. Underneath her sundress, she wore a bright yellow bikini swimsuit. "I knew this would happen," she remarked, smiling. "We left the boys on the boat with a full bar!" It took less than a minute for her to transform. When she emerged, she was the prettiest woman on the beach.

Antonella was gorgeous with long brown hair, long legs, and a perfect statuesque and tanned figure. Somehow, she looked even better than me; only she did not bother to diet. How did she do it? I was very jealous! I remembered that she ate not one but two cinnamon rolls for breakfast.

As we stood there on the beach feeling bloated from our lunch, Antonella dived into the water and began swimming towards the yacht. Ten minutes later, she returned in the dinghy to ferry us out to the boat.

"Did you find the boys?" Julie asked.

"Yes," Antonella replied. "They were swimming on the other side of the boat."

Once we returned to the boat, we set about doing different things. Antonella and Robbie continued their swim. Harry and David sat on the back deck enjoying cold beers and Julie, and I went to the front of the boat to fish. I would have preferred to lay in the sun, but Julie wanted to try fishing.

We had only one fishing pole, but that fact did not seem to bother Julie. "You take the pole;" she said, "while I improvise." Watching Julie fish was entertainment in and of itself. Lacking a pole, she tied a fishing line with a hook onto the end of her finger and lowered it over the side.

"Where did you learn that trick?" I asked.

"From my grandfather," Julie replied. "We used to fish off the dock at the cottage this way. My grandparents had a cottage on Baron Lake, near Niles, Michigan," she continued. "One day when we were sitting on the dock dangling our legs in the water, we noticed that the fish were biting our toes. We did not have poles, so we decided to improvise. Did you know that the little fish like to hide under the boat?"

"No," I replied.

"The bigger fish are scared to swim next to the boat," Julie continued. "They think the boat is a large fish." Julie was teasing me as she lay on her stomach, looking over the side. She let the bait sit on the surface until it attracted fish, and then she would gently lower and raise it, trying to entice them to bite.

"You are not fishing," I said; "you are stalking the fish." Julie laughed at me. The technique worked. She caught her first fish. It was a small fish, no more than four inches in length, but it would be the first of many.

"What are you using for bait?" I asked.

"Canned corn," Julie replied. "It's easy to put on the hook, and the fish cannot get it off."

"Hand me some corn," I suggested, as I was getting no bites using an artificial lure. The corn did the trick. Soon, I was getting nibbles also. "What happens if you catch something bigger?" I asked. Julie smiled and winked at me. "I suppose I will go for a swim," she replied.

As we sat there fishing, I then changed the subject to matters more serious. A matter which had been weighing heavily on my mind the last two days ever since Saddam Hussein had invaded Kuwait. "Do you think there will be a war?" I asked.

Julie took her eyes off the water below and turned her head towards mine. "Yes," she replied.

There was a heaviness in her voice as if she knew something horrible might happen. "Will you have to go?" I asked.

"I do not know," Julie replied, "so far, no one is saying. I have trained for this possibility; however, I think the first people to go will be coming from the States," she replied. "Our hospital may receive wounded."

"What about Robbie, Harry, and David?" I asked.

"I think for sure, Robbie and Harry will have to go," Julie replied. "They have been to the Persian Gulf twice now. They go there to retrieve sailors who get into trouble on shore leave. Getting the sailors out of the local jails can be the biggest challenge," Julie continued.

"What about David?" I asked. I was really worried about David.

"I do not know," Julie replied.

"How long do you think the war will last?" I asked.

"It is difficult to say," Julie replied. "It could be over in a couple of months or could last years. It is anybody's guess at this point." I remembered as she said this, that America's last war in Vietnam had lasted decades. The thought sent a chill up my spine. I could not bear the thought of losing David. What if it lasted for years? What would I do if something happened to David?

As I sat there tending my fishing pole, deep in thought, Julie continued to speak. "Harry and I have been talking about going to the States for Christmas," she remarked. "It may be the last time we get to go home for a while."

"Where are you going?" I asked.

"We are going to Chicago for Christmas," Julie replied, "and then on to Boston for New Year's Eve." Then she asked me a question. "Has David spoken to you about coming with us?" She asked.

"No," I replied, "he has not."

"Sorry for giving away the secret," Julie continued. "At some point soon, David is going to ask you to go with him to Chicago for Christmas."

It was the first I had heard this. Did David want to introduce me to his family? Would he ask me to marry him at Christmas? I remembered stories about how other soldiers had asked their girlfriends to marry them before going off to war. It seemed like our time together might be about to end. I was both excited and sad at the same time.

Elsa and David Go Swimming in the Blue Grotto

Later that afternoon, after a two-hour boat ride around the island, we anchored offshore opposite the entrance to the famed Blue Grotto for the night. It was now 6:00 pm, and the tour boats had departed for the day.

"Would you like to go for a swim?" David asked, "before dinner?" I nodded my head and smiled. Neither of us had been swimming yet. Soon David and I were in the water, swimming toward the Blue Grotto. The water felt warm against my skin. It was a beautiful summer evening. Above us, on the cliff, I could hear the noise of dishes rattling, as waiters set tables for dinner.

When we entered the tiny entrance to the grotto, we entered an enchanting world. The room was fifty meters long and fifteen meters wide with a ceiling that appeared to extend upwards indefinitely. Below us, the water glowed a deep and incandescent blue. It was more beautiful than I had ever realized. It was much more beautiful than the nymphaeum at Antonella's parent's house.

Below us, I could see small fish swimming. The water was very deep, and yet the water was also crystal clear. As we swam, letting our eyes adjust to the darkness, I looked around the room. Over towards one side, I could see a ledge, a place where we might be able to touch the bottom. David saw it too and motioned for me to swim towards it. When we arrived, we rested our arms on the rock ledge. The water was still too deep to touch the bottom, but at least we could hold on to the ledge.

As I turned toward David, I gazed into his eyes. He looked so handsome. I could not bear the thought of losing him. He smiled and gazed back at me, unaware of what I was thinking, reaching toward my face to remove the hair from my eyes. For a moment, we admired each other intensely, and then we kissed.

Behind us, I could hear splashing sounds as Harry and Julie entered the grotto. Both were laughing. Harry called out to David. "Are you two coming to Chicago with us?" He asked.

"I still need to ask her," David replied. He then turned towards me and asked me the question I knew was coming.

"Yes," I replied, wrapping my arms around his neck. "Yes, I would love to spend Christmas with you!" David smiled and gave me another kiss. I had made his day.

CHAPTER 35:

KIMMY'S SUMMER IN LONDON (AUGUST 1990)

I departed New York two days after my night at the Plaza Hotel to spend the remainder of the summer in London with my mother and grandmother. The last time I had been to London to visit my grandmother had been in 1983, the year I graduated from high school.

My grandmother lived in Belgravia, in a second story flat on a street known as Wilton Crescent. London's Belgravia neighborhood was a quiet residential community consisting of tall white row houses overlooking leafy green parks. It was a neighborhood built in the early 19th century filling up an area once known in Tudor times for robbers and highwaymen. It was now, however, one of the City of Westminster's most beautiful neighborhoods.

Belgravia had a wonderful, centralized location, excellent for accessing the rest of the city. Two blocks to the north lay one of the city's best shopping streets, Knightsbridge, and north of that, Hyde Park. To the west, eight blocks away, stood my favorite department store, Harrods, as well as museums surrounding the Royal Albert Hall. To the south lay Belgravia square, surrounded by foreign embassies, and further south, Victoria Station.

To the east sat the backside of Buckingham Palace's gardens, hidden behind a leafy wall and wrought iron fence. It was a wonderful neighborhood, the section of London my mother grew up in, and a place where nothing bad could ever happen. For two brief months, the movie set for "My Fair Lady" became my home.

My grandparents first moved to this quiet part of London in the 1930s before the war. They bought their flat at a time when the big row houses were being subdivided into smaller apartments, and it was here that my mother lived before and after World War II.

During the Blitz, my mother was sent off to a safe location to live with relatives in the country. She lived in a town known as Shaftsbury, close to Salisbury, while my grandparents remained in the city.

During the fall of 1941, Grandfather spent his days in the air as an RAF pilot, returning to his wife in the city whenever his busy schedule allowed. After the Battle of Britain, grandfather trained other pilots as a reward for his service. Somehow, he survived the war, even though many brave pilots did not.

After the war, grandfather worked as a banker in central London, while grandmother worked in the credit department at Harrods Department Store. Banking and finance ran in our family. My mother was just the most recent example, following in a line of bankers stretching back at least four generations. Someday I would be a banker too, I thought, if I could ever get Robbie to leave the Navy.

Moving to London brought peace to my life. My anxieties, which had been building during my stay in New York, gradually faded away. I needed stability in my life, something that felt comfortable and reassuring. There was something restful about London's beautiful West End neighborhoods which soothed my soul. I understood why my mother returned here. She needed stability also following her most recent turbulent year.

Our morning routine would begin with breakfast with grandmother and mother before mother left for work. We would eat scones with clotted cream, jam, and coffee while discussing our plans for the day. After my mother departed for work, I would go for a morning walk. Sometimes I would walk towards Hyde Park and, on other days, east into the city.

In the morning, I would visit museums or go shopping, and in the afternoon, I would often meet my mother somewhere either for lunch or for tea. Three times in the evening we went to a musical followed by dinner. We saw plays like "Cats," "Miss Saigon," and "Starlight Express."

Our favorite place for lunch was a pub in the Mayfair district that served wonderful bangers and mash (a pile of tasty sausages seated on mash potatoes and covered with a rich brown onion flavored gravy.) It was only a short "Tube" ride from my mother's place of work in Central London. According to mother, she discovered the pub during the year she dated father, before they married. He was working at the time at the U.S. Navy's headquarters on North Audley Street, across the square from the U.S. Embassy.

Our favorite place for tea was Fortnum and Mason's, a three-hundred-year-old department store on Piccadilly Street. Every little cake there was a work of art.

Dinner at a Chinese Restaurant

One night in August, after attending a play at a theater near Leicester Square, my mother treated me to dinner in nearby Chinatown at one of her favorite restaurants. Listening to her say the name always made me giggle. It was, however, a particularly excellent restaurant.

London had many excellent ethnic restaurants. It was quite different from Naples in that department. In Naples, there were only three types of restaurants, Italian, Italian and Italian. Occasionally I might find a Chinese restaurant tucked in a back alley. However, they were exceedingly rare.

All the restaurants had the same basic menu items. The only difference was the prices. If you wanted your spaghetti with clams, that would cost at least 11,000 lire. If you paid less, you might get spaghetti with empty shells. All of this said, however, Naples did have incredibly good restaurants.

There were the pizzerias with the wood-fired ovens, the elegant seafood restaurants, and the local family trattorias. We even found restaurants that specialized in grilled meats (Robbie's favorites). My favorite restaurants, however, were the ones where we could sit outside with a view of the sea.

In London, by contrast, all the restaurants were indoors. Cuisine variety replaced beautiful views. In London, I was able to sample every type of food on the planet. That summer, I ate Indian, Bengali, South African, Ethiopian, Malaysian, Thai, and many other types of food. If you wanted to sample traditional English food, however, you might have to leave the city.

For instance, I would not get to try traditional Yorkshire pudding, which is not a pudding at all but is rather a pastry filled with gravy, until I visited York in the north of England five years later.

One of my favorite aspects of London was the desserts. Mother's favorite was a traditional dessert known as "Spotted Dick." Every time she ordered it, I had to suppress my laughter, picturing in my mind a banana with spots. The dessert had nothing to do with bananas. Instead, it was a moist type of cake containing currants. The "dick part was English slang for the word pudding.

Puddings were not, however, puddings in the American sense of the word. Instead, they were moist cakes, which sometimes contained ingredients not appropriate for a cake. I learned this the hard way one time when I ordered Figgie Pudding, a dessert made with beef suet. Another of my mother's favorites was "Treacle Dick," another interesting named dessert, which was really a sponge cake with tasty syrup.

That evening we dined on crispy duck, a local specialty, which we ate with our fingers wrapping it in tiny pancakes. The skin was crispy, but thankfully not the duck meat inside. It was a high-end Chinese variation of a Mexican taco and very tasty.

After dinner, as we sipped our tea, waiting for the waiter to bring us a dessert menu (so that mother could order "spotted dick"), I showed my mother a letter I received just before leaving New York. The letter arrived the day before my departure. It was from an unknown sender and carried a concerning message.

As mother read the letter, I watched her face to glimpse what she might be thinking. Several times she scrunched her nose, but other than this, she gave no hint of her thoughts. When she finished, she set the letter down on the table and resumed sipping her tea. "What do you think?" I asked. Mother studied me intently.

"What do you plan to do?" she asked.

The truth was, I had not decided. I was thinking of confronting Robbie. I could tell from mother's face she did not think that a prudent idea.

"Be careful," mother replied, "you know he will deny it." I knew mother might be right. Robbie never confessed his infidelities. Instead, he would deny them or make excuses.

"Should I break up with him?" I asked. I really did want my mother's opinion.

"Are you ready to leave him?" Mother replied. She had a way of diving straight to the point of the matter.

"No," I replied. "I suppose I am not ready." Why did I keep doing this to myself? Why did I always have to be the adult in the room? When Robbie made a promise to me, he seldom kept it, and yet I always kept my promises to him, except, of course, the one time I did not.

"What should I do?" I asked. I could tell mother was uncomfortable with my question. I was putting her on the spot, asking her to make a difficult decision for me. I then modified my question. "What would you do?" I asked.

Mother's expression changed. She seemed willing to talk. Momentarily, the mother-daughter vail which separated us has brushed aside, and my mother became my confidant. "You need to be careful," she said. "Sometimes it is best to give your partner space. You know the truth, but sometimes it is better not to say what you know. Words can be hurtful, and once said, they cannot be un-said. The fact that Robbie cheats is not a new fact; you have known this for a while now." Once again, Mother had a way of separating facts from wishful thinking. Then she continued.

"The important question to ask is whether it matters to you. Kimmy, marriage is not just about sex. There are many more reasons why people get married. What does Robbie bring to the marriage? Does marrying Robbie offer anything for you? Does he support your hopes and dreams? Does he want the same things you do? Does he want to start a family? Can he support himself? Is he able to give you the type of life that you desire? If the answer to these questions is yes, then perhaps his latest infidelity can be forgiven; if not, it may be time to break up."

It was interesting to hear my mother frame the idea of marriage as a business decision, as I had never viewed it that way. I suppose I was love drunk, so wrapped up in the emotions of being in love that I failed to see the truth of the arrangement. Did nature do that to everyone on purpose? Was I really in love with Robbie, or was I in love with the idea of being in love? The truth was I did not know but feared it was the latter. Why did I return to someone that continually hurt me?

As I sat there pondering my situation, my mother asked me another interesting question. "What happens to Robbie when his dreams fall apart?" She asked.

"What do you mean?" I asked.

She continued her question. "Does he break down? Does he cry? Does he get angry? Does he drink? What does he do?"

I was not sure how to answer the question. I tried to remember what happened the first time he proposed, and I refused. That time he fell into a bottle. I remember that he went on a drinking binge for three days. For four weeks afterward, he would not speak with me as he wallowed in self-pity. He became temporarily mentally ill. Would he do that again?

"He lost it," I replied. "For several weeks he was a "basket case" until he finally pulled it together."

Mother stared at me again intently. "Be careful, Kimmy," she replied. "Toying with people's emotions can be dangerous. Men oftentimes appear rational on the outside, but it is important to remember that deep within, we are all emotional animals. Smashing another person's hopes and dreams can bring terrible consequences, particularly if they cannot manage rejection. You need to decide what you are going to do before you do it. If you plan to break up, it may be better to do so from a distance."

As usual, Mother's advice was sound. She had a way of cutting through the fog to understand essential truths. The truth was I was not willing to overlook Robbie's latest sins. It was too hard to forgive the sinner again if he had no intention of changing his behavior.

If mother was correct, it might be time to return the ring. What did Robbie offer me? That was the question. As I pondered that question, I realized he did not offer much. Love had blinded me to the reality of my situation. I was beginning to realize an uncomfortable fact. I was engaged to a jerk!

Dinner with Marcello at a Thai Restaurant

Marcello came to London early in September 1990, just before the start of the regular season. His team, S.S.C. Napoli had just won the Supercoppa Italiana, beating the previous season's champion Juventus, with a score of five to one. He happened to be visiting London on other business and offered to meet me one night for dinner. It would be nice to see him again, as I had something important to tell him. That night, we dined at a Thai restaurant near Trafalgar Square.

Since we last met in July, the stock market had done poorly, beginning a steep decline following Saddam Hussein's invasion of Kuwait in August 1990. The market would hit bottom in October 1990; however, we did not know that yet. Despite the losses on Wall Street, Marcello had managed to maintain his position, however. He had not made money, but he had not lost any either. Our strategy seemed to be working, even if we were doing so entirely by accident.

That night Marcello was in high spirits and very handsome as usual, eager for the start of the 1990-91 soccer season. We met at the base of Lord Nelson's column in the center of Trafalgar square. It was a beautiful "Indian summer" evening. Before dinner, we took pictures of each other standing next to the giant lions.

That night during dinner, we toasted our business relationship and looked forward to future success. Then as we finished sipping our tea, I brought up the subject near to my heart. I was incredibly nervous and had difficulty finding the words, but somehow that did not show in my demeanor.

"Marcello, I have news," I began. Then I paused to catch my breath. Marcello smiled. He seemed so relaxed and happy.

"Di Mi," he said (which means "speak to me" in Italian). He could tell I was nervous and was trying to make me more comfortable.

For a moment, I paused to reconsider what I was about to tell him. I had only just taken the test that evening. I still needed to confirm with a doctor. I then began. "Marcello," I said. "I am late."

For a moment, Marcello stared at me in silence. His eyes looked so gentle. Then he began to smile. "I knew there was something," Marcello began. "You have this healthy glow about you."

"Are you upset?" I asked.

"No," Marcello replied. "I am very happy!"

For a moment, I was delightfully surprised. Robbie was never happy when we had this conversation. Twice, I had told him I might be pregnant. Both times he looked at me as if, I told him he had cancer. Fortunately, both incidents had been false alarms. It was so refreshing to get a different response from Marcello.

"Have you taken the test yet?" Marcello asked. He seemed eager to confirm the news.

"Yes," I replied, "I did today. I am pregnant!"

By this point, Marcello was beaming and offered me a cigar. He wanted to celebrate. I smiled but also politely declined. "Is that good for the baby?" I asked.

Marcello laughed. "I feel this need to celebrate," he continued. "What to do?" He was now beside himself. "We should order a cake," he suggested.

That sounded like a better plan than smoking a cigar. Unfortunately, the restaurant did not have cake on the menu. All they had was mango sticky rice for dessert. This, however, did not stop Marcello. We ordered the rice with a big candle on top.

After we finished, we went for a walk back to the square. It was a beautiful evening. As we stood at the top in front of the National Gallery, overlooking Lord Nelson's column, Marcello got down on one knee and proposed to me. He did not have a ring, but it did not matter.

"Kimmy, will you marry me?" He asked.

"Yes," I replied without hesitation. It was the happiest day of my life. Years later I would learn he planned to propose with or without the added news I was pregnant.

The next day, we went ring shopping with mother and grandmother. It was another beautiful fall day. We went to Harrod's, my favorite store and bought a ring. It was beautiful. Afterward, we retired to the food court for lunch. All my plans had changed. I would be returning to Naples in October as originally planned, but not as Robbie's girlfriend. I would be returning to Naples to marry Marcello instead.

CHAPTER 36:

DAVID & ELSA'S SUMMER HOLIDAY IN SWEDEN (LAST WEEK IN AUGUST 1990)

It was the latter part of August 1990 when I first traveled to Stockholm to meet Elsa's parents. The upcoming month would bring two significant milestones for Elsa and me. First, it would mark our one-year anniversary together as a couple, and second, it would signal my tour of duty in Naples was entering its second and final year.

I knew I would need to make two major decisions in the upcoming six months. First, I would need to decide whether to leave the Navy and second, whether to propose to Elsa. The unexpected approach of war, however, was complicating both decisions. Elsa had one year of school remaining at the University of Naples. For the moment, our decision points were aligned. However, the war would change that in unexpected ways.

Did I want to marry Elsa? I had reached the conclusion I did. We were wonderful together as a couple. On many levels, we were happy. There was, however, a hidden divide between us. There were issues we needed to discuss, but which instead, we avoided. We both viewed our relationship through rose-colored glasses, thinking that our love could overcome any obstacles. Deep down, however, I knew we had cultural differences which might cause problems.

In many respects, Elsa was a chameleon. She had an innate ability to assume the identity of any nationality she wanted to be. She could be Italian, American, Dutch, German, or English. If you met her on the street, you would never know she was from Sweden. Most of my friends thought she was American. My problem was I could not adapt like that. No matter where I went, I would always be an American.

What did it mean that Elsa was Swedish, and how did that affect her motivations? I wasn't sure of the answer to that question. I needed to meet her family to better understand her nationality. I could take the woman out of Sweden, but could I ever take the Swede out of the woman?

I had no doubt Elsa could survive in Italy, America or anywhere else. Like a cat, she could drop from any height and land on her feet. The problem was I could not. For the first time in my life, I felt at a serious disadvantage. I should have studied foreign languages in school, however, I did not.

Studying foreign languages was not important nor required in American schools. When I moved to Italy, I told myself I would learn Italian, that it would be easy. However, it was not. The problem was not just learning the words. The problem was I needed to think in Italian. After a year in the country, I could still not do that. Instead, I kept translating in my head, which made it impossible for me to follow conversations.

I could survive simply fine as a tourist. I could order in a restaurant. I could even ask for directions, but I would never be able to work in Italy independent of the U.S. Government. My only possible employment option was to work for Uncle Sam, either as a government employee or as a contractor.

This brought me to a serious dilemma. What would happen if Elsa wanted to return to Sweden? She had mentioned a desire to return to Sweden several times. Could I learn the language? Could I earn a living, or would I become her dependent? I knew our love would not survive if I became her dependent. Elsa might be fine with the arrangement, but I never would be. If Elsa insisted on living in Sweden, I knew our marriage would never work.

Did we discuss this topic? No, we didn't! Instead, we talked around it. This was one of our major problems as a couple. We avoided difficult topics, anything which might lead to the end of our relationship. I had learned my lessons well. There were certain topics that were best avoided, such as her modeling career, and our future together as a couple.

When difficult topics presented themselves, we avoided them. We both understood our relationship had a potential expiration date of September 30, 1991 (the ending date for my tour in Italy). If we did nothing to prepare for the next step, our relationship would end. We needed to begin having the difficult conversation. The first step in that process was to visit Elsa's homeland to meet her parents.

Trip to Stockholm

We spent our first two days together in Sweden in Stockholm alone, at Elsa's parent's apartment. Elsa wanted to show me the city where she grew up, the place she called home. Afterward, we would join her family on the island of Vaxholm, where they owned a summer house.

I learned from Elsa that owning a summer cottage was a very Swedish thing to do. Everyone aspired to own a summer cottage. In this regard, Swedes were no different than Americans. It did not matter how small the cottages were. To be considered a "cottage," the house needed a front door, a window box, and an address. Beyond that, it could be the size of a privy.

Some people hauled their cottages around with them. Tiny trailers were immensely popular in Sweden. Other people opted for tiny houses on a lake. Elsa told me about the first lakefront cottage her parents owned. It was not much larger than a tent, comprising only one room. The house did not have a bathroom. Instead, everyone used a privy.

We arrived late on Friday afternoon and took a taxi to Elsa's parent's apartment. Elsa grew up in a section of Stockholm known as Osterholm. It was a nice neighborhood within close walking distance of the city center. It was quite different, however, from where I grew up. I grew up in a typical American neighborhood with single-family homes surrounded by green lawns and trees. Elsa's neighborhood, by contrast, was entirely paved. There were no trees, no grass, and no apparent places to park a car.

The building itself was modern and bland, five stories and not particularly attractive. It did, however, have a convenient location. The family apartment itself was small, with just two bedrooms, a living room, a tiny kitchen, a bathroom, and a small balcony, enclosed to form a laundry room. The apartment was furnished entirely with modern-looking furniture. For the first time, I realized Elsa shared a room with her twin sister Kristina.

During our first evening together in Stockholm, Elsa showed me her city. Just three blocks from the apartment, we entered a beautiful street known as the Strandvagen, which ran along the water towards the city center. On one side of the street sat a long row of elegant 19th-century buildings overlooking the water, and on the other side sat a row of houseboats lining a quay next to the harbor. Stockholm was a beautiful city, built on multiple islands, like a Nordic version of Venice.

As we walked towards the center, I could see a row of white ferry boats in front of a large hotel, on a point known as the Blasieholman. The historic center is behind those hotels, Elsa pointed out. She then added an interesting bit of info. "Here in Stockholm, people commute to work by ferry boat," she said. "During the summer, father uses the ferry boats to travel to work from the cottage."

After we passed the hotels, the city center came into view. Medieval Stockholm, known as the Gamla Stan, sits on an island surrounded by water. At one end of the island sits the massive royal palace, and in the center rises several tall, very German-looking church steeples. The waterfront was particularly charming. On the quays were several sailing ships. As I gazed at the harbor, admiring the view, I tried to picture it as it might have looked two hundred years before, filled with the masts of sailing ships. The view was magnificent.

Our first night, Elsa and I dined outdoors in the old town square, a place known as the Stortorget. We sat across from the Nobel Prize Museum. We began our meal with an assortment of Swedish appetizers, including various marinated types of fish, cheese, and meatballs with lingonberry preserves. For the main course, I ordered reindeer, while Elsa ordered trout. My reindeer was excellent, even though it seemed undercooked. Elsa's trout was a work of art. It had a rich butter sauce with almonds and was accompanied by five long stems of fresh asparagus.

That night we ate dinner late, enjoying the long summer evening. When we returned to the apartment at 11:00 pm, it was still light out, as if it were only 7:00 pm. I had entered the land of the midnight sun.

Day 2, Touring Stockholm's Museums

During our second day, Elsa and I visited two museums, the Vasa Ship Museum, and the Nordic Cultural Museum. The Vasa ship museum had only been open two months at the time of our visit, and Elsa wanted to see it even though it meant standing in a line for three hours. She had worked on the Vasa as a student at the university and was eager to show me the exhibit.

Inside the museum, sat a completely intact and restored wooden sailing ship, recovered from the floor of the harbor in 1961. It was gigantic and once carried over sixty large bronze cannons. It was constructed in the early part of the 17th century during the height of Sweden's maritime power. It sank on its first voyage, in front of a crowd of spectators, only three hundred feet from shore.

At the time, it was one of the most powerful warships of its age. Unfortunately, it had a major problem, a problem that no one wanted to tell the king about. It was top-heavy. The ship sank on August 10 in the year 1628, as it was leaving the harbor, when a breeze filled its sails, causing it to lean too far to port. The gunports were open at the time, about to fire a salute. When the ship leaned, water rushed into the open gunports on the lowest level, causing the ship to sink within a matter of minutes.

After we visited the ship, Elsa and I next visited the nearby Nordic Cultural Museum, where I learned, among other things, the story of the Swedish people's immigration to America. My grandmother's parents had both immigrated to Illinois from Sweden in the 1880s. My great-grandfather John came as an adult, while his wife Mathilda came with her parents as a young girl. Both families settled in Rockford, Illinois. My grandmother never visited Sweden, nor did she speak Swedish, but she did inherit its customs.

For instance, we opened our Christmas presents on Christmas Eve rather than Christmas Day. We also ate a traditional Swedish dinner with the family in Rockford until I was five years old. The dinner was served smorgasbord-style and consisted of traditional Swedish food, such as Bond-Ost cheese and Lutefisk (a type of dried fish, reconstituted in lye).

I loved the cheese but hated the fish. The best part of Christmas, however, was the rich desserts. Grandmother always had desserts in the house, often with multiple choices available. It was common to finish our meal with more than one helping of dessert.

It was not, however, until I visited the Nordic Museum that I understood why desserts were so important to my family. Within the museum was a large exhibit on desserts. It turns out that Sweden had serious issues in the 19th century. It had problems which eventually led to the socialist country existing today. The country was ruled by an out-of-touch elite. A considerable proportion of the population was poor, uneducated, exploited and living on small subsistence-level farms. This problem was particularly acute in Wester Gotland, the part of Sweden where my ancestors came from. During the years after the American Civil War, the problems worsened when crops failed, resulting in an exodus from Sweden.

It started in the 1840s and rapidly increased by the 1880s. Nearly thirty percent of the population left Sweden for a better life in America. Most immigrants settled in the American Midwest in the states of Illinois, Wisconsin, and Minnesota.

So why did my ancestors eat so much dessert? Because they could not do that in Sweden. Sweden had laws known as the "Dessert Laws," which said that only people of noble birth could eat rich desserts.

Boat Trip to Vaxholm Island

The next day, Elsa and I caught the ferry boat to Vaxholm Island, arriving shortly before noon. When we stepped off the boat, we entered the village. Across the water, I could see the outline of a fortress sitting on a separate island. The village was deserted as if all the sidewalks had been rolled up. "Is the village always this quiet?" I asked.

Elsa looked at me and smiled. "This is not Italy," she replied. "What do you do for fun here?" I asked.

Elsa laughed. "We read books and play card games."

It took us fifteen minutes to reach the house as we wandered through the village center past closed shops and businesses. I was expecting to see a seafood restaurant; however, the only restaurant we passed was Greek. After four twists and turns, we came to a narrow one-way road running along the water. On both sides of the road sat pretty houses behind picket fences. Three houses were painted pastel colors, while two houses sorely needed paint. The houses were an assortment of vintages, some appearing old and others modern.

"Can we see your house yet?" I asked.

"Yes," Elsa replied. "Our house is the long green colored house up ahead. It is just after the red garage." Ahead I could see a long one-story house, painted green with fancy white windows and shutters. The house seemed almost Russian in character. "Our house is the oldest house on the street," Elsa explained. "The original house is a log house, which has been modified three times."

"Where are the logs?" I asked.

"The log part is at the end closest to us," Elsa replied. "It dates to the 1700s when this area was a farm. The house was altered in the 19th century when two additional rooms were added."

"How many rooms does it have?" I asked.

"Three," Elsa replied. "There is a kitchen, a bedroom, and a combined living-dining room."

"Does the house have a bathroom?" I asked.

Elsa smiled. "It does now," Elsa replied. "Father converted the old woodshed into a bathroom when I was in high school. It is behind the garage."

When we arrived at the front gate, we were greeted by two small dachshunds (Sigmund and Glinda) belonging to Elsa's parents. Behind them stood Elsa's sister Kristina. Kristina smiled and gave us each a hug. "It is good to see you again," she remarked. Then she added, with a hint of mischief in her voice, that we had a guest for dinner.

"Who is it?" Elsa asked.

"It is Sven," Kristina replied.

For a moment, Elsa's face changed. Her smile turned into a look of panic. Her old boyfriend had stopped by to pay her a visit. "Does he know I am with David?" She asked.

"Yes," Kristina replied. "Father invited him to dinner today so that he could meet the competition."

There was a story that Elsa had not told me. It turns out Sven's family cottage was nearby, and that Sven and Elsa's father were good friends. When we arrived at the front door, I met Elsa's father, the blond, middle-aged college professor. I also met Elsa's boyfriend Sven, and Kristina's new Dutch boyfriend, Peter.

Elsa's father was tall and blond, with a gracious smile and a handshake to match. Sven looked like a Viking, with thick curly reddish hair, a mustache and beard and strong muscular arms. His handshake nearly broke my hand. Kristina's boyfriend Peter looked like Neal. Neal may have had a chance with Kristina, I thought to myself.

Elsa's parent's house was quite charming inside. Elsa described the house as very traditional Swedish in style. It was a warm and cozy house. The living room, which was once the only room, had a large walk-in fireplace big enough for roasting a pig. Within the fireplace, Elsa's father had installed an antique spit roasting gadget that had three rotisserie spits linked together by medieval-looking chains and gears. "Do you ever use that?" I asked.

"No," Father replied smiling. "We use the gas stove."

Near the fireplace stood a bookshelf, a TV on a stand, an end table, and a pullout sofa. At the other end of the room sat a large dining room table surrounded by cabinets containing dishes. The traditional Swedish family room revolved around the dining table, not the TV.

After we entered the house, Elsa took me into the kitchen to introduce me to her mother and then proceeded to give me a tour of the house. The tour lasted less than five minutes, including the outdoor bathroom. When we finished the tour, we walked down to the water to speak for a moment, away from Sven.

"Where are we going to sleep?" I asked.

"We get to sleep on the pullout sofa," Elsa replied with a smile. "Kristina and Peter get to sleep in the loft, and mother and father of course, get the bedroom."

"So, what is with Sven?" I asked. "Does he know we are dating?"

"He does," Elsa replied. "He lives three doors down. It is hard to avoid him when at the cottage. Now you understand why I wanted mother and father to come to Stockholm to meet you."

"Why is he such a pest?" I asked.

Elsa smiled. "Now you know why we broke up," she replied.

When we returned to the house, dinner was ready. That afternoon we ate smorgasbord style. We ate pickled herring appetizers, followed by candied ham balls with au gratin potatoes. For a moment, I was back again in Illinois. At the end of the meal, we had a choice of desserts. There were cookies, cake, and apple pie, and then, of course, after the meal, we drank coffee. After we finished, I felt like I had eaten a watermelon. The only thing missing from my first Swedish family meal, thankfully, was the Lutefisk.

The Card Game

After dinner, we cleared the table, washed the dishes, and then sat down for a family tradition, a card game known as "Scat." Soon, neighbors joined us until there were fourteen people seated around the table, all eating dessert and drinking coffee. The room had become quite crowded. We had to break out the folding chairs stored in the garage attic to seat everyone.

I was no stranger to this game, as my family had played this game back in Illinois. Grandmother thought it was a Swedish game. However, Elsa's mother knew the true origin. The game originally came from Prussia. The object of the game was simple. The person to survive to the end would win the "kitty", which in our case, was the Swedish equivalent of $200.

At the start of the game, each person would receive three cards and three poker chips plus one "free ride." As each hand was played, each player would have a choice. They could either pick up an unknown card from the deck, or they could pick up the last card discarded (face up). If you picked up from the discard deck, it would show the other players the suit you were collecting. What you discarded would also show them what you were not collecting. After several rounds, either someone would score thirty-one, or someone would "rap," signaling the round of play was complete.

If someone "rapped," everyone would have one additional chance to play (in the reverse direction) and then would have to show their cards. All players with hands scoring less than the hand of the "rapper" would have to forfeit a chip. If someone scored a thirty-one, they would say "scat," which would require that everyone forfeit a chip. Once a player lost all their chips (plus their free ride), their participation in the game would end.

The game sounds simple, however, it was not. Once the game started, the shenanigans began. The men would light up pipes or cigars to create the proper atmosphere. To facilitate the smoking, Elsa's Father brought a box of cigars to the table. Even Elsa lit up. Kristina and her mother liked to hide their poker chips. Kristina would hide her chips under her beer can while her mother kept her chips hidden under her coffee cup. Elsa would occasionally get up to refill the coffee cups, using the opportunity to peek in other people's hands.

Elsa's father seemed the cleverest of all. Elsa's father was the smartest. The professor seemed to know what was in everyone's hands. It turns out he was counting cards, watching what every person discarded and then backward calculating the cards remaining. He did this without taking any notes. This was no small feat, as we were playing with four decks of cards.

Once I realized his trick, I started making discards to throw him off track. I also learned to keep my cards face down on the table so that Sven, who was sitting beside me, could not peek. The worst cards to discard were aces. Giving someone an ace to pick up could cause them to "Scat." This forced me to hold on to aces I didn't want until I was certain the person next to me was not collecting that suit.

The game, which seemed so simple, lasted all evening. By the end, only two players remained, me and Elsa's father. As we smoked our cigars, everyone else watched. The game finally ended at 11:30 pm, when I laid a clean thirty-one on the table and said, "Scat."

Elsa's Father smiled. I had won the professor's respect. Afterward Elsa congratulated me. "Father likes you," she said. "Sven has never been able to beat him."

You may ask, Did Sven stay for the entire card game? Yes, and no. He started the game but soon wasn't doing well. Midway through the game, after eight rounds of play, Elsa got up to heat water for tea. Sven followed her into the kitchen, where loud words were exchanged in Swedish.

Soon thereafter, we heard the kitchen door slam shut. Sven had gone home, taking his one remaining chip with him. When Elsa returned to the game, she informed us that Sven had decided to leave. "What did you say to make him leave?" I asked. Elsa smiled and winked at me.

"I told him we were engaged," she replied.

When she said this, everyone stopped talking for a moment. Then Father smiled. "Are you two really engaged?" He asked.

Elsa looked at me with a twinkle in her eye. "Not yet, papa," she replied, "we are still working on that." It was the first time that Elsa had ever suggested she was working on marrying me.

Later that night, after everyone had gone to bed, Elsa and I took a walk beside the water. It was twilight time, but not quite dark. Even in the middle of the night, nature had left the lights on. When we reached the dock, Elsa motioned for me to sit beside her on a log.

She began our conversation with an apology. "David, I am sorry I mentioned we might get married, given the fact we never discussed it. I needed to say something to Sven to make him go away."

"What happened between you two?" I asked. For a moment, Elsa stared into the water. Then she told me something she had told no one else.

"Before I came to Italy, Sven hit me," she replied. "We had a big fight. Sven wanted me to buy a house with him and I said no. He accused me of running away from life. I slapped him hard, and then he punched me in the face. For several minutes afterward, I saw stars. He really scared me."

"Do you still have feelings for him?" I asked.

"No," Elsa replied, "not after he hit me. It is over between Sven and me. I have told him several times, but he doesn't give up."

"Have you told your parents what he did?" I asked.

"No," Elsa replied, "I have not been able to bring myself to do it. Father and Sven became close while we dated. It would break his heart."

"You need to tell him," I replied. "He needs to know."

For a moment, Elsa wrapped her arm around my waist. I could see she had tears in her eyes. She leaned over and kissed my cheek. "Thank you for listening to me," she said. Then she changed the subject. "David, I meant what I said in the dining room. I know we have not discussed it, but I really meant that."

"I know you did," I replied. Then I asked her a question. "Do you think we can make it work?" I asked.

"What do you mean?" Elsa replied.

"We are from two different worlds," I replied. "For the present, we live together in Italy. However, that will not last forever. Someday you will graduate, and my tour of duty will end. What will we do after that?"

Elsa smiled. "Maybe you could move to Stockholm?"

This was the answer I feared. I needed to phrase my response delicately so as not to burst her bubble. "Elsa, I am not sure I can make it here," I replied. "I am not like you. Learning a new language is hard for me. I need to be able to work and earn a living, and I am not sure I can do that here." Elsa nodded her head. It seemed she understood.

Then she asked another question. "David, do you love me?"

For a moment, I was silent, thinking of the right thing to say. I did love Elsa but wanted to find a more beautiful way to say it. I didn't want her to think I was willing to move to Sweden. What did she want to hear? I wanted to say something she would remember for the rest of her life. For a moment, I hesitated, then I offered a reply.

"Elsa, when I look at you, there is nothing that I see that is not perfection." I had answered her question without answering it. Elsa smiled the biggest smile I had ever seen her smile. Somehow, she understood me. We connected at a level too hard to describe in words.

Then she embraced me and whispered in my ear. "I love you," David, she said.

"I love you too," I replied, kissing her on the lips.

CHAPTER 37:

TRIP TO THE SOUTH OF FRANCE

(LATE AUGUST 1990)

During Ferragosto, that two-week period at the end of August when half of Italy goes to the beach, Harry and I decided to take a road trip to the French Riviera accompanied by our girlfriends, Antonella, and Julie. Originally, we planned to take Julie's car. However, it blew a head gasket two days before departure. When it came to cars, Julie's luck was always bad. Instead, we drove Harry's big mean green machine as it was the only car able to fit everyone.

The plan was to drive from Naples to San Raphael-Frejus, a place recommended by Antonella, where we would spend two nights. Afterward, we would spend one night with Antonella's parents in Monte Carlo and would then drive home. In retrospect, we spent four days on the road to spend three days on vacation.

On the first day, we drove as far as Lucca, a small walled city west of Pisa. We stopped to see the twelfth century leaning tower of Pisa and ended up visiting the entire cathedral complex. The most beautiful sight, however, was the interior of the eleventh-century cathedral and its magnificent art. Afterward, we bought our replica leaning towers and went on our way.

The first night we stayed in the city center of Lucca, just a short drive from Pisa, in a hotel near a large medieval tower. The tower was unique in that it had several large oak trees growing on the roof.

During our second day on the road, we traveled from Lucca around the end of the Italian Boot past Genoa to San Rafael. We passed several places worth visiting however, Harry was determined to reach the French border and did not want to stop to see any sights.

Any thought of stopping to admire the scenery was not considered. It would not be until many years later that I finally visited the Italian Riviera and realized what we had missed. Instead, we admired the engineering excellence of the Italian Autostrada. We must have passed through at least 200 tunnels before we stopped counting.

Driving with Harry was always an exhilarating experience. The entire trip, he kept his foot glued to the floorboard, oftentimes exceeding one hundred miles per hour. All through the trip, Julie kept hitting her imaginary brake on the passenger side of the car. I thought we were flying. However, Antonella thought we were barely moving. "This is nothing" she said. "Father's Ferrari is much faster!" I had not met the Ferrari yet. Perhaps I would meet it in Monte Carlo.

When we finally arrived at our hotel, it was not on the beach as advertised but instead sandwiched between two yacht clubs. We would have to find the beach another day.

Robbie's Day at the Beach

On our first day in France, the girls suggested we go to St Tropez for the day. They wanted to sunbathe on the famous nude beach. Harry and I thought about the offer and then declined to go with them, however. It's not that we were not interested but rather that we might embarrass ourselves. The girls did not seem to mind.

After the girls departed, Harry and I decided to find the beach. Harry had been reading the travel book. There is a big beach somewhere near here, he remarked. The Allies landed here in 1944. We found the beach without any problems.

San Rafael was a pretty and very modern resort. Clearly, the Allies did major damage during the landings as all the buildings were new. The town had nice wide sidewalks along the beach, as well as particularly good sand, but the part Harry and I liked best was the long row of restaurants and bars on the opposite side of the street.

Once we found the beach, we rented an umbrella and sat down to admire the view. It was now 11:30 am, and the beach was beginning to fill up for the day. Unfortunately, we sat down in an area surrounded by old women. This was not the French Riviera we expected. "Where are the babes?" Harry asked. He had one thing on his mind. He had come to see tits.

After spending $30 to rent a spot, and 30 minutes laying in the sun, we had had enough. "Let us find a place to get lunch" Harry remarked. I agreed. The last thing I wanted to do was get badly sunburned my first day on vacation.

This was when we began our search for the ultimate place to eat. I thought we were looking for a place with tasty food, whereas Harry had different ideas. As I looked at the menus, Harry kept walking. "What is wrong with this place?" I asked.

"Nothing," Harry replied. He just kept walking. It seemed he wanted to walk the entire length of the beach. Perhaps he wanted to check out all the restaurants before deciding, I thought.

"Is there a particular type of food you are looking for?" I asked.

"No," Harry replied. "It's not the food I am looking for."

Finally, after a mile of walking, Harry found his spot, one of the most decrepit bars on the beach. "What is so special about this spot? I asked."

"Look across the street," Harry replied.

It was then that I saw the object of Harry's search. He had found the one bar on the beach opposite the showers. He was now ready to see the babes.

That day, we sat at the bar, drinking beer, and eating appetizers all afternoon, while we watched hundreds of beautiful young women rinse off at the showers. Many women were quite lovely, while others were not. We saw all shapes and sizes, including women we admitted; we would have paid to put their tops back on. By the end of the afternoon, I was glad I had decided to study law rather than medicine.

That afternoon we tried all manner of French appetizers, which Harry referred to as "bait." We ate snails, tiny silver anchovies marinated in lemon juice, and frog legs, which resembled miniature chicken drumsticks. We also tried the fish soup, which contained no fish at all. Harry had his theory about the soup. He thought it was the rinse water used to clean the fish market. I pointed out it was a vehicle in which to eat croutons and mustard. The croutons and mustard did make it taste better. In fact, it was quite good once I stopped looking for the fish. Harry preferred to eat the croutons without the soup.

The highlight of our afternoon was watching a young woman eat an ice cream cone. She was a goddess, perhaps 20 years old, with a beautiful tan perfect figure. She had just finished showering. She stood across the street in front of an ice cream stand, eating her cone piled high with multiple scoops of ice cream, while her friends finished ordering.

It was a sweltering day, and it was clear she was struggling to keep control of her cone. She would lick one side of the cone and then the other, deftly catching the melting ice cream trails before they reached her fingers. It seemed as if she might finish the cone before it melted. Then it happened. One of the balls of ice cream on the top gently rolled off in slow motion. It did not land on the ground but instead landed on her naked breast, slowly rolling down until it dropped to the ground.

As Harry and I sat mesmerized, with our tongues touching the ground, she cleaned herself up with her index finger. She would wipe and then lick, wipe, and then lick until all the ice cream was gone. Then she turned, smiled, and winked at Harry and me before walking away with her friends.

That afternoon Harry and I had a wonderful time. We experienced the French Riviera in summer, enjoying tasty food and great scenery without having to apologize for being men.

Harry & Julie's Conversation at the Bar

Julie and Antonella returned from their day in St Tropez around 5:30 pm to find Robbie and me, seated at the bar beside the hotel pool. "Care to join us?" I asked.

"No thanks," Julie replied, "I am going to go upstairs to change. We are both a little sick to our stomachs right now."

"How was the beach?" I asked.

Julie smiled. "It was wonderful; however, the aftermath was not so great. How red am I?" Julie asked.

"Not too bad, I replied, for a lobster." Julie smiled. "Did you rent an umbrella?" I asked.

"No," Julie replied. "They wanted $100 for the umbrella. I wanted to rent it, not buy it. We decided to go without. Would you believe we used sunscreen?"

"How long did you lay on the beach?" I asked.

"Only an hour," Julie replied. "Unfortunately, we did so in the middle of the afternoon."

"Did you show the birthday suit?" I asked.

Julie laughed. "No, she replied. Antonella chickened out."

At this, Antonella gave us a sheepish grin. "Do not tell anyone," Antonella replied. Then she excused herself to visit the bathroom.

"What is with her?" I asked.

"She ate some bad sushi," Julie replied. "We had to stop twice on the way home so that she could revisit her lunch."

"What did you eat?" I asked. "I had French onion soup" Julie replied.

"So, what did you do all day?" I asked.

"Mostly we shopped," Julie replied. "St Tropez has an interesting city center and market. We also looked at the beautiful yachts moored in the harbor."

"What did you do today? Julie asked.

"Robbie and I found the beach," I replied. "This town has a pleasant beach."

"Obviously, you did not play in the sand all day," Julie remarked, noting we were not sunburned.

"No," I replied, "we tried that for 20 minutes and had enough."

"Did you end up on the old lady beach?" Julie had read my mind. "So, what did you do after the old lady beach?" Julie asked.

"We spent the day sitting on the boardwalk at a bar, watching people," I replied.

Julie smiled. She was having fun with her line of questioning. "Let me guess," she replied. "Was the bar in front of the shower?"

I laughed. "How did you guess?"

"I asked myself what John Belushi would do," Julie replied laughing!

Later That Night in Bed

Julie's sunburn did not take full effect until after the sun went down. That night, I slept under the covers trying to stay warm in our over-air-conditioned room, while Julie lay on top of the bed wearing shorts and a t-shirt. Everything hurt. It hurt to lay on her back as well as her stomach. The part of her body which hurt the most, however, was the top of her feet. That was the one place she did not apply sunscreen. As we lay in bed, unable to sleep, Julie told me more about her week.

"I learned something interesting this week," Julie began. "I spoke to Kimmy last Wednesday."

"How is she?" I asked.

"She is doing well. She is in London now with her mother. It sounds like she is having lots of fun. Marcello visited her in New York just before she left."

"Who is Marcello?" I asked.

"The soccer player from across the street," Julie replied. "You met him at the party, don't you remember?" At that moment, I did not know who she was talking about. The only soccer player I could remember was Mendoza.

"So, what else did you learn?" I asked.

"Kimmy knows that Robbie and Antonella are dating," Julie replied. For a moment, there was silence in the room.

"How did she find out about that?" I asked.

"Someone sent her an anonymous letter," Julie replied.

"And she called you to confirm?" I asked.

"Yes," Julie replied, "and I did so."

For a moment, I heard the screech of brakes and then the sound of breaking glass. Someone outside our hotel had just gotten into an accident. Julie smiled at the perfect timing.

"Did she sound upset?"

"No," Julie replied. "She was detached about it as if she were reading the weather report. It did not seem to affect her at all. What is with that pair?"

"I honestly do not know," I replied. "I stopped trying to figure them out a long time ago."

Julie then added, "Harry, do not take this the wrong way, but I do think your best friend is a jerk!" Julie always had a way with words.

"Kimmy's no peach either," I replied. Julie smiled in agreement. Then I changed the subject. "So, what is happening between Antonella and Robbie?" I asked.

"Antonella seems quite smitten," Julie replied. "She is a woman in love."

"Does she understand what she is getting into?" I asked.

"She does," Julie replied. She then added an interesting observation. "I think in Antonella, Robbie has met his match!"

Julie's Next Day

After our miserable sunburned evening, Harry, Robbie, Antonella, and I, spent the next day touring the French countryside between San Rafael and Monaco. We had had enough of the beach.

During the morning, we visited Antibes, a pretty town on the coast with an old and interesting fort. Afterward, we traveled to a small hilltop village named Vence for lunch. We thought about driving to nearby Grasse to visit lavender farms; however, the boys persuaded us instead to go for a drive high above Monaco to see the view. Harry wanted to travel the road traveled by Carey Grant and Grace Kelly in the movie "To Catch a Thief." In retrospect, it was the better choice.

The best view of the Cote D'Azur was from the hills above the coast. It was not down along the water. That afternoon we drove the Corniche Road from Villefranche-sur-Mere to Menton. We drove high above Monaco, following the route of the old Roman road, which once connected Italy with Gaul.

It was as beautiful a drive as the Amalfi Coast. At one point, we stopped to look out over the tiny Kingdom of Monaco. Monaco looked like Manhattan, a sea of high-rise buildings, all jammed into a tiny space between the mountains and the sea. We also stopped to visit a Roman ruin known as La Turbie midway on the drive. It was a monument, now covered with scaffolding, marking the boundary between Italy and the Roman province of Gaul.

After our drive, we returned to Monaco to spend the evening with Antonella's parents. We did not, however, stay with them, as their apartment was too small to sleep six people. Instead, we checked into our hotel, which was within walking distance of the Casino.

Robbie & Antonella's Evening in Monte Carlo

It was not until 7:00 pm that Antonella finally emerged from the bathroom, fully transformed. When she went in, she looked like a woman who had spent the day riding in a car with all the windows opened. When she came out, she had become a bronzed goddess.

Antonella wore an evening dress that perfectly complemented her tan. It was not red nor purple, but a lovely shade in between. Around her neck, she wore a string of white pearls. Without a doubt, I knew I would have the most beautiful date in the Casino.

We met Antonella's parents, as well as Harry & Julie, in the hotel bar and then proceeded to the rooftop restaurant for dinner. Outside the bar in the lobby, we stopped to view a race car parked there. It was the car that had won the Grand Prix earlier in May.

After ogling the car, we went upstairs to the roof for dinner. That evening we ate dinner on the roof of the hotel, overlooking the Mediterranean Sea. The brilliant blue colors of water and sky from earlier that afternoon had transformed into shades of grey making it impossible to discern the dividing line between water and sky.

That night we ate small but expensive, artistic meals with multiple courses. In between the courses, the waiter brought us little dainties to cleanse our palates. They were items that were not on the menu. One of the miniature appetizers was a single strawberry; another was a tiny ball of lime sorbet. I think one appetizer might have been pancreas. Antonella's favorite dish was the goose liver pate. I tried a bite and was delightfully surprised. I thought it would taste like liver; however, instead, it tasted like butter.

During one of the courses, the waiter offered to shave truffles onto our food. Antonella and Julie agreed to try. However, Harry declined, opting instead for the pepper. I tried the truffles but had to admit afterward that it did give the food an earthy taste. Harry laughed. "I told you so," he remarked. My favorite food of the night was pepper steak. The steak was cooked perfectly and served with a cream sauce containing red peppercorns.

The crowd at the restaurant was particularly interesting. Everyone was impeccably dressed, and yet I felt surrounded by a rogue's gallery of characters. It seemed like we were sitting in a section reserved for villains and spies.

As I gazed at a balding, fat gentlemen nearby I shared my observations with Antonella. She laughed and then responded in her Russian woman accent. "Really, darling, you've been watching too many movies", she said. For a moment, Antonella became a Russian secret agent. She reached into her purse and discreetly handed me a roll of film. "Here is the microfilm darling," she remarked. I couldn't help laughing.

That night, Antonella was stunning. Everything she did was mesmerizing. Her smile, the look in her eyes, the way she folded her hands, and the way she laughed was all enchanting to me. At times it was as if there were no one else in the restaurant. I had no inkling about what would happen after dinner.

Conversation between Antonella and Robbie

That evening, Robbie was enchanting. It was like dining with Harrison Ford recently returned from his latest adventure. As I sat there admiring my man, I reminded myself not to chicken out. That night I had a mission. Something I needed to do to win my man. It would be hard, but I needed to do it.

Two days before, Julie had told me a secret. A secret concerning Robbie, as well as a secret he did not know. We had tried to be discrete. However, Kimmy had found out about our affair. In addition, she still planned to return in October. Robbie had not broken their engagement. He had lied to me.

After the meal, everyone retired to the Casino, leaving Robbie and me standing outside. I did not want to go in until I had a chance to talk to Robbie. "Let us go for a walk," I remarked. "I need to walk off our big meal before we go into the Casino." Robbie agreed, having no idea what I wanted to discuss. It was the first time we had been alone together since before St Tropez.

I had thought about bringing up the subject after my day at the beach with Julie but had been too sick that night to bring it up. As we walked down the hill towards the old city, I finally mustered the nerve to say what was on my mind.

"Robbie, Julie, and I had an interesting conversation in St Tropez," I began. "Julie told me several things. First that Kimmy knows about our affair." I stopped a minute to let that fact sink in. Robbie's face turned as white as a sheet.

"How did she find out?" He asked.

"I do not know," I replied. "Suffice it to say, she knows!"

"What else did Julie tell you?" Robbie asked.

"Julie told me that Kimmy is returning to Naples, the first Wednesday in October. She bought her ticket last week. She is flying from London Gatwick directly into Naples."

Robbie looked perplexed. "Didn't I already tell you that?" He asked. He was trying to cover his tracks. Then he added insult to injury. "Can you please move out before she arrives?" What a thing to say! He wanted me to just disappear.

"Robbie, why is Kimmy returning to Naples?" I asked. "I thought you said you broke up."

For a moment, Robbie stopped talking, trying to think of something to say. I had just caught him in his lie. "It's not what you think," he stammered.

"What is it then?" I asked.

He then backtracked. "Well, technically, it is what you think. I am sorry I lied to you. I could not bring myself to do it. Kimmy still thinks we are getting married."

For a moment, I listened, letting his words sink in. Once again, Robbie was trying to have it both ways. "Are you going to tell her it is over?" I asked.

"I do not know," Robbie replied. He was becoming a weasel.

"Look, Robbie, I like you," I replied. "You know that, but I am not willing to participate in this love triangle any further. I have been through this before, and it did not end well. Robbie, I am in love with you. You know I want you, but I do not need you! If you want us to be a couple, you must leave Kimmy!"

As I said, this Robbie looked at me with pleading eyes. "Why do we need to discuss this now?" He asked. "It's only the end of August. Kimmy does not come home until October. We still have a full month to be together!"

Robbie was vacillating. "Dammit, Robbie!" I replied. "Kimmy may be willing to put up with your bullshit, but I am not! If you want me, you need to understand I will not share you, not with Kimmy, nor with any other woman!"

"Can't we at least finish the vacation?" He asked.

"No!" I replied. "Tonight, I will stay with my parents!"
"How will you get home?" He asked.

"That is not your problem!" I replied.

I had played my chip, the only chip I had to play. I wondered if it would be effective. I left Robbie standing by the railing and walked back to the hotel, trying not to cry. It was not how I wanted our vacation to end but things needed to be said.

Julie and Harry's Night in the Casino

After dinner, Harry and I proceeded into the Casino with Antonella's parents. Inside, the Casino was dazzling. It was not what I expected, however. I expected the Casino to resemble a hotel in Las Vegas, a large room filled with slot machines, bright lights, and gaming tables. Instead, we entered an elegant room with only gaming tables. We had entered the world's oldest Casino, the place that defined all casinos which followed.

Seated at the tables were the rich, and the wannabe rich, beginning their night of gambling. I remembered that Harry had told me about Monte Carlo, that the citizens paid no taxes. He told me that all the Kingdom's revenue came from the gaming tables.

That night Harry and I played Blackjack and Roulette. Once I lost my $200, I wisely stopped playing. However, Harry kept going. Soon he won enough money to pay for our trip. Once he achieved his goal, he stopped also. We then decided to watch Antonella's parents play. Antonella's father, Charles, was doing well at the Bacharach table.

As we watched him play, trying to understand the game, I managed to catch Antonella entering the room out of the corner of my eye. She was smiling her usual radiant smile; however, I also noticed her eyes were red. She had been crying.

"How did it go?" I asked. I knew why she had been crying.

"It was difficult", Antonella whispered. "I do not know what he will do." She had taken a big gamble, bigger than any gamble made in the Casino that night. She had bet her future that Robbie would do what she wanted.

"What happens if it does not work?" She asked.

"Do not worry," I replied. "I think it will work. He is crazy about you. He never looks at Kimmy the way he looks at you!"

CHAPTER 38:

KIMMY'S RETURN TO NAPLES

(EARLY OCTOBER 1990)

AFTER THE DECISION

After Marcello departed London to return to Naples, it seemed as if life had not changed, and yet it had. Suddenly the grass was greener, and the skies were prettier than they had been before. A giant weight had been lifted from my soul, and I now walked with a spring in my step. For a moment in time, I felt happier than I had ever felt before.

I had not realized the toll that the previous year had taken on me. Living with uncertainty and disappointment had been painful. Robbie had no idea of the pain he had caused me. It was a pain that multiplied seven-fold when I returned home to discover my parent's divorce. When I needed him most, Robbie was not there for me.

During the weeks following my engagement to Marcello, I learned much more about my mother and grandmother than I knew before. I thought they might be unhappy with my impetuous decision to marry Marcello; however, they were not. They were genuinely happy for me and the decision I had made. During our conversations, I learned that Grandmother had only known grandfather four months before their engagement. (I had known Marcello for five months).

Mother turned out to be more impetuous than I. She had met my father at a Christmas Party in 1959 and became engaged one week later. "We knew of each other for several years." Mother pointed out. "I just did not know that he was in love with me."

Grandmother laughed. "You two were crazy," grandmother exclaimed. "Your father and I never thought it would last, but it did."

It turns out my family had a history of "short engagements." "Long engagements are highly overrated," grandmother added. "Spending too much time with someone before becoming engaged is like wading slowly into freezing water." She thought it better to just jump in.

It seemed to work for my grandparents, as they were married for 50 years before grandfather passed away. As for my mother, I was not so certain. She, however, was, admitting she would do it all over again if she had the chance.

Getting to Know Marcello

After our engagement, Marcello called me every day, no matter where he was or what he was doing. He was very attentive, sending me little presents each Wednesday to celebrate our anniversary. One week it was a single rose; the next week, it was a box of chocolates and then a tin of cookies. Every Wednesday, there would be something.

Once during the month of September, he returned to London for several days to visit me between games. We spent our time together walking in the park, eating out, visiting museums and shopping. During our week together, we decided to get married at the Naples Courthouse in October. This would enable me to become an Italian citizen. We decided to have a big church wedding in Capri the following summer after our child was born.

We also had several interesting discussions about where our baby should be born. Already Marcello was thinking hard about the baby's future. We both agreed the baby should be born in America so that he or she could be born an American Citizen. Marcello also encouraged me to pursue a British Passport through my mother as well, so that we might have our choices of places to live. Marcello held two passports (the United States and Italy), and soon I would hold three. (United States, Italy, and Great Britain).

As the date for my return drew closer, I had one bit of business I needed to finish. I needed to return Robbie's ring. I would turn to Julie for help with that matter.

Saying Goodbye

I was a bundle of nerves the day I returned to Naples. I was happy as well as sad, about to begin a new life with Marcello and close my life with Robbie. All through the flight, I practiced in my mind what I might say. Mother had suggested I tell Robbie over the phone or write him a letter, but I could not do that. It did not seem right. I needed to tell him in person so that we might be able to part as friends if that was possible.

During the flight, Marcello offered to come with me, but I declined. It would not be right, and it might embarrass Robbie. I politely declined his generous offer, reassuring him that Julie would be nearby. I needed, however, to do this myself.

Ever since the engagement, Julie had become my best friend. She was there for me during the previous summer when Robbie was not. She did not tell me about Antonella but did confirm what Robbie was doing after I found out. She, too, was walking a tightrope between caring for Harry and caring for me.

The day before my arrival, her kindness continued when she did a huge favor for me. She told Robbie about Marcello, about his proposal and about the baby. It must have hurt Robbie terribly to hear that news, as he was already dealing with the loss of Antonella, but it needed to be done. I needed him to know the truth before our meeting. Perhaps if he got past the emotional shock, we might be able to communicate. I wondered how it would be. Would he be ready? I did not know.

We landed at the Naples Airport at noon, following our morning flight from London Gatwick. By 2:00 pm, we were home, at the apartment, my new home with Marcello. Our plan for the first day was to relax. I would meet with Robbie, return the ring and then Marcello and I would go out to dinner. The big event would be tomorrow when we went to the courthouse to declare our intention to marry.

Getting married in Italy had many interesting steps. It was not just about going to the church. First, we needed to declare our intentions, sign many papers, and then get them stamped. After we completed that step, the city would post the announcement establishing a time for public objections, and only after that would we be able to marry.

After the public comment period ended, Marcello and I would get married at the City Hall. It would be a simple ceremony, involving more paper signing, witnessed by our friends. Julie would sign as my witness, and Marcello's brother Vincenzo would sign as Marcello's witness. Once our official wedding was complete, we would go upstairs to buy more stamps. The Italian Government always had to be paid.

At 5:00 pm, just after Julie arrived home from work, I walked across the street to join her in the garden. When I arrived, she was seated at the little table in the garden next to Maria and Rosa, sipping tea. Seeing them there, I remembered how my odyssey started last spring.

"How was your flight?" Maria asked.

"It was nice," I replied.

Out of the corner of my eye, I could see Bari wagging his tail, happy to see me. He looked at me, then at Rosa's broom, and then back at me. He then lay at my feet. At last, he had learned to behave. The two-hundred-pound puppy had been tamed.

Turning towards Julie, I asked her a question. "How did he take it?" I asked. She smiled at me and replied.

"He took it well," she remarked. "Robbie's been through a lot," she continued. "He thought it ironic that he had lost both of his girls. He was not, however, surprised. I could tell he was hurting, however. He was trying to be brave. Afterward, Harry took him for a pizza and a drink at the Officer Club."

"Did he get drunk?" I asked.

"Not too bad," Julie replied. "Robbie was a little tipsy when they got home, but not as bad as I have seen him."

That afternoon, Julie, Maria, Rosa, and I sipped tea, waiting for Robbie to come home. In the end, he never did. When 7:00 pm finally arrived, I decided to leave him a note on the dining room table next to the ring box. It was not how I wanted to say goodbye, but perhaps, it was for the best.

Roma (May 2018)

The next time I saw Robbie again was twenty-seven years later in Rome on the Spanish Steps. Marcello and I had come to Rome for the week, and we're staying at a hotel nearby.

Robbie was seated on the steps, holding shopping bags, while waiting for his wife and daughter, who were still shopping below on the busy Via Condotti. As I walked up the steps through the seated crowd of young people, our eyes met. His temples were now gray, but he was still the magnificent man I had fallen in love with thirty-four years before.

"Hello Kimmy," he began.

"Hi, Robbie," I replied.

For a moment, we stopped what we were doing and stared at each other. Then he reached out his hand towards mine to offer me a seat beside him. "Fancy meeting you here," I replied.

Robbie smiled; "what brings you to Rome?" He asked.

"I am here with Marcello," I replied, "and you?"

"I am here with Antonella and our youngest daughter, Maria," he replied.

"Do you still live in Italy?" I asked.

"No," Robbie replied. "Antonella and I live in California now."

"Do you still live here?" Robbie asked.

"No," I replied. "Marcello and I still have a house in Capri. However, we now spend our time in London. Marcello is part-owner of a soccer team there."

For a moment, we sat together in silence, considering what to say next. Then Robbie began to speak. "Do you have any children?" He asked.

"Yes," I replied, "we have a son named Michael, who is married and now lives in Florence. We also have a daughter, Donatella, who lives with her boyfriend on Capri. Do you have children?" I asked.

"Yes," Robbie replied. "We have three daughters. Their names are Silvana, Elena, and Cinzia. The two oldest are married now and live in Los Angeles. Cinzia is still in college."

"Do your in-laws still live in Naples?" I asked.

"They do," Robbie replied. "We are going there next week to visit them."

We had reached the end of our conversation and had no more to say to each other. Instead, we sat together in silence as I mustered up the courage to say what I was thinking. "Robbie, I am sorry I hurt you," I replied. "I did not want to hurt you."

"I am sorry too," he replied. "I should have been there for you when your parents split up. I should have called. I should have visited you. It was wrong of me to cheat on you. I did not know what I wanted."

"Neither did I," I replied. "We certainly made a mess of things."

"We certainly did," Robbie replied. He then asked me a question. "Are you happy?"

"Yes," I replied, "are you?"

"I am," Robbie replied.

"Do you ever wonder how our lives together might have turned out?" I asked.

"No," Robbie replied. "I try not to look backward. It was for the best. I would never have met Antonella if it had not been for you." He then told me something interesting. "Do you remember when I told you about my first kiss in the second grade?"
"Yes," I replied.

"I did not know it at the time, but that little girl was Antonella," Robbie replied.

I now understood something I had not understood before. Our lives had been guided by unseen hands. "Do you want to hear something else interesting?" I asked.

"Certainly," Robbie replied.

"I owe you my life," I replied. "If it had not been for you, I would have gone to work at the World Trade Center."

Robbie smiled. I could see tears in his eyes. He did know. "Thank you, Robbie," I replied! I then gave him a hug. Life had come full circle. "It has been good to see you," I continued. "We need to do this more often."

Robbie laughed. "I am not sure Antonella would agree," he replied. "Even so, it has been good to see you." He then squeezed my hand and bid me farewell.
As I watched him walk down the steps, carrying his wife's shopping bags, I could see Antonella now standing beside the fountain, looking for her husband. She was as beautiful as ever. She had become her mother.

PART V. FINAL

CHAPTER 39:
CHRISTMAS IN CHICAGO

ELSA DESCRIBES THE TRIP TO CHICAGO

In 1990, just before the start of Operation Desert Storm, David, Harry, Julie, and I traveled to Chicago for Christmas. The purpose of the trip was clear but not necessarily stated. I was going to meet David's parents, and Harry was going to meet Julie's parents. Engagements might be in the offing; however, as I said before, it was only implied.

We departed the Saturday before Christmas, flying from Rome to Newark and from there on to Chicago. As usual, the flight into Chicago was delayed, not because of the weather in the New York area, but because our plane to Chicago had not yet left Chicago. As usual, Chicago was having a blizzard, just in time for Christmas.

We spent our first night in America on the top floor of a hotel near Newark airport. Outside the window, we could see the airport sitting beside a freeway. Below us sat a parking lot surrounded by barbed wire. All night long, the freeway never stopped moving, presenting an endless stream of headlights coming toward us and red brake lights moving away from us.

On the left side of the freeway sat a row of hotels, each with a neon sign, and at the end of the row sat a brewery with the words "Anheuser Bush" emblazoned on the side.

In the distance, however, beyond the airport sat the focus of our view, the World Trade Center's twin towers shimmering in the distance. They were beautiful that night; all lit up with their tall antennas piercing the night sky. New York was temptingly close however we never went there. Perhaps some other time, I thought. Even so, I felt as if I had come home.

We ended up sharing the room with Harry and Julie, as it was the only room left near the airport, and of course, the airline made us pay for it. Weather delays were not compensable.

That night, Harry, Julie, David, and I had our own little improvised Christmas Party. We dined on wasabi-flavored almonds, candy bars, little sausages in tiny cans, and aerosol cheese with crackers. We had no rental car, and it was the only food available at the hotel. We rinsed down our banquet with the contents of our minibar, mixing the soda pop with the tiny bottles of assorted liquor. Some combinations were excellent, and some were not. As an aside, never mix beer with tequila.

Our surroundings and refreshments did not matter. We were happy. Afterward, we enjoyed falling backward onto the bed, practicing our "Nestea plunges." Surprisingly, we had fun.

After our unexpected night in Newark, New Jersey, we were delighted to find a plane waiting to take us to Chicago the next morning.

We arrived in Chicago on a Sunday, shortly before noon, where we parted company. Harry and Julie left for Evanston with Julie's parents, while David and I proceeded to Skokie with David's parents.

As we waited for our bags at the carousel, we exchanged phone numbers agreeing to get together the next day to go shopping. Then we stepped outside. Once again, it was snowing as I stepped off the curb. A passing airport bus splashed slush onto my new white tennis shoes, reminding me that I was no longer in Italy. David smiled, holding my hand. "We need to get you some real boots," he exclaimed!

That first day, we attempted to drive into the city on the Kennedy Expressway but soon gave up, deciding instead to travel north on the Toll Road. Even though it was a Sunday afternoon, the road was a sea of taillights. Unfortunately, none of them were moving.

Finally, we reached our exit and proceeded across the city, passing through one suburb after another, all looking the same. First, there was Des Plaines, then Niles, then Morton Grove and then Skokie. Everywhere there were neon signs and little shopping centers. It was what David referred to as "Generica" (meaning generic America). We had arrived. After forty-five minutes of stop-and-go driving and endless traffic lights, we finally entered David's hometown, Skokie, Illinois.

When we finally reached David's house on Lee Street, I was greeted by a familiar sight. It was as if I had entered the land of the TV sitcom, "The Brady Bunch."

David grew up in what Americans refer to as a "ranch house," a long one-story house with a bay window in the living room and an attached two-car garage. Over the garage door was mounted a basketball hoop and in the front yard stood an apple tree.

"Does your mother use the apples to make pies?" I asked. Didn't all Americans eat apple pie? David laughed.

"No," David replied, "we buy our pies from the store."

"Do you eat the apples?" I asked.

David smiled. "Have you ever bitten into an apple with half a worm?" He asked. No, I had not.

"Why half a worm?" I asked? David once again smiled, teasing me. At last, I got the joke. "So, you do not eat the apples?" I replied.

"No," David replied. "The apples are mostly there to prevent us from parking in the driveway. When they fall, they dent the car. Dad keeps threatening to cut down the tree, but the mother will not let him."

As we stood in the driveway talking while father unpacked the car, I could see David had mischief in his eye. Reaching for snow, I made a ball and threw it at him. Unfortunately, I missed. David stuck out his tongue and then picked up snow and launched it back at me. It landed short, sliding down inside the front of my winter coat. Our snowball fight had begun.

For the next twenty minutes, we stopped unpacking the car and had an old-fashioned snowball fight. Our fun ended when David's mother finally stuck her head outside the back door, inside the garage, inviting us in for lunch. That afternoon we ate Chinese takeout leftovers warmed in the microwave oven. Welcome to Illinois, I thought.

David's parents were delightful. David's mother was short and thin with a gregarious personality. She was a musician who taught piano on the side. Everywhere in the house were signs of her three passions, music, books, and photography. In the living room sat her prize possession, a baby grand piano that she used to instruct her students.

That afternoon I was also introduced to the family dog, a grey miniature schnauzer named Charlie. Charlie could do a special trick. He could sit on the piano bench and put his paws on the keyboard. It did make for some extremely cute pictures.

David's father was a high school physics teacher, avid skier, duck hunter, and rock climber. He was the quintessential American outdoorsman with a droll sense of humor, like George Burns. After lunch, while puffing on a cigar, he showed me his collection of duck decoys and even let me make duck noises using his assortment of duck calls.

Once we finished cleaning up and touring the house, mother broke out the photo albums to show me pictures of David as a child. David was adorable as a child. In one picture, I got to see David sitting in the bathtub as a three-year-old, and in another picture, I saw David dressed for Halloween in his pirate outfit. My favorite, however, was a picture of David lying next to his mother on a beach blanket. It was taken perhaps when he was five years old.

After the trip down memory lane, the attention turned toward me. "Elsa, I understand you once lived near here," mother began.

"Yes," I replied. "My father attended graduate school at Northwestern University. We lived here for three years, from 1968 until 1970."

"Where did you live?" Mother asked.

"The first year we lived in graduate housing in Evanston, near the elevated train track," I replied. "We only lived there for one year. My parents got tired of the train noise. We lived the last two years in a small apartment in Rodgers Park. The apartment was on Touhy Avenue, near Clark Street. We lived near a Romanian kosher sausage store."

David's mother smiled. "I grew up in that neighborhood," she replied. "I lived on Chase Avenue, near Touhy Park." It was a small world.

I then continued my story. "My sister Kristina and I had a small bedroom that we shared. We decorated it with stuffed animals and posters of our heroes. My favorite poster was of Neil Armstrong. Kristina's favorite was David Cassidy."

Turning towards David, I asked him a question. "Did you see the moonwalk?" I asked.

"Of course," David replied. "Everyone saw the moonwalk!"

"Kristina and I watched the moonwalk on a small black and white TV," I said. "It was the first time we got to stay up past midnight. Father kept having to adjust the rabbit ears to keep the picture tuned to CBS news. As he described it later, it was like watching "cows in a snowstorm.""

"Did you actually see the moonwalk?" David asked.

"Yes," I replied. "For a short second, the static cleared, and we got to see Neil Armstrong step off the ladder onto the surface of the moon. Afterward, the picture became "cows in a snowstorm" again. Fortunately, the audio worked." David laughed, describing his experience as basically the same.

"What did you like most about Chicago?" Mother asked.

"Baseball," I replied. "Father used to take my sister and me to games at the ballpark. During the summer of sixty-nine, we loved to go to the afternoon games. The Cubs were good that year until they fell apart towards the end of the season." David's father groaned, remembering the season. I then continued my story.

"I especially enjoyed the sights and sounds of the ballpark, the organ playing short songs, the crowd yelling at the batter, and the occasional home run followed by cheering. One game father even caught a foul ball, which we later had signed."

"Who signed it?" David asked.

"Ernie Banks," I replied. "Kristina still has that ball." I then continued my story. "Kristina and I loved the hot dogs. Sometimes a man would come on the field and use a giant slingshot to shoot hot dogs up into the stands. It was fun to watch. The hot dog would go in one direction, the bun would go in another direction, and the mustard and ketchup would go in a third direction. Once the mustard and ketchup landed on Kristina's ball cap. We nearly died laughing."

"What did she do?" David asked.

"She took it in stride," I replied. "She wiped the condiments on her hat, off onto her hot dog and went on with life."

David's Christmas Eve Day Shopping at Marshall Fields

The next morning, on Christmas Eve Day, Elsa and I joined up with Julie and Harry to go shopping at Marshall Field's main store on State Street. During the drive over, Elsa gave us the history of the store. It was the third-largest department store in the world. It was also where the founder of London's Selfridge Department store got his start. Elsa's mother had once worked at the department store, and Elsa wanted to see it again. She had fond memories of the toy department there.

That morning we drove the short distance to Julie's parent's house, a large English Tudor House on the north side of Evanston. We then changed cars, driving Julie's family Cadillac into the city. Elsa had never ridden in a Cadillac before.

We decided to take Lake Shore Drive south rather than take the freeway, to give Harry and Elsa the best view of the city. Throughout the trip, Elsa kept looking up through the front windshield, admiring the tall buildings, and asking Julie questions.

"Did your father design that one?" She asked, pointing towards a tall building beside Lincoln Park.

"No," Julie replied. "He worked on the design of the tall building with the "x" cross-bracing up ahead."

Elsa beamed. It was the tallest building on the street. "You must be so proud," Elsa exclaimed!

When we finally reached a bend in the road, we exited and traveled south on Michigan Avenue until we passed over the Chicago River and parked the car. As we drove south, Elsa provided us with more commentary, having studied her Chicago travel book during our flight over. Elsa had missed her calling. She should have been a tour guide instead of a history major.

That morning I witnessed Elsa and Julie in their natural habitats. Both women loved to shop, or I would say try on clothes. Fortunately, they did not buy everything they liked.

Elsa came prepared with a list. She was always prepared. On the list were flannel pajamas for her and me, an electric blanket, stocking caps, gloves, and a dress for the upcoming Seabee ball.

Surprisingly, we spent as much time in the men's departments as we did in the women's departments. Elsa ended up buying me a sweater, even though I already had a drawer full of sweaters. Fortunately, she passed on the sweater with the reindeer on the front.

As we went down the list, exploring all thirteen floors of the building, we took turns paying until we had each racked up several hundred dollars in charges. When we finally reached the dress department, Harry and I sat on a bench, as our feet were tired, and watched the women model dresses. Elsa was obsessed with buying a dress for the Seabee Ball. She already owned several nice dresses but insisted she had nothing to wear.

I had loaned Elsa a pair of my old winter boots to wear. They were the tall type of boots worn on frigid winter days. Boots I referred to as "moon boots." Each time Elsa tried on a dress, she would model it to Harry and me while wearing the moon boots. It was hard not to laugh. "Why are you laughing," she exclaimed? "Do I look that bad?"

Harry chuckled. "It is not you; it is the boots." Elsa took the hint and removed her boots, standing barefooted in front of us.

"Where are your stockings?" I asked.

Elsa blushed. "I left them in the dressing room," she replied.

After trying on several dresses, Elsa finally found the perfect dress she wanted. When she emerged from the dressing room, she handed me the dress and asked me if I liked it. I did not reply but instead dropped the dress on the floor.

"Why did you do that?" Elsa asked.

"I want to see what it will look like," I replied.

Elsa stopped talking and stared at the floor. Then she looked up at me and smiled, understanding my joke. "Am I really that bad?" She asked. I said nothing and smiled. For a moment, Elsa blushed, then picked up the dress and kissed me. She had learned her lesson. After that, she no longer left her clothes laying on the bedroom floor.

Conversation Between David & Elsa on the Plane

Elsa and I had a wonderful Christmas in Chicago. During the plane ride home, we snuggled together on the seat. Elsa asked me if we could visit the following year again.

At the time, I did not realize it, but Elsa had made a provocative statement. The independent woman was fishing for a commitment. It seemed as if the marriage bug had bitten her. Was it something in the mint chocolate ice cream pie?

"Yes," I replied. "We can certainly do this again; in fact, we can do this every year if you want."

Elsa stopped talking and looked up at me, smiling. "Are you asking, what I think you are asking?" She asked.

"That depends," I replied.

"Depends on what," Elsa replied.

"It depends on your response," I replied.

She had forgotten the story I told her of my last attempt to propose to Dana. I was not about to ask the big question again unless I knew the answer first. She was not following me. "Would you like to do you know what?" I asked.

For a moment, Elsa's face changed. She looked startled. This was no longer a hypothetical question. I could tell she was not ready to respond.

"Are you being hypothetical? She asked. Sensing she was not ready, I replied in the affirmative.

For a moment, she relaxed. "Hypothetically speaking, I would marry you in a minute," she replied. "However, it is not that simple." Where was she going with this?

"Where will we live?" she asked.

"Where do you want to live?" I asked.

"Stockholm," Elsa replied. "I think we should live near my parents so that our children can know their grandparents."

This was a start. Not only had we finally broached the subject, but she also wanted children. Unfortunately, she seemed determined to return to Sweden, a place where I would not be able to find work.

"What about Chicago?" I asked. "Our children will have grandparents in Chicago."

"Touché" Elsa replied, waving her index finger!

I had deftly trumped her argument. She did seem to like Chicago. She knew all the city's nicknames; the city of the big shoulders; emporium of the world; makers of meat on a bone et cetera.

Then she frowned. This was not a good sign. Finally, she replied. "I do not know," Elsa replied. "I do not know if I can leave my country and family behind. It is not just about the children. You are asking me to give up a way of life."

I was asking a lot; of course, she was asking a lot as well. It was ironic that she did not seem to realize she had already left her family and homeland behind.

"Can I have time to think about it?" She asked.

"Certainly," I replied. "We have all the time in the world. Just remember, however, my tour of duty in Naples ends next September." She understood. For a moment, we had a meeting of the minds. Our love now had a deadline.

After the conversation, we relaxed and drifted off to sleep. Elsa was blissfully happy again. The seed was planted. We had finally gotten through our first difficult conversation about the "M" word.

Julie's Kitchen Conversation on Christmas Day

After our eventful day before Christmas with David and his family, Christmas Day went over like a lead balloon for Harry and me. I could sense that he felt awkward around so many people he did not know.

After dinner, while we washed the dishes, the men retired to the living room to watch "It's a Wonderful Life" through their eyelids. Harry wanted to watch the movie where the little boy gets a BB gun for Christmas. However, that was not on until 4:00 pm. As usual, there was no football on TV. It was, after all, Christmas Day, and a Tuesday.

At last, I could speak to my mother alone. "What do you think of Harry?" I asked. Mother had never met Harry before.

"I think he is cute," she replied. "He is also very funny." She was trying to be nice. Harry was funny, but cute seemed a stretch. "It is not important what I think," Mother replied. "At least he does not carry a gun with him everywhere."

My sister Emily smiled. Mother was once again teasing her about her husband. "Wayne needs to carry his gun for work," she protested. "He is a policeman!"

"Did he really need to bring the gun to Christmas dinner?" Mother replied. She did have a point.

I tried over again with the conversation. "Mother, what do you think of Harry?" Once again, she punted, turning the question back to me.

"What do you think about him dear?" Mother replied. "Is he good to you?" I felt like I was looking in a mirror.

"I like him but am frustrated," I replied. "We have dated for fourteen months and not once as he tried to get, you know, frisky. I am afraid he only wants to be friends."

"Friends are good," mother replied! "I thought all you wanted was to be friends."

"I did, but now I am thinking we need to take the next step," I replied. "My clock is ticking."

"Have you told him this?" Mother asked.

"No," I replied. "I 'm chicken. I am not sure he is interested. Maybe he does not like the way I look."

"Nonsense," mother replied. "You are very pretty when you want to be." She then urged me to stand up straight. "Do not slouch, dear! Does he remember your birthday?"

"Yes," I replied.

"Did he remember the anniversary of your first date?"

"Yes," I replied.

"Did he buy you something nice for Christmas?"

"Yes," I replied.

"Then he likes you!" mother replied. "What is not to like?"

"Then why isn't he interested in you know what?" I asked.

"It is called sex," mother replied.

"Yes, why isn't he interested in sex?"

"Maybe he is just being polite," mother replied.
It was interesting that my mother was referring to my boyfriend as polite. This was the man that passed gas at the dining room table. Was Harry polite? Well, maybe in bed he was. He could be a sweetheart when he wanted to be. Perhaps mother was right. I then remembered Harry standing by the statue in the Vatican Museum. He was rather handsome when he wanted to be.

"Was father like this?" I asked.

"No," mother replied. "With your father, I had to beat him off with a stick. I wish your father were more like Harry, but unfortunately, he is not."

I then turned to my sister Emily. "What about Wayne?" I asked. Emily smiled. I had hit paydirt.

"Wayne talks a big show," Emily replied, "but deep down, he is a mama's boy. I am sure he told his friends we were sleeping together long before we slept together. He was, however, timid in the bed department at first."

"How do I get past the "just friends" stage?" I asked.

Both women stopped for a moment, and then each offered their advice. Mother suggested the best way to win a man was through his stomach. I should bake him cookies. Emily suggested I greet him at the front door after work, naked.

There was my answer. Somewhere between baking cookies and getting naked was the key to catching my man. Immense help, you both are, I thought. Suppose life were only that simple.

The word "Cookie" did, however, get attention from inside the family room. No sooner was the "C" word mentioned than Harry walked through the kitchen door.

"Did I hear someone is baking cookies?" He asked. Mother smiled.

"I told you so," she winked. After Harry left the room, we broke out the recipe box. It was time to bake cookies.

Robbie's Christmas 1990

December 1990 was a cold and rainy month in Naples. One day blended into another as our world moved slowly towards war. The weather outside seemed to reflect my mood inside. Ever since receiving Kimmy's note on the dining room table, I had been despondent. I never thought losing Kimmy would hurt so much, but it did. I missed her, everything about her, especially the many little things she did during the holidays. I now understood what it felt like to lose a spouse. It was my first Christmas in seven years spent without her.

Several times during the past two months, I had walked across the street to ring the buzzer to her apartment, but she was never there. Rosa said she had returned to London. Maria said she had moved to Capri. It was clear that neither woman knew where she went. The only thing I knew for certain was that she was gone.

I tried calling Antonella several times, leaving messages on her machine. However, she never returned my calls. She still wanted nothing to do with me. Finally, the day before Christmas, someone picked up the phone. It was her mother, Silvana.

"Is Antonella there?" I asked.

On the other end of the phone, I could hear two people talking. After several minutes Silvana returned to the phone. "Are you doing anything for Christmas dinner?" She asked.

"No," I replied. "I have no plans."

For a moment, there was silence again on the phone as Silvana spoke to someone on the other end. I could hear a man's voice. It was Charles. Then Silvana returned to the line. "Charles is coming by at noon to pick up Maria and Rosa," she began. "We would love to have you join us for dinner."

For the first time in four months, it seemed as if there might be a glimmer of hope. At least I would be able to eat dinner in a warm house, I thought.

When Christmas day arrived, I woke early and went to the base. Everything was closed, except the gym. That morning I played basketball with the Marines and afterward took a hot shower. They were all excited, eagerly awaiting their expected turkey dinner at the Mess Hall. That would have been my plan A had I not been invited to dinner.

At 11:30 am, I returned to the house and changed. That day, I decided to wear a new grey flannel suit I had purchased from the base tailor in the fall. Ever since the breakup, it had hung in the closet. Afterward, I lit a fire in the fireplace and waited for Charles to arrive. I did not have to wait long, as Charles showed up early. Charles was his usual jolly self that day. He was always gregarious. For the next hour, he and I sat by the fire while we waited for the women downstairs to finish dressing.

"Does Antonella know I am coming?" I asked.

"Yes," Charles replied smiling. "It was her idea to invite you. She has been cooking a gigantic fish all morning just for you."

"Massive fish?" I asked.

"Yes," Charles replied. "Here in Italy, we do not eat turkey for Christmas; we eat fish." Then he whispered. "I also asked Silvana to cook a turkey, just in case the fish does not taste so good."

"Does Antonella know what she is doing? I asked.

Charles smiled and replied. "She has not a clue," he replied. "I think we are going to be waiting until midnight for the fish to cook."

"How big is it?" I asked.

"A little smaller than Moby Dick," Charles replied, laughing. It was good to laugh again.

That day, we dined well. We began with cocktails and then moved to the pasta while we waited for the fish to cook. At 5:00 pm, we began our next course, turkey with dressing, mashed potatoes with gravy and fish with broccoli rabe.

Unfortunately, the monster fish was not yet fully cooked. Back it went into the oven. By 6:00 pm, we were full of turkey. Charles, Silvana, and Antonella would end up eating the fish for the next two weeks.

Antonella was incredibly beautiful that day, although a bit frazzled by her fish debacle. After dinner, I joined her in the kitchen to watch the fish cook through the oven door. For a moment, we were alone, in awkward silence. Then finally, Antonella began to speak.

"I am sorry to hear about Kimmy," she began. "Maria has told me you have been very depressed." This was an interesting beginning to the conversation.

"How are you doing?" I asked.

"Not so bad," Antonella replied. "I have missed you."

"I have missed you too," I replied.

For a moment, our eyes met. Then Antonella leaned forward and gave me a gentle kiss. That simple gesture was all it took to get the ball rolling as soon one kiss led to another and then another. At last, Antonella was back in my life.

CHAPTER 40:

ROBBIE & HARRY'S ADVENTURE IN THE SANDBOX -THE GULF WAR (JANUARY 1991)

ROBBIE'S ACCOUNT

Harry and I arrived in Bahrain on January 10, 1991, on a mission to retrieve a sailor from a ten-day sojourn in a local jail. Harry would function as the defense attorney, and I would perform the duties of the prosecutor.

A certain Seaman Spuds had abandoned his career as a potato peeler on a U.S. Navy Destroyer to enjoy a night of liberty on the town with his shipmates. He did have a pass. The problem was he didn't return to the ship on time.

After two hours of drinking, he decided to try his luck with an 18-year-old Asian prostitute. One thing led to another, and soon he found himself in jail, accused of rape. How, you may ask, does a sailor rape a prostitute? In a word, he did not have enough money to pay her.

Getting the sailor out of the local jail took two days. The matter turned out to be simple enough once Harry loaned Seaman Spuds the money to pay the prostitute. She then dropped the charges. The local magistrate released the sailor and turned him over to us.

After his release, we tried to return the sailor to his ship to await courts-martial. However, the ship would not accept him. He had missed ships movement in time of war and the skipper would not take him back. He had a war to fight, after all.

Unfortunately, the sailors ship had put to sea and would not be coming back. For the next two days, Seaman Spuds became our roommate at the hotel. Nobody wanted him. Eventually, we unloaded our wayward sailor on the base security officer, who found a room for him at the barracks.

Normally, Harry and I would conduct our investigation and then return to Naples until a Courts Martial could be convened; however, the war intervened. Operation Desert Shield became Operation Desert Storm, and all commercial air traffic ended, stranding us in Bahrain. Our adventures in the sandbox had begun.

We had three choices we could make. We could wait for civilian air traffic to resume (i.e., for the war to end), we could try to return by military aircraft, or we could attempt to drive across the Arabian Peninsula, hoping to find an airport open. Harry and I were willing to take our show on the road; however, our Commanding Officer, Captain Simpson, instructed us to sit tight, and so we did. The area CINC (Commander in Chief) did not want American Servicemembers wandering all over the Arabian Peninsula.

For the next month, we sat tight at our hotel following orders, spending our days watching the war unfold on TV. Once a day, we drove to the airport to see if flights had resumed (of course, they had not) and to visit the tiny U.S. Navy base to visit our client, make phone calls, and meet with witnesses. After that, we returned to the hotel to watch TV.

Sometimes we watched CNN and sometimes we watched the local TV (even though we could not understand a word of what they were saying).

To break up the monotony, we often played poker at night, in our room, with other hotel guests. The war was bad for tourism; however, the hotel was still doing a brisk business catering to U.S. Navy contractors. We now had three Americans to play poker with.

After several days stuck in the hotel room playing cards, we decided to venture out and visit the local souk. The skipper wanted us to blend in to avoid making ourselves targets for would-be terrorists. Wearing khaki pants and logo golf shirts was not enough. We were tired of playing cards.

The trip to the souk was a bit disappointing from a clothes perspective; however, we did find much better luck at the indoor shopping mall. As Harry later described it, we went "full Arabian." I opted for a traditional white gown with a keffiyeh, a white handkerchief-type hat, while Harry bought a white gown with a Ghutra, the red and white table-cloth pattern headscarf worn by Saudi Arabian men. Afterward, we looked like extras from the movie "Lawrence of Arabia."

That evening we ate falafel at the mall food court. It was hard to tell there was a war going on. If it were not for the news, it might have been a typical day in Bahrain.

Then on January 16, the shooting war began. Every day we listened to CNN provide live coverage of the air raids over Baghdad. It was like watching a made-for-TV movie. Was it real or just TV? Only CNN Correspondent Peter Arnett knew for sure.

All-day we stayed in the hotel ordering our usual room service. The menu had many items; however, the hotel was out of them. Instead, we ate the only item available, falafel, falafel, and more falafel. Harry didn't mind the food, however I found himself in "vegetarian hell." What I wanted most was a good steak.

After dinner we ventured out in our bedsheets, sometimes to the local hotel bar beside the pool and sometimes to the hotel bar down the street. After our first foray, attempting to pass as Arabian tourists, we went back to wearing our khaki pants and logo shirts.

While most U.S. soldiers dug in, waiting for the fighting to begin, Harry and I enjoyed martinis and appetizers at the hotel bar. I particularly liked the "Moroccan Cigars," a type of Chinese eggroll resembling Filipino lumpia. Harry enjoyed dipping pita bread in assortments of hummus.

Throughout our time in Bahrain, the highlight of our days was calling the girls back in Naples. Antonella had moved into the house shortly before my departure, and each evening we would telephone the girls to say hello. It was great to hear their voices through the phone. Like us, they were watching the war on TV. Unlike us, they were freezing cold as usual. At least there was one advantage to spending the winter in the sandbox. It was warm.

On January 18, the war became more interesting when Iraq began firing Scud missiles. Harry referred to these as "Crud missiles" as they never hit anything. Sometimes they fired the missiles toward Israel, and sometimes they fired them at Saudi Arabia. Provided the missile went in the general direction intended, the Iraqis considered it a success. Fortunately, the Iraqis could not hit the broadside of a barn. Also, fortunately for us, they had no interest in bombing our hotel.

Antonella, however, was very worried. "What if a missile accidentally hits you?" She remarked. I reassured her that Harry and I would proceed to the hotel basement if the air raid sirens went off. However, we never did. Instead, we went outdoors and stood beside the pool. Harry and I decided if a missile were going to hit us, we would like to at least see it first. There was something reassuring about standing in the open-air drinking a martini during an air raid.

After a week of the air war, we began to see clouds of black smoke on the horizon. The Iraqis had begun setting oil wells on fire in Kuwait. This brought the war home. It was not just a made-for-TV movie anymore.

On January 29, the Iraqis launched a ground attack on Saudi Arabia 140 miles north of us. The attack was rapidly repulsed by coalition forces; however, it did cause our skipper to worry for our safety. They might hit something by accident. He did not feel comfortable letting us remain in Bahrain any longer. He wanted us to move over to the nearby Air Force Base in Dhahran, Saudi Arabia, and try to secure a military flight home.

The next day, we loaded our bags into the rental car and drove across the long King Fahd Bridge from Bahrain to Saudi Arabia. Soon we reestablished ourselves with a group of army lawyers in new quarters at the King Abdul-Aziz Air Base in Dhahran while we awaited a flight home.

Our days in the four-star hotel were over. Our new home would be a shipping container sitting in a parking lot. There would be no more martinis and appetizers at the hotel bar, either. From now on, our meals would be MREs (meals ready to eat), washed down with desalinated water. The war had entered a new phase. The ground war had begun.

The Flight Home

After days of competing without success for a seat on a military flight back to Europe, we decided to try our luck at a nearby commercial airport. While in Dhahran, we learned that an airline had begun operating air flights out of a small airport nearby. We informed our skipper of the situation, and he authorized us to return by commercial air.

Later that day, Harry and I went to the airport and bought two tickets from Dhahran to Cairo. We were finally going home, at least we thought. We would change planes in Cairo and then proceed on to Rome via another airline.

Later that night, I tried to call Antonella from a nearby payphone to inform her of our plans. However, I was not able to reach her.

The next morning on February 25, 1991, Harry and I arrived early at the airport and boarded our flight. It was not the jet we envisioned, but instead, a small and rickety two-engine propellor plane seating nine people plus the pilot.

Our flight to Cairo flew far to the south of the war zone over Riyadh and then over Medina crossing the empty Arabian desert. Below us stretched mountains and endless desert. Off towards our right, we could see dark clouds of smoke on the horizon. Somewhere over towards the smoke was the war in Kuwait.

When we reached the edge of the Red Sea, our plane banked right and flew north up the length of the Red Sea on the Saudi Arabian side, flying towards Cairo. It seemed as if all were going according to plan. Then unexpectedly, the pilot turned around in his seat and told us he needed to land at the nearest airport.

Looking towards the right, I looked out the window. The propellor on the starboard engine had stopped turning. Ten minutes later, we landed at a small airstrip in the Sinai, at a place known as Taba.

Harry's Account of the Return Home.

For the next two days, Robbie and I spent our time at a small hotel on the beach in the deserted Egyptian resort of Taba while we waited for the airline to fix our plane. Aside from three lonely palm trees around our hotel, it seemed as if we had landed on Mars.

During our first night in the hotel, we watched a fitting movie on TV. Someone in Cairo had a sense of humor. It was the movie "Flight of the Phoenix, "starring Jimmy Stewart. The movie was in English with Arabic subtitles and told the story of a group of men who crashed land in the Sahara Desert. Eventually, they work together to repair their plane and fly out of the desert.

Unlike Jimmy Stewart, we, however, did not know how to build a plane from spare parts. We would need to wait for the mechanics at our airline. Little did we know that Israel was only five miles away.

After the movie, we tried to call home. Unfortunately, our phone did not work. It was not connected to anything. It was only there for show.

During our second long day, we sat at the bar and drank local Egyptian beer, waiting for word from the airline. The beer tasted dreadful. Robbie thought the beer tasted like formaldehyde, whereas I passionately believed the beer was made from fermented camel piss. That said, it tasted better than the water.

For lunch, we ate what the hotel referred to as "lamb." We were tired of falafel. In retrospect, we should have ordered the falafel, as our lamb was more like an "old goat." The meat was very tough.

After lunch, around 2:00 pm, word finally arrived concerning the status of our plane's repairs. The news was bad. Our plane needed a new engine.

The airline promised to dispatch another plane to retrieve us in three days. However, Robbie and I decided not to wait. We had learned that morning that the Israeli border was only five miles away. After finishing our beer, we checked out of the hotel and persuaded the desk clerk to drive us to the border. (There were no taxis.) Ten minutes after leaving the hotel, we walked over the border into Israel.

Israel

During our first night in Israel, we stayed in a four-star hotel close to the border. For a moment, it seemed like we had entered a Hawaiian resort. We were now in Eilat, Israel's only port on the Red Sea.

That night we ate well at a local seafood restaurant. Robbie and I both ate fried shrimp with cocktail sauce and baked potatoes with sour cream. For a small moment in time, we felt like Americans again. Then after dinner, we attempted again to call home. Once again, no one picked up the phone.

The next day, after a restful night's sleep, Robbie and I boarded a bus and rode the length of Israel from Eilat in the south, up through the Negev Desert to Tel Aviv. During the trip, we passed many places named in the Bible. We drove around Beersheba, which was now a large metropolis, and then passed Gaza, Gath, Lachish, Ashkelon, and Ashdod until we arrived in Tel Aviv.

During our second night in Israel, we stayed at a resort hotel on the beach in Tel Aviv, where we watched fireworks over the Mediterranean Sea while eating Moroccan Cigars with Tahini sauce. The Israelis were celebrating. The Gulf War was finally over. That night we managed to reach the skipper by phone, but once again we were not able to reach the girls. It seemed strange that they were never home in the evening.

The next day, March 1st, we caught a morning flight back to Rome. When we arrived, it was shortly before noon. It was good to finally return to Italy again. It was also reassuring to find my car waiting for us in the long-term parking lot, exactly where I had left it almost two months before.

Chapter 41:
The Accident, January 18, 1991

DAVID'S NARRATIVE

It was 4:00 pm on a Friday when I received the phone call at work informing me that Elsa had been involved in a collision. The accident occurred sometime around noon in Naples' Vomero Quarter while Elsa was making a delivery. She had been weaving in and out of traffic and had lost her balance when a vehicle suddenly swerved, hitting her, causing her to tumble onto the street.

Exactly what happened was not clear, as the driver who caused the accident fled the scene. All that was known for certain was that Elsa was found lying on the pavement beside her motor scooter. When she was transported to the hospital, she was in good spirits, although in considerable pain. She had broken her arm, trying to catch herself, and had also bumped her head. She reassured everyone that she would be fine. Thankfully, she had been wearing her helmet.

The situation became worse, however, shortly after she arrived at the hospital when she began to lose consciousness. Realizing her head injury was more severe than originally thought, the doctors did tests that confirmed Elsa had a brain hemorrhage. Elsa was in serious trouble.

For the next several hours, as the surgeons operated, the staff at the hospital attempted to determine Elsa's identity. It was not easy as Elsa had left her wallet under the seat of her moped rather than in her coat pocket. When they finally reached the police, the only clue to Elsa's identity was her student ID card and my business card.

David's Long Evening at the Hospital

The hospital was lucky to reach me when they did. If they had called just five minutes later, they would not have reached me until the following Monday.

After the phone call, I drove home to change and then proceeded to the hospital. I left a note on the dining room table for Julie and Antonella. They were not home from work yet. Before leaving the house, I made two calls. First, I called Antonella's parents to let them know, and afterward, I called Elsa's father at his work number. As luck would have it, I caught him at the end of the day, just before he left for a weekend at the cottage.

When I arrived at the hospital shortly before 6:00 pm, Elsa was still in surgery. That night, as I waited, I had a candy bar for dinner. I did not feel much like eating. Charles, Silvana, and Julie arrived shortly thereafter, followed by Antonella around 8:00 pm.

Together and individually, we paced the halls, sat in the waiting room, and visited the chapel. Often, I thumbed through the waiting room magazines for something to do, even though I could not read Italian. Instead, I remained preoccupied, remembering my time with Elsa.

She looked so beautiful that morning when I left for work. I thought about waking her up to say goodbye but decided to let her sleep. She was sleeping soundly that morning, her face surrounded by blankets, with a stocking cap on her head. I never realized at that moment that I might never see her alive again.

At 9:00 pm, the doctor finally came to the waiting room following six hours of surgery. He looked very tired but also relieved. It was clear he brought good news. Elsa would live.

"How is she?" We asked in unison.

"She is doing well," he replied. "She will recover. The surgery went well; she is out of the recovery room and is now in the ICU."

"Can we visit her?" I asked.

For a moment, the doctor did not answer but instead looked at his watch. He then replied. "Its past visiting hours," he replied, "but I will let you visit her for five minutes." He then led us down the hall towards the ICU.

When we entered the intensive care unit, we found Elsa lying in her hospital bed, unconscious and covered in blankets. She had a cast on her left arm and bandages around her head, partially covering her face. It looked like she was wearing a beehive on her head.

It was strange seeing Elsa that way. She was connected to tubes and monitors, but thankfully she was breathing on her own. For several minutes I watched her breathe, her chest slowly rising and falling, then rising and falling again. I never thought I would be so happy to simply watch her breathe.

The truth was I had fallen in love with Elsa during our time together and could no longer imagine life without her. We stood around Elsa's bed in silence for several minutes. Then we said our goodbyes for the evening. When it came to my turn, I gently squeezed her hand to let her know I was there. There was no response. She was somewhere far away from us in dreamland.

After we left the ICU, we turned toward the doctor and began asking him questions. "When do you expect she will regain consciousness?" I asked.

"It could be two to three days," the doctor replied. "She is heavily sedated right now, as we do not want her moving. We will begin to reduce the sedative Monday. She should regain consciousness sometime Monday afternoon."

Charles then asked the question I was dreading to ask. "Do you know if she has suffered any brain damage?" He asked.

"No," the doctor replied. "Unfortunately, it is too early to tell. We will not know the full extent of her injuries until she regains consciousness. Fortunately, the hemorrhage was limited to a small area. There is one thing you should be aware of, however."

"What is that?" Charles asked.

"When she wakes up, she may be blind," the doctor replied.

For a moment I felt a lump in my throat. What would I do if Elsa were blind?

"Will she get her sight back? Silvana asked.

"It is too early to know," the doctor replied. "As the swelling goes down, she may recover her sight. The recovery may be full, or it may only be partial," he added. It was clear he was preparing us for a potentially bad outcome.

David's Account of Elsa's Recovery

For the next five weeks, while the rest of the world watched the Gulf War on TV, I visited Elsa every evening after work. Oftentimes I ran into her family. During the first three weeks we spent much time together.

During the first week, Elsa's progress was terribly slow. As the doctor expected, she regained consciousness on Monday afternoon. When she woke up, she was blind.

That evening, it was difficult to watch her. She had trouble speaking and oftentimes did the opposite of what the doctor asked her to do. When he asked her to raise her left leg, she would lower it instead. When he asked her to touch her nose, she would instead touch her chin. The wires in her brain were crossed.

She complained of a bad headache, difficulty seeing and often giggled for no reason. Fortunately for me, she remembered me. Unfortunately, she could not remember what day it was or what she had for lunch.

As she described it later, she felt as if her brain was enveloped in a fog. She described it as watching herself from a distance. The loss of her eyesight troubled her the most.

Elsa's family arrived the day after the accident and remained by her side throughout the first three weeks until her father and sister returned to Sweden. After that, Elsa's mother remained in Naples, staying with Charles and Silvana. It was the most time I had ever spent with either of her parents. It was also clear that they planned to take her home with them. Elsa's time in Italy would soon come to a premature end. I would learn they were never entirely supportive of her plan to move to Naples in the first place.

From the start of her recovery, the doctors monitored her continually, even after she left the ICU. She could not get out of bed on her own, even when she wanted to. If she tried, an alarm would go off, summoning the nurse. This was very frustrating to Elsa.

When she did get up, she had considerable difficulty walking. Her sense of balance was compromised and would take four weeks to regain. Fortunately, Elsa's eyesight returned during the second week. This improved her attitude considerably.

Basic walking was difficult and painful for Elsa, even though neither her legs nor back were injured. It was strange. The pain was all in her head, and yet it was very real. Oftentimes she did not want to try to walk, but between her mother and I, we made her walk. Progress was slow, but by the end of the fourth week, thanks to our efforts, she was able to finally walk without our assistance. Her cognitive recovery, however, was much slower.

It was interesting to see what she remembered and what she did not. She could remember our days vividly together as a couple but could not remember anything that happened the day before. She could remember endless historical trivia about Naples, but not what she ate for breakfast. She could still add up numbers in her head without pencil and paper but then had difficulty reading. As I watched her struggle, I wondered if she would ever be the same again.

During her fourth week in the hospital, we began to discuss plans for Elsa's discharge. Elsa's doctor and parents wanted her to return to Sweden to continue her rehabilitation. Elsa did not, however, want to leave. She was extremely stubborn and determined to stay in Italy, even though it was not in her best interests.

One evening during that fourth long week, I had a frank discussion with Elsa, her mother, and the doctor. The doctor was adamant that Elsa was not ready to live in a house with stairs. She needed to live in a place where everything was on one floor. He also insisted that she needed to continue her daily rehabilitation appointments with the occupational and physical therapists for at least an additional two to six months. She was not ready to return to school.

That night, after everyone left, Elsa cried and cried on my shoulder. "What is to become of us?" She asked. "What is to become of me?" The realization that her life might never be the same had taken a terrible toll on her. I tried to comfort her, to make her believe that everything would turn out right but had difficulty convincing either her or myself. The truth was I did not know if everything would turn out right. Our relationship was now in a difficult and uncertain period.

Discharge from the Hospital- February 27, 1991

Elsa was discharged from the hospital on Wednesday, February 27, 1991. It was the same week that Harry & Robbie went missing and the same week that the war ended. I was immensely proud of Elsa that day. She walked out of the hospital on her own two feet, determined to show her parents that she could return to a normal life. Unfortunately, she was still not ready.

This became painfully obvious when we returned to the house to collect her things. The day before, I had decided not to pack her things but instead to let her pack them. It would give her a chance to return home to say goodbye. That day she struggled. She struggled to climb the stairs and struggled to pack.

Twice she grew weary and sat in our bedroom chair, exhausted from her efforts. It was a difficult day and, unfortunately, very cold in the house. That evening Elsa and I slept together in our freezing cold bed for the last time. It was wonderful again to hold her in my arms as we tried to keep warm.

"Promise me; you will not forget about me," she said.

"I promise," I replied.

"When will I see you again?" She asked.

"I promise to visit you in two months," I replied, "provided the war is over and I am able." I could tell that Elsa was disappointed with me. She would have preferred to either stay in Naples or take me to Stockholm with her.

"David, do you think we will ever be the same?" She asked.

"Of course, we will," I replied.

I am not sure I convinced her, even though I tried. The truth was I was not certain anymore. The doctor had told Elsa's parents that she might not fully recover. How would we get through this, I asked myself? Would we get through this? I did not have all the answers. We had entered a rough patch in our lives together.

I blotted out the fears from my mind. Somehow, we will get through this, I told myself.

CHAPTER 42:

HOMECOMING (MARCH 1991)

During the months when Harry was away, with Antonella's assistance, I finally got to know my landlady Maria and her housekeeper Rosa. Both women had fascinating stories, which helped me cope with my separation from Harry. I will admit it was difficult to talk to them. I only knew a little Italian, and they knew almost no English.

Maria and Rosa both had remarkably fascinating stories. Both had experienced war, loss, and years of absence from their husbands. Rosa's husband, Silvio, went missing during the Battle of El Alamein in 1942.

His division, the Pavia Division, was abandoned in the desert by the retreating Axis Armies. For years afterward, Rosa waited for Silvio to come home from the war, but he never did. The entire division was lost during their retreat through the Sahara Desert. Silvio's fate was never determined. Officially, he was listed as missing in action. Unofficially, he was presumed dead. Rosa ended up raising her son alone, with the help of Maria, but never remarried.

As for Maria, she was luckier. Her husband, Giovanni, returned from the war many years after it ended. Giovanni, served with the Eighth Italian Army in Russia as a Colonel. He fought with the Air forces supporting the German Army, and was taken prisoner, by the Soviets in 1942, following the German surrender at Stalingrad. After the battle he disappeared into a Siberian prisoner of war camp.

For six years Maria did not know if he were alive or dead. Then after the war, with the aid of an American General, she learned of his whereabouts and secured his release. Giovanni returned home from the war in 1949. After the war, his health was poor, but he did manage to finish his career, retiring as a General in the Italian Air Force in 1958. His last assignment was as the commander of the nearby Italian Air Force Academy in Pozzuoli. Giovanni passed away in 1960.

So why, you may ask, did Maria love the Americans so much? The answer was simple. They helped bring her husband home after the war. Like most Italians during the war, Maria feared the Allies. They were the enemy. Then when the American Army "liberated" Naples, she finally met an American.

The Germans had been occupying the Villa Nike next door for six months and had commandeered her house as well. She, Rosa, and their children lived for four months in the garden, in a makeshift tent, while soldiers lived in her home. Several times they had to take shelter in a foxhole during heavy shelling. They also had little to eat.

After the city was liberated, The Americans moved into nearby Villa Nike, just as the Germans had, but they decided not to occupy Maria's house. It was an extraordinary act of kindness that Maria never forgot. They gave her food, and treated her with compassion, even though she was the wife of their enemy.

During a week in October 1943, Maria became friends with the Commanding General of American Forces in Italy, General Mark Clark, and it was with his help, that Giovanni finally came home. General Clark would remain Maria's friend until his death in 1984. Maria kept a photo of the General on her living room wall.

Listening to her story, made my situation more bearable. The truth was, I had fallen in love with Harry and missed him terribly. For two months, Antonella, David and I lived alone in the giant villa following the war news closely. Elsa's accident had been a sobering wake-up call for all of us. We now understood the fragility of our lives.

During the frigid winter months of 1991, our days revolved around the nightly calls with Harry and Robbie, visiting Elsa at the hospital, and visiting with Maria and Rosa. During the winter of ninety-one Antonella, and David became my best friends. They were always there for me, and I for them.

Julie's Phone Call at Work

Friday, March 1st I received a phone call at work shortly after returning from a late lunch at the cafeteria. I had stopped into my office to retrieve my clipboard before starting my afternoon rounds of the maternity ward, when the phone rang. On the other end of the line was Harry. For a moment, my heart skipped a beat.

"Where are you?" I asked.

"I am in Rome," Harry replied. "Robbie and I arrived ten minutes ago on a flight from Tel Aviv. We should be home by 5:00 pm." Glancing at my watch, I noticed it was shortly after 2:30.

"Tel Aviv?" I asked.

"It is a long story," Harry replied. "I will fill you in on our adventures when I get home."

"Have you heard about the war?" I asked. For a moment it seemed like the line had dropped. Then Harry's voice came back on the line.

"Sorry," he replied. "I almost lost you there for a minute. I had to deposit more coins in the phone. What were you saying?"

"Nothing" I replied, "I am simply happy to hear your voice." Once again there was a clicking sound. Then Harry returned.

"I am about to be cut off;" Harry replied. "I will see you when I get home." Click, and the call ended.

For the first time in weeks, I felt happy. Harry was coming home! For the past four days, ever since we last heard from Harry and Robbie, Antonella and I had been nervous wrecks. The crisis began on February 25th, when an Iraqi missile hit a barracks in Dhahran, Saudi Arabia. It landed somewhere near the place Robbie and Harry were staying.

Shortly after the missile strike, news began to circulate in the media that a substantial number of Americans had been killed and wounded. Was Harry among the casualties? It was not clear.

That night, I waited by the phone, anticipating Harry's call at the usual time, but no call came. Where was Harry? The next day, I called his office to see if they had heard from him. The secretary did not know his whereabouts. For a moment I was filled with dread. Where was Harry?

After speaking to the secretary, I tried calling my counterpart at the clinic in Bahrain to confirm what I heard on the news. The news was not good. Two dozen people had died and another one hundred were wounded. "Do you know what barracks were hit?" I asked.

"No," the doctor replied. He was not much help after that.

That night, I waited again by the phone, anticipating Harry's call. Surely, he would call me if he could, I thought. Once again, the evening came and went without a call from Harry.

The next day, Tuesday February 26th, dawned cold and rainy in Naples. The weather fit my mood. The war news had moved on. Coalition forces were doing well. Kuwait's leaders claimed control of their capital, and President Bush began calling for a cease-fire.

That morning, like everyone else, I was glued to the TV, watching images of the war. Over and over CNN showed images of a road in Kuwait filled with the burned-out wreckage of retreating Iraqi vehicles. Yesterday's ground offensive had turned into a rout of the Iraqi Army. I could not believe how quickly the war ended.

As I watched the news, I tried calling several doctors I knew in Ramstein, Germany, thinking they might know if Harry and Robbie were among the wounded. Their responses were textbook responses, the same type of response I had been trained to deliver. They could neither confirm nor deny. One doctor asked me if this was a business call or if I was family.

If I said business he might give me info, however I did not go down that road. Instead, I said the truth. "I am his girlfriend," I replied. For a moment, the man on the other end of the phone stopped talking. "Are you still there? I asked.

"Yes," he replied. He then whispered something on the phone. "He is not here," the voice replied.

"What about Robbie?" I asked. Once again, he stopped to check his list.

"Robbie is not here either," he replied. This was both good news and bad. Neither Robbie nor Harry, were among the wounded. That said, they could still be among the dead.

After the call, I thought about phoning Harry's parents. If he were dead, they would be the first people to know. I started to dial their phone number but then stopped. What would I say to them? Is your son dead? The question made me shudder. I was letting my fears get the better of me. Calling Harry's parents would be a huge mistake. I set down the receiver and decided to wait. I was confident if something had happened, they would eventually call me.

Harry's Homecoming Present

That afternoon, I returned home to a radiant Julie, waiting for me at the front door. She was all dolled up with bright red lipstick. Her long, curled hair was down. She looked the cutest I had ever seen her. She was wearing her Wisconsin Sweatshirt and blue jeans. She looked gorgeous that day.

Julie had a look of mischief in her eyes, as I entered the house. "I have a present for you," she smiled. I could see her hands were empty. I gave her a long kiss on the lips and then asked her where it was. "It is upstairs," Julie replied. "Come upstairs and I will show you." She then took my hand and led me up the stairway, stopping twice to kiss me along the way. This was getting good. I wondered what the present was.

When we entered the bedroom, Julie closed the door behind us and sat on the edge of the bed, beckoning me to join her. She gave me a smile, looking like the cat that ate the canary. "Harry, could you please roll down the shutters," Julie remarked.

Roll down the shutters? I now understood where this was going. "What are you up to?" I replied. Julie just smiled, and then got up to begin unbuttoning my shirt. "Shouldn't we roll down the shutters?" I asked.

"I do not care if you do not care," she replied.

I reached over and began turning the crank on the shutter, hoping the spring would not break.

Soon Julie had removed my shirt. "This seems a bit one sided," I remarked. "Shouldn't you also take something off?" Julie smiled at me.

"You will have to help me," she replied, as she removed her bra from underneath her sweatshirt, dropping it on the floor. She did not have to ask me twice. It was great to finally be home.

Robbie's Homecoming Present

When I arrived home from the war, I found a note for me, from Antonella, lying on the dining room table. Antonella had gone to work but bade me to visit her at the dress shop. That evening, the drive to the dress shop, seemed to last forever. Although her work was only three miles from our house, it seemed it was two hundred miles away.

The traffic was crawling like an inchworm around the city. Once again, Naples was gridlocked. It seemed that happened every time it rained. Twice I circled the business district looking for a parking space. Even with my tiny car, there was no place to park. I thought about double parking or parking on the sidewalk but decided against that course of action. I didn't want my car impounded.

Finally, after two passes, I parked in a garage three blocks from Piazza Vanvitelli, handing the keys to the parking attendant. It would cost me 50,000 lire, but at least I would have a car to return to. It would be a considerable walk to the shop, but at least I would get there sometime that evening versus never.

When I finally arrived at the shop, Antonella was waiting on a customer. She smiled at me from across the room. I could tell she was incredibly happy to see me. Then when the customer finally left the store, Antonella walked over to me and embraced me, giving me a long kiss.

"Welcome home my love," she smiled. I now understood how Odysseus felt when he returned home from the Trojan War. Like the hero of legend, my odyssey had finally ended in the arms of my beloved.

"Did you miss me?" She asked.

"Like, life itself," I replied. Antonella once again grinned with tears in her eyes.

"Robbie, I missed you so much," she replied.

"I missed you too," I replied.

For a moment we held each other tightly, not wanting to let go. "Robbie, I was so worried," Antonella began. "When that missile hit Dhahran and you went missing, I thought maybe you were dead. Please promise me you will never go to war again."

"I promise," I replied.

From Christmas until my departure for Bahrain, Antonella and I had been inseparable. It was as if we had never broken up in Monte Carlo. It was like a dream. All had been forgiven. Each day during my sojourn in the war zone, I thought of her wondering what she was doing, wanting to embrace her. I pictured her constantly in my mind, remembering how beautiful she looked our last weekend together.

I could see her standing on the balcony in her bathrobe gazing out to sea, as the birds sang their early morning songs. If only I could get home, I would never leave her again. I had never felt that way about any woman before. It was clear to me that Antonella was the one.

Later that evening, after the shop closed, Antonella and I walked back through the deserted streets of the Vomero, towards the car holding hands. It had been raining hard just before we left the store, however now the rain had stopped, leaving the paving stones glistening in the moonlight. When we finally reached Piazza Vanvitelli, it was 9:00 pm.

We stopped to get a bite to eat in a local family-owned trattoria. The menu was remarkably simple and delicious that night. We shared plates of mixed antipasti, including mixed marinated vegetables and mixed fried seafood. The fried calamari rings tasted particularly good.

We then followed the first course with Pasta Genovese (pasta with onions) and ended our dinner with tiny cups of espresso.

After the meal, as we sipped the last of our wine, I admired Antonella's beautiful face, trying to muster the courage to ask her my question. She could tell, I wanted to say something, and reached for my hands across the table.

"What are you thinking?" She asked.

"Will you marry me?" I asked. I did not have a ring, but it did not matter. At last, I knew what I wanted. I wanted Antonella.

Antonella smiled, and blushed, as a tear came to her eyes. For a moment we stopped talking and savored the moment. "I thought you might ask," she smiled. "I was hoping you might ask."

"So, what do you say?" I asked.

Antonella paused. "You need to ask my father first," she replied with a twinkle in her eye. Once again, we paused to gaze into each other's eyes. Antonella looked so beautiful. That night she was the most beautiful woman in the world to me.

After dinner we walked slowly back to the car, stopping to look over the city from the street beside Castle San Elmo. Far below us sat the narrow lanes of the historic center, its streetlights twinkling, reflecting off the wet cobblestones below. The city was coming back to life, following the end of the rainstorm.

"Let's go ask Papa," Antonella exclaimed!

"Do you think he will say yes?" I asked. Antonella just smiled. She knew he would.

That night, we woke up Antonella's parents at midnight, to ask their permission to marry. Antonella's parents were quite a sight. Charles stood before us in his pajamas, wearing his "bulldog face," his hair standing up in all directions, resembling Albert Einstein. Beside him stood Silvana, yawning, in her nightgown and curlers. We wished we had a camera to capture that moment.

"What do you two want at this ungodly hour?" Charles asked!

"Robbie wants to ask you a question," Antonella replied.

For a moment Charles' face softened. "Are you asking what I think you are asking?" Charles replied.

"Yes," I replied. "Will you give us your blessing?"

Charles and Silvana looked at each other, and then at us, their faces positively radiant. He then grasped my hand and gave me a hug, kissing me once on each cheek. "Of course," he replied. "Come on in and let's celebrate." That night we celebrated until 3:00 am. It was great to finally be back home.

Saturday April 27th– David's Account

The month of April was a beautiful time in Naples. Winter was finally over, and our house was warm again. I thought this would be my last winter in Naples. It turns out I was wrong.

It was another beautiful Saturday in Napoli. That day we had our first cookout of the season, to celebrate not one, but two engagements.

Since March 1st, Cupid had been busy at our house. Robbie and Antonella announced their engagement on March 3rd, shortly after Robbie and Harry returned from Saudi Arabia. They decided to get married in July and were busy planning their wedding.

From the start, Antonella and her mother took command of the preparations. Not only would the wedding be the event of the season featured in the family magazine, but it also would be used to launch Antonella's new line of wedding dresses.

They decided to hold the wedding and the reception at the Villa Cimbrone Gardens in Ravello, one of the most beautiful wedding venues on the Amalfi Coast. It would be a grand U.S. Navy-style wedding complete with choker white uniforms and swords. The centerpiece of the wedding, however, would be Antonella, in her latest designed wedding dress.

The second engagement, which came as a surprise to everyone, occurred after the first weekend in April. Harry and Julie went on a trip to Florence and when they returned, Julie was wearing a ring. Cupid's arrow had struck a second time. Neither Robbie, nor I, saw that one coming.

To return to our cookout story, that morning I drove to the base to buy a steak for myself, another six-pack of beer, and some French fries. I invited Julie to come with me so that I could hear what happened in Florence. She was quite talkative that day.

"So, what happened?" I asked. "The rest of us thought you would never get together."
Julie grinned. "Guess we showed you," she replied.

"I suspected something," I replied. "You two seemed to be getting chummy in Chicago last Christmas. What's with all the cookie baking lately?" I asked. "Is there something in those cookies?"
Julie smiled once again. "Harry and I like cookies," she replied.
"What do you call them again?" I asked.

"Love drops," Julie replied. It seemed an interesting name for chocolate chip cookies. They were however quite good, especially when they were warm. I wondered what the special ingredient was that she put in them.
"Love" Julie simply replied.

We had now entered the base. It was car wash day and the high school students were beckoning me to pull over and get the car washed. It did need a wash, I admit. The car was always dirty in Naples. "Do you mind if we stop?" I asked.

"No," Julie replied. "Go ahead."

Soon thereafter, we pulled into the area where they were washing cars and stepped out of the car to watch, as a dozen teenagers descended on my car with their soap covered sponges. It seemed they were more interested in flirting with each other rather than in washing my car.

"So, when do you plan to tie the knot?" I asked.

"Next spring," Julie replied, "after we return to the States. We thought about doing something this fall in Italy, however many of our family members cannot attend. Also, we don't want to steal from Antonella & Robbie's show."

"Where are you planning to do it?" I asked. "Either Chicago or Boston," Julie replied. "We still haven't decided. We plan to go back to the States this summer and begin setting things up."

"Do you know where you will be stationed next?" I asked.

Julie grinned. "Harry and I started talking to the detailers the minute we came home from Florence," she replied. "At present we're either going to D.C. or to San Diego next. Harry and I both prefer San Diego." Julie seemed incredibly happy. She then changed the conversation. "So, what's happening with you and Elsa?" She asked.

"Elsa's improving slowly," I replied. "We talk every day. Some days are better than other days. She misses Italy."

"Are you ever going to tie the knot?" Julie asked.

I smiled. "I have bought a ring," I replied, "and am planning to ask her when I visit in May for her birthday."

Julie grinned. "You're not planning to give her the "bad luck ring" are you?" She asked.

"No," I replied. "I told Robbie he could keep that ring. I bought a ring that Elsa and I saw last Christmas in Chicago. It was a ring she liked."

"When did you buy that?" Julie asked.

"While you and Elsa were walking around the Marshall Field's furniture department," I replied.

Julie laughed. "I knew you and Harry were up to no good," she replied. Then she asked me a question. "Why didn't you give Elsa the ring during the holidays?" She asked.

"I was waiting for the right occasion," I replied. "Elsa was a little tentative at Christmas. I wasn't sure she would say yes, so I decided to wait."

The truth was, I still wasn't sure she would say yes, but I decided to ask her anyway, during my upcoming visit to Stockholm. Elsa's father and I had spoken the night before. Elsa's recovery was stalled. Moving back to Sweden did not have the effect her parents had intended. Perhaps it was the wintry weather or the loss of her independence. It seemed as if Elsa was slipping backwards. She was missing her medical appointments and was also losing weight. "She needs a goal, something to live for," father advised. "Something that will inspire her to work hard to recover." He asked me for my help.

The Liberation Day Air Show

After our trip to the base, Julie and I returned to the house, to find Robbie busy preparing the grill. That afternoon we ate well, enjoying the fine spring day. Rosa and Maria joined us on the terrace, contributing a delicious assortment of antipasti to the meal. Both were quite happy toasting their success in getting everyone hitched (even though they had nothing to do with it.)

After we finished eating, we all went to the roof to watch the Italian Air Force. It was Liberation Day, the Italian Holiday celebrating the end of World War II. The air show began with a loud sonic boom as a squadron of jets swooped in over the bay from the north, leaving green, white, and red smoke trails in their wake.

For the next half-hour, the jets raced from one end of the Bay of Naples to the other, flying in tight formations over the water, performing stunts, and barrel rolls for the amusement of the cities and islands surrounding the bay.

Several times they came screaming up the hill from below us, leaving contrails of smoke in the colors of the Italian flag. They flew so close, that it seemed like we could almost reach out and touch them. It was a memorable day and a fitting end for the Gulf War.

CHAPTER 43:

DAVID'S SECOND TRIP TO STOCKHOLM (MAY 1991)

I flew to Stockholm to visit Elsa on a Sunday in the month of May. It was my first opportunity to get away from work. Ever since the end of the war, I had been terribly busy. All the Flag officer retirements, which had been postponed because of the war, were now moving forward, creating mountains of work for Enzo and me.

When I arrived at the airport in Stockholm, I was met by Elsa's father, John, who was eager to see me. "Elsa has been excited about your visit" John exclaimed. "Your planned visit has done much to lift her spirits."

Conversation between David & Elsa's Father (John)

During the drive into the city from the airport, I finally had an opportunity to talk to John in private. In the past, whenever we had spoken, Elsa had always been standing nearby. "How is she doing?" I asked.

"She is doing much better," John replied. "Much better than the last time we spoke. She has started reading books again, he continued. It has been good therapy for her and has helped her relearn how to concentrate again."

Before the accident, Elsa had been a voracious reader. The accident had changed that, however. After the accident, she had considerable difficulty focusing. She started many things but never finished them.

"What is she reading?" I asked.

"This week she is reading Robert Louis Stevenson's "Treasure Island,"" John replied. It was reassuring to hear that Elsa was reading again. She always loved adventure books.
"Has her sense of balance improved?" I asked.

"She is doing much better," John replied. "She is still carrying her cane, however its now mostly a security crutch, rather than a necessity. The past week it has been raining a great deal, so she has not been walking as much as she should. The forecast is for sunny weather this week. While you are here you should take Elsa for long walks," John suggested.
"Is she still having difficulty handling stress?" I asked.

"Yes," John replied. "She still gets frustrated very easily. Something happened yesterday which made her very anxious. I am not sure what happened. She was very jittery when mother and I returned home from work yesterday. She did not sleep well last night.
"Maybe she was anxious about my visit," I offered.

"I do not think so," John replied. "She has been looking forward to your visit. I think something else is bothering her. I am not sure what, however."

Reunion with Elsa

When we arrived at the apartment, Elsa greeted me at the front door, wrapping her arms around my neck and hugging me tightly. It was the sort of greeting I had hoped for.
Later that afternoon, after lunch, we took a long walk together. Instead of walking towards the city center, we decided to walk to the island with all the museums. Elsa wanted to show me the open-air museum, a place known as Skansen.

That afternoon we wandered the world's oldest open-air museum, enjoying its seventy-five acres of historic houses and farms, gathered from all parts of Sweden. Many of the houses resembled houses from a "Grimm's Fairy Tale." There were tiny summer cottages, no larger than a privy, a house that looked like an old shoe, several windmills, nomad Sami houses, (Sweden's version of Eskimos) and decorative wooden barns which stood on stilts.

One of the houses belonged to a family named Lindstrom, said to have immigrated to America. I wondered if it once belonged to my great grandfather Lindstrom.

At the end of our tour, we visited the gift shop where Elsa purchased brightly colored winter stocking caps for each of us. She offered to buy me the matching Sami shoes. (Felt shoes with curled toes with bells) but I declined.

Note that the Sami people are Sweden's version of Eskimos. They dress in brightly colored knit clothes and look like Santa's elves.

Back to our story, Elsa bought two pairs of Sami shoes anyway. She bought one pair for herself and a matching pair for me.

That afternoon Elsa was delightful again. It was as if the accident had never happened. Elsa seemed almost normal. She continued to walk with the cane, however it was clear she no longer needed it. Occasionally she twirled it or used it to point, illustrating she no longer needed it to walk.

"Do you still use that?" I asked, pointing towards the cane.

"Not really," Elsa replied. "Mother insists I take it with me everywhere I go." Elsa then sat down on a bench offering me a seat.

"I hear you are reading again," I responded.

"Yes," Elsa replied. "I have managed to finish two books in the last ten days." She was quite proud of herself.

"How is "Treasure Island,"?" I asked.

Elsa laughed then replied like a pirate. "Argh by thunder," she replied. "Do you know why John Silver is known as "Long John Silver"?"

"No," I replied, "is it because he wears long john underwear?"

Elsa smiled. "Not exactly" she replied, "although you are close." She smiled at me with a look of mischief in her eyes. I could tell what she had in mind.

"Are you feeling up to it?" I asked. Elsa smiled, nodded her head, kissed me, and then changed the subject. "When do you think you will be able to return to Italy?" I asked.

Elsa stopped talking and looked at the ground. "I do not know," she replied. "Mother and father insist I complete my therapy first."

"Is there an end date to this therapy?" I asked.

Elsa looked sad. "No," Elsa replied. "The therapy is endless. I have five sessions a week. Monday, Wednesday, and Friday, I visit the occupational therapist."

"What is "occupational therapy,"" I asked.

"Remedial high school," Elsa replied. "Currently I am relearning algebra. I never used algebra the first time and now I am having to relearn it again. On Tuesdays and Thursdays, I visit the physical therapist."

"How is that going?" I asked.

"Both good and not so good," Elsa replied. "I still have not recovered the peripheral vision in my right eye."

"Is it noticeable?" I asked.

"No," Elsa replied. "It is strange, my mind fills in the image of what should be there, only it is not there. Sometimes, I bump into things."

"Will you be able to drive again?" I asked.

"Yes," Elsa replied. "The doctor says I will be able to drive. I can see fine. That is not the problem. The problem is in my perception, not my sight. I now need to turn my head towards the right before I move to the right. I am no longer able to trust what I think I see. I need to confirm it first before I act."

Elsa seemed incredibly sad. Her new handicap was clearly frustrating. She had hoped for a full recovery and was realizing that would no longer be possible.

For a moment, I noticed tears forming in her eyes, then she looked up at me, smiled, and wiped her eyes. "I wish I could return to Italy with you," she replied. "Too bad I cannot fit in your suitcase."

"Have you heard about the upcoming weddings?" I asked.

"Which weddings?" Elsa replied.

"Kimmy is getting married the first weekend in July," I replied, "and Antonella and Robbie are getting married, three weeks later, at the end of July." Elsa had received an invitation to Antonella's wedding but not Kimmy's. "Will you be able to come?" I asked.

"I plan to attend Antonella's wedding," Elsa replied. "I have managed to convince my mother and father to let me go. Perhaps, they will let me stay."

"Isn't that your decision?" I asked.

Elsa smiled. "You've met my parents she replied. Even when I am fifty, they will still view me as their little girl."

The "Conversation"

My four-day trip to Sweden was much shorter than I would have liked, but I needed to get back to work. A new Army General was moving in the following week, and I needed to work over the weekend to prepare his house.

My week with Elsa was wonderful. Each day we took long walks together into the city. We even spent one day together wandering the halls and gardens of a nearby Royal Palace, known as Drottningholm, which was located outside of the city.

During our last night together, we walked into the old city to eat dinner at the same place we had eaten the previous summer. When we returned from dinner, we stopped to sit on a bench, and look out over the harbor. I needed to ask Elsa a question but was having difficulty mustering the courage. Elsa could tell there was something weighing heavily on my mind. Finally, she held my hand and asked me what was troubling me. I did not reply, but instead reached inside my front coat pocket to retrieve a small box. On the box, were written the words "Marshall Fields" and inside was a ring.

When Elsa saw the box, tears came to her eyes. "David, is that what I think it is?" She asked.

"Yes," I replied opening the box. Elsa stopped talking and gazed into the box. Inside sat a small but very elegant diamond ring. Elsa was now crying.

"What is wrong?" I asked. Elsa did not reply, but instead reached inside her purse.

"David, there is something I need to tell you" Elsa sobbed. "Something happened last week before you arrived." For a moment she searched inside her purse trying to find what she was looking for. I could tell she was becoming frustrated. Then she pulled out a small box. Another box containing a ring.

"Sven gave me this last week," she said.

For a moment I felt faint. Sven had proposed before me. For the next five minutes, Elsa and I stared at the water in silence. At last, I thought I knew what was bothering Elsa. She might still have feelings for Sven, I thought.

It took several minutes to recover my speech. I then asked my question. "What did you tell him?" I asked.

Elsa coughed, clearing her throat. "I told him I needed time to think about it," she replied. She then added something interesting. "I was hoping you would ask first."

"So, what are you going to do?" I asked.

"I haven't figured that out yet," Elsa replied. "Sven's proposal was so unexpected. Everything is happening too fast right now. When I think about it, it gives me a headache. Why is life so complicated?"

"What do you want?" I asked.

For a moment Elsa wiped her eyes. "I wish it were that easy," Elsa replied. I wasn't sure what she meant.

"What do you plan to say to Sven?" I asked.

Elsa continued looking at the ground. "I plan to tell him no," she replied. "I honestly don't love him anymore. I haven't found the courage yet to tell him, however."

"What about us?" I asked. "Do you want to marry me?"

Elsa continued staring at the ground. Then she turned towards me and smiled. "David, you know how I feel about you," she replied. "I love you. What I'm not sure about is leaving my family," she replied. "Saying yes to you means leaving them!"

For a moment we sat together silently. We had returned to the same place we had visited at Christmas. Elsa was not ready to say goodbye to her life and family in Sweden.

At that moment I also began to get a headache. Why was this happening to me again? I certainly had reasons to be upset. I was angry at life and at my circumstances. Even so, there was little I could do to change our situation. Elsa needed to make a major decision. It was not a decision I could make for her.

For a moment I considered what to say. It would have been easy to show my pain, but that would not be helpful to the situation. I decided instead to control my emotions. I squeezed Elsa's hand and gave her a kiss on the cheek.

"Elsa, you do not have to decide today," I said. "I realize this is hard for you. I want you to take as much time as you need to decide. You know how I feel about you. Do remember when we first met? Do you remember what you asked me?"

"Yes," Elsa replied, "I asked you if a boy like you, could fall in love with a girl like me?" Elsa smiled. "Have you?" She asked.

"Yes," I replied. "I am in love with you."

For a moment Elsa gazed into my eyes, then she wrapped her arms around my neck and whispered in my ear. "I love you too, she replied." Then she added something to her statement I had not expected. "I wish it were that simple David," she said.

"Unfortunately, marriage is not just about love. It is also about the rest of my life. David, the truth is I do not know what I want. I wish I did, but I do not. I guess, I need to figure out what I want first."

Then she asked me a question. "When do you need my answer?" She asked. "Can I have until Antonella's wedding?"

"That will be fine," I replied. "The important thing is that you get better first."

Plane Ride Home

It was cold and rainy the day I returned to Naples. The brief sunshine that Elsa and I enjoyed together in Sweden, ended when I boarded the plane.

I will never forget our last embrace, just before I started my walk down the jetway. Elsa had a faraway look in her eyes, once again feeling overwhelmed by her situation. I reminded her that she was lucky. "Most women never had the chance to choose between two men," I said. I expressed confidence she would make the right choice, wondering as I said it if I would ever see her again.

Saying goodbye was exceedingly difficult. Had I done the right thing? I had let go, hoping she might return to me. At that moment I realized I did not own Elsa, nor did she own me. Even if I wanted to, I could not make time standstill. Elsa would need to decide what she wanted most in life. It was a decision she would need to make on her own. It was not a decision I could make for her.

CHAPTER 44:

ELSA'S DECISION (JUNE 1991)

      After David returned to Naples, Sven renewed his efforts to convince me to marry him. Sven and I had a history together. It was a history which went back to early adolescence. I didn't want to marry Sven. Of this I was certain. I couldn't tell him, however. I was still afraid of him.

      I first met Sven during the summer of our seventh-grade year. His parents had purchased a house on the island near our cottage. That summer, Sven and I made eyes at each other each day on the beach. We were very shy, afraid to talk to each other. Instead, we communicated through notes delivered by our friends. Although Sven was skinny and shorter than I, I thought he was cute and enjoyed flirting with him. That first summer Sven chased me, while I played hard to get.

      At the end of the summer, we had our first date. Sven finally mustered the courage to ask me to go to the movie with him at the village theater. All through the movie, Sven attempted to wrap his arm around me. It was very annoying.

      After our first date, I did not see Sven again until the following summer. By that point, he had changed. He was much taller and more handsome. I was smitten. During our second summer together, I chased him while he, in turn, played hard to get.

By our third summer together, our ninth-grade year, we overcame our shyness and became friends. All through high school, we remained friends. I had my boyfriends, and he had his girlfriends. Occasionally we double-dated and went to the movies together. It seemed we would always be friends until the summer after high school graduation, when we first kissed.

It was an innocent enough kiss at the time, but it soon led to more kisses. The dam broke. Soon we were inseparable. Our romance that summer was intense, and then it flamed out. For six months afterward we broke up, and then we got back together again. After our first reunion, we loved intensely, fought intensely and then repeated the cycle.

During our first year together, we had sex for the first time. It was awkward. Afterward, I avoided Sven. Our relationship was moving too fast and needed to slow down. I was afraid of getting pregnant. Then, during our last year at the university, after three years of on-again, off-again dating, we decided to take the next big step. We moved in together.

Living with Sven was much different than dating him. When we dated, I could always go home at the end of the evening. Now that we lived together, I could not.

Sven was very jealous of my time as well as my affections. For the first time in my life, I had no privacy. Sven could be kind and gentle, but he could also be overbearing. Our struggle for dominance had begun.

Once I missed my period and thought I might be pregnant. Sven was very unhappy with me. He blamed everything on me. He said it was all my fault. He even questioned if I had sex with another man. Nothing could be further from the truth, however. Sven was the only man in my life.

That night, the situation became ugly. Sven tried to hit me. Afterwards I moved out. For three weeks afterward, he pleaded with me, begging me to move back in. He said he was sorry, and I believed him.

After graduation from the university, we continued living together. It seemed as if our difficulties were finally behind us. Then Sven decided he wanted more.

After graduation, Sven wanted to get married, whereas I did not. I was not ready to make that level of commitment. Unfortunately, I was not assertive. When Sven proposed, I meekly refused. My no came across as a maybe. I should have moved out but did not. I was in love, or so I thought I was. I just was not ready to get married.

Our troubles came to a climax during our first year together after graduation. Sven wanted to buy a house together. At first, I thought it was a promising idea. I had always wanted a place I could call my own. Then I realized it was a trap. Sven was trying another tactic to pressure me into marriage.

The day after we signed the offer to purchase our cottage, I suddenly had buyer's remorse. In a moment of weakness, Sven had tricked me into signing my life away. For the next three days, as we waited for the home inspection, I was deeply depressed. I knew what our purchase meant. It was not just that we were buying a house. It also meant giving up all my childhood hopes and dreams.

I would never get to see the world. I would never get to pursue the career I wanted to pursue. Instead, I would spend my life doing what others expected of me. It was overwhelming. I felt like I was choking, dying inside. I could not allow this to happen to me.

On the day of the home inspection, I backed out of the contract. My decision, in turn, forced Sven to back out of the contract as well. Fortunately, we did not lose our deposit. Later that evening, he was incredibly angry with me, and rightfully so. He lashed out, hitting me. He accused me of running away from life. An accusation that was true. I was running away from life. I was running away from my life with him.

That evening, I moved out of the apartment, abandoning my stereo and record collection. He could have it. I was not going back. Two weeks later, I moved to Italy to begin a new degree program, completely severing all my ties to Sven. I had applied for the program months before and had never told Sven.

Given all our bad history together, you may ask yourself, why I ever let Sven back into my life. The answer was simple. When I returned home after the accident, I was deeply depressed. Sven was nice to me.

Relationship Rekindled

During my first week in Stockholm, Sven came to visit, bringing flowers. He was overly sweet. Each day thereafter, he stopped in after work to visit me. He offered me encouragement, took me for walks, made me smile and rekindled my hope. I saw the potential danger but decided to look the other way. He apologized for the way he had previously treated me and promised to be good. He promised he had changed, that he had grown up.

The day he asked me to marry him, we were returning from a walk into the old city. It was our first beautiful spring day together since my return. That afternoon we ate comfort food together at our favorite restaurant and afterward walked along the water. When we reached the park, we sat on a bench in front of a statue. It was there that Sven proposed.

His proposal caught me completely by surprise. I had no inkling he would do that. He knew I had a steady boyfriend, and yet he proposed anyway. "I have missed you so much," he said. "You would make me the happiest man in the world if you said yes."

For a very brief second, I smiled, caught up in the moment and then my smile turned to a frown when I remembered our previous life together. Sven only saw the smile. He never acknowledged the frown.

That day, I dodged Sven's question. I did not say yes, but I did not say no either. Instead, I accepted his gift and placed the ring in my purse, telling him I would think about it. Afterward, I reminded Sven that I had a boyfriend.

The week of David's visit, Sven stayed away. After David's departure, however, Sven resumed his pursuit, reminding me that I still owed him an answer. He asked if David had asked me to marry him. I told him yes, even though it was frankly none of Sven's business.

In the days and weeks which followed, Sven continued his pressure campaign taking advantage of my weakened condition. Then he took the next step to box me in.

On Sunday, June 9, 1991, my parents invited Sven to dinner. During dinner, Sven informed my parents that we were engaged, even though I had not yet decided. I was quite angry at his actions.

At first, mother and father reacted with happiness. They failed to notice the expression on my face. Then I kicked mother in the shin under the table and invited her to join me in the kitchen.

When we emerged from the kitchen several minutes later, mother whispered in father's ear. "Sven's lying," she whispered. "Elsa has not yet accepted his proposal. She doesn't want to marry him."

For a moment, father's expression changed. Then he smiled and invited Sven to join him in the den for a glass of brandy and a cigar. Soon thereafter, Sven departed. Father had called his bluff.

Conversation between Elsa and Her Parents

After Sven left for the evening, mother, father, and I sat at the dining room table for a long discussion. I told them what had happened between Sven and me. I told them everything, including why I had fled to Italy two years before.

I told them how Sven had hit me. I also told them about David's proposal. When I finished my story, we sat together in silence. Then father began to speak.

"Why didn't you tell us sooner?" Father asked.

"I do not know," I replied. "I suppose I should have told you, but I did not. I am sorry. It is hard to talk to one's parents about one's love life."

Mother smiled and laughed. "You are extremely fortunate, she replied. You have two men who want to marry you. That does not happen every day!"

"What do you plan to do?" Mother asked.

"I want to marry David," I replied. "The problem is he doesn't want to move to Sweden. Saying yes to David will mean I have to say goodbye to both of you."

For a moment mother and father both smiled. "Elsa, I suppose there is something we should tell you." Mother replied.

"What is it?" I asked. "What is the big secret?"

Your father and I are thinking of retiring and moving to the south of France," mother replied. "We are tired of the long Swedish winters. If Sweden joins the EU, we are moving to France."

"Are you saying, I will be the only person left in Sweden?" I asked.

"Yes," mother replied. "We are moving to France and Kristina is moving to Amsterdam."

For a moment, I realized my excuse for not marrying David was an illusion. "You do not mind if David and I live far away from you?" I asked.

"No," mother replied. "We will still see you. You will still be our little girl. Nothing will ever change that." Then she asked me a question. "Do you love David?" Mother asked.

"I do," I replied. Mother and father both smiled. I had their consent.

CHAPTER 45:

KIMMY'S WEDDING

JULIE'S PIZZA LUNCH WITH KIMMY

It was May 1991 when Kimmy finally returned to Naples following the delivery of her baby boy, Michael. Little Michael was born in March 1991 at the Georgetown University Hospital in Washington D.C, close to his grandfather's rowhouse in Georgetown.

From the start, Kimmy referred to her baby boy by his nickname, Michelangelo (Michael the angel). I gave him an additional nickname during our lunch at the pizzeria. I named him, Il Principe (meaning the little prince) as he was born with a silver spoon in his mouth. Kimmy got a good laugh at my proposed nickname. It seemed to fit.

That day, Michael was a delightful and well-behaved baby. He had his mother's face and his father's dark curly hair. No doubt he would grow up to be a soccer player like his father, I thought.

I had not seen Kimmy since the previous December and was eager for us to catch up. Since her wedding to Marcello at the city hall, Kimmy had lived in many places.

She spent the fall of 1990 in Marcello's apartment in Naples, frequently traveling with her husband to attend his soccer matches on the weekends. During one such weekend, Harry and I managed to attend a soccer match with her in Rome. It was the one time that Harry got to see Mendoza play.

After Christmas, Kimmy moved to London to spend the winter with her mother. Then in the spring, she moved again to Washington D.C. to visit her father and have her baby. I did not see her again until early May.

It was a lovely spring day in the middle of the week, the day we went for pizza. I had off that day, having worked the previous Sunday. We met for lunch at our favorite local pizzeria, Da Pasquale's in Piazza Sannazaro.

I ordered my usual pizza Margherita (pizza with tomato sauce and buffalo mozzarella), and Kimmy ordered her favorite, the pizza capricciosa (pizza with ham, mushrooms, artichokes, mozzarella, and tomatoes). As we waited for our pizza to arrive, we sipped our wine and caught up on the latest gossip.

"How do you like married life with Marcello?" I asked.

Kimmy smiled and laughed. "Marcello and I have a delightful marriage," Kimmy replied. "He is on the road often, but when he is around, he is a wonderful husband and father. Marcello is a world of difference from Robbie," Kimmy continued. "We think alike and seldom ever fight. We are natural together.

In our family, the drama is between Marcello's sister Cinzia and her boyfriend, not between Marcello and me. Being married has taken a little getting used to but was not as difficult as I thought. Marcello is a wonderful attentive husband. Despite being apart much of the past year, we have spoken every day."

"Are you getting help with the baby?" I asked.

"Yes," Kimmy replied. "Between Marcello's family and mine, I am getting a great deal of help and more than enough free advice. This summer, I expect we will have many visitors, which we will need to entertain. Marcello has graciously agreed to hire a live-in nanny to help me."

"Have you been following the latest soccer news?" Kimmy asked.

"No," I replied. "As you know, we live within an American bubble. The only news we ever get is from CNN, Stars and Stripes and the International Herald Tribune."

Kimmy smiled. "I forgot," she said. "Since I married Marcello, I have been trying harder to become Italian." She then continued.

"Mendoza is leaving Naples and returning home," Kimmy continued. "The story is currently dominating the local news." I remembered Kimmy telling me that Marcello planned to retire if Mendoza left.

"Is Marcello planning to retire also?" I asked.

"Not yet," Kimmy replied. "Mendoza's departure has caught him by surprise. Marcello has two more years on his contract. He plans to retire when his contract ends. Between now and then, I have given him an assignment," Kimmy continued.

"What is that?" I asked.

"He needs to figure out what he wants to do in retirement," Kimmy replied smiling.

"What do you plan to do?" I asked.

Kimmy smiled. "We are working on another baby," Kimmy replied.

"Besides that," I replied.

Kimmy continued. "This summer we are going to begin working on the house," Kimmy replied. "That will be our major project during the upcoming year. After the wedding, the contractors arrive to begin replacing the roof."

"This fall I also plan to open my own financial management business in Capri. Marcello's lawyer, Luciano and I are forming a partnership. Luciano knows many wealthy people on the island. He also already has a financial advisor license. He and I plan to expand the business to provide financial advice to his clients, offering them access to U.S. financial markets. There are many people who have expressed interest in investing in American & International Markets." Listening to Kimmy, it was clear she had no intention of being a stay-at-home mom, hence the need for a live-in nanny.

"What has been happening here while I have been away," Kimmy asked.

"A lot of things," I replied. "First, Harry and I are getting married." For a moment, I stopped talking to let that news sink in. Kimmy smiled and fanned her face. She was clearly happy for me. Then I continued. "We plan to marry before Christmas in Chicago. We have not firmed up a date yet, however. Do you think you will be able to attend?"

Kimmy smiled. "Just tell me when she replied, and I will try to attend. It may just be the baby and I, but I will try to come." "What is happening with David & Elsa?" Kimmy asked.

"Did you hear about the accident?" I asked.

"Yes," Kimmy replied. "Maria told me in a letter. It sounded terrible. How is Elsa doing?"

"She is doing much better," I replied. "She has regained her eyesight and seems to be making a full recovery. David recently visited her in Stockholm. He said she seems fully recovered, although she is still completing her therapy."

"Are David and Elsa still getting married?" Kimmy asked.

"They were headed in that direction before the accident. David proposed during his last visit to Stockholm, however Elsa did not decide," I replied. "It turns out, David has competition. Elsa's old boyfriend, Sven, proposed the day before."

For a moment I stopped talking to let that bit of news, sink in. Kimmy's jaw dropped. "That must be awful for David," Kimmy replied! "How is he taking it?"

"It is hard to tell," I replied. "You know David, he tends to keep to himself." Kimmy nodded her head in agreement.

"So, what is happening with Robbie and Antonella?" Kimmy asked.

"They are engaged," I replied.

For a brief second, Kimmy looked down. I wondered if she still had feelings for Robbie. If she did, she did not show it, however. Little Michael was fussing in his basket. Once she finished adjusting his blanket he settled down. Kimmy returned to the conversation. "So, what is happening with Robbie," she began again.

"Robbie and Antonella are getting married at the end of July," I replied.

Kimmy smiled, frowned, and then replied. "I knew he was infatuated with her even though he denied it. Where are they getting married?" Kimmy asked.

"In Ravello, at the Villa Cimbrone Gardens," I replied.

Once again Kimmy smiled. "That is a lovely place," she replied. "Not as nice as my wedding location, but nice, nonetheless."

"Does it bother you?" I asked.

"No," Kimmy replied. "It might have in the past, but not anymore. I am happy with how my life has turned out. If Robbie is happy with Antonella, I am happy for him."

"Did he send you an invitation?" I asked.

Kimmy laughed. "You must be kidding," she replied! "Robbie might do something stupid like that, but fortunately, Antonella would never allow it." Then she added something interesting. "Did you know I am buying my wedding dress from Antonella's shop?"

"I did not know that" I replied.

"Yes," Kimmy replied. "Marcello insisted I buy the dress from Antonella's shop. He did not know about Antonella & I. He just liked the shop. I bought the dress last week. Fortunately, Antonella was not working that day. Currently it's being adjusted. I go to pick it up later this week on Thursday. You should come with me," Kimmy offered.

"Thanks, but I will not be able," I replied. "I need to work that day. Did she offer you a discount?" I asked.

"No," Kimmy replied laughing. "I paid full price. Antonella knows, I am already married. She has no reason to offer me a discount. I should have bought the dress before we married at the city hall!"

"How much longer do you have in Naples," Kimmy asked.

"Two more months" I replied. "Harry and I are moving to San Diego in September. He received orders to the Legal Service Office there, and I will be working at the new Balboa Naval Hospital."

Kimmy nodded her approval. "San Diego is wonderful" she replied. "Make sure to visit Balboa Park."

"How much longer does Robbie have here," Kimmy asked.

"Three months, I think," I replied. "He plans to ask to stay in Naples for another year."

"What about David?" Kimmy asked.

"I am not sure what is happening with David," I replied. "His obligation ends in September. He still wants to get out of the Navy however his plans are on hold until Elsa makes her decision."

That afternoon Kimmy and I had a wonderful time together. The pizza was excellent as usual, as was the company. Throughout our lunch, the baby never made a peep. He was sound asleep in his light blue, Napoli team pajamas.

The Wedding Rehearsal (1st Weekend in July 1991)

The day before the wedding, on a Friday, Harry, and I travelled to Capri for Kimmy's wedding rehearsal. Kimmy had asked me to serve as one of her bridesmaids. Harry came along for the ride. We arrived on the island at 11:00 am and proceeded to the church, where we met the wedding couple's families for the first time. It was interesting to see the two families interact for the first time.

Kimmy's parents looked rather unhappy. They were adorned in their best Sunday clothes and wore their most sober faces. The only thing missing from the family portrait was the barn and the pitchfork. I later learned the reason for their grim faces. Kimmy's father had brought his new wife, Jillian, to the wedding. It was the first time the old wife met the new wife.

Marcello's family by contrast, was enormous, boisterous, smiling, and laughing. There were children running everywhere playing tag. It seemed as if Marcello was related to the entire village.

The wedding rehearsal was chaos as usual. We tried to go through the ceremony twice but gave up. Between the frequent trips to the coffee bar, the side conversations and the constant interruptions of tourists entering the church, it was impossible to get through the ceremony.

By the time we came to the exchange of rings, the ring bearer, a cute five-year-old boy, could not be found. We found him afterwards selling flowers to the tourists in the sidewalk café.

After the wedding rehearsal at the church everyone traveled by taxi to the hotel where we were staying, the Caesar Augustus in Anacapri for dinner.

That afternoon we enjoyed the rehearsal dinner, our first of two wedding feasts. This feast occurred on the terrace at the Caesar Augustus Hotel. The meal lasted from two in the afternoon until six in the evening. The view from the outdoor terrace was spectacular. I did not want to leave. It was as if we were perched on the top of the world.

After the meal we proceeded to Kimmy and Marcello's house in Capri, for dessert. The party then continued late into the evening. It was the first time I had visited Kimmy's new home. What a fabulous house! Kimmy had chosen very well.

The Wedding

The next day, David arrived on the early hydrofoil from Naples. He looked incredibly happy as he checked into the hotel. He had good news. Unfortunately, I did not have a chance to talk to him before I was pulled away for my bridesmaids' duties. Elsa had said yes to his marriage proposal.

Soon after his arrival, the men went over to the house to prepare, while Kimmy, I and the other bridesmaids traveled down to the village of Capri to dress. Kimmy was extremely nervous that morning. She was already married and yet she was so nervous. "Why are you so tense?" I asked.

Kimmy laughed. "Donatella (Marcello's mother) called this morning to tell me that the dress has problems," Kimmy replied. "She did not say what the problem was."

When we arrived at the church, we learned the problem. A few stitches had come apart. It was no big deal.

That morning we mended the dress and then primped for what seemed hours, in front of the mirror. Kimmy thought she looked fat, whereas her mother and I thought she looked perfect. Having a baby had been good for Kimmy. She had gained a little weight and had filled out her figure nicely. She, however, did not see it that way. Where we saw curves, she saw fat.

While we stood in front of the mirror admiring and adjusting the dress from every angle, the men waited patiently in the church. The dress was magnificent and worth every penny of the thirty million lire Kimmy paid for it. Besides, a wedding was not a wedding if we did not keep the men waiting.

After we achieved perfection, we crossed our fingers and then proceeded across the village square, from Donatella's apartment to the nearby church of Santo Stefano. At the entrance Kimmy's father greeted us. He looked handsome in his black tuxedo. For the first time, I saw him smile.

After we left Kimmy at the entrance to the church, I proceeded with Cinzia, (Marcello's sister) and the other bridesmaids to the front of the church to await the procession. It was now noon, time for the wedding to begin. The church was beautiful inside and full of people. The entire village had turned out to see their favorite son get married. Everywhere there were yellow flowers, offering a contrast to the church's brilliant white baroque interior. Then the organ began to play.

When Kimmy entered the church, she was the very picture of beauty in her white lace dress. She seemed to glide effortlessly down the aisle as if floating in the air. If there were feet under the dress, they were invisible. She had been so worried about her shoes. Nobody could see them. She could have walked barefoot.

The ceremony was long. Out of the corner of my eye I could see David and Harry sitting in their pew towards the back, yawning. Seeing them yawn almost made me yawn. The wedding was beautiful unfortunately I couldn't understand most of what was said. Everything was in Italian. The only clue I had that it was ending was when the wedding couple turned towards each other and finally kissed.

After the ceremony, we stopped to take pictures, and then walked out of the church. For Harry and me, the short walk down the aisle was a rehearsal for things to come. Afterwards the wedding couple climbed into a convertible taxi for a tour of the island and more pictures while the rest of us proceeded to the village square to begin the wedding reception. Our eight-hour wedding feast had begun.

The Wedding Feast

Weddings are big events in every culture however, I swear, in Italy they are bigger. Kimmy's wedding was no exception. Her feast was a meal of biblical proportions. We began the feast in the village square at 2:00 pm and continued until long after dark. That day, Harry and I dined with David, Maria, and Rosa at a small round table barely able to contain our dishes, while waiters moved between the tables constantly bringing out new dishes, clearing old dishes and refilling glasses.

Each hour, on the hour a new course arrived. First, we ate Caprese salad. This course was followed by more antipasti, marinated vegetables, meats, cheeses, and cold seafood. Harry, Maria, and Rosa ate the raw oysters, while David and I split the cocktail shrimp.

After the antipasti courses came the first course, linguine with seafood. This was no restaurant version however, as each plate contained a whole lobster tail. Most of the courses were small, however over time they added up. Fortunately, the chef left ample room between courses for digestion. Even so, in the end I felt as if I had eaten a pumpkin. Everything smelled wonderful.

Throughout the meal, the waiters constantly refilled our water and wine glasses, making it impossible to track the number of glasses we each had. I drank somewhere between six to eight glasses of wine. Harry drank at least ten. Maria and Rosa drank more than either of us. Despite the quantity, the drinks were spaced well apart so that Harry and I never really felt drunk.

After the first course, came the meat courses, not one course, not two courses, but three courses. First came the grilled calamari. It was wonderful. Then came the scallopini with white wine sauce, and last came the porchetta with rosemary potatoes. The porchetta (roast suckling pig) was by far the best meat course. I have never tasted meat so juicy and delicious! Harry loved the potatoes which were also particularly good.

After the meat, came the ubiquitous salad. I never really liked Neapolitan lettuce salad. It was always served warm, covered in olive oil, salted, and served with lemon. It was not my idea of a tasty lettuce salad. I prefer my lettuce salad crisp, cold and covered with Thousand Island dressing. This course, I could have skipped.

After the salad came the desserts, wedding cake, and after that came the Rum Baba's (tiny little rum-soaked cakes), coffee and Limoncello. By the time the meal was finished, it was after dark. The party was not however over. At the end of the meal, Marcello's mother invited the cooks out of the kitchen to receive our applause. Afterward, they returned to their duties.

After the meal, we continued to sip our drinks and dance in the village square until the wee hours of the morning. During the dinner musicians serenaded us walking between the tables, playing classic Italian favorites. Several times we were serenaded with the classic tune of "O Sole Mio." After dinner a disc jockey began playing modern Italian disco music for us to dance to. Normally I could not get Harry to take me dancing, however that night he was in rare form enjoying himself immensely. It was not until 3:00 am that Harry and I finally returned to our hotel room in Anacapri. Years later, Harry and I had to admit, Kimmy's wedding was the grandest wedding we ever attended.

CHAPTER 46:

Wedding in Ravello

HARRY DESCRIBES THE NATIONAL GASOLINE TRUCK DRIVER'S STRIKE OF 1991

The strike began the day after Julie, and I returned from Kimmy's wedding. We expected the strike to be short, as all Italian strikes were short. This strike, however, would be different and would go on for twenty days, bringing the entire country to a standstill.

From the beginning David was prepared. He had been advised the strike might last several weeks. He filled his gas tank immediately and began creating plans to carpool to work. Julie and I filled our gas tanks the day after the strike began, just before the gas station near the base ran out. Robbie, by contrast, did not fill his tank at all. It was a decision he would live to regret.

I seldom saw Robbie during the three weeks before his wedding. Robbie and Antonella had moved out of the house and onto her parent's boat for the remainder of the summer, to enjoy their last days in Italy together.

They planned to marry at the end of July and move back to the States at the beginning of September. Robbie had landed a great new assignment. He would be moving to Los Angeles to work in a film liaison unit.

He learned about the job from the base public affairs officer who had recently moved from Los Angeles to Naples. During the previous years, the Navy had built a solid relationship with the film industry, collaborating on several successful movies, including "An Officer and A Gentlemen" and "Top Gun." They now wanted to produce movies involving the Navy's JAG Corps, hence the opportunity for Robbie.

Antonella was thrilled about moving to America. She saw it as an opportunity to live her dreams and promote her dress designs. Her mother and father encouraged the move, seeing within it the possibility to enlarge their business empires. It seemed a good move for all.

I wondered however if Robbie's marriage would survive the experience. I remembered something I had heard from a woman at the office. She warned Robbie that Antonella might not adjust well to American life. "You can take the woman out of Italy," she said, "but you will never be able to take the Italy out of the woman."

Robbie insisted the secretary was wrong, that Antonella was already part American, and therefore everything would be fine. It turns out he was quite naïve. Their first few years together in Los Angeles would prove difficult, as Antonella was constantly homesick for Naples.

Robbie's new married life began with the strike of 1991, as Antonella began to take charge of their life together. The fruit had not fallen far from the tree. Antonella was becoming her mother.

As the strike dragged on, threatening to cancel the wedding, Antonella doubled down on her plans to continue. She was relentless, developing backup plans for every contingency, determined that no strike would ruin her wedding. Neither hell, nor high water was going to disrupt her wedding plans.

From the start, David, Julie, and I were part of the plan. David and I were provided minor roles to play. Antonella wanted us to wear our white uniforms and swords. Other than that, she did not care much about us.

Robbie's brother would play the role of best man. Julie was offered the position of bridesmaid to secure my participation. Elsa would serve as the maid of honor.

Antonella was determined to marry Robbie with or without guests. The primary plan remained to marry in Ravello, however she developed secondary plans as well. If the strike dragged on, she planned to move the wedding to her parent's house. She did not bother to ask them for permission first.

She also developed a plan to ferry the guests to the wedding if necessary. Athena's gas tank was full. If people could not get to the wedding by car, she would transport them to the wedding by boat. Every plan and the backup plan had a backup plan. I now understood why her family was so rich. Antonella was woven from the same cloth as her mother and father. They appeared spontaneous but left nothing to chance.

Despite Antonella's best efforts to avert disaster, during the second week, the situation seemed beyond her control. Local food stores began closing. I wondered if we would have anything to eat at the wedding. They were not getting their deliveries and the national economy was beginning to falter.

The gravity of the situation came home one night after work. Antonella had telephoned Robbie asking us to pick her up at the dress shop. She was carrying her wedding dress and did not want to carry it back to the boat in the rain. Robbie had no gasoline in his car, however, so I was drafted to pick up Antonella.

David and I picked her up around 5:30 PM at the dress shop and began our trip back to the house, driving the usual route which ran through the center of the Vomero Quarter.

The Vomero has one major street which runs through the center. The name and the direction of the street constantly change. It starts with the name Via Scarlatti, then changes to Via Cilea, then to Corso Europa, and finally turns into Via Manzoni.

Every few blocks, through the center of the Vomero, the street also changes direction. First, it is one way westbound and then it changes to one way eastbound, and then changes back again. With each change in direction, traffic is diverted onto narrow side streets which wander aimlessly. Clearly it was a street engineered by an idiot.

If one followed the posted signs, one might become totally lost. I made that mistake just once and resolved never to do it again. After my first efforts to obey the law, I followed the Neapolitans and ignored the signs. Each time the street direction changed, I joined the funnel, as three lanes of traffic merged into the single lane reserved for buses only. It was what Americans referred to as the "funnel effect."

I enjoyed driving into funnels. It reminded me of the white-knuckle, slow motion, test of wills driving I had learned from my father growing up in Boston. Within the funnel no one was my master.

Once we entered the bus lane, the test of wills would briefly end, and traffic would resume moving at its usual snail speed, until we reached another change in direction, at which point we would emerge from the funnel.

When we emerged from the funnel, we would experience, the "reverse funnel effect." Everyone's pent-up frustrations were released in a burst of speed, resembling the start of an auto race. This would last for two blocks followed by the screeching of brakes, as everyone entered the next funnel.

Also, the bus lane was more than stripes on the pavement. It was a single lane flanked by tall curbs on either side. Once a car entered the bus lane there was no way out, except through the other end.

This brings me to the story of the evening, in question. That night, after we picked up Antonella, it began to rain. It was not a mere drizzle. It was a downpour. Napoli can be crazy, in normal weather, however it gets worse when it rains.

As we inched our way down the Via Scarlatti, we entered the bus lane as usual. Then midway, through the block, the car in front of us stopped moving. He had engine trouble. Rather than help him, as usual, everyone behind us decided to use their horns.

For at least 10 minutes we sat in traffic waiting for the car to move. I could tell he was trying to start the car. Unfortunately, the car would not start. He then got out of the car, closed the car door, locked it, and proceeded to walk away! Apparently, he lived nearby.

Oh no, I thought, we are screwed! David saw the situation also and immediately got out of the car, chasing after the man in the rain. A few minutes later, David returned to the car, now thoroughly soaked, bringing the man with him. "He is out of gas and needs us to push," David exclaimed!

That night, at the end of the second week of the strike, David and I pushed the man's car a full city block while Antonella drove behind us. The reality of the gasoline strike finally sank in. This car would be the first of many cars I had to push out of the road during the coming week. Eventually the streets of Naples were strewn with abandoned cars. Fortunately thanks to David's foresight, we never ran out of gas.

As the strike dragged on into its third week, more cars were abandoned wherever and in whatever position they were, when they ran out of gas. By the middle of the third week, we had the streets of Naples entirely to ourselves. Everyone was now walking.

Conversation between Antonella and Robbie

The evening before our wedding neither Robbie nor I could sleep. He paced in his room, and I paced in mine. Robbie wanted to share a room together. However, I felt, it was bad luck to see each other before the wedding.

The past month had been one of the most stressful months of my life. All the forces of hell had conspired to ruin my wedding day. At times I was a nervous wreck, however Robbie remained my knight in shining armor. Never once did he falter. It is just a party he reminded me. His words of reassurance helped me weather the storm. Now that the stress was released, I found I could not sleep.

During our last night together on the boat, the night before, we spoke for hours, excited to begin our lives together. It was during the conversation that I revealed mother and father's secret wedding present.

Our plans for after the wedding were considerable. First, we planned to travel to Positano after the wedding to spend our first night together as husband and wife. Robbie had made reservations at Le Sirenuse Hotel in Positano.

After our first night in Positano, we planned to drive to Rome and then fly to Los Angeles for a one-week honeymoon. Our time remaining in Italy was becoming limited. Robbie wanted to spend our honeymoon in Los Angeles so that we might find a place to live.

He had booked a beautiful place for us to stay. It was an elegant pre-World War I era, hotel in Pasadena, known as the Langham Huntington Hotel. It looked like the kind of place where movie stars might stay.

Our goal was to see the sights and find a place to live within our one-week vacation. Both of us wanted to find a house in Pasadena. Afterwards we would return to Naples and begin preparing for the move.

That night, our last on the boat, as we lay in each other's arms, I revealed mother and father's secret. "We have a tradition in our family," I began. "It is more than our family tradition. It is an ancient Neapolitan tradition. When a Neapolitan couple marries, their parents give them a place to live. My grandparents did this for my parents, as did their parents before them. Mother and father have offered to help us buy a house."

The look on Robbie's face was priceless. "Are you kidding?" He asked.

"No," I replied. "I am serious. Mother and father have offered to buy us a house."

For a moment, Robbie stared at me in silence. Then he smiled and asked me a question. "How much can we spend?"

I had not thought of asking that question. "I am not sure" I replied. Then I added a suggestion. "I think we should keep our request modest," I replied. "We are after all, just starting out."

Robbie smiled. "You are always full of delightful surprises," he said. Then he reached over and kissed me.

"How many bedrooms should we look for," I asked, "two or three?"

Robbie smiled once again. "We need at least three" he replied. "One for you and me, one for a baby, and one for your parents to stay in when they come to visit."

A baby? Robbie could see my eyes light up when he mentioned the word baby. "What about my brother Tony?" I asked.

Robbie laughed. "He can sleep on the couch," he replied.

I laughed! "How long do you think before your parents buy a house in California?" He asked.

I laughed again. "That depends on when we have a baby, I replied."

Robbie smiled. "Do you want a baby?" He asked.

"Very much," I replied. "Once we have a child, mother and father will buy a house for sure."

Robbie smiled. "You and I will live in a small house in Pasadena while your parents live in a grand house in Beverly Hills."

I laughed. Robbie understood my parents. Afterwards he asked me a serious question.

"Are you ok with moving so far away?" He asked. He could tell I was less than certain.

"I think so," I replied. I tried to sound confident. I wondered if I would miss Naples. "Do you think we will ever move back?" I asked.

"I do not know," Robbie replied. "I suppose we will at some point. If your mother and father are any example, we will return to Naples someday."

I smiled. It was good to hear that Robbie was open to the idea of living in Naples again. I was excited about leaving Naples to see the world, but also felt a twinge of sorrow at the thought of leaving.

I reached over and gave Robbie another slow kiss on the lips. Then I stood up beside the bed and let my nightgown drop onto the floor. Robbie did not need any coaching as he soon joined me beneath the covers. At last, we were a couple. Although we were not yet married, I no longer felt any fear about getting pregnant. For the first time in my life, I was eager to make a baby.

David's Trip to Ravello

I checked into the hotel in Ravello on a Friday afternoon around 2:00 PM, following an anxious drive from Naples. I remember the day. It was July 26, 1991. The strike which had paralyzed the country had ended the night before, just in time for Robbie and Antonella's wedding. Unfortunately, the end of the strike did not mean that everything had instantly returned to normal.

I left work shortly after lunch hoping the gas station near the base had finally received its delivery. It had not. Gazing at the gas gage, I had less than a quarter of a tank remaining for the drive to Ravello. I did not have enough gas to get there. The first station I came to on the Autostrada was jammed with cars waiting to buy gas. Clearly, it had received its delivery, however, it would take at least an hour to fill up there. I decided to keep driving.

As I drove south around the bottom of Vesuvius, now with my gas gage firmly on "E," I passed more gas stations, each crowded with cars. I was beginning to run out of options. I needed desperately to find gas before I reached my exit. Finally, as I neared Pompeii, I saw an empty gas station and decided to pull in. The chain across the entrance had been removed, however there were no cars in the station. Fortunately for me, the station had received its delivery.

Finding gas, just in time, saved me from an anxious drive over the mountains. I would never have made it to Ravello. For the first time in two weeks, a tremendous burden was finally lifted.

That afternoon, I took my time driving over the mountains, stopping several times to admire the view. I had driven this route before several times with Elsa but had never been able to see the city through the air pollution. That day, the skies were clear. A week without cars on the road, had finally revealed the beautiful slopes of Vesuvius.

After several miles, I reached the top of the mountain pass and began the slow winding descent towards Ravello. The scenery had changed completely. I had entered the Amalfi Coast. All around me, behind the garden walls, were vineyards and the sounds of tinkling bells hidden within the foliage. I had entered the realm of shepherds. Twice during the last ten miles, I had to stop and wait for sheep to cross the road. It was hard to believe I was less than fifty miles from the congested heart of Naples.

When I arrived at the hotel, I checked in and inquired about Elsa. I had last spoken with her five days before and had given her the name of the hotel where I was staying, as she had not yet made a reservation. When I checked in, I learned she had not reserved a room. Perhaps, the reservation was in her parent's name, I thought. I tried their names also. They had not made reservations either. For a moment, I felt a chill, wondering if Elsa had decided not to attend the wedding. Then I remembered that Antonella had asked her to be her maid of honor. I felt relieved. Certainly, she would come, I thought.

The Villa Rufolo

That afternoon, I decided to take a walk. I needed fresh air. I decided to visit the nearby Villa Rufolo. I remembered Elsa's description of the house, from the first day we met. Instead of walking towards the village square, I turned left and entered the path leading to the villa. Up ahead stood a tall and ancient stone tower at the end of a dirt path flanked by cypress trees. As I entered the arched gateway, I passed through the old tower entrance, finding myself all alone. The gate was left open however the attendant was nowhere to be found.

I had visited the house once before with Elsa. I remembered the story she told me, of how the castle was built by a noble family from Amalfi during the 13th century on the ruins of a more ancient house. A member of that family, a certain Landolfo Rufolo, had been immortalized by the 14th century Italian poet, Boccaccio, in his book, "The Decameron."

Over the course of hundreds of years, the ownership had changed many times, until the house was finally purchased in the 19th century by a Scotsman who attempted to restore portions of it.

In 1880, the German composer Wagner visited the house. He was so impressed with the ruins and garden that he used it as the inspiration for a scene in one of his operas, an opera known as "Parsifal," about the search for the Holy Grail. I had entered Wagner's magical garden.

It was a beautiful day to visit the villa. The smell of flowers from the garden was heavy in the air. The first thing that I came to as I entered the villa was an interior courtyard surrounded by a columned arcade.

Surrounding the multistory courtyard on all sides was a façade of interlaced black and white, horseshoe-shaped arches. I entered an enchanted realm, a middle eastern-like place more like Morocco, than Italy.

On the opposite side of the courtyard, stood a beautiful woman with blond hair standing between a pair of columns. She was bending over to smell a flower. It was Elsa.

For a moment, I stood transfixed in absolute silence, as I gazed at her beautiful form across the courtyard. Elsa was more lovely than the first day we met. She did not see me, but instead, she turned away from me and walked through a doorway into the garden beyond.

A few minutes later, I walked through the doorway into the garden passing through a loggia of gothic arches, leftover from the crusades. Elsa had disappeared into the garden. The view from the loggia was breathtaking that afternoon. Below the house stood a tall umbrella pine next to the twin belltowers of a small church, and beyond that, far below, spread the brilliantly blue, Mediterranean Sea.

At last, I understood Wagner's fascination with the place. I was standing in one of the world's most beautiful gardens. Surely Eden itself was not more beautiful.

As I walked into the garden and gazed towards the sea, I saw Elsa standing beside a railing overlooking the water. I noticed she was playing with a ring on her finger. She was wearing my ring. I wondered what she might be thinking. As I approached her, she heard my footsteps, and turned to face me. Then she smiled and bade me to stand beside her by the railing.

"I was hoping you might find me here" she said. "I wondered if you might arrive early."

"How was your flight?" I asked.

"It was good," Elsa replied. "Mother, Father, and I arrived about an hour ago."

"Where are you staying?" I asked.

"We are staying in a little pensione near the Villa Cimbrone," Elsa replied. "The hotel where you are staying was full."
"I notice you are wearing my ring," I said.

Elsa looked down at the ring and spun it on her finger. "Yes," she replied. "I am still trying to get used to it. As you can see, I have lost weight. Do I look too thin?"
"No," I replied. "You look beautiful."

Elsa turned and smiled. "Really, you are not just saying that?"
"Yes, really," I replied, "you are stunning!"

"Do you like my new hair?" She asked.

"I do," I replied. "You should always wear your hair this way."
Elsa smiled once again. "It is nice to reveal my real hair again. For months since the accident, I have been wearing a wig. Can you see my scar on the back?"

"No," I replied. Elsa smiled once again. She looked positively radiant.

"David, I have a confession to make" she continued. For a moment, I stopped to catch my breath. Before she started, I began to speak. I asked her a question.

"Elsa, did you break up with Sven?" I asked. Elsa smiled.

"Of course," she replied. Then she laughed. "Sven was only interested in my body!"

"So, what happened?" I asked.

"I rediscovered the reason I left him the first time." Elsa giggled. "Sven is not the right person for me. You are the right person!"

For a moment, we stopped and gazed at each other. Her eyes were dancing, revealing a secret hidden within.

"Really, what happened?" I asked.

"I told father and mother about Sven" Elsa replied. "Afterwards, father told Sven to leave me alone. In the end father returned Sven's ring."

"I have missed you so much," Elsa began.

"I have missed you too," I replied.

"David, I have something to tell you," Elsa began again. Once again, I took a deep breath. "David, the past few months I have had lots of time to think. I realize now that I have been running away from life. When I first came to Italy, I ran away from Sven, and for the last several months, I have been running away from you. I suppose, in ways I am still a little girl, full of hopes and dreams about the man I will marry. I always thought I would recognize him when I saw him, that God would give me a sign to let me know I had found "the one." Before the accident I was not sure you were the one. I adored you but I was not sure. I wanted a sign."

"Seems like you got your sign," I replied with a smile.

Elsa smiled back. "I sure did," she replied. "I suppose I should be more careful with what I ask for."

Then she continued her story. "Do you remember last summer?" She asked.

"Yes," I replied. "You wanted us to get married and move to Stockholm" I replied.

Elsa laughed. "Do you want to hear something funny?"

"Sure," I replied.
"Everyone is leaving Stockholm," Elsa replied! "Mother and father plan to retire to the south of France, and Kristina's moving to Amsterdam to live with her boyfriend. Mother and father have even decided to sell the cottage. If you and I moved to Sweden, we would find ourselves alone."

"So, I take it, you are no longer interested in moving back to Sweden?" I asked.

"Yes," Elsa replied. "That is correct. There is no point moving there if everyone else has left. It's liberating to finally realize that. I suppose, home is not a fixed place. It is instead, wherever I am at. I suppose I can live anywhere, anywhere we want to go."
For a moment, the realization of what she said began to sink in. She was ready to go anywhere with me. I suddenly felt very happy indeed. Then she continued her story. "David, there is something else you should know she began. Do you remember when I was unconscious in the hospital?"

"Yes," I replied.

"I knew you were there," Elsa replied. "It felt as if you were far away, but I knew you were there. I could not see you, but I could feel your touch and could hear your voice. I wanted so much to respond but I could not. I called out to you, but my lips would not move. I could only greet you with my mind. While I was in surgery, I saw you praying in the chapel. I do not know if I saw you in my mind, or if I really saw you."

"I realize now that you were there for me during the most difficult moment in my life. I realized how deeply you loved me. When I saw you in the chapel, I thought I had died. In that moment I wanted more than anything else, to live again."

As she said this, I could see tears begin to fill her eyes. She wrapped her arms tightly about my neck and whispered in my ear. "I love you David," she said. "Do you still want to marry me?"

For a moment, I held her tightly, feeling her warm body against mine. It was wonderful to hold her in my arms again. "I do," I whispered. I could feel Elsa's warm tears against my neck as she whispered in my ear, accepting my proposal.

"I fell in love with you, the minute I saw you drive up in that pickup truck" she whispered. My Elsa was finally home again.

The Wedding (End of July 1991) – Julie narrates

Antonella and Robbie were married at noon on a Saturday in Ravello's 11th century Church of Saint Pantaleone, in the same church where Antonella's father and mother had married thirty years before. The grass was green, the sky was blue, and the sun was shining. It was neither too hot nor too cold. It was a perfect day for a wedding.

As usual Harry saw the humor in everything that we experienced in Italy. He loved the name of the church and enjoyed making jokes. He would later refer to the church where Robbie was married as the "Church of the Holy Pants." I reminded him the patron saint was known as the saint of healing, not of blue jeans, but even so I could not help laughing.

After the ceremony, which seemed to go on for hours, the wedding couple exited the church through an archway of white clad naval officers with drawn swords, while spectators pelted them with rice. Harry looked quite dashing in his white uniform. Harry would have preferred to cook the rice first.

Afterwards we walked a mile in the hot afternoon sun to the nearby Villa Cimbrone gardens for the reception. Antonella and Robbie's reception was held outdoors on the grassy lawn overlooking the Mediterranean Sea.

By the time we reached the reception, Harry was quite warm and had unbuttoned his collar. He hated wearing his white uniform, even though it looked wonderful. Antonella loved the Navy's Choker White uniforms however Harry thought them extremely uncomfortable. He referred to them as "dirt magnets", as the dirt seemed to literally jump off the walls onto his uniform.

I had never visited the Villa Cimbrone before, however David and Elsa had. According to Elsa, it was the place where they first kissed. Elsa was beautiful and radiant that afternoon. She had fully recovered from her accident earlier in the year and had become more beautiful than ever. David looked handsome as usual in his white uniform. Elsa was right, David did look like Robert Redford.

As I sat there admiring my roommates, I also noticed for the first time that David resembled Elsa's father. Had Elsa fallen in love with David because he resembled her father? The resemblance was uncanny. She of course would deny it, but it did seem a plausible theory. For a moment the thought gave me pause for reflection. Then I sighed and reached a conclusion. Maybe we are attracted to people we admire, I thought? The notion had never registered in my mind before.

As I thought this thought I realized there were aspects about Harry that reminded me of my favorite person, my grandfather. Grandfather had an irrepressible wit like Harry. I loved to listen to grandfather as a child. He was my favorite person in all the world. Now that he was gone, I missed him terribly.

Maybe there was something to my newfound theory. Maybe we are not attracted to movie idols after all. Maybe we are attracted to people we loved and admired as children? The thought sent shivers up my spine. At last, I began to get a glimpse of the impenetrable secrets that drive human desire.

After letting my mind wander, I focused again on Elsa and David. They made a handsome couple. The week before, they had joined our club, and were now amongst the engaged to be married. Clearly, there was a marriage bug in the water at our house.

That afternoon we dined outdoors on the lawn. Harry and I were seated at a round table with David, Elsa, Maria, Rosa and Elsa's parents, John & Tilly. The wedding couple were seated at a round table with their parents, brothers, and sisters. Antonella had insisted that they sit with the guests, rather than set apart from everyone, isolated at a head table.

We ate very well that afternoon enjoying the finest foods the Amalfi Coast had to offer. We began the meal with a mix of appetizers including incredibly good fried zucchini flowers, then proceeded to a rice dish with mixed seafood, followed by swordfish fillets swimming in butter and capers, followed by salad, tiramisu dessert, and tiny shots of espresso and limoncello. Between each course we sipped our wine, admired the scenery, and conversed about every subject under the sun.

Maria and Rosa were quite proud of themselves that afternoon, insisting it was they, that had arranged each of our engagements. Harry and I tried hard not to laugh. We did learn interesting things, however during the conversation. First, we learned who told Kimmy, about Robbie's affair with Antonella; It was Rosa. We also learned who persuaded Marcello to pursue Kimmy; it was Maria.

We also learned a secret that even Robbie and Antonella had never heard before, that Charles and Silvana had once shared the same bedroom, which Robbie and Antonella now occupied, thirty years before.

Had Maria and Rosa played a role in bringing Harry and I together? Only a small amount, I concluded. Maria had rented her house to Harry, and of course she also refused to fix the heating system.

Life is what brought Harry and I together. There were mishaps and accidents, funny moments, robberies, car troubles and acts of kindness. Sometimes we laughed so hard we cried. There were evening walks and ice cream cones, road trips, and wonderful meals shared together.

We shared our electric blanket to keep warm and took turns resetting circuit breakers in the middle of the night. During the summer, we tended to our buckets, and washed the dishes at 2:00 AM.

We enjoyed parties together, days at the beach, shots of liquor sitting around the dining table, grilled steaks on the back terrace, and enjoyed watching football games on the TV. We baked cookies and spent evenings playing fetch with the dog. We made hundreds of memories together.

In the end it was a thousand tiny things that caused Harry and I to fall in love. So, when did I finally realize I loved him? I suppose it was when I thought I had lost him.

For sure I could have gone on living alone. I had a good life as a single woman, however life with Harry was so much richer than life by myself.

Harry had a way about him that made every day I spent with him wonderful. When I feared I had lost him, I realized I wanted him back more than life itself. That was when I finally knew the truth. I had fallen in love with Harry.

After the dinner, as the afternoon transformed into the evening, we posed for pictures together on the Balcony of Infinity. Far below us sat the tranquil waters of the Mediterranean Sea. David posed with Elsa, I posed with Harry and last of all Robbie posed with Antonella. Then we posed together as a group.

When the picture-taking was complete, we stood together and watched the sun slowly descend over the horizon marveling as the scenery softened from brilliant blues and greens to the soft evening shades of purple, dark blue and black. It was the perfect ending to a perfect day, as well as a wonderful culmination of our time together in Italy.

PART VI: APPENDIX

Figure 1

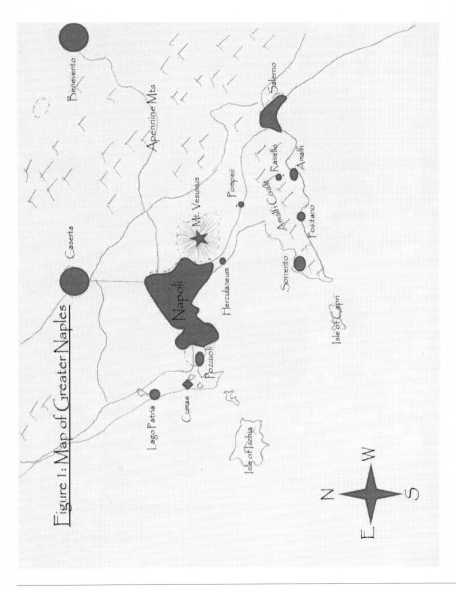

Figure 1: Map of Greater Naples

Figure 2

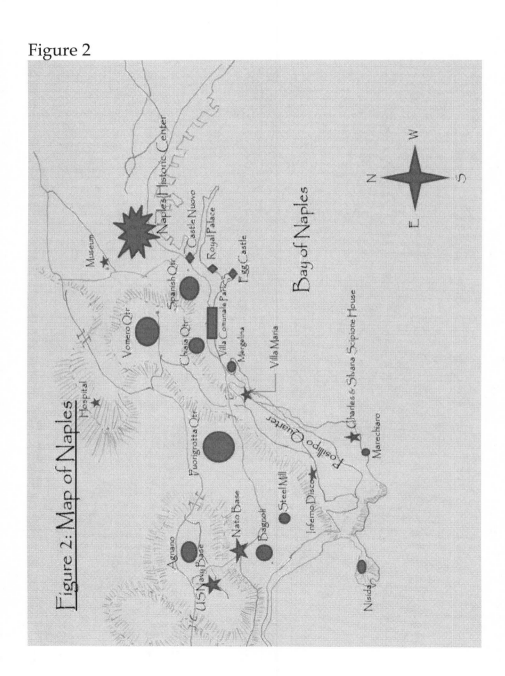

Figure 2: Map of Naples

Figure 3

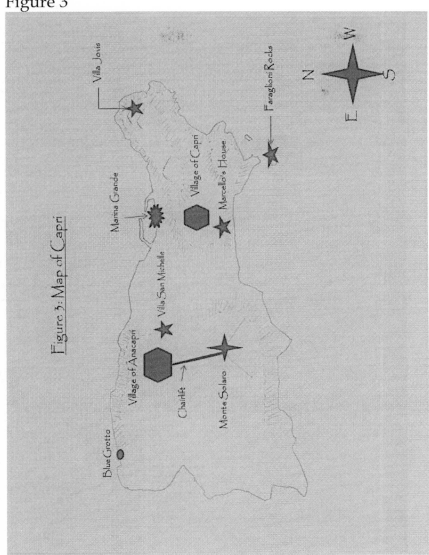

Figure 3: Map of Capri

AUTHORS NOTES

I would like to start by saying that "The Villa; A Neapolitan Love Story" is a work of fiction. While it is inspired by my years living in Naples, the characters in the story are not real. The people described in this book are all fictional characters. As such they live happily ever after. Real people's stories only occasionally turn out that way.

I considered sixteen different titles when picking a title for this book. In the end one of my friends from Naples made the most convincing argument. The house, she said, is what brings everyone together. Without it, the characters never would have met. There is a fundamental truth in that statement. All our relationships in life begin with random occurrences that bring us together. After the initial meeting however, our actions determine how our relationships develop.

I first came to live in Naples during the late 1980's. I agreed to accept a job that no one wanted, to manage Flag Housing, so that I could experience life outside the United States. Before I moved to Naples, my Navy colleagues in San Diego told me that Naples was like Detroit. They did not think I would like it. They could not have been further from the truth.

For two years, I shared a large house on Napoli's Posillipo Hill with two other bachelors. We had fun. Looking backwards now, I can say that my first two years in Naples were some of the happiest years of my life.

After I left Naples, I returned to San Diego. I missed Naples terribly and yearned to go back. My passion for the place was contagious, inspiring several of my co-workers to see Naples for themselves. They in turn, brought more friends, until many people from my old office in San Diego, had moved to Naples. For at least ten years, Naples attracted a steady stream of U.S. Navy employees from San Diego.

I returned to Naples a second time in the mid 1990's, following a tragedy in my life. I had lost my smile and was unable to find it again. Moving back to Naples renewed my joy for living again. The second time I stayed for almost five years.

My most recent trip to Naples occurred in 2018 before the start of the COVID Pandemic. Naples had improved considerably since I last lived there. The old buildings had received a fresh coat of paint, and much of the historic center had become pedestrian only. The city had also become much cleaner.

The square in front of the Royal Palace, which was once used as the central bus station during the 1980s, is now a wonderful place to take an evening stroll. The main street along the waterfront in front of the Egg Castle, is now filled with outdoor restaurants instead of idling automobiles stuck in traffic.

The U.S. Navy Base in Agnano, where I worked, is now closed. The building where I worked is now an auto dealership. The NATO base has also moved from Bagnoli. The food, however, remains as wonderful as always. My favorite places, Capri, Sorrento, Positano, and Ravello have not changed.

The house where I lived on the Posillipo Hill has changed considerably since I lived there in the 1980's. During my last visit it had changed colors and was undergoing a major renovation. The once beautiful garden is now overgrown with weeds.

The house where the Admiral lived has changed also. Admirals no longer live in Villa Nike. The house has been renovated and converted into condominiums. Someday someone should write a history of Villa Nike. Many important people passed through that house.

I wrote this book during the COVID-19 Pandemic, while the entire world worked from home. As part of my research, I searched the internet for videos and news articles concerning the Miracle of San Gennaro. It was reassuring to learn that San Gennaro's blood failed to liquify during the Pandemic. The mystery of the miracle continues.

In closing I encourage everyone to visit Naples. It is the best place I know to regain a sense of wonder and joy in life. The people, the culture, the history, the food, and the scenery are all fascinating. As I said in the book, living in the shadow of Vesuvius has transformed the people who live there. The people of Naples have learned how to enjoy life in a way that I have not experienced anywhere else. You will see more people kissing in Naples than anywhere else.

No matter how difficult your life may be, enjoying tasty food in a beautiful place is always a good cure for life's troubles. As a writer once wrote over two thousand years ago. "The Region of Campania is the most blessed land, the fairest of all regions in the world." Remember this quote as you sit out of doors, sipping your wine, while enjoying the breathtaking splendor of the Amalfi Coast, the Isle of Capri, or Napoli itself.

There is a reason so many Roman Emperors built their villas here. The region's coastline is one of the most beautiful places on earth.

BIBLIOGRAPHY

Books
- Inside the Vatican – by Bart McDowell – National Geographic Society-1991
- Capri New Coloured Guidebook with Map – by Loretta Santini – Plurigraf Narni -1987
- Axel Munthe's San Michelle Visitors Guide – by The San Michele Foundation Stockholm -1980
- Southern Italy: An Archaeological Guide -by Margaret Guido – Faber and Faber Ltd -1972
- Insite Guides Naples Capri & The Coast – APA Publications (HK) Ltd – 1992
- Naples With Pompeii & The Amalfi Coast – Dorling Kindersley – 1998
- Rome – DK Publishing – 1993
- Italy – Dorling Kindersley – 1996
- Rome of the Caesars – Leonardo B. Dal Maso – Bonechi Edizioni – 1989
- The Vatican Museums – SCALA, Instituto Fotografico Editoriale, Firenze – 1972
- Pompeii – Francesco Paolo Maulucci -Publisher Carcavallo-Naples – 1987
- Sweden -Dorling Kindersley -2005

Periodical Stories
- Italy Before the Romans – National Geographic Society – Feb 2005
- Who Were the Phoenicians – National Geographic Society – Oct 2004
- Rome's Bad Boy, Nero Rises from the Ashes – National Geographic – Sep 2014
- Naples Unabashed – National Geographic – Mar 1998
- Palio, Siena's Wild 90-Second Horse Race – National Geographic – Jun 1988
- The Persian Gulf After the Storm – National Geographic – Aug 1991
- Roman Empire – National Geographic – Jul 1997
- Vesuvius Countdown – National Geographic -Sep 2007

Articles
- Vesuvius's big daddy: The super volcano that threatens all life in Europe – by Phil Robinson for MailOnline – 3 Jan 2011.
- Miracle of the Blood – by Katherine Wilson
- How to Become an Italian Citizen – by Marco Permunian

Videos
- In The Shadow of Vesuvius – National Geographic Video – Warner Home Video - 1987

Websites
- https://en.wikipedia.org/wiki/Campanian_Ignimbrite_eruption
- https://en.wikipedia.org/wiki/Eruption_of_Mount_Vesuvius_in_79_AD
- https://en.wikipedia.org/wiki/1990_FIFA_World_Cup
- https://en.wikipedia.org/wiki/Augustus_of_Prima_Porta
- https://en.wikipedia.org/wiki/Basilica_of_Saint_Paul_Outside_the_Walls
- https://en.wikipedia.org/wiki/Battle_of_Monte_Cassino
- https://en.wikipedia.org/wiki/Capri
- https://en.wikipedia.org/wiki/East_Germany
- https://en.wikipedia.org/wiki/Fall_of_the_Berlin_Wall
- https://en.wikipedia.org/wiki/Gaeta
- https://en.wikipedia.org/wiki/Gulf_War
- https://en.wikipedia.org/wiki/Hayreddin_Barbarossa
- https://en.wikipedia.org/wiki/It_Started_in_Naples
- https://en.wikipedia.org/wiki/When_Harry_Met_Sally...
- https://en.wikipedia.org/wiki/The_Way_We_Were
- https://en.wikipedia.org/wiki/La_Dolce_Vita
- https://en.wikipedia.org/wiki/Januarius
- https://en.wikipedia.org/wiki/Marshall_Field_and_Company_Building
- https://en.wikipedia.org/wiki/Marshall_Fields
- https://en.wikipedia.org/wiki/Posillipo
- https://www.officeholidays.com/countries/italy/2022
- https://en.wikipedia.org/wiki/Saint_Peter%27s_tomb
- https://en.wikipedia.org/wiki/Swedish_emigration_to_the_United_States

- https://en.wikipedia.org/wiki/Timeline_of_Gulf_War_(1990%E2%80%931991)
- https://en.wikipedia.org/wiki/V%C3%A1clav_Havel
- https://en.wikipedia.org/wiki/Velvet_Revolution
- https://en.wikipedia.org/wiki/Vasa_(ship)
- https://en.wikipedia.org/wiki/Vatican_Museums
- https://en.wikipedia.org/wiki/Vatican_Necropolis
- https://en.wikipedia.org/wiki/Villa_Jovis
- https://en.wikipedia.org/wiki/Lake_Avernus
- https://en.wikipedia.org/wiki/Cumaean_Sibyl
- https://en.wikipedia.org/wiki/Sibylline_Books
- https://en.wikipedia.org/wiki/Tiberius
- https://en.wikipedia.org/wiki/Villa_San_Michele
- https://en.wikipedia.org/wiki/Circus_of_Nero
- https://en.wikipedia.org/wiki/Villa_Rufolo
- https://en.wikipedia.org/wiki/Ravello
- https://en.wikipedia.org/wiki/Duchy_of_Amalfi
- https://en.wikipedia.org/wiki/Villa_Cimbrone
- https://en.wikipedia.org/wiki/University_of_Naples_Federico_II
- https://en.wikipedia.org/wiki/Castel_Nuovo
- https://en.wikipedia.org/wiki/Solfatara_(volcano)
- https://en.wikipedia.org/wiki/Tutti_Frutti_(game_show)
- https://en.wikipedia.org/wiki/Pozzuoli
- https://en.wikipedia.org/wiki/Odyssey
- https://en.wikipedia.org/wiki/Pliny_the_Elder
- https://en.wikipedia.org/wiki/National_Archaeological_Museum,_Naples
- https://enchantingsorrento.com/baths-of-the-queen-giovanna-i-bagni-della-regina-giovanna/
- https://en.wikipedia.org/wiki/Nymphaeum
- https://en.wikipedia.org/wiki/Nile_God_Statue,_Naples
- https://en.wikipedia.org/wiki/Spaccanapoli_(street)
- https://en.wikipedia.org/wiki/Naples_Cathedral
- https://en.wikipedia.org/wiki/Cappella_Sansevero
- https://www.greekmyths-greekmythology.com/pandoras-box-myth/
- https://en.wikipedia.org/wiki/Galla_Placidia
- https://en.wikipedia.org/wiki/Roman_Forum

- https://en.wikipedia.org/wiki/Victor_Emmanuel_II_Monument
- https://en.wikipedia.org/wiki/Arch_of_Titus
- https://en.wikipedia.org/wiki/Palatine_Hill
- https://en.wikipedia.org/wiki/Piazza_Navona
- https://en.wikipedia.org/wiki/Fontana_dei_Quattro_Fiumi
- https://en.wikipedia.org/wiki/Sulla
- https://en.wikipedia.org/wiki/Social_War_(91%E2%80%9387_BC)
- https://en.wikipedia.org/wiki/Siena
- https://en.wikipedia.org/wiki/San_Gimignano
- https://en.wikipedia.org/wiki/Plaza_Suite
- https://en.wikipedia.org/wiki/Plaza_Hotel
- https://en.wikipedia.org/wiki/Belgravia
- https://en.wikipedia.org/wiki/Mark_W._Clark
- https://en.wikipedia.org/wiki/Skansen
- https://sirenuse.it/en/
- https://www.langhamhotels.com/en/the-langham/los-angeles/

Other:
- Google Maps, Images & Website links for various locations including Naples, Ravello, Capri, Rome, Siena, San Gimignano, Lucca, Montalcino, Chicago, New York, London, Monaco and San Rafael-Frejus